Left to Die

Left to Die

LISA JACKSON

HODDER &
STOUGHTON

First published in Great Britain in 2008 by Hodder & Stoughton
An Hachette Livre UK company

First hardback edition published in 2010 by Hodder & Stoughton

1

A CIP catalogue record for this title is available from the British Library

ISBN 978 0 340 96196 4

Typeset by Hewer Text UK Ltd, Edinburgh
Printed and bound in the UK by CPI Mackays, Chatham ME5 8TD

Hodder & Stoughton policy is to use papers that are natural, renewable
and recyclable products and made from wood grown in sustainable
forests. The logging and manufacturing processes are expected to
conform to the environmental regulations of the country of origin.

Hodder & Stoughton Ltd
338 Euston Road
London NW1 3BH

www.hodder.co.uk

Acknowledgments

Dozens of people helped me with the creation, writing and research for this book. I'm sure I won't remember them all, but I would like to thank the following individuals for their time, effort, support and, as always, sense of humor while the author sometimes lost hers:

Ken Bush, Nancy Bush, Matthew Crose, Michael Crose, Kelly Foster, Marilyn Katcher, Ken Melum, Roz Noonan, Gayle Nachtigal, Fred Nachtigal, Mike Seidel, Larry Sparks, Niki Wilkins and probably a zillion others who remain nameless.

Prologue

Bitterroot Mountains, Montana
November

He's going to kill you.
Right here in the middle of this snow-covered godforsaken valley, he's going to kill you! Fight, Wendy, fight!

Wendy Ito struggled, battling with the ropes that cut into her bare flesh, feeling the sting of a fierce arctic wind as it howled through the mountain ridges that surrounded them.

She was alone. Aside from the psychopath who had captured her.

God, why had she trusted him?

How in the world had she thought that he was her rescuer? That his mission was to heal her until, after the blizzard, he could call for help or take her to the nearest hospital?

Had she been lured by his sincere concern as he'd come upon her wrecked car? Had it been those blue, blue eyes? His smile? His soft words of assurance? Or had it been because she'd had no choice, because without his aid she would surely die alone in a deep, forgotten ravine?

Whatever the reason, she'd believed him, trusted him. *Fool! Idiot!*

He'd proved himself to be her worst nightmare, an evil wolf in sheep's clothing, and now, oh God, now she was paying the price.

Shivering, certain she would die, she was naked and lashed to a tree, the thick rope cutting into her bare arms and torso, a gag so tight over her lips that she could barely breathe.

And he was close. So close she could feel the warmth of his breath sifting around the trunk of the sturdy pine, hear him grunt as he put all his strength into securing her, see a flash of white neoprene ski pants and parka from the corner of her eye.

Another tug on the rope.

She gasped, her whole body jerking even tighter against the scaly bark of the tree. Pain shot through her and she set her jaw. She just needed him to get close enough so that she could kick him hard. Hit his shin. Or his nuts.

She couldn't let him get away with this. Wouldn't!

Her heart raced and she tried to come up with a way to save herself, to break free of her bonds and climb up the snow-covered deer trail he'd dragged her down. Oh, she'd fought him. Wriggling and fighting, flinging herself at him, trying to find some way to free herself, to avoid being brought down here to whatever fate he'd planned. She could still see the fresh tracks in the thick snow. His steady, evenly placed big boot prints and her smaller, wild, erratic barefoot tracks made when she'd tried to get away, even as he'd prodded her with his damned knife. There were drips of blood in the white snow, proving that he'd cut her, that he'd meant business.

Dear God, help me, she silently prayed to the gun-metal gray heavens threatening more snow.

He laced the restraining ropes ever tighter.

"No!" Wendy tried to scream. *"No! No! No!"* But the foul gag covered her mouth and kept her cries muffled and weak while the panic surging through her blood caused her heart to thunder.

Why? Oh God, why me?

She blinked back tears but felt the salty drops fall from her eyes to stain and freeze upon her cheeks.

Don't cry. Whatever you do, do not let him see that you fear him. Don't give the son of a bitch the satisfaction. But don't fight, either. Pretend to give up; fake it and act like you've accepted your fate. Maybe his guard will slip and you can somehow get hold of his damned knife.

Her stomach clenched even tighter and she tried to keep his weapon, a hunting knife used for gutting game, in her sights. Razor sharp, it could slice through the ropes easily. Just as easily as it could pierce and cut her flesh.

Oh God . . .

Her knees went weak and it was all she could do not to bawl and beg, to mewl and plead, to offer to do anything he wanted if he would just not hurt her.

Go ahead, let him see that you're resigned to your fate . . . but keep your eye on the knife, with its menacing, deadly blade.

She was shivering harder now. Shaking so violently that slivers from the bark were digging into her skin. Was she trembling because of the bitter Montana wind, gusts she was certain were blowing down from Canada and the arctic? Or was she quivering from the fear that tore at her insides?

Beneath the gag her teeth chattered and she felt the raw wind buffet her as he worked. She caught glimpses of his legs, warmed by thick hunting socks and the white ski pants, his heavy, fur-lined parka protecting him from the very elements to which she was exposed.

This lying son of a bitch had no intention of saving you, of healing your wounds after the horrible car wreck. All along, the sick bastard kept you alive, citing the storm as a reason he couldn't get help, only to kill you. In the time he wanted. In the manner he wanted. He was savoring the anticipation, while you half fell in love with him.

Bile rose up her throat and she nearly wretched at the thought. He'd known it. She'd seen it in his eyes, that he'd read her utter dependency, her silly, stupid and pathetic desire to please him.

If she could, she'd kill him.

Right here. Right now.

She heard him grunt in satisfaction again, as he pulled the taut rope even tighter, forcing her buttocks into the sharp bark, her shoulders to be held fast. She could still kick, but he kept himself far from the damage she might inflict. Even with one leg still sore from the accident, she thought she could wound, and wound badly, because of all her training in the martial arts.

But he was careful to stay on the far side of the tree and keep away from her heels. And the cold was beginning to take its toll. She had trouble focusing, thinking of anything but the ice in her flesh, the sheer frigidity settling in her bones.

Blackness pulled at her vision.

Each breath she drew was labored and thin, her lungs on fire from lack of oxygen.

Maybe unconsciousness would be the way out. The blackness was soothing, taking the sting out of the wind.

But then she saw him move so that he was in front of her, staring at her with his cruel, relentless gaze.

How had she ever thought him handsome? How had she ever fantasized about him? How had she ever considered making love to him?

Slowly he removed the knife from his belt. Its cruel metallic surface winked in the shifting gray light.

She was doomed.

She knew it.

Even before he slowly, inexorably raised the blade.

Chapter One

"Goddamn, son of a bitch."

Ivor Hicks usually didn't mind the cold, but he didn't like the thought that he was being forced to hike in this section of the mountains after the recent blizzard. For the love of God, there could be an avalanche if he coughed too hard, and he was liable to 'cause his lungs felt heavy, as if he might be coming down with something.

Probably from the damned aliens, he decided, though he quickly rid himself of the thought. Criminy, no one wanted to believe that he'd been abducted in the late seventies, used for an experiment that involved his lungs, blood and testicles. The blasted ETs had left his drained and exhausted body in a snowbank two miles from his mountain home. When he'd come out of the drug-induced coma, he'd found himself half frozen, lying in his jockey shorts, an empty bottle of rye whiskey on the other side of a hollowed-out log that was home to a porcupine and beetles. But not one of them damned law enforcement boys wanted to listen to him.

At the time, the deputy he'd complained to, a smart-ass kid of about thirty, hadn't even bothered to swallow his smile of disbelief. He just took a quick statement, then hauled Ivor to the local clinic for treatment of frostbite and exposure. Doc Norwood hadn't been so outwardly disbelieving, but when he'd sent Ivor to the hospital in Missoula he'd suggested psychiatric testing.

Damned fools.

They'd all just played into the aliens' hands. Crytor, the leader of the pod, who had teleported him into their mother ship, was probably still laughing at the earthlings' simpleton explanation of alcohol, dehydration and hallucinations that the doctors were sure had been the cause of his "confusion."

Well, they were just dumb asses all around.

Using a walking stick, Ivor trudged up Cross Creek Pass, his hiking boots crunching in the snow, the sky as wide and blue as an ocean, not that he'd ever really seen one, but he'd seen himself Flathead Lake, which was one big-ass lake. Must be the same, only much, much larger, if those televised fishing excursions on the Fish and Game Channel could be believed.

Breathing heavily, he trudged up the trail, winding through an outcropping of snow-dusted boulders and ancient hemlocks with branches that appeared to scrape the sky. He stopped to catch his breath, watching it fog and cursing the aliens who had forced him up the mountain trail when his arthritis was acting up. The pain now was exacerbated, he was certain, by the experiments they'd done on him and the invisible chip they'd slipped into his body.

"I'm goin', I'm goin'," he said when he felt that little pinch at his temple, the prod they used to urge him on, the one that had pushed him out of bed before the sun climbed over the mountain crest. Hell, he hadn't even had a swallow of coffee, much less a sip of Jim Beam. Crytor, damn his orange reptilian hide, was a more intense taskmaster than Lila had been, God rest her soul.

He made the sign of the cross over his chest in memory of his dead wife, though he was not a Catholic, never had been and had no intention of becoming one. It just seemed like the right, reverent thing to do.

Even Crytor didn't seem to mind.

Through a stand of fir he noticed elk tracks and dung in the snow and wished he'd brought his rifle, though it wasn't hunting season. Who would ever find out?

Well, besides Crytor.

Rounding a bend in the path, he caught a glimpse of the valley below.

And he stopped short, nearly slipping.

His seventy-six-year-old heart almost quit on him as his gaze, as good as it ever was, focused on a solitary pine tree and the naked woman lashed to the trunk.

"Holy Mother Mary," he whispered and headed faster down the hillside, his walking stick digging deep through the snow to the frozen ground below as he hurried downward.

No wonder the aliens had wanted him to see this.

They'd probably abducted her, did what they wanted and left her here in this frigid, unpopulated valley. That's what they did, you know.

He wished he had a cell phone, though he thought he'd heard that the damned things didn't work up here. Too remote. No towers. He slid and caught himself, moving quickly along the familiar trail. She was probably still alive. Just stunned into submission. He could wrap her in his jacket, and hike back and get help.

Digging his stick deep and fast into the snow, he descended rapidly, hurrying down the switchbacks to the valley floor, where a snow owl hooted softly in an otherwise eerily quiet canyon.

"Hey!" he cried, half-running, nearly out of breath. "Hey!"

But before he reached the woman strapped to the tree, he stopped short and froze.

This was no return of a body from an alien ship.

Hell no.

This was the work of the very devil.

The hairs on the back of his wrinkled neck lifted.

This woman, an Asian woman, was as dead as dead can be. Her skin was blue, snow dusting her dark, shiny hair, her eyes staring without life. Blood lay on her skin, dark and frozen. A gag covered her lips. The bindings strapping her to the tree had cut deep bruises and welts into her arms and chest and waist. Not quite hog-tied. But close enough.

Somewhere a tree branch groaned with the weight of snow and Ivor felt as if unseen eyes might be watching.

He'd never felt more fear in his life.

Not even as Crytor's prisoner.

Again, wishing he had his hunting rifle, he stepped backward slowly, easing out the way he'd come, until, at the edge of the mountain trail, he turned and started running as fast as his legs dared carry him.

Who or whatever had done this to the woman was the purest and deadliest form of evil.

And it lingered.

God in heaven, it was still here.

Detective Selena Alvarez dropped into the chair at her desk. It wasn't yet seven, but she had piles of paperwork to sift through, and the unsolved case of the two dead women found nearly a month apart, linked by the way their bodies had been left in the snow, was uppermost in her mind.

The images of those bodies—naked, tied to trees, gagged and left in the snow to die—chilled her to her bones. For years any dead bodies discovered in and around Pinewood County were few and far between, usually the result of hunting, fishing, skiing or hiking accidents. One time a jogger was mauled nearly to death by a cougar, and there had always been the domestic disputes gone bad, fueled by alcohol or drugs, a firearm or other weapon in handy reach. But murder had never been common in this part of the country. Multiple murders rarer still. A serial killer in this neck of the woods? Unheard of.

But one was here.

She had only to look on her computer screen and see the dead bodies of Theresa Charleton and Nina Salvadore, two women with little in common, to know that a psychopath was either nearby or had passed through.

She clicked her mouse and the dead body of the first victim, Theresa Charleton, came into view on her monitor. A few more clicks and she split the screen with several images: the woman's driver's license picture, procured from the Idaho DMV; a photo of the wrecked green Ford Eclipse, labeled *Crime Scene One*; and another shot of a lonely hemlock tree in a snowy valley with the woman lashed to the trunk, tagged as *Crime Scene Two*. The final image was of the note left nailed above the woman's head: her initials, T C, in block letters, written below a star that had been not only drawn on the white paper but also carved into the bole of the tree about five inches above her head. The lab had found traces of blood in the carving, blood belonging to the victim.

Alvarez's jaw tightened as she stared at what had been left of the schoolteacher from Boise. She'd had no known enemies. Married for two years, no children, the husband devastated. He'd claimed she'd been visiting her parents in Whitefish and his story had checked out. The victim's parents and brother were beside them-

selves with grief and anger. Her brother had insisted the
police "find the monster who did this!"

"We're working on it," Alvarez said to herself as she
opened a file and saw a copy of the note.

The star, similar to the one cut into the tree over the
victim's head, had been drawn high over the letters:

T   **C**

Why? Alvarez wondered. What did it mean to the
killer? The sheriff's department had checked on the
people who had seen her last and come up with nothing so far. They'd thought the incident was a single
murder—until the next victim had been found in an
identical situation.

Again Alvarez clicked her mouse and another image,
so similar to the first that it turned her blood to ice,
flickered onto the screen. A naked woman with long
dark hair was bound to the trunk of a fir tree. Different
location, but eerily similar.

Victim number two was Nina Salvadore, a single
mother and computer programmer from Redding, California. She, too, had been found tied to a tree in a tiny
valley within the wilds of the Bitterroots. Her body had
been two miles from her vehicle, a Ford Focus wrecked
into a nearly unidentifiable crush of red paint, metal
and plastic, found several weeks earlier.

The star cut into the tree over Salvadore's body was
located in a slightly different position in relation to her
body, and the note that had been left at the scene was
slightly different as well. This time, though the star had
been drawn on a standard-size piece of printer paper,
new letters had been written on it. It appeared that
both sets of the victims' initials had been interwoven:

* * *

T   SC   N

Was the killer playing with them? Trying to communicate? If he wanted credit for both killings, why not
write *T C N S*, the order of the women's first and last
names? Why mix the initials up?

Alvarez narrowed her eyes. She was a computer wiz-
ard and had run several programs trying to find out if
the four letters meant anything. So far, she'd come up
dry.

"Bastard," she muttered, trying to imagine what kind
of monster would do something so brutal and cruel as
to leave a woman to freeze in the wilds of Montana in
the winter.

Interviews with those closest to Nina Salvadore had
provided no additional clues. She'd been on her way
back to California, though she'd planned to meet up
with friends in Oregon first, and had driven from Helena, Montana, where she'd been visiting her sister. The
missing persons report had been filed in Oregon first,
when she hadn't arrived in the small town of Seaside
and had been missing for twenty-four hours. In Helena,
Nina's sister had filed a similar report that same day.

Despite combing the crime scenes, bodies and wrecked
cars, and working with police in the hometowns where
the women had lived, the department had no suspects.

Random killings?

Or victims who had been targeted and stalked?

Alvarez bit her lip and found no answers.

After staring at the screen for a few minutes, she gave
up, left her cubicle and made her way down a long hallway. She veered to the left and through a doorway to
the lunchroom, a windowless area complete with small
kitchen and a few scattered tables.

A glass pot of congealing coffee sat on a warmer. Left

over from the night shift. Selena dumped the dark liquid and the pre-measured packet of grounds and started over, rinsing the pot, filling the reservoir with water and finding a fresh package of dark roast in a drawer.

All the while the coffee machine sputtered, dripped and brewed, she considered the bizarre killings. The lab had found traces of bark in both victims' hair. The wood splinters matched those of the trees to which they had been lashed. The bruises and contusions on their bodies had been consistent with being tethered to the trees, and they each had a cut or two from a knife, nothing deep, just a quick little slice, or prick, as if whoever had been urging them to their ultimate place of death had prodded them along.

But other wounds had begun to heal, according to the autopsies. Injuries consistent with what had been sustained in their car wrecks had begun to heal: broken metacarpals, cracked ribs and a fractured radius in Theresa Charleton's case; a broken clavicle and dislocated knee for Nina Salvadore. Each woman's bones appeared to have been set, her abrasions tended to. Salvadore even appeared to have had recent stitches on her right cheek and an area of scalp where some hair had been shaved away.

Where had he kept them?

And why?

Why bring them somewhat back to health only to leave their naked bodies out in the weather? Why heal them only to let them die?

According to the ME, neither woman had been sexually molested.

The case was odd. Nerve-wracking. And Alvarez had spent dozens of hours of overtime trying to get into the killer's head. To no avail.

The FBI was being consulted. Field agents from Salt Lake City had come and left again.

On the kitchen counter the coffee machine gurgled and sputtered its last drops just about the same time Joelle Fisher, secretary and receptionist for the department, breezed in.

"Oh, you already made the coffee. That's my job, you know," she said with one of her ever-present smiles. Nearing sixty, Joelle looked ten years younger except for the fact that she insisted upon wearing her platinum hair in some kind of teased hairdo reminiscent of the fifties screen sirens Alvarez remembered from watching old movies with her mother.

"Yeah, I know."

Joelle's pretty face squinched up as she quickly picked up some old napkins and stir sticks left on one of the tables, then wiped the surface. "You'll get me in trouble with the sheriff."

Pouring herself a cup, Selena didn't think Dan Grayson gave a flying fig about who made the coffee, but she kept her views to herself. Joelle's smug self-satisfaction about all things domestic was no big deal. If she considered the kitchen her little kingdom, so be it.

"Hey!" Cort Brewster, the undersheriff, strode in with a newspaper tucked under his arm.

"How's it going?" Alvarez asked, offering him just a hint of a smile. Brewster was a good guy, happily married, the father of four, but there was something about him that put her on edge a bit. A glint in his eye, maybe, or the way his smile didn't always meet his gaze. Or maybe she was being super-sensitive. Brewster had never done anything untoward to her, or to anyone else in the department as far as she knew.

"If the coffee's not to your liking, I'm sorry," Joelle said, flinging up her hands in resignation. "It was, er, already brewing when I got here." Her perfect little pink-tinged lips puckered a bit and her eyebrows shot up as if she were a schoolmarm pointing out that little Timmy had been playing with himself under the table.

"My fault if the coffee tastes like sewer sludge," Alvarez admitted. "I made it."

Brewster laughed as he found a ceramic mug in the cupboard and poured himself a tall cup.

Joelle, miffed, strutted out of the kitchen, her high heels tapping indignantly down the hallway.

"Looks like you stepped on someone's toes this morning," Brewster observed.

"It's *every* morning." Selena poured herself a cup. "Working here should be considered hazardous duty."

"Meeeow," Brewster murmured into his cup.

"Comes with the territory." She shrugged and headed to her desk. Her shift wasn't due to start for another forty-five minutes, but a few of the night crew were trading stories and packing up.

Her phone rang and she answered it with a grunt of acknowledgment as she sat down.

"Alvarez? This is Peggy Florence in dispatch. I've got a call I think you should hear."

From the tone of the dispatcher's voice, Selena guessed what was coming and braced herself.

"Came in two minutes ago. From Ivor Hicks. If he can be believed, we've got ourselves another one."

". . . and it's another sub-zero-degree day in this part of Montana, blizzard conditions on the roads and another storm rolling in this afternoon." The radio announcer sounded way too chipper considering the news he was delivering. "Coming up after this, we've got an extensive road report and school-closure list, so stay with us at KKAR at ninety-seven point six on your FM dial."

He segued into the first notes of "Winter Wonderland."

Regan Pescoli buried her face into her pillow and groaned at the thought of rousing. Bing Crosby crooning about the joys of snow wasn't exactly what she wanted to hear, not this morning. Her head was thundering, her mouth tasted like garbage and the last thing she needed was to roll out of a nice warm bed and head to the sheriff's department office where all hell was surely breaking loose with this last storm.

Besides, it was still only November. There was still a lotta time before Christmas.

She slapped at the damned radio without opening her eyes, missed and realized belatedly that she wasn't in her own bed. Holy crap! Lifting an eyelid, she focused on her surroundings only to recognize the scarred, shabby furniture of room seven at the North Shore, a small, local motel where she stayed overnight with her sometime lover. Never mind that the low-slung concrete-block motel was situated at the south end of town, near the county line, and there was no shore, no river, no lake and certainly no ocean for miles.

She blinked at the mocking, red digital display of the clock radio: 7:08. If she didn't get cracking, she'd be late for work.

Again.

"Oh hell," she muttered, untangling her legs from the faded striped quilt of the queen-sized bed.

He was just lying there, snoring softly, his incredible, muscular back to her, his hair black and gleaming against the pillowcase.

"Sweet dreams, hotshot," she muttered ungraciously as she searched in the dark for her clothes. Black lacy undies, matching bra, slacks and a sweater.

"Back atcha, sunshine," he whispered without so much as lifting his head.

"Some of us have to work."

"Really?" He rolled over then, instantly awake, and grabbed her hard, pulling her back down onto the bed.

"Hey! I don't have time for this—"

"Sure you do."

"Really, I—"

But he'd already stripped her of the bra she'd just put on and had yanked off her panties in one quick, sure motion. He rolled her atop him and she felt his erection, thick, hard and ready.

"You miserable son of a bitch," she said as he thrust up inside her.

"That's me."

God, he was good. Her juices began to flow within seconds and his hands, kneading her breasts before he rose up to suckle her nipples, made her cry out in pleasure.

His movements were quick. Sure. Long.

She was panting, her breath fast and shallow, her blood coursing hot through her veins, her mind spinning in images of lovemaking and desire.

Her fingernails bit into the muscles of his shoulders as she felt herself begin to spasm. One rocking contraction after another as she leaned back her head, her eyes shut. An orgasm started deep inside and shook her to her soul. "Oh God . . . Oh God . . ."

He held her tight, strong hands gripping her waist, keeping their bodies pressed together as he jerked upward, thrusting in and out, faster and faster, causing her breath to get lost somewhere in her lungs and her mind to spin out of control again. "Oooooh," she whispered as at last he lunged upward, thigh muscles straining and taut. With a growl and one last, hard, mind-numbing thrust, he let go, releasing himself into her.

She felt him stiffen, his back muscles convulse, and

when she opened her eyes she found him staring at her, as he always did whenever they made love.

"Damn you," she said, sweat running down her back and curling the hairs around her nape. "Damn you straight to hell."

"Too late," he said and laughed, pulling her down into the rumpled bedclothes. "I'm already there."

"I know." She let out a long sigh, telling herself she really, really had to get up. "Me, too."

"You're late, you know."

"You love it, don't you?"

"Love what?"

"Being a prick."

His grin was a wicked slash of white in the semi-dark. "No, darlin', you love it."

She snorted and rolled off the bed, swiped up her clothes and, before he could grab her again, dashed into the bathroom, where the air was so cold her breath came out in clouds of steam. What was it about him that was so insidiously tempting? Why could she never say no and mean it? What was it about him that she found so damned sexy? Hadn't she sworn over and over again that she was going to get over him, that she wasn't about to tumble into his trap again?

Yeah, well, a lot of good that did.

If only he weren't so unabashedly good-looking.

Oh hell. She'd known a lot of men. Many good-looking. Most with rock-hard bodies. But this one . . . this one was different.

Really? Isn't he just another bad boy in a long line starting with Chad Wheaton in the eighth grade? Face it, Regan, you have horrible taste in men and enough signed divorce decrees to prove it.

She glanced in the mirror and cringed. Bloodshot eyes, messy hair, ruined makeup, a hickey the size of

New Hampshire on her neck. What was the phrase? Rode hard and put away wet? That's what she looked like. And she didn't have time to go home and step into a long, hot shower.

Deftly she cleaned herself with warm water and a cloth. Dampening her face, she scrubbed off the traces of last night's mascara and lipstick. Then she dabbed the cloth at her armpits and between her legs.

Within five minutes she was ready. Clothes on and somewhat unwrinkled, makeup refreshed, hair snapped back into a curly knot at the base of her skull, she stepped into the darkened bedroom and heard him snoring again.

"Bastard," she muttered, trying to sound angrier than she actually was.

"I heard that." Muffled, from within the pillow.

"Good." She pulled on the boots she'd kicked off at the door and snagged her jacket from the back of a chair. Then she slipped on her shoulder holster, checked the safety of her sidearm and tucked her wallet with her badge in her pocket.

Without another word Detective Regan Pescoli pushed open the motel room door and stepped into the bitter cold of another Montana winter morning.

What was wrong with her? she wondered as she walked to her Jeep, unlocked the rig and climbed behind the wheel. Her cell phone chimed as she backed out of the pockmarked parking space and she checked caller ID. Luckily, the caller wasn't her ex-husband or his sickening Barbie doll of a wife calling about the kids.

But it wasn't good news. She recognized the cell phone number: her partner, Selena Alvarez.

"Pescoli," she answered, eyeing her rearview mirror, then shoving the Jeep into drive.

"We got another one."

Regan's heart nose-dived. She knew what was coming.

Another dead body had turned up in the icy crags and valleys of the Bitterroot Mountains, compliments of their very own serial killer. "Shit. Where?"

"Wildfire Canyon." Alvarez was all business as she gave Pescoli directions to the killing ground.

"I'll be there in thirty," she said and hung up. The remains of yesterday's super-sized soda, probably frozen, sat in the cup holder between the bucket seats. She didn't think twice, just grabbed the soggy paper cup, placed her lips around the straw and took a long swallow of the flat diet cola. As she nosed her way onto the county road, she dug in her glove box for the single pack of Marlboro Lights she kept hidden inside. She was down to one pack a week. Not bad considering her habit had once been three packs a day. But this son of a bitch who was killing women and leaving them in the freezing cold, he was playing havoc with all her good intentions.

She planned to quit all together after the New Year, less than two months away, but between the pressures of her ex-husband, her job and this sicko numb-nuts who got off torturing his victims in the Montana cold, she feared all her good intentions and resolutions might just go by the wayside.

She flipped on her siren and lights and trod hard on the accelerator. The man in the motel room flitted through her mind for a second, then she pushed him steadfastly to that locked corner of her brain she rarely opened, the one that reminded her she was still a sensual, sexy woman with needs.

For the moment, and for most of her life, she was a cop.

Bad boys be damned, she had a homicide to investigate.

Chapter Two

Alvarez ignored the bite of the wind as she surveyed the crime scene where a naked woman was lashed to a solitary tree. Tree branches rattled and snow blew off the heavily laden branches.

Selena Alvarez had never felt so cold in her life.

Dressed in county-issued coat and pants, she stared at the frozen corpse, and her own blood seemed to freeze in her veins.

The victim was Asian from the looks of her. Straight black hair capped with snow, once-smooth flesh showing bruising and contusions, blood discoloring the snow at the base of the tree. Snow that had at one time been mashed beneath boots and bare feet, then crusted over, was now, with a fresh blanket of white, slightly uneven.

Forensic techs were hoping to take casts of what remained of the prints or gather evidence in the form of soil, hair, fibers or any kind of debris that might have dropped from the attacker's clothing or the soles of his boots.

Alvarez held out little hope, as the killer, so far, had been either meticulous or just damned lucky.

As in the other cases, a note had been left at the scene, nailed over the victim's head, and a star hewn out of the bark a few inches above her crown. Though again, the star seemed in a slightly different position, the same being true of its placement on the single sheet of paper.

This time, the note read:

W   T   SC   I N

"What the hell does that mean?" Brewster, who had driven out with Alvarez, asked.

"Don't know."

"Is it some kind of warning, explanation?"

Alvarez shook her head. "He's just screwing with us. Obviously the victim's initials are W and I, though who knows which is her first name and which is her last."

"You mean like Wilhelmina Ingles or Ida Wellington?"

"Yeah," she said sarcastically, slowly walking around the tree, though at a short distance away. "Like Wilhelmina." Already the forensic techs and ME were examining the body, trying to establish a time of death and maybe a cause, as well as searching the area for any other pieces of evidence, anything at all.

As for the cause of death, Alvarez was willing to bet the cause was the same as the others: exposure. Though this woman's body had a few more bruises and cuts upon it, Alvarez thought the end result would be the same. Maybe the killer was growing more violent, getting off on torturing the women first. Or maybe this small woman fought harder than the others, or had fewer injuries from the "accident" where her vehicle had skidded off the icy road.

"No car found," Brewster said, as if reading her thoughts.

"Yet." She glanced up at him. There was no playful flirting now. "Only a matter of time." From the corner of her eye, she saw movement coming down the trail they'd used to access this canyon, then her partner, Regan Pescoli, all five feet ten inches of her, appeared and signed in to the crime scene with the road deputy who'd been first to arrive at the site.

Pescoli was wearing sunglasses, though it wasn't all that bright and clouds were rolling in, and the same unflattering outerwear as the rest of the detectives and road deputies on the scene.

"So we got ourselves another one," she said as she reached Alvarez and Brewster. Her face was flushed, red hair coiling wildly from beneath her stocking cap, and the smell of cigarette smoke clung to her like a shroud.

Alvarez didn't doubt for a minute that Pescoli had been partying the night before, hooking up with yet another loser, but she kept her mouth shut. As long as what her partner did off-hours didn't affect her ability to handle her job, it wasn't really any of Selena's business.

"Yep, looks like," she agreed. She brought Pescoli up to speed about the fact that no vehicle had been found, there were new letters on the same kind of note as left at the previous scenes, there was a slight repositioning of the star and the body had been found by Ivor Hicks.

"Old Man Hicks was up here?" Pescoli repeated, her eyes, behind shaded lenses, scanning the desolate area.

"Walking."

"Who the hell walks up here before dawn?"

"It was the aliens again," Brewster explained. "They made him do it."

Pescoli's lips twisted into a wry smile. "Was it Crytor, the reptilian genius, who sent him up here?"

"General, the reptilian general. Not genius," Brewster corrected. Everyone in the department knew about Ivor Hicks's transportation to the "mother ship" for experiments and tests by the aliens. The story had been written up in the local paper in the seventies, and then again recently, on the thirtieth anniversary of the abduction.

"Ivor been drinking?" Pescoli asked.

Alvarez shook her head. "Doesn't seem like it."

"He drinks a lot."

"I know."

Brewster snorted. "The aliens who did all those tests on him? Wonder if they ran a Breathalyzer."

Alvarez smiled faintly.

"Yeah, they probably think all humans run around blowing a point-three-two in a blood alcohol level."

Pescoli stared at the victim as the paramedics bagged her hands and feet, then cut her free and placed her into a body bag. "I don't think Ivor has the strength, smarts or wherewithal to be our guy. What's he tip out at, maybe a hundred and twenty, a hundred and thirty pounds?" She shook her head. "You talk to him?" she asked Alvarez.

"At length. He's in Deputy Hanson's rig, if you want a word."

"I do," Pescoli said.

"You know he'll go to the press as soon as he gets back into town."

Pescoli pulled a face. "We've kept some details from the press but if Ivor shoots off his big mouth—"

"Every nutcase who wants a little publicity will come forward," Alvarez said, unhappily considering the wasted man-hours that would be spent separating the wannabes from the real deal. The time ill-used sifting through the BS would take away from time that could be spent trying to find the killer.

"He's all yours." Alvarez hitched her chin toward the trail they'd all used to make their way into the canyon and Pescoli took off in the hopes that she could jar a little more information out of Ivor Hicks's alcohol-shriveled brain.

"Good luck," Alvarez muttered.

"Thanks." Pescoli's smile held no warmth. "I'll radio in to missing persons, ask them about any missing Asian or Amer-Asian women with our vic's description. I'll also have them look for anyone missing in the last week with initials that include W and I."

"Make it more than statewide. Have missing persons check Idaho, Washington, Oregon, Wyoming and California."

"Got it." Pescoli was already walking along the trail toward the idling rig where Ivor Hicks was waiting to insist everything he did was because of aliens.

Not exactly the most credible witness.

Alvarez watched as the body bag was carried out. "Guess we're done here."

"Yeah." Brewster shook his head. "What the fuck is going on?"

"Don't know." They, too, began walking out of the snow-covered open space. "Before the next storm sets in, we need choppers and vehicles searching all the roads in a two-mile radius from this point. The other two victims' bodies were found about a mile and a half from the point where their vehicles slid off the road. Pay special attention to the roads that curve sharply over a ravine."

Brewster snorted. "You're talking about every damned road in this part of the county."

"I know." She looked up at the sky where clouds were definitely gathering. They didn't have a lot of time, but the longer they waited the more likely the Asian woman's vehicle would be buried until the spring thaw and any evidence from the car would be lost or degraded. In the meantime she'd go back to the office and chart out each crime scene, see where, if at all, the two-mile radius from each separate area intersected.

Maybe then she'd be one step closer to finding the son of a bitch.

Sheriff Dan Grayson's day had gone from bad to worse.

And it didn't look like things were going to improve any time soon. With his heartburn acting up, he stood behind the desk in his office and stared out the window at the approaching storm. At five in the afternoon, the lights of the city were already glowing, reflecting bluish in the snow-covered streets. As the sheriff's office and jail were perched on the top of Boxer Bluff, he had a view of the river and the falls, located nearly a mile downhill, where much of the town, including the brick-and-mortar, hundred-plus-year-old courthouse, was located.

The press, in the form of microphone-wielding television reporters, had come en masse to the heretofore small, unnoteworthy town of Grizzly Falls.

The last big news in the area was the flood of eighty-eight that had wiped out the boat landing and wildlife refuge located on the banks of the Grizzly River.

But now some goddamned psycho had decided to start leaving naked women bound to trees in this section of the Bitterroot Mountains and that had brought the camera crews, with their recording equipment, lights and vans sprouting satellite dishes, descending like Ivor's aliens upon this sleepy, usually boring town. Freelance reporters and photographers for the local, statewide and even national newspapers were filling the local motels. Armed with pocket recorders, sharp rapid-fire questions and a sense of importance, they, along with their television counterparts, had been mixing it up with the locals.

One idiot of an innkeeper had winked at Grayson over coffee and said, "Well, I'll tell you one thing, Sheriff, all this press is damned good for business."

Grayson had wanted to shove Rod Larimer's cherry Danish down his throat. Instead, he'd finished his coffee in one swallow and said, "What's happening around here, Rod, isn't good for anything. Including business."

Now, Grayson found a bottle of antacids in his desk, opened the plastic lid with one hand and popped a pill dry before settling into his squeaky, old leather chair. Earlier in the day, just after noon, he'd held a press conference, warning the public, explaining the severity of the situation. You would think that'd satisfy them, but when he was finished, the reporters had still clamored for more information. He had given them what he could, had held back only a few vital bits of knowledge, and he'd locked Ivor Hicks up on a trumped-up charge just to keep him away from the press.

Ivor's son, Bill, had gotten wind of his father's predicament and had insisted the old man be released. "You can't hold him, Sheriff," he'd insisted on a telephone call earlier in the day. "For God's sake, Dad helped you, didn't he?"

Grayson hadn't been able to argue that point and had promised to let Ivor go free as soon as the detectives had interviewed him again and taken his statement.

"I'll hold you to it," Bill Hicks had growled before hanging up. It wasn't the first time Ivor's son had tried to bail his father out of a tight spot. It wouldn't be the last.

The truth of the matter was that Ivor's son had called his bluff. Holding the old man was really a load of cock and bull. Several detectives had interviewed Hicks. Grayson was convinced that the sheriff's department had learned everything they could from the old man, yet he hated to think what would happen if one reporter offered to buy Ivor a drink. Ivor could very easily give the guy details of the investigation only the police knew, though, if pressed, he would start talking about the aliens prodding him to the killing site and the reporter would rule the old man out as a credible source.

Or not.

"Hell," Grayson grumbled.

As soon as he figured out a way to keep Ivor from spouting off to the press or neighbors or anyone who would buy him a drink for a good story, he'd release him.

But Ivor Hicks wasn't his only concern. The Feds were involved, too, though this wasn't necessarily a bad thing. Right now, he felt he needed all the help he could get, from the state police to the Feds.

Absently, Grayson tugged on his moustache and stared at the snow blowing in from the north. Predictions were that another blizzard was heading their way. Which was only more bad news. The department was stretched to the limit as it was. Roads were closing, power crews were working double time to keep the electricity and gas flowing, and meanwhile there were some people who didn't have heat, idiots were still trying to drive and ending up wrecking their cars and, if that weren't enough, somewhere in the frigid coming night, a psycho was plotting his next move.

Grayson's jaw slid to one side. "Not in my county," he said, but even to himself the words sounded hollow. Already three murders had been committed, all within the boundaries of Pinewood County.

He just hoped there wouldn't be more.

A rap on the door snapped him out of his reverie.

"Sheriff," Selena Alvarez said as he looked over his

shoulder. "I thought you'd like to see what we came up with on the third victim."

"Just tell me you figured out who the bastard is."

Alvarez's brown eyes darkened a shade. "Not yet," she admitted. She was serious, even more than usual, her mouth drawn down at the edges, her black hair twisted into a knot at the base of her neck, a few thin lines appearing between black, arched eyebrows. Smart as a whip, Selena Alvarez worked at a hundred and twenty percent but kept her private life locked away, as if she had some secret.

Not that it mattered.

He followed her down a short hallway to what had become a special room for a task force that was coming together. Tacked to the scratched green walls were panels of pictures and information on each of the victims, along with details of their deaths. Photographs of the bodies, the wrecked vehicles and the victims' driver's licenses were part of the tableau as well. Theresa Charleton's pictures and info were next to Nina Salvadore's, and in the third space the name Wendy Ito was written next to a question mark.

"We've IDed her?" he asked.

"Not positively, but we think her initials are W and I, or I and W," Alvarez said, "and in our statewide search looking for a missing Asian woman, we found Wendy Ito. Single hairdresser from Spokane, Washington, missing since the second week in November after she spent a weekend with friends in Whitefish. We're checking with those friends now, and the parents." She shook her head. "Still waiting for photo identification from the Washington state DMV."

She pointed to a large map of Pinewood County on one of the other walls. Pushpins had been shoved into the map indicating where the bodies and wrecked cars had been discovered. Three red pins pointed out where the bodies were found, all in different small valleys of the mountain range. Two yellow pins signaled where the crumpled vehicles had been located. A large circle had been drawn around the area and other marks showed the distance between the existing crime scenes.

Grayson stared at the map. "You've talked to all of the people who own property or live here?" he asked, tapping the circle's center.

"We're working on it. Pretty isolated country. Some summer homes, but not many. A few full-time residents." She glanced up at him. "We've talked to most of them." Before he could ask, she added, "No one knows anything."

The knot that was his stomach tightened. "Keep asking. Have we located the last victim's car?"

"Not yet."

He glanced at the map again. "And keep looking."

"We are," she assured him and the set of her jaw convinced him she'd leave no stone unturned in her quest. He just wasn't sure that was going to be good enough.

At six thirty the sun wasn't quite up in Seattle. Jillian Rivers poured herself a second cup of coffee and nearly sloshed it onto the sleeve of her robe as her cell phone beeped from somewhere in the bowels of her purse. She glanced at the digital clock in the microwave and wondered who in the world would call her so early.

The same idiot who called three days ago at five a.m. and didn't leave a message. Like it's a big joke.

She felt an immediate flush of anger before trying to convince herself she was overreacting. The call might be from someone on the East Coast forgetting how early it was three time zones away. Hadn't her college roommate made the mistake not once, but twice before?

Digging through her handbag, she found the phone just as it quit ringing, and called "hello" to no one. "Great." Using the cell's menu, she clicked onto a list of received calls. The last one appeared with no information.

"Wonderful," she said with more than a trace of sarcasm as the cat door clicked loudly.

Marilyn, her long-haired calico, pressed her head against the plastic door, slithered through the opening and slunk into the kitchen. Jillian had installed the door herself upon moving to this townhouse on the shores of Lake Washington. "What, no mouse? No rat? No disgusting headless snake?" she asked as Marilyn did figure eights around her ankles, rubbing and purring loudly. "All right, mighty huntress. Even the best mousers have off days." She picked the calico off the floor and whispered into a pointed, flicking ear, "You're still the fairest of them all, you know."

The cat, snow white with only a few patches of orange and black, had been named Marilyn after Marilyn Monroe by Jillian's mother.

"She's just so beautiful. She has a Hollywood quality, don't you think?" Linnie White had gushed upon delivering the eight-week-old kitten to her youngest daughter. "I tell you, I saw her and couldn't resist. Let's name her Marilyn."

"Wouldn't Norma Jean be a little more . . . I don't know . . . subtle . . . or intellectual? Kind of an inside joke?" Jillian had offered.

"Well, for God's sake, Jillian, it's a cat, for crying out loud. Who needs subtle and intellectual?"

"I'm not sure I even want a cat."

"Of course you do." Linnie had handed Jillian the adorable little bit of fluff and the tiny thing had shown the insight to look up at Jillian with wide green eyes and purr wildly, as if Jillian were some kind of savior. Upon being held closer to Jillian's neck, the kitten had kneaded her with those petite paws and that was, as they say, that. Jillian had fallen instantly in love. Her no-animals decree was null and void. "Oh God, she's already working me," she'd said, knowing she'd been snared. Jillian could have protested to the ends of the earth, but she'd begun bonding with the little feline immediately. Even though she'd never been a "cat person," and even though, after the death of her old, blind dog, another rescued animal from the pound, Jillian had sworn off animals, none of that mattered when Marilyn purred against her neck.

"That's what cats do. Work you," Linnie had agreed, smugly satisfied that Jillian was hooked by the kitten and there would be no returning the little calico to the Humane Society shelter. "And it's why they're so much like husbands."

"Fine, fine, Marilyn can stay. Just don't go to the ex-husband pound and bring me one back, okay?"

Linnie smiled. "Funny girl. Didn't I tell you not to marry Mason, huh? I distinctly remember mentioning something about you not being over Aaron when you took up with him."

"Mom, Aaron was dead four years when I married Mason."

"He was *missing* for four years. And you always suspected something else was going on with Aaron before he disappeared."

"So did the police. But it's ancient history now," Jillian reminded her, not wanting to think what her ex had done, how he'd set her up, how she'd been hounded after his death.

Linnie had clearly wanted to say more, but for once had thought better of it. "So stick with cats for a while."

"Oh, I will," Jillian had agreed. "Believe me."

"No men?"

"No, Mom, no men. Not for a long, long time."

And so the cat had stayed, and so far, Jillian had kept her vow. Which didn't answer the burning question: who was calling her at the crack of dawn? No, make that *before* dawn.

She took a sip of coffee, set a squirming Marilyn onto the ground and was about to walk up the stairs to her bedroom when her cell, still in her hand, jangled.

She answered before the second ring. "Hello?"

"He's alive," a reedy, paper-thin voice whispered.

"Pardon?"

"He's alive."

"Who? Who's alive? Who is this?"

"Your husband. He's alive."

"I *know* he's alive. And by the way, he's my ex." She *knew* Mason Rivers was very much alive and still driving a BMW, practicing law and most likely cheating on his most recent wife. Lots of women wished him dead, but Mason was just too damned egotistical to die. "Who is this?"

"Not your ex."

"I'm hanging up," Jillian said after a moment. A cold sensation was climbing up the back of her neck as she stared out the kitchen window at the gray waters of the lake. Her own pale reflection in the glass looked frightened. "Who are you?"

Click.

The phone went dead and as she stared at it she saw that her hand was shaking. Trembling. Her throat as dry as dust.

Aaron. Whoever was on the other end of the phone was telling her . . . warning her . . . that Aaron was alive? What the hell was that all about? And it wasn't true!

But they never found his body, did they?

You *never quit believing that someday he would walk back through your front door to explain how he'd left you alone after he'd embezzled all that money. After the police had suspected* you *were in on the plot to steal over half a million dollars in funds from people who had invested with him, trusted him.*

"Oh God," she whispered and dropped the phone, sending it clattering across the tile floor. Tears welled in her eyes and her heart was pounding as she slumped against the side of the sink. Aaron was dead. As in forever. An accident while on that damned hiking trip in Suriname. Just because his body had never been recovered from the rain forests of South America didn't mean he was alive.

And then she was angry. Infuriated with whomever had called her. She hated practical jokes. Hated them. Aaron was dead and gone and had been for years.

With an effort, she calmed herself down slowly. Marilyn was staring at her in an unnerving way and it sent a funny little chill down Jillian's spine.

"He's dead," she told the cat firmly. For an answer, Marilyn uneasily flicked her tail and scurried back out the cat door. Jillian was left staring after her . . . and wondering.

Chapter Three

"Rise and shine," Regan Pescoli ordered from the open doorway of her son's bedroom. Posters of grunge and heavy metal bands battled for space on the walls and ceiling with oversized pictures of pro basketball players. Clothes, DVDs and dishes, complete with the dried-on remains of spaghetti or pizza, littered the floor, desk and top of the small television. In a word, the ten-by-ten room in the basement was a sty.

No response from the huge lump in the middle of the futon he'd claimed as his bed.

"Hey, Jeremy, did you hear me? It's time to get up for school."

This time she heard a grunt.

"You know you're not out of the woods yet. One more tardy and Mr. Quasdorff is going to—"

"I don't give a . . . a rat's ass what Quasdorff will do!" her son declared, throwing back the covers. Glaring at the ceiling, he looked so much like her first husband, Regan felt as if she'd been kicked in the gut. "He's so damned gay!"

"I wouldn't be spouting that off. Especially to his wife and kids."

Jeremy rolled morosely out of bed and Cisco, their mottled terrier of some kind, hopped onto the floor. Cisco was ten and graying but still thought he was a puppy. "I could use a little privacy," Jeremy groused, all six feet two of him. Regan sipped her coffee and didn't move. "I get it, Mom, okay?"

"And give your sister a ride to junior high."

"I *know*." He glanced at her with eyes still filled with sleep and she saw only a glimmer of the happy-go-lucky kid he'd once been. Now, he was trying to grow a soul patch, scraggly, uneven whiskers, a darker spot on his chin, and talking about getting tattoos and piercings despite her protests that he wait at least until he was eighteen.

If only his father were still alive. If only Joe hadn't been a hero and died in the line of duty. If only I'd been a better wife . . .

Jeremy nearly ran into her as he made his way up the stairs to the single bathroom and slammed the door. Through the thin panels she heard him turn on the shower, and as the water warmed, flip up the toilet seat and pee like a racehorse.

Things would have been better if Joe had lived, she thought. No, check. Change that. Things would have been *different*; that much she knew. Better? That was just conjecture.

She walked the few steps to the kitchen, where her daughter, perched on a bar stool, was ignoring a slice of peanut butter toast and text messaging as if she'd been born with a cell phone trapped between her slim, be-ringed fingers. With thick, reddish curls, smooth Mediterranean skin and hazel eyes, Bianca was a small, feminine version of her father, Luke Pescoli.

She'd often wondered why, after carrying her children for nine months in her womb, neither had the courtesy to look like her. Jeremy was the spitting image of his father, Joe Strand, while Bianca was a miniature Luke. Sometimes Regan felt like little more than the vessel in which her husbands' DNA had sprouted.

"Eat up," she said, her gaze sliding through the dining area to the living room, where, beside a tired mock-leather couch, a Christmas tree festooned in a billion lights and innumerable strands of tinsel was shoved into the corner, inches from a non-working fireplace. The chipped porcelain nativity scene that had been in her family for generations was strung along the mantel, atop glittery cotton that once had resembled snow but now was tattered and torn. This would be the snow's last year.

Bianca, fingers still flying, the phone clicking, ignored her. The toast was untouched. "Bianca, Jeremy will be ready soon and you know he won't want to wait around. Eat your breakfast."

Click, click, click, click. "Ugh, Mom. Gross! Don't you know that peanut butter is just fat?"

"I believe there's some protein in there."

"Whatever." Bianca didn't bother looking up. The tiny keys kept clicking softly.

Not in the mood to argue, Regan refilled her cup from the pot warming on the coffeemaker. The kitchen was cramped, like the rest of the house—a small "starter home" that Regan worked hard to pay the mortgage on each and every month. The furnace was rumbling loudly, trying to make up for the cold air seeping through the cracks in the caulking around the windows and doors.

Cisco was whining and scratching at the slider door leading to the deck. "Need to go out?" Regan walked to the dining area and opened the door. "Hurry back," she said as the terrier, spying a squirrel trying to break into the bird feeder on the rail, took off on all cylinders, his bark low and gruff, the hackles on the back of his neck raised at the audacity of the rodent.

"I'll cook you an egg," Regan said to her daughter as she closed the door.

"Are you even remotely serious? Do you want me to puke? Geez, Mom, Michelle doesn't make me eat breakfast."

Bully for Stepmom. Though Bianca's father, Luke "Lucky" Pescoli, and Regan had been divorced three months before he began dating Michelle, Regan had never liked the woman, who was still in her twenties, for God's sake, and had *no business* trying to be the kids' second mother. *No business!* Built like a Barbie doll, if not an airhead, Michelle had the dumb-blonde routine down pat. Regan figured the ditziness was an act worthy of an Oscar. Beneath those long blonde tresses and behind the impossibly wide blue eyes, there was a cunning twenty-six-year-old who had graduated from college. Michelle knew exactly what she wanted and how to get it. She just needed enough lip gloss and stiletto heels to make it happen.

The fact that she'd wanted Lucky was a mystery, one Regan hadn't yet been able to solve.

Not that it mattered much.

Rather than think about the twit, Regan found a glass on the counter, rinsed it out, filled it with water and poured some into the rapidly wilting speckled poinsettia on the counter, adding a few drops into the soil surrounding the Christmas cactus, which was going nuts with vibrant pink blooms.

Bianca, never one to leave an argument alone, added, "Michelle says a person should only eat when they're hungry."

"Does she?" Not that Regan cared.

"Uh-huh, and she never has a weight problem."

Good for her, Regan thought as she picked up Bianca's rejected toast and bit into it. No reason for it to go to waste. Or was that *waist?*

"I'll make you some of that instant oatmeal."

Bianca glanced up, her pretty face twisted into a knot of disbelief. "You really do want me to throw up!" Her cell phone beeped again, another text that had her absorbed as a bellow of rage echoed from the bathroom. Old pipes groaned as a faucet was slammed off.

"Shit!" Jeremy yelled loudly enough to be heard throughout the small house.

Regan sipped her coffee and nibbled on the toast. "Guess your brother is finally awake."

The door to the bathroom opened so hard it banged against the wall. Jeremy, towel slung over his slim hips in an attempt to hide, or maybe call attention to, his nether regions stormed into the kitchen. "Who the hell used all the hot water?" he demanded, skewering his sister with an intense stare of hate that could have come straight out of a teen horror flick.

"The tank's small." Regan dusted her fingers of crumbs. "Want some breakfast? Peanut butter toast."

Jeremy wasn't about to be derailed. "So that means *she* has the right to hog it all? Jesus, Mom, aren't you always preaching about consideration?" He walked to the refrigerator, pulled out a carton of orange juice and held it to his lips.

"Get a glass."

"I'm finishing it."

"You brought up consideration."

He guzzled juice and left the carton on the counter next to last night's pizza box.

"Jeremy?"

"What?" he called as he hurried down the stairs.

"We need to talk about your chores around here."

"I thought my chore was to take the dingbat to school."

Bianca snorted. "The dingbat who's on the honor roll. What a creep. He hasn't seen anything above a two-point for so long, he wouldn't know what it was." One eyebrow lifted in prim smugness, though the truth of the matter was that her grades had been slipping lately. Something was up.

"About those grades," Regan said. "Yours have been—"

"Yeah, yeah, I know." Bianca finished her text and looked up. "I'm bringing them up. I told you Miss Lefever has it in for me."

"Maybe it's all the time you're spending with Chris."

At the mere mention of her boyfriend's name, Bianca absolutely lit up, her bad mood disappearing for an instant. Her lips twitched into a happy little smile, which Regan found more than slightly disturbing. "Chris has nothing to do with my grades."

"Since you started"—Regan made air quotes—" 'going with' him, you haven't been so interested in school."

"Big deal."

"Bianca—"

"Oh, what? I've got a boyfriend?" she mocked. "Yeah, that's right. But he's *not* affecting my grades, okay? Maybe you're just jealous or something."

Regan stared at her silently.

"I mean, it wouldn't hurt you to date. You know, get a life. Then maybe you'd be off my . . . case." She swept her backpack from the counter and slid off the bar stool as Jeremy's heavy tread pounded up the stairs again.

"Gotta go," Bianca said quickly and slid her phone into her book bag.

"We're not finished with this discussion," Regan warned as Jeremy appeared in an oversized sweatshirt, sweat-pants and a stocking cap pulled low over his forehead. As he slipped on a pair of sunglasses, Regan thought her son was a dead ringer for the Unibomber or half a dozen other police sketches of wanted men.

Bianca had already grabbed a jacket and was out the door as Jeremy, keys jangling from one hand, followed after her.

"What about your backpack?" Regan asked, eyeing her son.

"In the car."

"So you didn't do your homework?"

"Oh, Mom." One hand on the doorknob, Jeremy rolled his eyes just as Cisco shot into the house.

She fought the urge to light into her son about his schoolwork. Now wasn't the time. "Drive carefully. Some of the roads have been closed and there's another blizzard predicted, for this after—" The front door slammed behind them and Regan walked to the living room to stare through the window as her son dutifully turned on the old pickup's engine, then went about scraping off the windows as the defroster heated the glass from the inside. Even inside the house she heard the heavy beat of some indefinable rock music.

"At least it's not rap, at least it's not rap," she said, her mantra for the past five years. Within minutes, the windows were clear enough and he folded himself into his twenty-year-old Chevy truck.

When had it come to this? When the kids took off without saying good-bye or buzzing her cheek with a kiss? Or even listening to her?

She watched them drive away and waved, though, of course, neither of them turned to look back at the house. She felt a little like a fool. She had to do something about the kids. She knew they were both headed for trouble. Jeremy was still dealing with issues about his deceased dad and Bianca was trying to find a way to fit herself into her father's new family.

And it didn't help that Regan was a single mom, work-

ing with the sheriff's department on the first serial-killer
case in this part of Montana that anyone could remember. She'd spent almost every waking hour trying to figure out who the bastard was and when he would strike
again.

It had been two weeks since the last body had been
found. Wendy Ito had been identified by her two grief-
riddled parents, the father stoic and grim while Wendy's
mother had dissolved into a rage of tears and had to be
held up by her slight but rigid spouse.

It had been hell.

And all the interviewing in the world hadn't brought
the sheriff's department, or the friggin' FBI, for that
matter, any closer to the killer. Wendy Ito's new Prius
hybrid hadn't been located and none of the friends
she'd spent the weekend with had been much help. No
one, it seemed, had any idea as to the identity of the
girl's killer. Just like with Theresa Charleton and Nina
Salvadore. But it wasn't over.

"We'll get you, you son of a bitch," Regan said as she
walked back to the kitchen and dumped the remains of
her coffee into the sink. She rinsed out her cup and left
it with the ever-growing stack of dishes piling on the
counters. "We'll get you."

The trouble was, if the killer was still in his same pattern, it was about time for another "accident" where he,
presumably, would stage the scene, shooting out the
tire of his next victim, then showing up to "rescue" her.
That's how he did it. Shot out the goddamned tires.
Bastard. Regan set her jaw.

The ME was certain that the women who had been
found staked to trees in desolate parts of the mountains
had spent at least a week, maybe two, healing from the
injuries sustained in accidents where their vehicles had
skidded off the road. The medical examiner theorized
that each of the dead women had received basic first

aid, or medical care, before they'd been marched naked to the place where they would be forsaken and left to die.

She wondered vaguely if there were others—victims who hadn't survived the staged accidents, lucky ones, maybe, who hadn't been made to suffer and die in the elements—but she dismissed the thought. No other wrecked vehicles had been discovered.

After feeding Cisco and making sure the dog had ample water for the day, she walked to her cramped bedroom to change into slacks, a red turtleneck sweater because it was the holidays damn it, her shoulder holster, a jacket and boots. She then made certain the Christmas tree lights were unplugged and the exterior doors were locked, and headed through the attached single-car garage to her Jeep.

There was a chance that today would be the day they caught the prick.

Maybe they'd get lucky.

Though a gambling woman by nature, Detective Regan Pescoli wasn't ready to bet on it.

Not yet.

Jillian parked in her assigned spot under the carport, then made a mad dash to the front porch as raindrops assailed her from a nearly dark sky. Most of the row houses were decorated, their sparkling, colored lights tiny bright beacons in the gray drizzle that was Seattle in winter. Battling with her small umbrella at the curb where the bevy of mailboxes for her group of units was located, Jillian unlocked her box and found a large manila envelope wedged in, her name and address written in black marker and block letters that began to run in the rain.

"Great," she muttered, a gust of wind catching in her

umbrella and turning it inside out as thick raindrops pelted her face. Ducking her head and sidestepping puddles, she dashed past the front lawns of two other row houses, then hurried up her front walk. The rain, blowing sideways off Lake Washington, pummeled her as she finally unlocked her front door and scurried inside. "Honey, I'm home," she called as she entered, pulling the door shut behind her. It was her private joke, but every once in a while, as if on cue, Marilyn would come trotting from the kitchen at the back of the house, meow and greet her expectantly. Today, she wasn't lucky, and after tossing her keys and purse on the side table, she set about opening the mail, starting with the envelope with the postmark of Missoula, Montana.

Where Mason, her ex-husband, lived.

So what was this? Some post-divorce court order?

God, Mason could be such a bastard.

But, then, why no return address? No printer-generated label from his law firm?

Water from the hem of her coat dripping onto the hardwood floor, she tore the wet packet open without the aid of a letter opener. Several grainy photographs, the kind that looked as if they'd been taken by an amateur photographer using a cell phone and printed off a computer, slid onto the side table.

Three images.

All of the same man.

All fuzzy and a little out of focus, as if the subject were moving, walking away, his head turned away.

Jillian's heart nearly stopped beating.

Oh God, it couldn't be!

She switched on the lamp. Golden light poured over the pictures that she flattened so that they lay side by side, as if they were stills from a movie.

The man was profiled in the first two shots but in the third shot, he looked back over his shoulder and faced the lens so that she could make out his features beneath his beard and aviator shades.

"Aaron?" she said aloud, and her first husband's name seemed to reverberate off the walls. "Dear God, Aaron?"

Tears burned at the back of her eyes. She'd loved this man. *Loved* him. Lived with him. Married him. Lost him. And grieved for him. Oh Lord, how she'd grieved for him.

And now he was *alive?*

She let out a slow breath that she didn't realize she'd been holding. The envelope, the one from which the pictures had tumbled, was clenched hard in her left hand.

He was alive?

Aaron Caruso, her college sweetheart, the man she'd married so naively, hadn't died in a forest in Suriname? Had lied to her? Had wanted her to think him dead? Had heartlessly left her while absconding with investors' funds? Hadn't cared that she would be a suspect, too? That the police would believe she knew what had happened to him? Would he have been so cruel?

Her knees threatened to give way and she braced herself against the table. No. This man in the hastily snapped photo wasn't Aaron, just someone who looked like him. The beard hid his jaw. Aaron's had been square and strong. And the sunglasses disguised the color and shape of his eyes. Aaron's had been a deep brown and wide-set, his nose broken from an old basketball injury . . . She studied the pictures again and thought she saw the slight bump on his nose.

Of course it had been over ten years since she'd seen her first husband. He, if he had lived, would have changed. Like the man in the photo, who was at least ten pounds heavier and bearded. But the hair, that light brown hair with its distinctive widow's peak, was the same—thick and wavy.

So distinctively Aaron.

What did it mean if this photo was real . . . if Aaron was alive? He would have built some sort of life for himself. A wife and kids. A home.

Don't fall for this, Jillian, she warned herself, but it was too late. She was already half-buying into the fact that these photos showed her first husband, the one whom everyone, including the insurance company and the authorities, had presumed to have slid down a steep ravine to a raging river, where he'd been swept away by a swift current and drowned.

Presumably drowned.

The house phone rang and she nearly jumped out of her skin. Carrying the rest of the mail and the damned pictures with her, she walked through the hallway to the small family room and snapped up the receiver before the second ring. "Hello?" she said into the receiver and noted that, once again, the caller ID had been blocked.

"He's alive," the disembodied voice hissed again.

"Who is this? I'm not interested in playing any games."

"Check your mail and your e-mail."

"What do you want?"

Click.

"Damn it!" Jillian hung up and felt a rage so deep she could barely think. Who was doing this? Not Aaron, even if he were alive. So who? And why?

Jillian felt as if a ghost had just brushed against the back of her neck. Either the person on the other end of the call had been teasing her, playing a sick prank on her, or the unthinkable had happened and Aaron had come back from the dead.

Jillian closed her eyes. *Ten* years. A damned decade! He couldn't be alive. That didn't make any sense and yet . . . and yet . . .

Go to the police her inner voice suggested as she peeled off her coat, walked to the front of the house again and hung the garment on the wrought-iron coat tree near the front door. She found her tattered umbrella, fixed the broken spokes as best she could, then shoved it into the lower part of the same tree. Taking the steps two at a time, she climbed to the second floor and made her way to her den, which, when the hide-a-bed was opened, became her guest room. The computer was on and waiting, a screen saver of waving palms like wistful arms beckoning her to some sunny, remote destination where the sun always shone.

Kicking out her desk chair, Jillian sat down and clicked onto her e-mail account. She found one that had slipped through her spam filter with an attachment. When she opened it, sure enough, the same three pictures of the bearded man who was supposed to be her dead first husband appeared.

She checked the e-mail address, pressed REPLY, but, of course, her mail bounced back at her.

Damn.

She clicked back to her home page and a news item caught her eye. SERIAL KILLER STRIKES MONTANA. The story mentioned two women found dead in desolate parts of the Bitterroots, but she was too distracted to read on with these photos of Aaron taunting her.

She enhanced the pictures, enlarging them, then sharpening the images. As she worked with computer and photographic images for a living, this was a piece of cake. She'd spent the past five years creating brochures, both real and virtual, for clients ranging from universities to travel agencies and tour groups. In this room alone, the walls were covered with photographs she'd taken herself, colorful pictures of exotic locales and beautiful homes turned into inns. There were images of a brilliant sunset on the Oregon coast, the Cascade

Mountains deep in snow, a fishing excursion on the
Kenai River in Alaska and a hundred-and-fifty-year-old
hotel situated in the rugged Columbia Gorge.

Using programs that enhanced, enlarged, zoomed in
and recolored, she played with the photographs, eras-
ing the man's beard and sunglasses, growing his hair a
few inches, taking off ten pounds. With each change,
her heart beat a little faster, her nerves tightened and
anticipation coursed through her veins.

When she was finished, the altered image was a dead
ringer for her long-lost first husband.

*Anyone can make someone look different. You've seen
countless short movies of people morphing from one person to
another. You've seen the before and after pictures of models on
the covers of magazines. You know how to make an image
change shape.*

This could be an out-and-out scam.

But *why?*

And who was behind it? Mason, in Missoula?

She shook her head at the thought. If Mason wanted
to give her information, he'd just do it, call her up and
give her the facts. And if he were trying to be sneaky,
he'd mail the envelope from another town. He knew
she wasn't an idiot.

*But what about that new wife of his—Sherice? She always
had it in for you. And his mother, Belle—that woman never
did like you.*

It seemed far-fetched. She and Mason rarely commu-
nicated, and though Sherice, Mason's receptionist, had
outwardly despised Jillian when Jillian and Mason were
married, now, since she'd become the second *much younger*
Mrs. Mason Rivers, Sherice's animosity had faded. Sherice
had won the great prize of becoming a trophy wife. So
why try to stir up trouble now?

Jillian leaned back in her desk chair and tapped the
eraser end of her pencil on the arm of the chair as she

stared at the image on the computer. She heard a soft meow and then Marilyn padded through the open door and, spying Jillian's empty lap, leaped onto it.

"Hey, sweetcakes," Jillian said, absently rubbing the calico's head. "What do you think?"

The cat responded by curling up in her lap while Jillian tried to figure out if her long-dead husband had suddenly resurrected and why anyone would want her to know.

"It's a problem," she confided to Marilyn and knew in that instant that she couldn't leave it alone.

She had to find out the truth.

If for no other reason than to clear her name.

No matter what it entailed, how painful it happened to be.

Chapter Four

Naked, I stand at the window.

Alone.

Waiting.

While sand slips oh so slowly through the hourglass.

The coming night is near, shadows playing darkly. A hollow wind, keening and savage, cuts through the canyons with the promise of death upon its breath. I hear its plaintive cry from deep in the cabin.

It wants me, I think. *It wants her.*

It's as hungry as I am.

Good!

Feeling the ache, the low, insistent pulse, I peer through the windowpanes glazed in ice, frosted with blowing snow.

Naked branches of the lonely trees rattle and dance, like skeletal arms raised in supplication to the heavens.

As if God were interested.

I feel the urge to step outside. The tug of the cold tempts me to languish in the caress of frigid gusts upon my bare skin.

But it is too soon.

I won't let myself fall victim to that easy enticement. The timing isn't right. Not yet.

I have to be patient.

Because she is coming.

Unfailingly and without any inkling as to her fate, she is drawing near. I feel it.

And everything has to be perfect.

"Come on," I whisper quietly and feel that sensual twitch deep inside at the thought of her: lightly tanned skin, dusting of freckles, wide hazel eyes and untamed hair a deep brown that shines red in the firelight. "Come the fuck on."

The knowledge that she will soon appear causes my blood to race, my mind to fire with images of what's to come. I can almost taste her, feel the texture of her skin as she quivers at my touch. In my mind's eye I watch her pupils dilate until her eyes are nearly black with fear and a dark, unwelcome desire.

Oh, she will want me.

She will beg for more of me.

And I will give her what she wants . . . what she fears.

Her last conscious thoughts will be of me.

Only me.

But not yet . . . I have to hold back.

Tamping down my vibrant, exhilarating fantasies, I decide to savor them later. When the timing is right.

With one last glance at the window, I walk to the table near the fire, sit in the smooth wooden chair, feel the varnish against my bare skin. When my body is un-fettered by clothes, my mind is sharper. Clearer.

I study my maps carefully. Using a magnifying glass, charting my course. The worn, marked pages spread upon the table near the kerosene lantern glow softly. Scattered upon the scarred planks are the astrological charts, birth certificates and recent clippings of the deaths that no one will ever trace to me. In the articles

the beautiful release of souls is described as brutal slay-
ings, the work of a psychopath.

Reporters, like the police, are idiots.

I can't help but smile at all their wasted efforts.

The authorities are morons.

Cretins.

Fools who are so easily toyed with.

Burning wood crackles in the grate, anxious flames
devouring the mossy chunks of oak and pine. The scent
of wood smoke is heavy in my nostrils as I reread the stories about the "victims," tales that have been carefully
construed by the stupid cops to ensure that no details
they wish to keep from the public have slipped into the
articles. They have worked diligently to hold back information, clues that will keep every nutcase around from
claiming ownership of my deeds.

For if that should happen, the short-staffed sheriff's
department would have to sort it all out, spending valu-
able hours dealing with the fraud. Officers would have
to expose him or her as just some whack job trying to
get his or her fifteen minutes of fame. The department
would lose a lot of time uncovering the false murderer,
a lunatic pretender who in no way could understand
the divinity, nor the complexity, of the painstakingly ex-
ecuted sacrifices.

Sorry, imbeciles.

You'll have to find some other killer to emulate.

"Killer." The word tastes bitter. As do "criminal" and
"psycho." Because what I do isn't a crime, not just a
"killing," not some psychotic whim, but a necessity . . . a
calling. However, those who are unenlightened can
never understand. What I've done, what I will do again,
is misunderstood.

So be it.

A window rattles against a gust of wind and I feel a
sudden chill slither down my spine. Glancing up from

my work to the icy panes, I see fluttering flakes of snow in the steely day beyond. Feeling the storm seep through the cracks in the walls, the cold air taunting my skin, I envision her again.

Beautiful bitch.

Soon you will be mine.

God and the Fates are on my side.

I lick my lips as a thrill steals through my bloodstream. Turning back to the table, I see her picture. In black and white, the surroundings out of focus, her features clear and crisp.

In the glossy photograph, she appears happy, though, of course, her smile is a frail façade. She looks almost flirtatious.

A lie.

As I stare deeply into her eyes, I detect a shadow, a small hint of darkness that betrays her fear.

In that fragile moment when the camera captured her, she sensed that her life was far from what it seemed.

And yet she couldn't possibly comprehend the truth, then or now. Little does she know what is about to happen: that her fate has already been sealed, that she will soon join the others. . . .

Carefully I read the charts once more. The stars are in the right positions; the groundwork has been done and December, with its cold, stinging kiss, will soon be here.

As will she.

She will arrive before the turn of the calendar's page.

Closing my eyes I imagine our meeting: Her chilled flesh will press against mine. Her skin will have the salty taste of fear, her cheeks even more so, with the tracks of tears.

A frisson of expectation sizzles through my blood.

I glance down at the photograph again.

So clear.

So sharp.

So ready.

"Soon," I whisper, not saying her name aloud, not wanting to hear it echo through the rafters. "Very soon."

My groin tightens with expectancy.

Winter and Death are about to meet.

Jillian stepped on the accelerator.

Her medium-size station wagon engine whining, responded, winter tires digging into the icy terrain. She took a sip from her cup, a rapidly cooling cup of coffee that she'd bought at the last town she'd passed through, now nearly five miles back. Spruce Creek, the town, if you could call it that, was little more than a stoplight at two crossroads. The intersection had boasted a post office, gas station, coffee shop, two churches and, as if in perfect juxtaposition, two taverns. A few distantly spaced farmhouses had peppered the snowy landscape.

"Welcome to rural Montana," she said aloud, wondering, not for the first time, if she was on a fool's mission. The radio was tuned to a country/western station and Willie Nelson was singing over the underlying static, "White Christmas" no less.

"I'm dreaming of a white Christmas," he warbled in his nasal twang.

"Well, you got one, Willie Boy," she said, staring out a windshield threatening to fog over to a vast landscape of snow-laden trees and piling drifts. "You've got yourself one helluva white Christmas."

All around her, the mountains knifed upward, their peaks hidden by the thick clouds and driving snow. Here, in the Bitterroot Mountains, it looked like a second Ice Age.

The road twisted ever upward and her little car

climbed steadily, its wipers slapping the flurries off the windshield. One tire slipped before digging in. Jillian eased into the slide, sloshing coffee, and the car's all-wheel drive didn't let her down. Nonetheless, she was nervous and wondered how far it was to the next town.

This mountainous part of Montana was more desolate than she'd anticipated, and though she wasn't a coward or the least bit skittish, today, as dusk threatened and she met not one other vehicle on the road, she felt a little anxious, a bit edgy.

"Too much caffeine," she muttered as Willie's song faded and an announcer's voice cut in and out. Irritated, she switched off the radio and thought about the calls she'd received from the unidentified caller and the pictures he or she had sent.

Had they been of Aaron?

Or was this some elaborate hoax?

"Face it, you're on a wild goose chase," she told herself for the umpteenth time, but her hands tightened on the steering wheel as she remembered those whispered conversations all insisting the same thing:

"He's alive."

"Son of a bitch," she muttered as the Subaru's engine suddenly strained. She hadn't really believed the weirdo on the other end of the line and God knew the photos could have been doctored, but she wasn't one to live with any kind of doubt. So what if it was just a twisted joke? At least she could finally put Aaron's memory to rest.

Right?

She'd left Seattle without telling a soul other than to ask her nineteen-year-old neighbor, Emily Hardy, to take care of Marilyn for a few days. So now she was in the middle of the Montana wilderness, a blizzard brewing. "Turn around," she told herself, realizing she was chasing the same damned ghost she had been pursuing for years.

Hadn't Mason, her second husband, accused her of just that? "Damn it all to hell." The Outback's tires slid a bit and she slipped the gearshift into a lower gear. "Come on, come on." The mid-size car lunged forward, engine groaning in protest.

Spruce Creek wasn't that far behind her. If she found a wide spot in the road, she could turn around and give up for the night.

The thought of a bed and a warm room in a motel made her sigh. She could hole up and spread her map out, check out the best route between here and Missoula, where she would spring her surprise on Mason.

But turning back felt too much like quitting, and she'd never been a quitter. Not since third grade, when she'd been bucked off a horse and decided to give up horseback riding all together. Until her grandfather had stared down at her with kind blue eyes and said, "Hey, Jillie, don't you know, quitting's for sissies? I never figured you to be one to run and hide when things got a little rough." He'd helped her back on the wild-eyed colt, walked that painted pony for hours, until Jillian's confidence had returned. So she wouldn't give up now. Grandpa Jim had been dead and buried for over fifteen years, but she still felt as if he could see her every time she considered throwing in the towel.

Setting her jaw, she saw the next corner on this white, snow-flecked ridge. Maybe this was the summit. Maybe she'd finally reached a point where the road would wind down to the next town and she'd find a hotel or bed and breakfast where she could spend the night, take a long, hot shower and—

CRRRAAACCCKKK!

Jillian jumped.

The sharp report of a rifle echoed through the canyon.
BAM!
Her front tire blew.
"Oh Jesus!" Her heart flew to her throat. "No!"
The car spun crazily, wildly careening from one side of the icy road to the other.
"Oh God, oh God . . . oh . . ."
Don't overreact!
Drive into the spin.
Grandpa Jim's voice filled her brain and all the advice she'd heard about driving in ice and snow flashed through her mind.
Already skidding, the Subaru bouncing off the wall of ice on the mountain side of the road, shaving off snow and ice only to slide to the other side of this narrow ridge, toward the yawning canyon of the cliff face, as Jillian fought to control the Outback.
"Please, oh please . . ." She pressed the brakes and gripped the steering wheel.
Closer to the edge of the ridge, where the tops of trees were the only indication there was a bottom to the steep ravine, the automobile wavered and shuddered. "No, no, no!" she cried. To hell with the advice. She couldn't turn into the spin and steer toward the abyss. Frantically, she yanked on the wheel, cranking it away from the gaping hole and trying like hell to keep the car on the road.
She stood on the brakes.
The tires jerked beneath her, anti-lock mechanism working to grab the icy pavement.
"No," she whispered through her teeth, her heart tattooing wildly, her mind screaming. She stomped on the brake pedal, trying to slow the damned car down!
She braced herself against the steering wheel, her foot jabbing hard on the brake.
Stop! Stop the car, now!

One wheel slipped over the edge.

The car rocked crazily.

She cranked on the steering wheel again. Hard.

Too late!

Momentum propelled her Subaru over the edge.

And then the car was falling, plunging into the coming night.

Through the windshield, Jillian saw the tops of snow-covered trees, heard the scrape of branches tearing at the car's underbelly and sides.

Glass shattered.

Metal twisted and groaned.

She screamed, arms covering her face, both feet on the brake pedal, as the mid-size car hurtled into the dark, gaping abyss of the canyon.

Perfect!

The silver vehicle with Washington plates plummeted into the canyon.

Free-falling almost in slow motion.

A thing of beauty.

The "accident" planned to meticulous perfection.

The Subaru tumbled and dropped.

Brittle tree branches snapped.

Frozen snow fell in clumps.

Metal shrieked.

A scream rang through the ravine, a scream of pure, unadulterated terror.

Which couldn't have been more exquisite.

All of the waiting had been worth it.

Jillian Rivers, the bitch, was finally about to die.

Jillian's eyelids snapped open.

But she couldn't see . . . all around was darkness.

She groaned as a burning, grinding pain shrieked through her body. And her vision, oh God, why couldn't she make out anything? Her legs were on fire, her head thudding, something covering her mouth and nose, cutting off her air.

Oh, sweet God in heaven, what happened?

Where am I?

And please, please make the pain stop!

She tried to draw in a breath, gasping around whatever was over her face, suffocating her.

Panic engulfed her, but she attempted to put it at bay. It was dark, but not completely, and the object over her face wasn't pressing down, wasn't stopping the flow of air completely. Her mind cleared as she tried to bat it away. What the hell was it? A pillow? No. A damned balloon? No . . . oh dear God, it was an air bag!

Teeth chattering from the cold or shock, she flailed at the damned bag and pushed it to one side. Despite the pounding in her head, she tried to focus. Slowly she realized she was trapped in the twisted wreckage that had been her Subaru.

A car wreck?

I was in an accident. Oh Holy Mother, my ankle!

She sucked in a breath, tried to think back. She was trapped inside a car, her ten-year-old Subaru Outback, now mangled and dead. It was freezing cold, wind screaming through the shattered windshield. Her head pounded and she felt blood, sticky and warm, in her hair.

Her thoughts were scattered and disjointed, as if she were drunk, blackness threatening to pull her under, pain keeping her conscious.

You've got a concussion, you idiot. You've got a stupid concussion. That's why you feel light-headed. Wake up, Jillian, and figure this out! You're going to freeze in here.

She moved just a bit.

Pain stopped her cold.

Every bone in her body felt as if it were broken, her muscles and skin bruised, agony throbbing through her joints.

Gritting her teeth, she tried to move again, but her left foot, pinned beneath the crumpled dash, wouldn't budge. Pain jagged up her leg. Nausea boiled in her throat and she nearly retched. She felt the blood drain from her face and knew she was on the verge of passing out.

Don't do it. Don't let go. Hang on, whatever you do. Losing consciousness will kill you.

Taking deep breaths, her chest aching as if she'd cracked ribs, she struggled to stay awake.

God, it was cold. So damned cold. She tried the ignition, twisting the key, but nothing happened, as if the starter itself were ruined. She tried again and again, but there wasn't so much as a click indicating the engine was trying to spark.

"Damn it all to hell," she muttered, giving up on any hope of starting the car.

She stared out the splintered glass to the coming dusk and the snow blowing in wild circles, a million swirling flakes caught in the dim beams of headlights twisted at odd angles but still, somehow, giving off cock-eyed illumination.

Maybe someone would see her, find her because of the headlights splashing in macabre patterns upward through the trees.

And if they don't, what happens? You freeze. Right here in this wreck of a car. You have to get out, Jillian, and you have to get out now!

"Help!" she cried. "Someone, help me!"

Her voice was hoarse and faint against the wind.

Where had she been going on this stormy night? Why the hell was she in these mountains?

Why was she alone?

At that thought she froze.

Maybe she hadn't been traveling by herself. Maybe someone had been with her! She slid a glance to the side, but the passenger seat was empty. Ignoring the pain, she twisted her neck and glanced into the torn and buckled area that had been the backseat. Fabric was ripped, padding exposed, her suitcase wedged between the front seat and what was left of the backseat. But there wasn't any evidence of anyone caught in the mangled metal and plastic and shards of glass. No bloody arm peeked out of the torn cushions; no terrified face of a dead person stared at her through glassy, sightless eyes.

Shivering, she pulled at a blanket she always kept in the car and yanked hard, as it was caught in the folds of wrenched metal and plastic. The pain in her rib cage was excruciating but she didn't give up. "Come on, come on," she muttered, yanking hard on the damned piece of quilt her grandmother had made fifty years earlier. She heard it rend, old stitches giving way, but she managed to tear off most of it and wrap it around her as her damned ankle continued to pound and her head ached, the cuts on her face burning.

She yelled again and pounded on the horn. It gave out a sharp blast. Again she hit the damned thing, yelling, hoping beyond hope that someone would hear her.

What had she been doing driving in what appeared to be steep mountains with sharp ridges and sheer canyons? And where the hell were these damned mountains located? The Cascade Range in Western Washington? The Canadian Rockies? The Tetons? Or some other craggy range?

Montana, she thought dimly. *You were driving to Montana.*

Surely someone would be missing her soon when she

didn't arrive at her destination, wherever in Montana that was. And then, of course, a search party would be sent.

Unless this trip of yours was secret. Clandestine.

She had the uneasy feeling that no one knew where she was, though she wasn't clear about where she was going. It had something to do with Montana and her ex-husband, something secret . . . what was it? If she could only recall.

"For the love of God," she muttered and shook her head, only to wince at the pain. She didn't remember everything about herself, but she knew she wasn't some sort of spy and she wasn't one to keep secrets and she never really cared to keep anything on the "down low."

And yet . . .

A dark fear that she was completely alone snaked around her heart.

"Don't even think it," she told herself. Someone somewhere was missing her, looking for her. It was only a matter of time before she'd be found. She just had to stay alive long enough for the rescue.

Head throbbing, she glanced up again, searching for the road that had to be high overhead. All she saw was a sheer wall of snow and ice. There were trees in this grim crevice, a few foreboding sentinels covered in snow, but not much else. Obviously her car had slid down the steep embankment and landed in what appeared to be a frozen creek bed. Had she swerved to avoid hitting another vehicle? A deer? Someone on foot? Or had she just taken a corner too fast and hit ice, only to go careening over the ledge?

Try as she might, she couldn't remember. Yes, there were fleeting thoughts of packing the car, of planning a quick trip . . . a long trip, from Seattle, where she lived. She had a quick memory of checking a road map and heading east, out of the snarl of traffic of the U District and her row house near the campus of the University of Washington. She'd nosed her Outback across the Evergreen Point Floating Bridge, which straddled a narrow point in Lake Washington, and then drove on the freeway past Bellevue and further east . . . and then . . . nothing. She had an inkling that she'd been determined. Maybe even angry. Which wasn't a surprise if it had anything to do with her ex.

"Terrific," she muttered under her breath, unable to call up any memory more tangible. Not that it really mattered. Why she was on her hastily planned trip and even where she was going weren't of vital consequence. Getting out of the canyon and to safety was.

"Damn it all," she whispered, frustrated and shivering, her breath fogging in the freezing air.

Still staring upward, she swallowed back a new surge of despair.

The sheer face of the cliff was daunting. If the road was up there, high over this frozen creek bed, how would she ever be able to climb up the steep, frigid wall of rock and ice? Even if she weren't injured, if she were healthy, dressed for the arctic, with rock-climbing gear, she doubted she could scale the mountain.

Think, Jillian. Think! *There must be another way out of here!*

Holding the blanket tight, she slowly surveyed the creek bed. Was there a path or road, some other means, away from this ravine, toward civilization? Maybe she could follow the stream downhill.

Oh yeah right, Einstein. With an ankle that might be broken? A leg that moved so much as an inch causes you to howl in agony? Face it, you can't get out of here without help.

"Hell." She banged on the horn again. Urgently. Frantically. Desperately. Sending the sharp blasts ricocheting through the snowy gorge.

But it was useless; she knew it. To her own ears the

wild honking sounded like the forlorn bleating of a frightened sheep.

Pathetic.

But it was all she could do.

Still pounding on the horn, she yelled again until her throat was raw, hoping her pathetic din and the fading headlights would draw some attention. But no sound of a car's engine answered, no jumbled shouts of rescuers could be heard, no *whop, whop, whop* of a helicopter's rotors sounded over the sigh of the wind.

No . . . she was alone.

In this godforsaken wilderness, with the freezing night slipping ever closer, she was totally and frighteningly alone.

Chapter Five

"You suck!" Bianca grumbled under her breath as Jeremy lay on the couch watching MTV.

"You suck!" he threw back and tossed another handful of some trail mix into his mouth.

"Right now, I think you both suck," Regan broke in from the kitchen. "And for the record, I hate that word. Can't you come up with some other insult? Something a little more clever."

"Oh, Mom, don't be such a nerd." Bianca flopped into a side chair, red-blonde curls flouncing around her small face. A few freckles she tried desperately to hide with makeup bridged her nose and her big hazel eyes were rimmed with thick, dark lashes. Just like her damned father.

Cisco hopped into Bianca's lap. She usually adored and indulged the dog, but she was in one of her foul moods right now and, frowning, pushed Cisco onto the floor. He sat on the worn carpet and cocked his head from one side to the other, as if trying to understand the girl who had, before falling in love, lavished all her attention upon him.

"Can't help it, Bianca, I'm a nerd by nature. It's genetic, and as such, you, too, have the nerd gene." Regan plucked off a prematurely dying bloom from the Christmas cactus in the garden window.

Bianca rolled her eyes as if her mother were the most stupid woman on the planet. "I just want to go over to Chris's for a while. I don't think it's that big of a deal."

"It's a blizzard outside, if you haven't noticed. The only reason I'm going out is because I have to." Regan was bundling up in enough outer gear to battle the elements. She grabbed her stocking cap and gloves off the table, where the mail had been stacked and unattended for days. "I don't want either of you driving."

Again, Bianca rolled those huge Pescoli eyes.

Which ticked Regan off.

"And not only are you to have your homework done by the time I get home, I want the dishwasher unloaded and all the dishes in the sink washed."

Neither of her children responded.

"Jer, I'm talkin' to you, too," she said a little louder. He was glued to the set, didn't so much as look over his shoulder. "Jeremy!" She walked into the living room before realizing he was wearing earbuds buried deep in his ears so that he could blast his brain with music from his iPod while watching some reality show with what he called "hot whiny chicks."

"Jeremy!" she yelled, tapping him on the shoulder.

"Wha—?" He looked up and, when he saw her stern expression, said again, "What?"

She yanked out one of the earbuds. "You feed the dog and unload the dishwasher, then do the dishes. It's your week."

"But Bianca—"

"Did them last week. You're on, bud."

"Yeah, right," he groused, his gaze wandering back to the television.

"I mean it. And this mess"—she motioned to the paper plates and glasses stacked on the coffee table within easy reach of his highness—"needs to be picked up."

"I'll do 'em. Okay? Geez . . ."

"Good. I've got a witness."

Bianca, too burned that she wasn't being allowed to leave, didn't even show any of her usual smugness or pleasure that Jeremy was being reamed. She was too busy texting what were probably notes of undying love to the man of her dreams, Chris, a lanky, dull-appearing boy who spoke in monosyllables and, unless Regan missed her guess, was a habitual marijuana smoker.

Which scared her to death.

Not that she hadn't done her share of weed back in the day, when she'd been a little older than Bianca, but she'd had the good sense to leave it at that. Nothing stronger. Ever. And she'd left pot alone with her first pregnancy and had never looked back.

But these days, kids were different. Weed was different.

"You, get your homework done, too," she said to her sullen, beautiful daughter. "And clean your room. It's a mess."

"It's better than *his*," she sneered, arching an eyebrow toward the couch while her fingers flew over the buttons of her cell phone.

"Yeah, I know, but he did make an effort last weekend. Believe me, he's not off the hook; I'm just prioritizing. Living room and kitchen first, then I'll tackle the mess in the dungeon."

If Jeremy heard her, which she doubted, he had the good sense to ignore the jabs about his living area. "Okay, Bianca," Regan said, "I'm serious about the room and homework. You're going to go to your dad's this weekend, so everything needs to get done before you leave."

Bianca let out a long, put-upon sigh as Regan petted Cisco, then walked through the back door to the garage, where the temperature dropped decidedly.

Usually when the kids took off for the weekend, she spent at least one night out, sometimes both. Being home alone wore thin quickly and she figured it was her time for a little fun. But all her plans for this weekend had been put on hold so she could be ready to report in. It was near the middle of the month, the time the psycho struck. Though the victims had always been found later, the ME and forensic techs thought that the killer's pattern suggested that he hunted his victims a week or so before the end of the month.

Which would be soon.

Everyone in the department was nervous, expecting to hear a call about an abandoned car or a dead woman tied to some lone tree somewhere in the mountains.

She wondered how many victims there might already be, women whose wrecked cars or frozen dead bodies, now probably picked at by animals, existed in the woods outside the small town where she'd lived most of her life.

"Don't go there," she told herself as she backed out of the garage, barely avoiding Jeremy's truck, then turned around and drove carefully down the lane. Her access street wound between several trees before meeting the main road, but the snow was dry, not much ice beneath, and her tires got plenty of traction.

She and the kids lived five miles out of town, in the hills surrounding Grizzly Falls, and there was little traffic. She passed a snowplow scraping snow to the side of the road and one abandoned vehicle. She stopped to make sure no one was inside, then called it in and returned to her Jeep. With snow melting on her shoulders, she took the main road into town. The amount of vehicles increased as the road split and she headed to the part of the city located on the ridge overlooking the river. Ice had collected along the banks and the water was the color of steel as it cascaded over the steep rocks that defined the falls.

Parking in the outside lot, she walked briskly inside, her breath misting around her, the cold air slapping her cheeks as she pushed through the glass doors, signed in, then headed toward a back hallway and the rabbit warren of cubicles and offices of the department.

She dropped her things in her locker, grabbed a cup of coffee, made a little small talk with Trilby Van Droz, a road deputy and single mother whose only daughter was one year younger than Bianca. Trilby's ex was worse than Lucky, skipping the state and paying child support just sporadically enough to irritate the hell out of her but keep her from running back to her attorney.

A few minutes later, she found Alvarez at her desk on the phone, her computer screen filled with images of the victims of the first serial killer in the history of Grizzly Falls.

"Brought you coffee," Pescoli said, knowing that Alvarez was forever pouring herself a cup and letting it cool untouched on her desk.

"Thanks." She took the cup and sipped without looking up.

"Anything new?"

"Nah. Not yet."

"Still haven't located Wendy Ito's vehicle?"

Alvarez glanced her way. Her dark hair was pulled back neat and tight while Regan's reddish curls were waiting to spring free of their clip. "I've been working on the notes," she said, pulling a spiral notebook to the front of the desk. On the lined pages were the initials of the victims' names, laid out in the order in which they had been printed in dark block letters, and between those letters Alvarez had filled in the blanks:

W   T   SC   I N

"Come up with anything?"

"Nothing that makes any sense. If it's a message, the first word could be 'what' or maybe 'wait,' or the T might be the start of the next word. It looks like the S and C are supposed to be linked. For a word like 'scene,' or 'school,' or 'scent' or who knows? The N might go with it or not. Or it could be one long word, a warning, or—"

"Or he could be screwing with us. Maybe he's laughing his ass off as he comes up with his whacko note."

Alvarez's eyebrows drew together and she shook her head. "No. He's too organized. He finds his victims, tracks them down, blows out the tires of their vehicles, goes down and retrieves them and their personal effects, all without leaving any trace evidence. Then he keeps them somewhere while they partially heal and finally takes them to a spot I'm sure he's picked out ahead of time and ties them up and leaves them and the damned notes."

"Why do you think the spot is chosen earlier?"

"From the few tracks we've found in the snow, there's no hesitation. They go in a straight line."

"Someone very familiar with the area. Geography. Access roads. Someone confident he'll get in and get out without anyone seeing him."

"Umm." Alvarez was nodding, tracing the letters of the note with the index finger of her right hand. "Hiker? Skier? Hunting or fishing guide? Someone who works in the woods?"

"Forestry service?"

Alvarez glanced up, her dark eyes intense. Pescoli felt a chill as cold as death and her heart nearly stopped beating. She lowered her voice. "You're thinking about someone in the department?"

"I don't know what I'm thinking," Alvarez said. "But whoever's behind this, he's smart, he's organized, he knows the area like the back of his hand and he's one step ahead of us. Worse yet, he's about to strike again. If he hasn't already."

Pescoli felt unnerved. Whoever was behind these atrocities, whatever sick mind had become compelled to prey upon the women he hunted, surely he wasn't someone they worked with! In a half-second, all the faces of the deputies of the department flashed in quicksilver images through her mind. "No way," she whispered but realized her fingers were wrapped tightly over the handle of her cup, her knuckles showing white.

Alvarez muttered tersely, "I'm just saying we can't rule anyone out. Not yet."

Regan nodded. She was right. That was the hell of it. Once again, Alvarez was spot-on. Everyone was a suspect. Even the men within the department that both of them trusted with their lives.

"Damn. Damn," Jillian said aloud, her teeth chattering wildly, some of her skin feeling numb. She'd fallen asleep for a few minutes, or had it been longer? It was a little darker now, the moon rising as the sun started to set. Her headlights were dim and yellow.

So this was it? She was going to freeze to death in a ten-year-old Subaru in the bottom of a frozen ravine?

What kind of ignoble end was that?

Dear God, Jillian, you're in deep trouble this time.

And you can count only on yourself.

She tried to think, to remember the crash, or the events leading up to it, but nothing but a yawning black hole filled her mind. Shivering, teeth chattering, she tried to remember as she worked at the handle of the door. It wouldn't budge. She reached across the seat, tried the passenger door. It, too, was locked solid, either from ice or wreckage.

She grunted in dismay.

She could push herself through the broken window. If she could stand the pain and dislodge her foot from its trap. Setting her jaw, she tried to free her ankle again. Hot, blinding pain ripped through her foot. She sucked in her breath, felt the cold, then gritted her teeth for another go at it. She couldn't just stay here. She had to free herself. Somehow.

Come on, Jillian, do something!

The cell phone! Oh God, where was it? Her purse? Wasn't her purse somewhere . . . not on the passenger seat, but there, on the floor beneath the glove box. She strained, reaching as far as she could, trying to ignore the agony tearing through her ankle and the pain in her chest. If she could just reach her damned purse . . . its strap only inches from her fingers. She pushed herself, lying over the console, stretching as far as she could . . . reaching . . . brushing the edge of the strap with her fingers. "Come on," she urged, her breath fogging in the air, determination in her voice. "Come *on.*" She strained. Harder. Felt something in her ankle pop. "Ow! Oooh . . ." Clenching her teeth, she inched her middle finger around the strap and drew back, bringing the purse with her. The damned cell phone fell out! Onto the floor.

"No!"

It was within reach. She snagged the slippery phone

before it slid away. Gasping, she held onto the slim device in a death grip, as if afraid it would jump from her fingers.

"Please let there be service," she whispered, ignoring the throb in her ankle, the pain behind her eyes, the blood she felt coagulating on her cheeks and forehead. The phone was turned on, but no signal-strength bars registered and the LCD screen flashed "No Reception."

Jillian groaned. "Great," she muttered through chattering teeth, thinking things could hardly get worse. She tried to place a call anyway, hoping that her phone would ping off the closest cell tower and that somehow someone would find her by the GPS chip in the damned thing. If the signal could reach a tower . . . if there was one anywhere nearby.

Refusing to think about the possibility that in this remote location there might not be a cell tower for miles, or that no one in his right mind would be out in this blizzard, she opened her purse and in the fading light saw that her wallet, sunglasses, makeup case and checkbook were still intact. There was a receipt for gas, at a station in Wildwood, Montana. Wherever the hell was that? Using a little illumination from her cell phone, she checked the date. December seventh. Was that today?

She had no idea, but found over three hundred dollars in her wallet, much more than she usually carried, and a half-full bottle of ibuprofen. "Thank you, God," she whispered and with trembling hands shook out two pills, thought about it and added a third, then tossed them down her throat and swallowed them dry. "Do your magic." Recapping the plastic bottle, she prayed the medication would help with her pain, then stuffed her wallet and the bottle into the handbag.

"Okay, so now . . ."

Shivering, she slid a glance at the cracked rearview mirror and spied her reflection. She flinched. The image staring back at her wasn't only distorted from the broken glass and dark with the fading light but appeared to have been through a war zone. Cuts and lacerations discolored her skin, blood had dried around her nose from a gash in her forehead and the whites of her eyes seemed slick and tinged pink. Bruises had already started to appear and her brown hair, cut chin length and layered, was matted to her head, glued with her own blood.

She turned away. "Don't think about it," she muttered, and tried her phone again. Nothing. She couldn't call anyone. Teeth rattling, she yelled, "Help!" And again. "Help!" At the top of her lungs. Was it possible for anyone to be nearby? If so, wouldn't they have heard her skid off the road, the car crash into the trees?

Where were the rescuers?

The police?

The firefighters?

Anyone?

She'd heard about cars sliding off mountain roads or small planes going down in the winter. The bodies of those inside the wreckage were often not found until the next spring, when it thawed. If ever. Shivering violently, she thought about her fate. Surely she wasn't destined to die in this unknown ravine, trapped in her own vehicle, all alone.

"Stay calm, don't think about it," she told herself as she spied a paper cup on the floor, remnants of a coffee drink splashed on the rug. Upon the cup was a brown logo, a picture of a moose backdropped by mountains. Beneath the logo were the words "Chocolate Moose Café, Spruce Creek, Montana."

She'd obviously been in that café, but try as she might, she had no memory of the place. Was it a mile down the road? Five? Twenty?

It may as well be a million.

She closed her eyes. Tried to concentrate over the pounding in her skull and the pain throbbing up her leg. How could she save herself?

Spruce Creek, Montana? Why the hell had she been there? What was it that had propelled her from her home to this frigid, forested wilderness? She couldn't quiet grasp it, but there was something that connected her to this state . . . something that bothered her, something she couldn't pull out of her subconscious. What was it? Oh God. Her pulse jumped. She *did* know someone in Montana, someone she was pretty certain she hadn't raced out in the middle of the winter to visit:

Mason Rivers.

Her ex-husband.

Her stomach knotted as she tried to conjure up Mason's face and came up blank. She had the vague feeling that he had brown hair and hazel eyes and kept himself in pretty good shape, but she couldn't recall his features, at least at the moment. Besides, he was in Helena, an attorney. No, make that a defense lawyer.

Though she couldn't remember why, she was fairly certain Mason was part of the reason she was in Montana in the first place.

The cold became a soothing blanket, drawing her under as she shivered. *Don't let go. Fight, Jillian. For God's sake, fight!*

She forced her eyes open. "Help!" she yelled again, determined to find a way out of this mess. "Can anybody hear me? I'm down here! For God's sake, someone, please! Help me!" Again she pounded on the horn.

But her words echoed back at her through the canyon, taunting her in their naivete and fear, the lights of the car dimming as the battery died, the horn becoming little more than a weak honk.

She kept at it, but within minutes the battery had failed. Jillian beat on the horn, but its sound had died away and her voice was little more than a desperate, croaky whisper, while the headlights had grown impossibly dim.

"Oh God," she murmured, alone in the dark.

Worn out, she could do nothing but wait and pray and try to stay awake, to keep the cold and unconsciousness at bay, until there was only silence.

Dark, disturbing silence.

She wondered about her life and those she'd loved. Would she ever see them again? Or was this it? Was her life truly over?

A shadow in the cracked rearview mirror moved. It seemed far away, and yet, oddly out of place, a scuttling umbra on this white landscape.

Her heart jumped.

She twisted her head. Searched the darkening terrain.

Had someone found her?

Was it her imagination? Or was someone or something out there? Maybe it was just the snow falling, an optical illusion.

She started to open her mouth to yell, then stopped before making a sound.

There was a chance it was nothing. Her mind playing tricks on her.

Nerves tight as bowstrings, she stared into the night, eyes straining, heart pounding.

A rescuer would have called out.

Anyone searching down here would have seen her car. Right?

Why else would anyone be in this lonesome, frozen canyon?

Another movement in the cracked mirror.

Her heart leaped to her throat.

Again she started to scream for help and again she snapped her mouth closed and bit her tongue.

Frantic, she tried to make out the movement in the shadows.

Was she hallucinating?

Or . . .

You have to take a chance. Friend or foe, you need help! You can't stay here in the car if you want to get out of this alive!

And yet . . . she didn't move a muscle and the world began to spin as if she were going to pass out. She struggled to keep her eyes open, her gaze vigilant.

Pinned in the car, unable to free herself and all alone, she was such easy prey. Too easy.

Paralyzing fear controlled her.

For the first time since the accident, she felt incredibly and ultimately vulnerable, entirely at the mercy of whomever or whatever was outside. The skin on the back of her neck prickled and she fought the urge to scream. Muscles tight, she stared through the broken glass. *Please be a good guy. Please . . . oh please . . .*

Another movement.

She gasped, nearly screaming, then held back. She grabbed a piece of glass, cutting her hand, needing something to use as a weapon.

Don't be silly, she told herself, but her blood was pumping, fear jetting through her veins, and yet she felt a wave of darkness threatening to pull her under. *Don't fall victim to your own wild imagination or fright. You've watched too many teen slasher movies. Call out to whomever's out there. You need help. You have to get medical attention or you will die.*

However, she resisted the urge to let out even the barest of whispers.

Because she knew.

Deep in her gut she knew.

Call it feminine intuition, or some kind of animal instinct, but, trapped in the twisted metal of her car, unable to get out of this steep ravine, she was as easy quarry as a rabbit in a snare. She felt her scalp wrinkle with foreboding and she was certain that whatever was prowling these snowy, night-darkened woods was the embodiment of pure, malevolent evil.

Her insides turned as cold as death and still the blackness tried to pull her under, tugging hard.

Shivering, struggling to stay conscious, she set her jaw and wondered if, within the wreckage of her old Subaru, there was anything other than the piece of glass she could use as a weapon. Her camera! It was heavy. She could swing the strap of the case like a bola or Mace and hurl the Canon .35-millimeter at—

Another movement, this time closer.

Swift. Dark. Scurrying.

In front of the car.

Her pulse skyrocketed for a moment, jarring her awake.

Jesus, help me!

Her every nerve was strung tight. Blood oozed through her fingers as she clenched the shard of glass. The blackness toyed with her brain, seducing her to let go.

She held her breath. Listened hard, her ears straining, her eyes trying to pierce the coming darkness.

But she saw nothing and the wind died inexplicably.

Goosebumps pimpled her flesh and she fought to stay awake.

Suddenly, the silence within that deep, frozen chasm was deafening.

Chapter Six

Alvarez was naturally suspicious.

But then again, it came with the territory.

She hadn't been born distrusting people; no, she'd been a happy child, but all that had changed about the time she'd entered high school.

You can't outrun your past.

She knew that, of course, but couldn't help trying. She probably always would, she thought as she hurried through the lobby of the courthouse, where she'd testified in a domestic violence case. She'd heard before that she was a good witness. Cool. Calm. Not rattled easily.

Defense lawyers hated to come up against her and today had been no exception.

She pushed open the doors of the courthouse and, feeling the bite of the wind, tightened the scarf around her neck. Despite the fact the temperature was hovering near freezing, she was wearing a knee-length skirt, high-heeled boots, a snug turtleneck and a jacket. Small silver hoops and a matching pendant necklace were her only accessories and she'd twisted her hair away from her face a little less severely. Her testimony had been clear and concise, no matter how hard the defense lawyer tried to make her say something that would let the sleazebag of a stepfather off the hook. No way. Not when he'd been abusing his wife's teenaged daughter for the past three years.

When the jury returned, she'd bet her badge the guy would be sent to prison for a long while.

Good. She found her car in the lot and drove directly to her studio apartment, where she changed into slacks and shoes with lower heels. She loved this tidy little space with its Murphy bed that flattened up against the wall, love seat, chair and ottoman. A small gas fireplace filled one wall, its mantel covered with framed pictures of the members of her large family, and a collapsible desk occupied the small space usually reserved for a kitchen table. As it had been for the past three months, the desk was littered with books, notes, diagrams and her laptop computer. She hated to think how many hours she'd spent at that very desk in the past few months, all trying to solve the latest murders.

She didn't begrudge herself the time, but it really ticked her off that she wasn't any closer to solving the crimes. "Patience," she reminded herself as she pulled on her heavy down coat and headed outside, locking the door behind her.

She noticed that in the short time she'd been in her apartment, the wind had kicked up again, thick-bellied clouds roiling overhead, promising another storm.

"Just what we need," she thought aloud as a sharp gust tossed dry leaves across the parking lot, sending them dancing and reeling over the snowy landscape.

As she crossed to her car, she felt as if someone were watching her. She actually looked over her shoulder but spied no one.

"Just your imagination," she told herself.

But as she slid behind the wheel, she felt it again, that sharp, clear premonition of death.

Hers?

Or another poor victim, bound naked to a tree, hoping and praying to be rescued but all the while knowing she was doomed to die.

"God help us," Alvarez whispered, and for the first time since she was fourteen, she fervently made the sign of the cross over her chest. "God help us all."

Bam! Bam! Bam!

Jillian attempted to open an eye.

God, it was cold.

So cold.

And dark.

An ear-splitting groan reverberated through her brain.

What the hell?

Where am I?

"Hey! Lady! Wake up!" a man's deep, anxious voice ordered. "Help me out here, would ya!"

What?

She tried to focus and felt the throb in her ankle.

What in God's name? Is this a dream?

In a flash, she recalled waking up in the mangled Subaru. She'd been trapped in the car, hoping for help, sensing an evil presence, when she must have slipped into unconsciousness. . . .

Her heart kick-started and she squinted into the darkness. The shard of glass she'd been gripping was still in her clenched fist, now nearly frozen solid.

Was this person who was trying to pry open the door the same one she'd thought she'd seen furtively darting through the snowy forest? The one she'd been certain was evil incarnate?

"Hey! Are you okay?" her would-be rescuer yelled.

Was he out of his mind? Of course she wasn't okay. Did she *look* okay?

"Can you push on the door?"

If only.

She caught a glimpse of him then through the thick flakes of falling snow. A ski mask and goggles, all in black, covered his face, making him look more alien than human. He was wearing a thick ski jacket but she saw no insignia indicating he was with the police or forest service or any agency. . . .

"Hey!" He reached through the broken windshield and touched her shoulder. "Wake up!"

"I—I am!" she tried to yell, but it came out as a faint whisper.

"Can you move?" he shouted so loudly she twitched with a painful jolt.

Dear God, had she slipped into unconsciousness again?

She tried to answer, but failed, fighting like hell to keep her eyes open.

Should she trust him?

Did she have any choice?

"I can't pull you through here . . . the roof's crushed. I'm gonna try the door."

Her teeth were chattering again and she no longer felt the same intense pain she had earlier. Probably because she was numb and frostbite was settling in.

Her eyes were so heavy. So damned heavy.

"Hey! Lady! Stay with me! Oh for Christ's sake! Come on, hang in there. What's your name?"

She blinked. Had she fallen asleep again? Blacked out?

"Son of a bitch." He had something in his hand, a crowbar, she thought vaguely . . . like the one in her trunk. If she could just sleep, only for a few minutes . . . five or ten . . . that was all she needed.

She heard a deep, tortured groan. Metal twisting and

resisting as the man used the crowbar on the driver's-side door. From the corner of her eye she saw him pushing hard against the lever, throwing his weight into it, grunting and straining with the effort. "Come on, you miserable son of a bitch," he said through clenched teeth. Metal squealed. Resisted. Frozen locks torqued but refused to give way. "Come on, come on, you bastard," he swore at the car as he tried desperately to pry the door open.

She should feel fear.

Or worry.

Or anything.

But all she wanted to do was be pulled back under, into a warm, soft cloud of unconsciousness.

"Stay with me!" he ordered.

She was drifting away. . . .

Snap!

Something broke, she thought, but didn't know what. Didn't care.

Metal shrieked, and somewhere, far away, she thought she heard a man's voice over the rush of a bitter cold wind. "Don't you die on me. Do you hear me? You'd better not damned well die on me."

She felt the icy wind and the jostle of someone touching her, feeling her neck, as if for a pulse, reaching over her. . . .

But she couldn't force her eyes open, and for the next few hours—or was it longer?—she was in and out of consciousness, hearing him yelling at her through a long, dark tunnel. She would drift off to blackness until she was jarred by movement or noise, which roused her back to the surface until she faded out again. She was barely aware of the noise of an engine, of movement, and it seemed as if she were gliding, floating through the universe, with stars falling all around her. . . . Her ankle and ribs still hurt, which was probably a good sign, but the numbness that had settled over her skin made her feel dreamlike and buoyant, her soul weightless.

"Don't you let go," he kept saying to her over the thrum of some engine, his voice seeming disembodied, coming from far away. "Whoever the hell you are, hang with me."

The call to the sheriff's department came in two days later, with a break in the weather. Another car had been found, wrecked, abandoned and covered in snow.

Selena Alvarez had been at her desk when dispatch phoned with the location of the vehicle and therefore she was one of the first detectives on the icy scene. She rode with Johnson and Slatkin in the county crime lab truck down a closed access road to the bottom of a canyon where the snow was nearly two feet deep.

"Hey, Alvarez, over here!" Deputy Pete Watershed's voice echoed through the desolate canyon.

She looked up from where she was crouched by the front wheel of the mangled car covered in snow. It had once been a Subaru, but with its shattered windshield, dented body and mashed frame, it was nearly unrecognizable.

She clicked off her handheld recorder. "Just a sec," she called over her shoulder, then returned her attention to the right front wheel of the sedan.

Pictures had already been taken of every angle of the wreckage, so she brushed away a dusting of snow and examined the hole torn through a snow tire.

Identical to the others.

No doubt the result of a bullet being shot from a long-range rifle.

"Son of a bitch," she muttered, though she wasn't surprised. She'd been at two similar crime scenes in just as many months. The right front tires of the cars registered to Theresa Charleton and Nina Salvadore had been shot by a high-powered rifle, causing the cars to careen off a high cliff, only to land, crunched and twisted, at the base of the steep hillside. They were still looking for Wendy Ito's vanity-plated, white Prius, but this car didn't belong to the dead woman.

Alvarez said as much into her pocket recorder, the quickest way to take notes in freezing conditions, then clicked the recorder off and straightened as she gazed over the snowbound ravine.

Today the normally empty canyon was transformed: detectives, deputies and criminalists working together, using the best equipment Pinewood County and the State of Montana had to offer, hoping for some bit of evidence leading them to the son of a bitch who was behind three, now possibly four, brutal murders.

As with the previous single-car crashes, all personal effects and the driver of the vehicle itself were missing from the scene. The killer had left each car's license plates intact, though that was of little help, as a car's owner could be traced from the vehicle identification number. Otherwise, all that had remained in each case was a twisted piece of metal that had once been a vehicle, skid marks on the road above and a few broken trees and branches that the plummeting vehicle had snapped in its free fall to the bottom of a canyon deep in the Bitterroot Mountains.

So far the right front tire had blown, and Alvarez was willing to bet her master's degree in psychology that upon further investigation, the reason for this latest blowout would be the same as the others—a bullet from a .30-caliber rifle.

"You sick son of a bitch," she muttered, her breath a cloud, and despite her down jacket, gloves, ski pants, thermal underwear and boots, she felt a chill deep inside, far colder than the icy breeze sweeping through the canyons.

She pointed at the tire and said to the tech with a camera, "Let's get a shot of this."

"You got it." Virginia Johnson, a black woman bundled in a county-issued jacket, gloves and ski pants, snapped off several shots as Selena picked her way through the crusted snow and downed branches littering the floor of the ravine.

"So what've you got?" she asked Watershed, who, as always, appeared impatient, his eyebrows pulled together, his thin lips in a perpetual scowl. He, too, was wearing a down jacket issued by the department and a wool hat with a wide brim that shielded his glasses while collecting the falling snow.

"Take a look here." He squatted down close to the ground and pointed one gloved finger to a spot in the thick, newly fallen snow where, beneath nearly two inches of the frigid fluff, bits of red were visible. "Blood," he said, "a trail." He motioned east, toward a bend in the creek bed where a forest service road was partially hidden. "Looks like he dragged her out on some kind of stretcher."

Alvarez shone the beam of her flashlight onto the drifts of snow and, sure enough, ruts were visible in the drifts and between them was a definite blood trail, dark drips of red beneath a thin crust of snow.

"Let's collect it," she said.

Mikhail Slatkin, one of the forensic techs who'd been attempting to take a casting of a boot print in the snow, nodded without looking up. Tall and raw-boned, the son of Russian immigrants, he was barely twenty-six and was one of the best forensic scientists Alvarez had ever met. "I'll get it in a minute. Just let me finish here." He worked fast, racing against the elements as snow was blowing through the canyon, covering evidence at the rate of half an inch an hour.

Over the whistle of the wind, Alvarez heard the rumble of an engine and looked up to see Regan Pescoli's rig grind to a stop behind the county truck. Pescoli was out of the car in an instant, pulling on a stocking cap to cover her tangle of reddish curls. She was pale and wan-looking, dark smudges beneath her large eyes indicating she hadn't gotten enough sleep.

Which wasn't a surprise.

Though Pescoli's private life wasn't any of Alvarez's business, she couldn't help but be a little ticked off. Nine times out of ten she had to cover for her partner, either because she'd had a long night waiting up for one of her kids, a battle royale with her ex or a late night at a bar with one of her many loser boyfriends.

Despite it all, Pescoli was a brilliant detective. And that's all that mattered. She had a knack for pegging a person on first meeting, for cutting through the usual BS and finding the truth. It bugged the hell out of Alvarez that all of her education and degrees didn't seem to stack up to her partner's gut instincts.

It was a slap in the face, but Alvarez would get over it.

Alvarez looked back at Watershed as Pescoli signed in to the crime scene with one of the deputies, her eyes already taking in the single-car accident as she scribbled her name on the sheet. "Same damned thing," she said, heading toward Alvarez. "Same bloody damned thing."

She smelled of cigarette smoke and looked like hell, but then, no one was their best at this hour of the morning, bundled in outdoor gear.

"So what've we got?"

"Nothing new. Take a look." Alvarez walked her partner through the trod-on snow to the car.

"Wendy Ito's?"

"Nope. Washington plates, but this is an older-model Subaru Outback. Ito drove a newer Toyota with vanity plates."

"A Prius. I remember." Pescoli's jaw tightened as she bent down to peer into the twisted wreckage. "So we've got another one."

"Looks like."

"Hell." She sighed as she straightened, her eyes, usually a gold color, darkening. "Driver's door jimmied open? Tire shot? No ID, no personal effects like a wallet or purse?"

Alvarez nodded, snowflakes drifting from the steely heavens. "Same as before."

"But no body found?"

"Not yet."

Alvarez walked Pescoli around what was left of the silver Subaru and gave Pescoli a rundown of what they'd found. She had to shout, as the wind began to shriek down the canyon again, tearing through the trees, rattling bare branches and blowing tiny sharp flakes of snow against Alvarez's skin.

"Just like the others," Pescoli observed, her full lips pulled into a frustrated scowl. "What the hell is the bastard up to?"

A moot question.

Pescoli squinted upward, toward the ridge, suspecting that this car, like the others, had been forced off the road, then plunged and careened down the canyon wall to land at the bottom of the canyon floor, in this frozen creek bed.

Alvarez followed her gaze and knew what her partner was thinking. It was a wonder anyone survived the crash.

But then, they weren't certain anyone had. Just that the driver had been removed. Damn.

"We know when this happened?" Pescoli asked.

Alvarez tugged her gloves on tighter. "It could've been as early as yesterday afternoon, judging by the snowfall."

"Then the victim's probably still alive." Pescoli glanced

around the bleak ravine with sheer walls of ice and rock. "The son of a bitch tends to them, nurses them like some damned Florence Nightingale, then ties 'em to a tree and leaves 'em to freeze to death. Sick bastard."

Amen to that.

"Who found the car and called it in?" Pescoli asked.

Beneath the brim of his wool hat, Pete Watershed winced.

Pescoli wasn't about to be coddled. "Tell me."

"Grace Perchant. Walking her dog."

"Walking her dog? When it's ten degrees below freezing? Down here? Why the hell was she doing that?"

"Why does Grace do anything?" Watershed asked with a lift of one shoulder.

Good question. Grace Perchant was another one of the town's oddities. Alvarez reminded her partner, "Grace claims to see ghosts, too, and talk with the friggin' dead, for crying out loud. And that dog of hers is half-wolf."

"Three quarters," Mikhail cut in, looking up with a knowing smile.

"You know this *how?*" Alvarez wasn't certain she really wanted to hear the answer.

"I'm interested in a pup."

"Oh, for the love of God! You know that Grace's dog is practically a wild animal! She probably wasn't walking it; the damned thing was walking her."

"She's right," Pescoli said. "We've had complaints about the wolf-dog more than once."

"It bit someone?"

"Nah. Howled. Kept the neighbors awake." Pescoli tucked a stray strand of hair beneath her cap.

"That's ridiculous," Alvarez cut in. "I mean, if the dog needs to relieve himself, why not just let him go outside? Why walk during a damned blizzard?"

"It's Grace," Watershed said, as if that explained it all.

Frustrated, her cheeks red with the cold, Pescoli looked around the scene, her gaze inching over the snowy terrain. "Damn it, where did he take her?"

Selena Alvarez shook her head. Deep inside, she experienced a chill, a frigid drip of dread sliding through her gut. She knew the woman inside the car was already doomed and eventually they would find her, just as they'd found the others. As the wind keened and the blizzard started ripping through this ridge of mountains, she and Pescoli walked back to the spot where Slatkin was taking samples of the frozen blood. "Maybe we'll get lucky and the son of a bitch cut himself. It could be his blood."

"Let's not count on luck." Another male voice broke in and Alvarez looked over her shoulder to spy the sheriff walking toward them from the direction of the forest service road. His big boots crunched in the snow and his expression said it all: repressed anger, and maybe even a touch of defeat. The wind had been so damned fierce, she hadn't even heard his rig arrive.

Alvarez nodded. "You're right, we won't."

"A little luck wouldn't hurt," Pescoli observed. "Personally, I'll take all we can get."

A bit of a smile cracked across Grayson's face. "Fair enough." A tall, strapping man with a thick, graying moustache and dark, deep-set eyes, Grayson was recently elected and recently divorced—the two, it seemed, had gone hand in hand. At least it seemed that way to Alvarez. "Tell me that Ivor Hicks didn't call this in."

"Not this time," Alvarez assured him.

"Nope." Pescoli shoved her hands deep into her coat pockets. "This time our witness is Grace Perchant."

"Oh for the love of God. Another nutcase." Grayson scowled. "First Ivor, now Grace. The next thing you know, we'll be getting tips from Henry Johansen."

Though Henry, a local farmer, hadn't claimed to

have been abducted by aliens like Ivor, nor did he commune with the dead, which was Grace's specialty, he had fallen off his tractor twenty years earlier and suffered an injury that had caused him to claim he could read people's minds. There had been no proof of this phenomenon, and yet Henry was convinced that the voices he heard were the random thoughts of people he'd met. He was a regular visitor at the sheriff's department, always insisting he had the inside track on some local crime.

"God help us," Watershed said.

As Grayson observed the scene, his expression only grew more grim. "We'd better wrap this up soon. The weather service is advising that we're in for another blizzard. A big one."

Alvarez's heart sank. The chances of finding the driver of the car weren't that great to begin with; add a blizzard and they dropped to nearly impossible.

Grayson glared at the half-buried car and the lines around his mouth etched even deeper. "Looks like he's at it again."

"Looks like," Pescoli agreed.

"Shit." Dan glanced up at the ridge and snowflakes caught on his moustache as he chewed on his lower lip. "Same MO?"

Watershed nodded. "Yep. Body and ID missing."

"Tire shot?"

"Blown for sure," Alvarez said. "Haven't been able to determine if—"

"It was shot." Grayson voiced what they all thought was fact, just not yet proven. "This isn't a coincidence. That bastard's hunting again."

"I'd bet on it," Watershed agreed.

Alvarez nodded.

"Run the license plate," Grayson said. "Find out who owns the car and we'll work from there. If the bullet isn't lodged in the undercarriage or somewhere else in the vehicle, check the ridge. Maybe it fell onto the road or became imbedded in the cliff on the farside. Anyone call a tow truck to haul the car in?"

"Truck's on its way," Alvarez said. She'd put in the call as soon as she arrived.

"Let's hope they can get down here. The roads are a mess. Half the staff is dealing with power outages and accidents." He rubbed his chin and shook his head, his gaze fastening on the crumpled car, which was quickly being buried in snow. "We need to nail this bastard."

"I'm all for that," Pescoli agreed.

Grayson nodded and met Alvarez's eyes. "But first let's find the victim. And this time, let's find her alive."

Chapter Seven

Scccrratttch!

The match head scrapes loudly against the stone hearth and the sharp smell of sulfur stings my nostrils. With a sweet hiss, the flame flares before my eyes.

Perfect little flicker of hot light.

I've always loved fire.

Always been fascinated at how it so quickly springs to life—a living, breathing thing that requires air to survive. The shifting yellow and orange flames are oh so seductive in their warmth and brilliance and deadly abilities.

Striking matches—bringing fire to life—is one of my passions, one of many.

Carefully lifting the glass of the lantern, I light the wick, another spot of illumination in the large, barren room. A fire already crackles and burns in the grate, red embers glowing in a thick bed of ashes, mossy wood licked by passionate flames, smoke rising through the old stone chimney, golden shadows dancing on the watery old windowpanes.

Outside the storm rages, winds howling, snow blowing furiously, and yet the stone-and-log cabin is a fortress against the elements. Here I don't have to bother with the burden of clothing that scratches and itches and bothers. No, I can walk comfortably over the smooth flagstones in bare feet, the heat radiating from the fire enough to keep my skin warm.

I keep a large store of firewood within the cabin, but should I need to walk to the outbuilding to retrieve more, I won't need the trappings of boots and jacket but can face the elements naked, bracing myself against the bite of the wind and the slap of ice.

The match burns down, licking at my fingertips, and I shake it out quickly.

With one ear to the police-band radio that spits and sputters, I sit on the chairs I've turned by hand. I spread out my forestry maps, along with the more graphic pictures I've printed from satellites, photos available on the Internet, on the long table. I've carefully pieced these images together and marked them with colored pins that correspond to the same colored pins on the forestry maps.

From a room down the hallway, I hear her quiet cough.

I freeze. Listening.

She groans, no doubt still unconscious.

A smile pricks at the corners of my mouth when I think of her. She is rousing and that's a good sign. Soon she'll be ready. A little sizzle of anticipation sweeps through my bloodstream and I quickly tamp it down. Not yet. Not until the time is right. Not until she is healthy enough to do her part.

Oh, it will be unwillingly, but she will partake.

They all do.

She groans more loudly and I know I'll have to attend to her. Soon. I look at the open closet, an armoire I've fashioned with my own hands and a few basic tools. I've carved it ornately, lovingly, with images of celestial beings cut into the dark wood. Inside are the cubicles where I keep my treasures, little mementos of the reluctant participants. The door is slightly ajar. I scoot back my chair and stand, stretching my muscles before walking to the closet. Opening the doors further, I note how the mirrors lining the inside catch the reflection of the fire and my own sinewy body. Toned muscles. Dark hair. Deep set eyes with 20/10 vision.

"A specimen," one foolish woman said of me as she let her gaze wander down my frame.

As if I would be flattered.

"A tall drink of water," another unimaginative would-be lover cooed, licking her lips slightly.

"Ah . . . a bad boy with bedroom eyes," a third whispered, hoping I would fall prey to her uninspired advances.

In the mirror my lips twist at the memories, my eyes darken a shade.

They found out, didn't they?

But those incidents were just the beginning, before I fully understood my mission.

Ignoring my reflection, I open some of the drawers in the closet and eye my treasures, little bits of the women who were to become immortal: a tooled leather bag with fringe, a small clutch made out of fake leopard fur, a snakeskin wallet filled with credit cards, driver's licenses, insurance information cards. Designer cases for eyeglasses, cigarettes and makeup. Nail files, tampons, cell phones, lipsticks in shades from wine to sheer, shimmering pink.

Treasures.

From those who were the chosen. I glance at one of the newspaper articles that has been written about the killings, the clippings all stacked neatly on a thin shelf. In this particular article, the reporter quoted some "source within the sheriff's department" who indicated

that the "acts" had been "random," and that a "maniac"
sharpshooter was behind the murders.

Maniac?

Random?

The police are worse imbeciles than I originally
thought.

Idiots playing at detection.

From a distance, through long-range binoculars, I
have watched the officers from the sheriff's department
swarm into the canyon, some up on the ridge, searching for clues, sifting for evidence, pawing through the
snow like dogs looking for bones in the sand. Others,
the lazier ones, huddled around the wrecked car,
scratching their chins, frowning and talking and getting
nowhere.

As I close the closet door I hear her cry out. Whimpering. Perhaps this one was a poor choice. She doesn't
seem to have much backbone.

But it's early. She will snap out of it. Her ferocity, her
passion, will surely appear.

I know she is one of the chosen. Just like the others.

Listening to the howl of the wind, I wonder just
where I will leave her to fight her battle with fate and
the elements. She is too injured from the "accident" to
move easily just yet, but within the week, she will have
healed to the point that she can be urged to the perfect
spot, a site I have yet to find. It has to be remote yet accessible, so that the imbeciles who work for the sheriff's
department can find her.

Eyeing the forestry map again, I run a finger down
the spine of one of the smaller ranges branching off the
Bitterroots and remember a valley I hunted in long ago.
Somewhat alpine, the meadowland has a few sparse
trees along its perimeter. I think hard, remembering,
bringing back the imagery of those few grassy acres. Just
at dawn, I once spied an elk across the lea, a muscular

bull standing near one gnarled pine, his rack five feet wide if an inch, his dark mane and coat barely visible in the thicket. I shot at him, missed, and he disappeared as if he were a ghost. I found the bullet from my rifle burrowed deep in the scaly bole of a solitary pine. That tree, if it is still standing, will be the perfect death post.

I study the map carefully. There are so many gullies and ridges, places a body won't be discovered until spring, and maybe not even then.

But those won't do.

I need the woman to be found.

I have to keep searching for the perfect spot.

I don't doubt that I will find it.

God and the Fates are on my side.

"Okay, so what have we got?" Alvarez asked as the Jeep, buffeted by the wind, slid on the icy terrain.

"You mean besides diddly-squat?" Pescoli was driving, her eyes narrowed as she tried to keep the rig on the road. Despite the windshield wipers slapping frantically at the continuous flakes, visibility was nil in the near whiteout. The road they were driving had already been closed, the plows unable to keep up with the storm. Ahead of them, the vehicles driven by the officers at the scene slowly eased along the uneven mountain terrain.

"Yeah, besides that." The police band crackled and the defroster blew enough hot air that Alvarez pulled off her gloves with her teeth, then unzipped her jacket. The interior smelled faintly of cigarette smoke and the cup holders were filled with half-full drinks.

"We've got his MO." Pescoli glared through the window as she drove, her gaze fastened on the snowy road, her eyebrows pulled together.

"Which so far only links the Subaru to the other cars

we found." Alvarez didn't like the turn of her thoughts. She was certain the crumpled Subaru would show up registered to a woman who had gone missing, a woman who even now was being held hostage somewhere within the surrounding five miles. So close, and yet eons away in this blizzard.

As Pescoli drove, Alvarez put a call in to the State of Washington DMV, finally connected, only to be placed on hold. When the clerk on the other end returned to Selena, he refused to give her any information over the phone but promised to fax the car's registration, as well as e-mail it to the sheriff's department. By the time Alvarez and Pescoli returned to the office, the car owner's identity would be available.

Not so the killer's.

"So if this car has been in the ravine two, possibly three, days, how much longer do you think he'll keep her alive?"

"Don't know," Alvarez said, concentrating on the taillights of Watershed's rig, the closest vehicle in their mini-convoy of county-owned pickups, SUVs and cars. The tow truck was behind them all, dragging what was left of the Subaru to the lot where it would be gone over again and again as investigators looked for evidence pointing to the killer. If only the guy would leave a fingerprint, or a hair, or some damned piece of evidence for them to work with.

So far, the killer had been lucky. No hairs, no fibers other than from the yellow plastic rope used to bind the victims to the trees, no fingerprints on the notes or vehicles, no witnesses to his crime. They had bullets, no casings, and poor impressions of boot prints in the snow. The blood samples the department had collected were all from the victims, and the damned carvings in the trees, all of which seemed to have been cut by some kind of hunting knife, gave no indication, except for a guestimate, of the killer's height. There had been no semen left in or on the victims, no evidence of rape.

Their profile of the killer was weak.

What they believed was that the killer was a male who wore a size-eleven shoe and was between the height of five feet ten and six three. But again, this was primarily assumption. The paper the notes were written on was common computer paper, available in any office supply store or department, the ink from the pens unremarkable, a common blue from disposable ballpoints.

And the notes he left, damn. What the hell did they mean?

Pescoli down-shifted as they came to a hairpin corner and Watershed's truck slipped a bit. "Son of a bitch," she muttered under her breath as her rig slid, then found enough traction to right itself. "Remind me why I don't live in Phoenix or San Diego. You know, where cold is seventy?"

"You'd hate Phoenix. And the desert gets cold at night."

"Not *this* cold. But okay, then San Diego. I think I might move there. Next week."

Alvarez couldn't help but smile at the image of Pescoli, in her boots, jeans and down vest, roller-skating on a sidewalk near a beach in Southern California.

"Laugh if you want to, but I'm doin' it. When we get back to the office, I'm searching for job openings from LA south."

"Good luck."

Pescoli actually flashed a quick we-both-know-I'm-full-of-crap grin.

The roads improved closer to town, where traffic had beat the snow into slush that was bound to refreeze. De-icer trucks were busily spraying the streets as both pedestrians and vehicles battled the elements.

Pescoli eased into the lot. She parked her Jeep as close to the main door as possible, then switched the engine off. Alvarez zipped up her jacket, pulled on her gloves and tugged her hood over her hair as she stepped out of the vehicle and hurried inside.

Once at her desk, she peeled off the layers again, then found the fax from the Washington DMV. According to the car's registration, it belonged to a thirty-six-year-old woman named Jillian Colleen Rivers, whose address was listed as Seattle. An e-mail came through as well, with a picture of Jillian Rivers as good as any of those licensing photos could be.

"Jesus," Alvarez said, staring at the picture of a woman who might already be dead. Shoulder-length dark brown hair, eyes listed as hazel on the license but appearing gray in the photo, strong nose, small mouth, easy smile, high, pronounced cheekbones, maybe the hint of freckles.

Alvarez dialed the number of the Seattle PD, connected to a detective who worked homicide and explained the situation.

"We'll check it out," Detective Renfro assured her. "Just give me a couple of hours."

"You got it. And see if this woman has any outstanding warrants or priors." But as Alvarez hung up, she knew that Renfro wouldn't be able to locate the woman.

No way.

Jillian Rivers was probably a model citizen, like the other women left in the forest to die. And as such, well on her way to being the sadist's next victim.

Thud!
Jillian heard the noise, tried to rouse, but couldn't.
What was it? A door slamming?

Vaguely she was aware of pain in her leg and ribs. Jesus, they ached.

Trying to think past the pain, she attempted to lift an eyelid. It didn't budge.

Dear God, where was she? She'd been in a car wreck, yes, that was it . . . and someone had come to help her . . . but she couldn't think, couldn't piece together her thoughts. In the distance she heard a high-pitched keen that, in her dazed thoughts, she decided might be the wind. As if it were racing through some deep ravine.

Oh God, what had happened?

Time was meaningless.

Her life seemed far away. Distant.

But she was no longer cold, and though she knew she should wake up, the blackness that had been her companion for God only knew how long kept her wrapped in its warm cocoon.

And she succumbed to its gentle lure.

She needed to sleep.

To heal.

She'd deal with the rest later. . . .

She is awake.

I am sure of it.

Something in the air has changed. Her moaning stopped a while ago, and I know she's awake and frightened.

They always are.

But I will placate her.

Get her to trust me.

For now, though, I need to let her be alone.

In the dark.

To learn to fear the isolation.

When she realizes I am her only human connection,

she will have no choice but to depend upon me. It will take only a few days and in those days she will heal.

Resisting the urge to open the door to her room, I pick up the heavy book of astronomy I've inadvertently dropped to the floor and return it to my worktable. After squaring it precisely with the other books stacked in one corner of the planks, I stand and stretch, my eye catching sight of the bar in the doorway to my sleeping area. The smooth steel rod is mounted near the top of the frame. Soundlessly I walk to it, reach up, grab the cool, smooth steel and take a deep breath. Then I flex every muscle, drawing my face up to the bar and lifting my legs at a right angle to my body. I hold the pose for several long, slow minutes, waiting until my muscles start to scream, and then even longer, as I tremble and sweat with the effort of maintaining the perfect pose.

Only when I am certain I can't hang on for a second longer, I count resolutely to sixty and release, dropping to the floor. I wipe my sweaty palms and jump up again, this time doing a hundred chin-ups in quick succession before I again lift my legs in front of me, again hold the position, legs outstretched, toes pointing, my strident muscles visible through taut skin, my body shaking from the effort.

This is part of my regimen.

Discipline.

Mental and physical discipline.

Directly in front of me, in a mirror on the far wall of the bed chamber, I see my reflection and check to make certain the pose is perfect.

It is.

Of course.

I hear her moaning again, more softly, and I smile, for soon I will open the door, "rescue" her all over again, hold her, reassure her, convince her that I will do everything possible to make her safe and bring her back to health. She will ask about her friends, her family, EMTs and hospitals and getting back to civilization, and I will explain about the lack of communication, but will tell her that as soon as the storm blows over, I will get help.

All I have to do is keep her alive for a few days.

And then, once the storm passes and she is able to hobble, the next phase will begin.

She will learn about discipline then.

About pain.

About mind over matter.

I release my pose and land deftly on the floor, barely making a sound. The moaning has stopped again.

Good girl. That's it. Be brave.

I nearly open the door to her room, but resist again, and walk to the window, where ice has crusted and white snow blows in great flurries. The panes clatter a bit over the rush of the wind, but the fire inside snaps and dances.

Though I am naked, not a stitch of clothing on my body, I am warm, sweating and satisfied.

Everything is going as planned.

"So what do we know about Jillian Rivers?" Pescoli asked the next day as she and Alvarez stopped for coffee at the Java Bean, Grizzly Falls's answer to Starbucks. While she poured herself a cup of coffee from the self-help pot, then paid for a double-cheese bagel, Alvarez ordered a soy chai latte, a frothy confection sprinkled with cinnamon and served in a mug that could double as a cereal bowl.

They sat at a small table near the window and stared out at the continuing storm. The coffee shop was nearly empty, one barista serving up the hot drinks to the few customers who had braved the bad weather.

"She's single, but been married twice. The first husband died in a hiking accident in Suriname about ten years ago. Body never found, but yes, the insurance did pay, and she remarried a defense lawyer from Missoula, Mason Rivers, but that didn't last long. She lives in Seattle, where she makes brochures and pamphlets, kind of a one-woman show. She takes the pictures, does the artwork and layout and writes the copy. No kids. One sister, Dusti Bellamy, who lives with her husband and two kids in one of your favorite towns."

"Which one is that?"

"San Diego."

"Oh." Pescoli grinned. "And I was betting on Phoenix."

"Jillian Rivers's mother, Linnette White, is alive and well, though her father is dead. Linnette also lives in Seattle, but not with her daughter. Jillian lived alone. The Seattle PD have sealed her home and checked the scene, but so far there's no indication of where she was going. I haven't called the mother or sister yet. That's on the agenda for this morning."

"You've been busy," Pescoli observed as she slathered peanut butter and cream cheese on her bagel with one of those cheap little plastic knives.

Alvarez looked up sharply. "I don't have kids."

"Yeah. I know." Pescoli nodded, scraping the excess cream cheese off the knife and onto her plate. "Sometimes, believe me, that's a blessing." She bit into the bagel, the flavors blending on her tongue.

Alvarez's eyes darkened just a bit, but the shadow, if it existed at all, disappeared in a second. "You wouldn't trade them for the world."

"Doesn't mean they can't be pains in the butt."

"Too much like their mother."

Pescoli grinned and took a long swallow of the hot coffee. "Don't tell them that. I like to tell them all their bad traits are genetic and not from my side of the family."

"They seem too smart to buy it."

Pescoli snorted. "Probably." She polished off her bagel while Alvarez sipped from the massive cup. They'd been partners for three years, ever since Alvarez had moved to Grizzly Falls from San Bernardino, and though they were about as alike as oil and water, they got along. Respected each other. In Pescoli's opinion Alvarez was wound too tightly and needed to get out more. Sure, she took all kinds of martial arts classes and had trophies for her abilities, from sharpshooting to archery. She'd also mentioned something about running a marathon, the Bay to Breakers in San Francisco or some other damned long race, maybe a butt-load of races, but Alvarez didn't have a social life. Spent her time with her nose in books, her fingers clicking a mouse as she searched for information on the Internet, and honing her mind and body to precision with classes at the university and athletic club.

In Pescoli's opinion, Alvarez needed to knock back a few double margaritas and get herself laid. Those two simple acts would do wonders for her partner's temperament.

Pescoli was certain of it.

Chapter Eight

The FBI agents weren't anything like they were portrayed in the movies, Alvarez thought, crossing one ankle over the other. She, along with other members of the task force working the serial murder case, sat at the big table in the task force room. Cups of cooling coffee, pens, notepads, gum wrappers and a crushed empty pack of cigarettes littered the long, fake-woodgrain surface of the table, while pictures of the crime scenes and notes about the victims hung on one of the walls, an enlarged map of the area on an adjacent wall.

At least, Craig Halden wasn't typical. Shipped out from the field office in Salt Lake City, Halden seemed like a personable enough guy. His brown hair was trimmed neatly, yes, but was far from a military cut. He had an easy, country boy charm about him, probably from growing up in rural Georgia. He called himself a "cracker" and he was jovial enough, though beneath the affable, easygoing-guy exterior Alvarez sensed that he was a sharp, dedicated federal agent.

His partner, however, was a piece of work, at least in Alvarez's mind. Stephanie "Steff" Chandler was a tall,

slim, humorless bitch. With long blond hair pulled
back into a tight knot, skin that still looked tanned, as if
she spent a lot of time outdoors, and little makeup, she
stood in front of the poster boards and stared at the information written near the pictures of the victims,
memorizing every word. At previous meetings she'd
been dressed in a dark suit, but today, with a nod to the
menacing weather, she wore a navy blue jogging suit
and long-sleeved, turtleneck sweater. She hadn't said a
whole lot so far, but her lips were folded thoughtfully
and there was an unspoken air of disapproval in her
stiff-backed stance and narrowed eyes. It seemed, though
it hadn't been said, that she thought she was the only
one capable of solving the crime.

Everyone else in the small room, including Pescoli
and Sheriff Grayson, were seated, but Chandler, one of
those nervous types, began pacing in front of the boards,
chewing on a corner of her lip. Alvarez was grateful that
she was partners with irreverent, bend-the-rules Pescoli
rather than this uptight woman.

At least Regan Pescoli had a sense of humor, dark as
it could be at times.

Moving her eyes to the final panel, where Jillian
Rivers's driver's license picture and mangled car were
posted, Chandler shook her head.

"This woman was never reported missing."

"Her family had no idea that she had even left Seattle. The only one who knew she'd taken off was the
neighbor who took care of her cat," Alvarez said. "Emily
Hardy, nineteen. Lives in the same complex of town-
houses as Rivers and goes to school at the university.
U-Dub." Chandler frowned as if she didn't get it. "University of Washington. Instead of U W, it's called U-Dub.
Rivers has her own kind of printing company and does
most of the work herself, so co-workers haven't missed

her and we've just started talking to her friends and ex-husband."

"The one that's still alive," Pescoli said. "I've got a call in to him."

Alvarez added, "Seattle PD found nothing out of place at her apartment. No desktop computer. Her laptop and purse are missing, likely with her."

"But not found at the scene?" Halden finished his coffee and tossed the empty paper cup into a nearby trash can.

"Just like the others." Pescoli frowned as she stared at the panels of the victims. "Same with the tire being shot."

"Same caliber rifle?"

"Couldn't find the bullet or the casing, but we're still looking."

"Anything different about this one?"

"The insurance information and registration were left behind," Alvarez admitted. "It's the one anomaly. But those docs weren't kept in the usual spots, not in the glove box or above the visor. They were hidden under the driver's seat and crushed when the car was wrecked. We didn't find them until the car was back here and the techs went over it."

"An oversight by the killer?" Chandler asked.

"Probably just couldn't find them. Maybe she was hurt and he had to get her out of the cold, or maybe he heard something that scared him off."

"Why would the car's information be under the driver's seat?" Chandler rested a hip against the table and her ice-blue eyes zeroed in on Alvarez.

"The papers could have slipped down there after a traffic stop, or maybe she just keeps them there."

"Or he dropped them as he was pulling her out of the car and didn't realize it?" Chandler was theorizing, her face tense, the wheels turning in her mind.

"No blood on them." Alvarez, too, was bothered by the one thing that was different at the scene. "We're checking for prints."

Chandler nodded.

Maybe she wasn't such a bitch after all, Alvarez thought, though she couldn't quite believe it. She unzipped her vest, as the room was warming up. The furnace was working overtime, wheezing as it blew hot air into the room packed with too many bodies. Through the bank of windows lay a view of the white-packed parking lot, a long plowed road and, less than a quarter of a mile away, the county jail, a two-storied cinder block building with a flat roof. Snow gathered near the foot of the jail's high fence and clung to the swirled razor wire, almost picturesque.

"Okay," Chandler said, walking back to the panels on the wall. "So no one has any idea what these notes mean?" Chandler pointed to the blowups of the papers left at each of the scenes.

"Not yet," Grayson drawled. The sheriff had been taking in the meeting, not saying much from his seat at a corner of the table. His attitude was almost why-don't-you-tell-us, Miss Know-It-All, but if he thought it, he kept it to himself.

"It seems odd that the position of the star is different in each case. He's so precise with these notes; the letters are all the same size, blocked out perfectly. So, the fact that the star isn't in exactly the same spot each time is for a reason. He's trying to tell us something."

"More likely taunting us," Pescoli said.

"Yeah, that, too. He seems intelligent and careful. These aren't rash, random killings. He's planned this, down to the smallest detail. He's organized. Thinks he's smarter than we are and it's unlikely that he would miss a detail like the car documents." Chandler walked to the panels and pointed to the enlarged notes. "Look at the placement of the stars. They're where they are for a reason, yet they vary from one note to the other. I think that's significant."

Alvarez nodded. She'd always thought so. "Then he's trying to leave us a message with the letters. The women aren't random."

"I think they're targeted," Chandler said.

Pescoli said, "But not raped."

Chandler's gaze swung to the taller detective. "Another anomaly. A lot of organized serial killers get off on holding their victims, getting close to them, torturing them and sexually molesting them." She rubbed her chin. "We've discounted the possibility of a female killer, right? Big shoe prints, strength necessary to get into the wrecked cars and haul the victims away."

"If it's a woman, she's big. Strong." Pescoli added her two cents. "Our female victims are all on the petite side, anywhere from a hundred and five to a hundred and twenty-five pounds. But most serials are men."

"A female killer feels wrong to me," Chandler admitted. "Off."

"To me, too," Pescoli agreed and no one argued. Outside the closed door Alvarez heard a phone ringing and footsteps as someone walked past the room.

Chandler went on, "We think he either kidnaps or leaves the women to die around the twentieth of the month. We've got three known victims and one potential, so let's check star alignment on those dates, September through December, and then if we find anything noteworthy, let's project to January."

"We haven't found the December victim yet," Pescoli pointed out, "and you're already thinking about January?"

"That's right." Craig Halden's usually affable expression was missing. His face was grim. "Our guy, he's not stopping." Halden shoved his chair back and walked around the table to the oversized topographical map that covered a large section of one wall. It was marked with the scenes where the wrecked vehicles and victims had been found. "Have we talked to everyone who lives or has a summer cabin in this area?" he asked, one of his hands arcing over the mountainous terrain on the map.

"Started," Grayson said. "We've got a list from the assessor's office. Lots of summer cabins. The area covers miles of rugged country."

Chandler said, "Vastly unpopulated."

Grayson nodded slowly. "We'll keep on it."

Between the pushpins, lines had been drawn in the hopes that some intersecting point would reveal the area where the killer lived, but the areas where the lines crossed were usually uninhabited.

But that was the way with organized serial killers, Alvarez knew from her research. These psychos went to great lengths to hide themselves and elude detection. They thought about their crimes long and hard, picked out their quarry, planned each move, got off on toying with their victims before they killed them. And all the while they enjoyed outwitting the police.

Sick bastards.

Halden walked back to his chair as his partner asked, "Have we had any ideas about the notes?"

That was a sore point with Alvarez, who had spent countless hours at night trying to figure out what the killer was trying to tell them. "*We* don't have much," she admitted.

"Let's put a cryptographer on it."

"Already have," Sheriff Grayson said. "One of the best in the country. So far nothing. Said he'd never seen anything quite like it."

Craig Halden settled into his chair. "We're getting the

same info. Nothing in the database matches up to this guy. He seems to be our own special loony."

"Ain't we lucky?" Pescoli muttered and slid Alvarez a glance.

Chandler finally took her seat and flipped through several pages of her notes. "Okay, about the people who discovered the crime scenes. According to your records, the car registered to Jillian Rivers was discovered by a woman who communes with the dead."

"Well," Grayson said, "we're not sure she actually makes contact. All we know is, she thinks she talks to spirits, but the jury's definitely out on her ability to . . . what do they call it, 'cross over'?"

"Something like that," Pescoli said.

"And Wendy Ito was found by a man who claims to be a victim of an alien abduction," Chandler said, looking pointedly at Grayson. "Isn't that odd?"

"Not around here," Pescoli said, and Grayson sent her a sharp look.

"They aren't exactly the most stable witnesses."

"Does it matter?" Pescoli asked. "It's not as if they were giving statements about the killer. All they did was lead us to one victim and one car. Yeah, they're both missing a screw or two, but they did help us out."

Grayson added, "Both Ivor and Grace were out in below-freezing weather, walking around. At least it was clear when Ivor made his discovery. Now, Grace, she was out with her dog in the middle of a damned blizzard. I don't think it's strange that they aren't rowing with all their oars in the water. Who else would be out in this weather?"

Touché, Sheriff, Alvarez thought, twirling her pen between her fingers. It bothered her that Chandler came in with "attitude," as if they were all country bumpkins and she was the big-city specialist. Alvarez altered her first impression. There was a good chance that Field Agent Stephanie Chandler was a little like the agents portrayed in movies after all.

Grayson was staring straight at both agents. "Theresa Charleton was found by hikers, Nina Salvadore by cross-country skiers. Charleton's car was seen by a trucker who happened to park his rig on a bridge and saw a glint of something up the creek bed, Salvadore's by teenagers out partying. None of them connect to each other; none of them knew the victims. None of them with priors—well, except for one of the kids who found the Ford Focus. He was driving on a suspended license."

"Good to know that all of the reports weren't from people guaranteed certifiable." Chandler offered Grayson a smile that wasn't the least bit warm. Yep, she was a bitch. "I'd like to look through your files on these cases."

"Be my guest," Grayson offered, the slightest of tics near the corner of his left eye belying a little of his irritation. "You can have copies of the files and see the vehicles, talk to anyone here. All the trace evidence collected is with the crime lab in Missoula."

"Thanks." Halden nodded, even though he had to have already known where the evidence was. He had turned his attention back to the map. "We're still missing the vehicle for victim three and the body for victim four."

"We're hoping to find Jillian Rivers alive," Alvarez said, and Stephanie Chandler caught her gaze.

There wasn't the slightest bit of hope in those ice-blue eyes. "Let's just hope there aren't others out there. We're all assuming our killer started with Theresa Charleton, but that's just because she was the first body found. He could have started earlier and we just haven't located either the victims or their vehicles. This is pretty rugged country."

"Wouldn't the notes have had other initials if there were other victims? Hell, is it hot enough in here?" Pescoli pushed back her chair and walked to the thermostat. "Seventy-five? That's like an effin' sauna! Aren't we in some kind of energy crisis?" She played with the electronic temperature control before returning to her seat. "Sorry," she said, but didn't appear the least bit contrite.

Chandler didn't miss a beat. "Signature serial killers rarely alter their signature, though their MOs can evolve as they experiment and learn. But this guy's different. We already mentioned that he's not raping them, there's no hint of sexual activity of any kind and he crosses race lines. Charleton and Rivers are Caucasian, Salvadore is Latino and Ito, Asian. This guy is organized, but he's all over the map." Chandler looked at the large topographical map on the far wall. "We've got our work cut out for us."

Sheriff Grayson's cell phone rang sharply and he shoved his chair back from the table. "All right, then. Anything we can do for ya, let us know. We'll take all the help we can get to nail this son of a bitch."

Jillian's head pounded.

Her ankle was on fire.

Her chest ached every time she moved.

She opened a bleary eye and looked around a darkened room lit by kerosene lanterns and a fire burning in a woodstove. She was warm, but sensed that was new. She'd been cold. So very, very cold.

And she'd heard someone moaning . . .

Or had she cried out herself?

She blinked, trying to figure out where she was. Bits of memory assailed her. The drive in the snow, spinning out, her tire blowing, glass shattering.

Someone had come to her rescue.

A man in dark ski wear who had yelled at her.

She remembered that and not much else.

So why wasn't she in a hospital?

What was this dark cabin all about? She was lying on a cot of some kind, tucked in a sleeping bag. She tried to push herself into a sitting position and the pain pounding in her ankle made her cry out.

Oh God, what had she gotten herself into?

She remembered the fear. First of being trapped in the car and never found this winter. Then she'd sensed a presence, something evil in those woods, and seen a dark shadow.

Obviously it was the man who rescued you.

Some rescue. She now seemed trapped in this stone-and-rough-timber room with a single small window that offered little light. Or was it dark? Dear God, how long had she slept?

She thought she remembered someone coming into the room and tending to her, but she wasn't certain . . . Oh God. She lifted one arm and saw that it was encased in a sleeve she didn't recognize. Some kind of thermal undershirt that was too big, the cuff of the sleeve pushed up. Her other arm was the same.

And she wasn't wearing a bra.

Someone had taken off the clothes she'd been wearing and redressed her in this oversized insulated shirt.

She tried to push herself up to a sitting position, but the pain in her leg made movement impossible, and when she lifted her head, she became dizzy. Her mouth tasted horrible, as if she hadn't brushed her teeth in a week, and she wondered how long she'd been lying here, unconscious. She shifted and realized she had some kind of splint on her leg. Touching her face, she felt bandages.

Whoever had brought her here had tended to her. On a small bedside table, little more than a stool, was a tube of some kind of antibiotic ointment and a plastic glass with a straw.

From the cot, she eyed the stone wall running up to the ceiling and the woodstove in front of it. Behind small glass doors were glowing coals, embers from what had probably been a larger fire.

She figured he had to come into the room fairly often to feed the fire and check on her and she remembered, vaguely, sensing another person close to her.

Damn right he was close . . . he undressed you, tended your wounds and put you to bed . . . he wasn't just close, he was damn near . . . intimate.

The rafters creaked loudly and then she heard the rush of wind and felt the walls shake.

Was she alone in the cabin?

Though no one was in the small room with her, there was a single door and beneath it a strip of light, indicating there was illumination in the next room. She thought about calling out, then decided against it. Something about this was off, really off, and she had to be careful. The man in the ski mask who had rescued her, the man whose face she couldn't identify, had brought her here rather than to civilization.

Why?

Because he didn't have a vehicle?

Because of the storm?

But he could somehow get her to this cabin? How did that work?

Was it near the spot where her car slid off the road? Was it near town? Or remote? There was no way to tell unless she dragged herself to the window and peered out. Currently, with her damned leg, that was impossible.

She lay quietly and listened but heard nothing over the rush of the wind, the creak of old timbers and the soft hiss of the fire.

The only way out of the room was through the single doorway, or the small window, mounted high and seemingly crusted with ice. Was it day? Night? She couldn't really tell. Maybe dusk? Or dawn? She had no idea. Out of habit, she looked at her left wrist, but her watch, which she rarely removed, was missing.

Great.

She eyed the window, situated six feet off the floor and so small she couldn't possibly push herself through.

Not that she could leave anyway. Not yet. She couldn't move her leg, and even if she did somehow hobble over to the wall, pulling the cot and hoisting herself to the glass pane, what then? The chance that she could slip through was slim, and then there was the problem, if she didn't get stuck, of being outside in a storm that continued to rage and pound this cabin in furious gusts.

For now, escape was out of the question.

But he must have a vehicle. A four-wheel-drive truck, or SUV or damned dog sled . . . If you could find a way . . .

Or she could ask him.

Just come out with the questions she had. The worst he could do was lie.

Right?

Or was she kidding herself? She thought she remembered something about some missing women in Montana, women whose cars had been wrecked or something. She couldn't remember the details, but the overriding memory of a menace gripped her. A man who had been hurting these women . . . single women traveling through Montana.

A fear like no other drove straight into her heart.

What were the chances that she'd had a wreck and the lunatic killer had found her and—

Stop! Don't even go there. Just play it cool.

But her heart was pounding so loudly she was certain it was echoing off the exposed beams of the high ceiling overhead. Her pulse raced as if she'd just finished a biathlon.

She swallowed back her fear, her mind racing.

From the next room, she heard the scrape of wood—a chair leg against the stone floor?

Her heart nearly stopped.

She saw a shadow in the space beneath the doorway, a quick movement as someone passed between a light source and the threshold.

Oh God, was he coming into the room?

You have no reason to distrust him. He saved you from certain death, didn't he?

Yeah, but he didn't get me to a hospital, or call the police or fire rescue. He brought me, unconscious, here. Alone. And I'm damned helpless.

For the time being all she could do was feign sleep and try to figure out if she should trust him.

Or if she shouldn't.

She didn't move a muscle as the door creaked open. Though her eyes were closed, she *felt* him walk into the room, come close to the bed and stare down at her.

Take even, slow breaths.

Relax your muscles.

Don't clench your fist.

You can move . . . people move in their sleep . . . just don't overdo it.

He seemed to stand over her for hours, when, in reality, it was probably less than two minutes. She kept her eyes shut, not risking a peek beneath her lashes.

Eventually he moved on, his footsteps fading, and then she heard the door of her room's woodstove rattle and open. She imagined that he was picking up short chunks of wood and stuffing them into the fire.

She couldn't resist, inching her eyelids up just a fraction.

It was shadowy in the room, and as he kneeled in front of the fire, his body was in silhouette. She couldn't see much, just got impressions, but yes, he was definitely male. Wide shoulders in some kind of dark sweater, hair that was either dark as coffee or black, enough to curl slightly over the turtleneck and dark pants.

The fire crackled loudly, hungrily devouring the new fuel, flaring behind him as he turned to one side, his face in quick profile as he reached for another length of wood. She caught a razor-sharp image of a strong jaw, long nose, deep-set eyes and thick eyebrows before she let her lids close completely.

She heard him stuff the chunk of mossy oak into the firebox and she hazarded another look, seeing that his sweater had ridden up above the waistline of his pants. No thermal undershirt was visible, just a crescent-shaped slice of firm flesh, taut skin over hard back muscles, as if he worked out all the time.

"Like what you see?" he asked, not turning around, his voice nearly echoing in the room.

She almost started. *Oh damn!* She let her eyes close and didn't move.

"I could say something like, 'Why don't you take a picture? It'll last longer.' But that seems a little sophomoric, don't you think?"

She didn't respond, but heard him brush his hands together, as if ridding them of wood dust or slivers. He was probably getting to his feet again.

He walked closer to the bed.

God help me.

"I know you're awake." He was standing over her again and she felt his gaze rake over her, studying her. "Jillian?" he said a little more softly and she died a thousand deaths. He knew who she was. Of course he did.

He had all of her belongings—her purse, her laptop, her cell phone, probably the registration of the car.

With all the restraint she could muster, she attempted to remain impassive, no twitch of nervous muscles showing, no signs of tension in her relaxed body.

"Jillian? Hey." He touched her then, warm fingers resting on her shoulder.

She wanted to scream.

"We need to talk. You and I, we're stuck here for a while, at least until the storm passes, and I need to know that you're all right. You need to eat and drink. . . . Jillian? Can you hear me?"

She kept slowly breathing.

"I know you can hear me, and to prove it, I could tickle the bottoms of your feet."

Dear God, no! He wouldn't! She was so sensitive to tickling. Maybe he was one of those fetish freaks. Weren't a lot of serial killers into all kinds of weird, macabre collections or rituals?

She tried to be rational. After all, he'd done nothing but be kind to her.

So far.

"Jillian, please. We don't have time for games. If I'm going to get you out of here, I'm going to need your help."

If?

Jillian's heart went into overdrive at the many connotations of that one little word. Oh Lord, her pulse was beating so wildly he could probably see it. What did he mean by *if?* Not *if,* but *when. When* he was going to get her out of here. Surely that's what he meant.

"So you might want to quit playin' possum." He took his hand away, and she wanted to let out a long, relieved sigh, but didn't.

She knew he was just looking for a reaction, some indication that she could hear him.

"You know, Jillian—"

Jillian. As if he knew her. As if they were friends, for God's sake.

Well, come on, do you expect him to refer to you as Ms. Rivers? Being that you're trapped alone with him in a snowstorm, you're going to get up on formality? Come on, Jillian. Get real!

She felt violated, as if her own life had been torn apart and studied.

"—you and I, we've got a lot to do. If the storm breaks in a few days like the weather service predicts, then we've got to figure out how to get you out of here before the next one hits."

He waited a few seconds, the weight of his gaze heavy on her, before saying, "Okay, do whatever it is you have to do, but I imagine that ankle of yours isn't feeling all that great. I don't think it's broken, but from the looks of it, it's sprained big-time. There are some pills here, in the bottle. Ibuprofen. You might want to take a few."

Then he walked out of the room and softly closed the door separating this room from the rest of the cabin. At least he was allowing her some privacy.

Or himself. Maybe he doesn't want you to see what he's doing, rather than the other way around.

She slowly counted to a hundred. Then two hundred.

Afterwards, her heart still beating crazily, she opened an eye. Just a crack. To make sure he hadn't faked her out. But she was alone. Thank God.

The fire was blazing and she wondered at his kindness. Was he truly a Good Samaritan, or just faking her out, trying to gain her trust?

Why?

To what end?

If he was going to hurt you, he would have done it by now. Right? You're not restrained, are you?

Well, not unless being hobbled by an injured ankle and trapped by a blizzard counted.

Could she trust him? Hell no! At least not yet. There

was a killer on the loose in the wilds of Montana, she did know that much.

Don't panic. Stay calm.

But her throat was dry with dread.

What were the chances that she'd met up with him? One in a million?

No way could she be that unlucky. No way!

Or was she kidding herself?

Chapter Nine

"So you don't know where your sister might be," Pescoli clarified, thinking she'd drawn the short straw by having to make the phone call to Dusti Bellamy. She sat at her desk, intent on the conversation, barely noticing other phones ringing, other conversations, the continuous click of keyboards or even when Trilby Van Droz shepherded an obviously inebriated man past her cubicle. Pescoli was too into her conversation with Jillian Rivers's only known sibling. Unfortunately, Pescoli thought as she listened to the whiner on the other end of the connection, it was obvious the woman didn't give a rat's ass about Jillian Rivers, sister or no sister.

"Sorry, Detective, I'd like to help you, really I would. And this business about Jillian's wrecked car, well, that just scares me to death, but it's really not that much of a surprise. She's always been so . . . outdoorsy. Kind of a daredevil. Not quite like Evel Knievel, but geez, she's done everything from barrel racing in rodeos to parachuting. And she can't stand a boss or anyone telling her what to do. No wonder she couldn't stay married. She's . . . well, she's just wild. What you're telling me worries me sick, but I don't think I can help you. We're just not that close. Never have been. I live in San Diego. She lives in Seattle. I have two kids and a husband. Jill isn't married—well, not right now," she said with the superiority of one who had landed a husband and held him fast. "And she never had kids. We don't have a lot in common."

"I see," Regan said, to keep her going. Dusti White Bellamy sounded a little breathless, as if she'd spent her day chasing kids or running up flights of stairs or working out on some kind of cardio machine. "As I told you, the last time I spoke to her was sometime near the tenth of November, I think, when she informed me she wouldn't be coming down for Thanksgiving. Just like that! She didn't say why and I didn't ask."

"Was she dating anyone?"

"Maybe. Probably. I don't really know. She never said anything about a new guy, and my mother, she would have told me. Linnie can't keep that kind of thing under wraps."

"Would Jillian have confided in Linnette?" Regan doubted it. Personally, she kept everything about her love life from her mother, as well as her daughter.

"Oh, probably not. My—er, our mom isn't one to keep her opinions to herself. She's old school and . . ." Her voice faded for a second. "Oh God . . . I've got to go. My five-year-old's on a chair near my husband's aquarium. Reece!" she screamed at the top of her lungs. "Don't!"

"If you think of anything else, would you call me at—"

Crash!

"No!"

The sound of shattering glass and a child's cry was cut off with a distinct click.

"So much for sisterly love," Pescoli muttered as she finished her notes and scanned them over. If Dusti White Bellamy knew anything about her sister's disappearance, she wasn't giving it up. Nor was the neighboring student who was caring for Jillian's cat. The Seattle police had interviewed Emily Hardy, who'd said only that Jillian had asked her to care for the cat, as she was "going out of town for a few days."

Pescoli looked over her notes to double-check. Emily Hardy had supplied the police with Jillian's cell phone number, but when they'd called, no one had answered. Pescoli, too, had tried to reach Jillian Rivers, but her call had gone directly to voice mail.

"Dead end, dead end, dead end," she said, clicking her pen nervously as she reached for the phone again. The Seattle PD had already talked to Linnette White, but Regan decided to call the woman herself. She waited through six rings but Linnette didn't answer. Leaving her name and number, she asked for a return call. If she didn't get one by tomorrow morning, she'd dial Jillian's mother again.

Or maybe the FBI would send a Seattle agent out to talk with her. They were supposed to be working hand in hand with them and so far Chandler and Halden hadn't gotten in the way. The agents had actually helped, so Pescoli wasn't complaining.

Yet.

She glanced down at the list of Jillian Rivers's known acquaintances. Written below the missing woman's sister and mother was Mason Rivers, Jillian's ex-husband. Pescoli tried not to let her experiences with Lucky color her judgment. Though she firmly believed there was no such thing as a "good" ex-husband, she tried to push her own prejudices aside. According to court records, Mason Rivers and Jillian had been married for four years and divorced for two. According to court documents, Mason had remarried about six months ago.

"Nothing ventured, nothing gained," she said, punching out his office number and leaning back in her chair.

"Olsen, Nye and Rivers," a no-nonsense woman answered. Pescoli asked for Mason Rivers but got nowhere. According to the receptionist, Mr. Rivers was "in court and not expected back until tomorrow afternoon."

Convenient, Pescoli thought, her detective radar on alert. Or was it her ex-wife radar? Or just her bullshit radar? She suspected the pert voice on the other end of the line was lying to her. But then, she always thought people lied to her. Especially anyone who was an ex to a missing person.

She left her name and number and asked to have "Mr. Rivers" return her call. She hung up and stared at the phone, again clicking her damned pen. What was it about this case that no one knew anything? Flipping through her notes on Theresa Charleton, Nina Salvadore and Wendy Ito, she was struck by the same theme. "No enemies" was the common thread. "Well liked" resonated with all the victims. "Can't imagine who would want to hurt her" had been said over and over again.

Had the victims been random? Had the killer just started writing down initials in no particular pattern? Chandler didn't think so. Neither did Pescoli. She turned to her computer and clicked on copies of the notes. Each one so similar to the others. Meticulous, as Chandler had pointed out. The victims had to have been chosen for some reason and their initials were part of it. So . . . the women were chosen *for* their names? Was that it?

What kind of nutcase were they dealing with? She read the initials again.

W   T   SC   I N

If she filled in missing letters, she got "WHAT SCENE" or "WANT SCORN" or "WILT SCAN." Or maybe there were more letters added to the front and end of the message, if indeed it was one. Like "SWAT" or "SWEAT" or "AWAIT" for the first word . . . or maybe it was all one long word waiting for missing letters.

Where would Jillian Rivers's initials fit in?

Though the room was warm, she felt suddenly cold inside, thinking of Jillian Rivers's fate. Was she dead already? Being tortured? Awaiting her ultimate doom?

"Crap!" she muttered and tossed her pen onto the desk.

Dear God, she hoped they would find the woman before she was left in the freezing weather, lashed to a tree, a star carved over her head and her initials added to the deadly enigma that was the killer's note.

Jillian had to pee.

No two ways about it.

And she still couldn't move.

Great. Just . . . great.

Her only option other than calling out to her captor/rescuer/whatever to help her to a toilet was to wet the bed.

Out of the question.

She listened.

The cabin was quiet, aside from the rush of the wind and creak of old timbers. She held her breath, but heard no footsteps, no rustle of clothing or papers, no snoring. It seemed as if she was completely alone.

Maybe he's abandoned you. Left you here alone in the blizzard.

She didn't know whether that was a bad thing, or good. Couldn't dwell on it, not with the pressure in her bladder.

Setting her jaw so that she wouldn't cry out, she forced herself into a sitting position, all the while feeling the dull throb in her rib cage. Once upright, she took a good, hard look around the room. Yes, there was a window, and it had to be daylight because there was more illumination within this small room than there had been, but snow obliterated any view from the cot. The only door into the room was the old scratched panel that connected this small bedroom to the next, which she thought was probably the heart of this rustic cabin, the area where *he* stayed, whoever the hell *he* was. She listened and heard nothing, as if he either were asleep or out of the house.

Was that possible?

In this storm?

How?

By the same way he brought you here.

She remembered feeling as if she were floating and, yes, hearing some loud engine, but it had been cold, so damned cold, and she'd been on the brink of consciousness, almost wakening, then settling deeper into the coma or whatever it was that had kept her unaware ever since the accident.

She couldn't damned well stay propped on this bed with her bladder about to burst, so she gritted her teeth and swung her good leg over the edge of the cot.

Now, for the real test of will.

Clenching her jaw, she tried to drag her injured leg to the side of the bed.

A sharp, excruciating pain shot up her calf.

Holy Mother of God!

Think beyond the pain, beyond the injury. She'd taken enough self-defense courses to train her mind and focus, but man, her leg hurt.

She sucked in her breath.

Again, she told herself. *You can do it.*

With effort she dragged her foot to the side of the bed and slowly rotated so that she could swing her leg over. For the first time she saw what he'd done and realized he'd taped her ankle, stabilizing it. Clean cotton gauze wrapped around a splint of two pieces of wood that stuck out a bit. It was old-school, not the molded plastic boots she'd seen on school athletes who had injured themselves, but it looked like whoever had taped her up had done a decent enough job.

But, of course, it wasn't a walking cast.

Then she saw the crutch.

Propped against the wall near the foot of the bed.

Her skin crawled a little. This guy was a lot more prepared than she'd thought. Who had a crutch just lying around? Maybe a doctor? Or . . . or someone who'd once hurt himself. But really, in this barren room, a crutch?

Don't second-guess it. Just nab that sucker!

Maybe, just maybe, he's a good guy.

No, she couldn't let herself think that way, not until she knew more about him. He'd shown up pretty fast after the accident. Why the hell was he out in the middle of a snowstorm? She thought she remembered the sound of a rifle report, as if someone had shot at her before the car started spinning. Though it was just conjecture, she had to be cautious.

Because, damn it, she was trapped here.

With a healer?

Or a killer?

Don't even go there. Not yet.

Willing herself to keep moving, she scooted down the length of the cot and snagged the single crutch. Somehow, she pulled herself to a standing position, though she kept no weight on the injured foot, and then, with her bladder full and her leg aching dully, she made her way to the doorway, hobbling awkwardly and making more noise than she'd intended.

Even so, she didn't hear a response. If he was inside, he hadn't heard her.

Taking a deep breath, she twisted the old metal doorknob and pushed gently on the oak panels. Soundlessly the door opened a bit and she peered through the crack to a larger room. No lamps had been lit and the stone and wood living area looked gloomy and dark, only a bit of light coming from the fireplace that butted up to the doorway from which Jillian was peering.

The room had a high ceiling, nearly two stories. On the far end was a ladder that led to an open loft. Bookcases filled the area beneath the loft's overhang and a massive table occupied the center of the shadowy room. An armoire of sorts was pushed against the wall and nearer the fireplace was another cupboard—no, a closet, like she'd seen at Grandpa Jim's house twenty-five years earlier, the locked, handcrafted cupboard he'd used to store his hunting rifles.

Jillian felt a trickle of fear.

Of course he's got guns. For God's sake, he lives in the wilderness! Maybe you can get hold of one and some ammunition. Just in case you need it.

A sharp shard of memory cut through her brain as once again she heard the crack of a rifle and then her car was spinning out of control, rotating fast toward the sharp ravine. . . .

Her heart froze and her throat went dry in fear.

She needed to leave.

To find a way out of this place.

Now!

Using the damned crutch, she gently pushed the door open further and braced herself, certain someone or something would leap out at her.

A beat-up leather sofa sat near the stone fireplace and backed up to her bedroom. Another chair with a lumpy ottoman was situated nearby and a recliner, complete with sleeping bag, was tucked into the corner that was dominated by floor-to-ceiling bookshelves. On the opposite wall, a bank of glass windows was protected by the overhang of a long porch with exposed rafters. The cabin was on a hill, but the view, if there was one, was obscured by a thick veil of heavy, swirling snow that had blown over the floorboards of the porch.

Outside was a whiteout.

She couldn't see ten feet beyond the porch. But she could hear the ferocity of the wind, feel it shake this old wood-and-rock building.

Her heart sank.

Any thought of leaving here, of seeking help, was obliterated by the storm. She was stuck here for the time being. "Wonderful," she muttered under her breath as she turned slowly to look around, a sharp pain in her chest reminding her she'd probably cracked a rib or two in the accident.

As she'd thought the cabin was empty. No one around. Inside the massive stone fireplace the flames eagerly licked at a chunk of wood, casting blood-red shadows and shifting shapes on the rock and windows.

It's not creepy. It's cozy.

"Yeah, right."

Steadfastly ignoring the pain in her ankle, she hobbled to what she thought was the gun closet. Sure enough, it was locked, no key in sight. So much for getting lucky.

Moving onward, she hitched her way through an open doorway and found a tiny kitchen with scarred wooden counters and rustic cupboards that looked over a hundred years old. But there was a sink and faucet, so running water did exist, evidenced by the slow trickle coming out of the tap. At least she didn't have to try and make her way through three-foot snowdrifts to an outhouse. She hitched her way through the kitchen to a narrow

door at the far end of the room. It opened to a cold,
compact bathroom with cracked linoleum and a tiny
window poised over a claw-foot tub with a shower. Along
one wall was a toilet and a small vanity with a sink. On
the other was a washer and dryer and an old cupboard.

"All the comforts of home," she muttered and wasted
no time closing the door, grabbing onto the sink with
one hand and, using the crutch, propelling herself to
the toilet. After relieving herself, she stood at the sink
and caught a glimpse of her face in the mirror. Her hair
was a mess, oily and tangled, her face bruised, the white
of one eye bloodshot. "Cute," she muttered as she took
the time to splash water over her face and refused to
think about the throb of her aching chest and injured
ankle.

She didn't have any time to lose.

She needed to figure out how to get the hell out of
here and somehow get in contact with civilization. She
could grab a gun and ammunition from his closet, pull
on the warmest clothes she could find and . . . and . . .
and what? Hobble down the hillside in the middle of a
blizzard with one crutch?

Maybe there was a vehicle. A four-wheel-drive truck
or snowmobile or something . . . even a damned horse.
She moved to the back door and peered through the
icy panels. Yes, there were a few other buildings. One
could be a garage. And one a barn. But they were slippery paths and huge drifts along the way. "Damn it all."

She opened two drawers before she found the knife,
a thin, long-bladed filet knife, perfect for cutting flesh
from bone. Or for protecting herself. Holding the
weapon tight, she worked her way to the living area
again and saw not only snowshoes but skis mounted on
the wall.

Lots of good those would do her.

The phone!

Damn it, Jillian, what have you been thinking? Where's the friggin' phone?

Propelling herself back into the kitchen again, she saw no evidence of a telephone, and when she flipped a light switch, nothing happened. The power was out. No surprise there, with the intensity of this storm.

No phones in the kitchen.

Back to that large hall-like main room.

Once through the doorway, she looked around for a land line, a cell phone or a computer, any device she could use to contact the outside world once the electricity was restored. She needed to get out of here, to let someone know where she was, to . . . Where the hell was it?

Her ankle throbbing, she moved around the perimeter of the main room. Wasn't there a land line? A modem for computer service? Even a stupid television?

Careful, Jillian, your city-girl roots are showing.

There had been a time when she and Aaron had backpacked through areas that had been undeveloped. They'd slept under the stars, washed themselves in mountain lakes, eschewed all the comforts and stress of modern life.

Aaron.

Memories of hiking through the wilderness assailed her. Pacific rain forests of the Olympic Peninsula, the mountainous trails of the Cascades in Oregon, exploring the alpine meadows of the San Juans, discovering remote sections of Colorado and the everglades in Florida. But the ultimate trip, the one they'd planned and saved for and talked about in every conversation for nearly a year, had been the adventure of a lifetime, a long backpacking trek through the wilds of South America, where he'd disappeared and died.

Or not.

She grabbed a corner of the table to steady herself as another wave of memories washed over her. Aaron was the reason she'd left Seattle. Someone had sent her pictures of a man claiming to be him, someone in Missoula. That's why she was driving through the mountains when she'd heard the rifle shot. . . .

Her knees quivered as she again remembered that distinctive crack of a rifle. Then her tire had blown and her car had spun over the edge of the cliff and . . . and *someone* had *intentionally* caused her car to careen into the frozen ravine? *Someone* had tried to kill her?

Why?

Who even knew she would be driving through these mountains?

The caller, you idiot! The damned person who sent you the pictures that were supposedly of Aaron. He lured you here and he's probably the stranger who "saved" you. Remember, there's a killer on the loose up here.

Oh God, oh God, oh God . . .

Her heart jackhammered. She couldn't run away. Couldn't get far at all in her injured state with a storm raging through these mountains. For the love of God, she didn't even know where she was. But somewhere, he had her cell phone and some means by which to leave this tiny cabin.

Thud!

Startled, she jumped at the noise and turned swiftly only to realize the sound had come from the fire, a chunk of wood that had burned through and broken.

Her pulse was beating out of control and she was all too aware that any second the man who had brought her here might return. *What then? What will you do then?*

Panicked, she started going around the room again, checking the outlets, searching for a phone jack.

Nothing!

She saw nothing.

Hurry, hurry, hurry!

Dear God, she was going out of her mind.

Think, Jillian, don't lose it, just think. There has to be a way to communicate with the outside world. He couldn't be up here isolated and completely cut off from—

Click!

She bit back a scream.

The sound of a deadbolt slipping out of place made her skin crawl. This noise wasn't the damned fire!

He was back!

The distinctive creak of a door opening and the stomp of boots on the kitchen floor met her ears.

"Get in here!"

Oh God, someone was with him? A partner? Or some other victim?

Frantically, she glanced at the door to the bedroom. If she could slink noiselessly across this room, slip through the door and sink onto the bed, she could hide there, again pretend to be asleep, but it was too far. She'd never make it. Her fingers curled over the hilt of the thin knife and she slid the blade up her sleeve, determined to hide it. Keep it.

In case she needed it.

The door in the kitchen slammed shut and she nearly jumped out of her skin as the sound of the wind became muted again.

Calm down, Jillian. It's time for the acting job of your life. Don't let him know you don't trust him. Don't slip up for a minute. Whatever his bullshit story is, pretend to believe it. Maybe his guard will slip. . . .

Terrified, she turned toward the kitchen, nearly falling in the process. Her heart was in her throat, but she maintained a placid expression that she hoped belied her fear.

More stomping.

No other voice.

Heavy footsteps resounded along with another sound, a quick click-click scratching sound.

She held herself up by the edge of his big table. The metal crutch was tucked under her arm, her fingers wrapped around the handgrip so hard her knuckles showed white, the handle of the knife hidden in her other palm.

Sweat beaded on her forehead though the temperature in the room was cold.

Okay, bastard, she thought, mentally gearing up for a fight. *I'm ready.*

He appeared, big as life, in the archway between the kitchen and living area. Tall and rugged-looking, he was dressed head to toe in black ski gear as he filled the archway between the kitchen and living area.

All the spit dried in her mouth.

"Well, look who's up," he said without a trace of a smile. Was he talking to her or whoever was with him?

"If it isn't Sleeping Beauty."

Chapter Ten

Alvarez offered the woman a cup of coffee and tried to keep her expression bland, as if she believed anything Grace Perchant, the ghost whisperer, had to say. She was alone with the thin, pale woman in the interrogation room, but both of them knew other people were observing the conversation on the other side of the mirror. More were watching the monitor, as the interview was being recorded. "You know, we're sorry to bother you again. You've been a big help, but we just want to make certain we have all the facts straight, that we haven't missed anything."

Grace didn't so much as nod. Sometimes it was hard to tell if she even heard a person. Pescoli always said it was because she had so many dead people screaming inside her head, she couldn't hear the living. But then, that was sarcastic, never-believe-anything-that-isn't-hard-fact Pescoli. "Tell me again about finding the car."

Grace Perchant sat in the straight-backed chair at the table, ignored the steaming cup and stared up with the palest green eyes Alvarez had ever seen. "I already told the other detectives. I was walking my dog, Bane, and I looked down into the canyon and saw the car. It glinted through the snow. Is that so hard to understand?"

"No, I guess not."

"And would it be too much trouble to get a cup of tea?" Grace asked. "Coffee's not good for you."

Alvarez nodded as she took a swig of her own detrimental brew. "Just a sec."

"With lemon and honey."

"We don't have—"

"Fine." One arched eyebrow lifted a fraction further as Grace said, "Plain will do. Herbal would be better. . . ." Then catching the skepticism in Alvarez's gaze, she amended her request. "Anything will be fine."

"Good." Alvarez scooted her chair back, walked through the door. It shut behind her as she met Pescoli in the hall outside.

"I heard," Pescoli said, rolling her eyes. "What does she think this is, damned Starbucks?"

"She's Grace Perchant," Alvarez said, as if that explained everything.

"Yeah, yeah, I'll get her tea. I hate to agree with Chandler but it's hell to think Grace and Ivor might be our star witnesses in this case."

If it ever gets to trial, Alvarez thought and hated herself for her doubts as Pescoli headed down the hall toward the break room. Alvarez slipped back inside. "It'll be just a couple of minutes." She slid into her chair. "You were telling me about being out there at September Creek."

Grace nodded, her graying blond hair moving against her shoulders as if it was nothing to be hiking through a blizzard.

"It was below freezing and snowing," Alvarez said.

"Bane needed to go out." Grace shrugged. "He's part wolf; the cold doesn't bother him. We take that route along the creek every other day or so."

"What about you? Doesn't the cold weather bother you?"

"Sometimes." Grace looked directly at the mirror, as if she could see the sheriff and FBI agents beyond. "It's often a situation of mind over matter."

"Did you see anyone else out there?"

Grace shook her head. "No. As you pointed out it was freezing."

"No other cars?"

Sighing, Grace folded her hands over the metal top of the table and leaned closer, her eerie eyes focusing hard on Alvarez. "If I told you what I saw out there you wouldn't believe me."

"Try me."

Her face was calm and without the least bit of guile. "Don't patronize me, Detective. You know about me, that I see spirits."

"And there were spirits out there?"

"They're everywhere." She smiled, her thin lips twisting a bit. "They don't mind the cold."

Was Grace for real?

"Did your dog act strangely? As if he saw anything?"

"He sniffed around, but no more than usual."

There was a soft knock on the door and Alvarez opened it to find Joelle on the other side. She held a Styrofoam cup of hot water, a tea bag steeping within.

"We only had Earl Gray," she said. "I think Grace likes those herbal calming ones that they serve over at the Java Bean, but we don't have anything like that." Joelle appeared worried, little lines threading between her eyebrows. Her glossed lips, the same exact shade as her jacket and slacks, pulled into a tight knot.

"It'll be fine," Alvarez said. "It's only one cup. If she doesn't like it, she'll get over it." She took the steaming cup from Joelle's reluctant fingers and slipped back into the stark room.

Grace took a small sip and didn't complain.

Good thing.

With a little prodding Grace told Alvarez the same story she had earlier, nearly verbatim. She hadn't seen anything out of the ordinary other than the wrecked car in the creek bed. "We were walking along the ridge road, and I could see it in the ravine."

"You were on the road above?"

"Yes, and I saw the point where the car had gone over the edge, so I hurried back to the house and called. Fortunately the phones were still working. Then I tried to get back to the car myself, to get down the embankment and see if anyone was inside, but the deputy arrived before I did, coming in from the other side. He was in the area, I guess."

That was right. So far so good. "So you can't tell us anything else?"

"If I could I would," Grace said simply, though her eyes darkened incredibly, her pupils widening as she stared at the detective.

Alvarez felt as if a cold, dark wind blew through her soul and it was all she could do to hold Grace's stare and not look away. "Well . . . if you think of anything, let us know." She pushed back her chair to end the interview. Quick as lightning, Grace reached across the table, knocking over Alvarez's near-empty cup. Strong fingers wrapped around the detective's wrist. "You'll find him," she vowed as the detective instinctively reached for her sidearm.

Concern etched the ghost whisperer's face and Alvarez let her hand fall from her pistol. "Of course we will." She carefully pulled her wrist away from Grace's cold grasp. "The son of a bitch won't get away with this."

"What? The man the police are looking for? He's not who I was talking about," Grace said, her eyebrows elevating a fraction.

"Then . . . what?" Alvarez asked, but she knew, deep in her heart, that this woman to whom she'd never before spoken, could see into the darkest reaches of her heart.

"Don't despair," Grace said with a calm that Alvarez found eerie. "You'll find him."

From the other side of the one-way mirror Pescoli nearly dropped her cup of coffee. She'd been on her way to the door when Grace had grabbed Alvarez, but the sheriff had held her back.

"It's okay," he said, and she'd waited, watching the weird scene unfold. "What the hell was that all about?"

"With Grace," Grayson said, staring through the one-way mirror, "you never know."

"Jesus, Mary and Joseph. First Ivor I've-been-abducted-by-aliens Hicks as a critical witness, and now a wolf-woman who speaks with ghosts." Pescoli crushed her coffee cup in her fist and threw it into an almost-full trash can. "You know, Sheriff, I hate to say it, but I'm thinkin' the odds are stacked against us."

"Sleeping Beauty my ass." Jillian glared at the man she'd decided was more her captor than savior.

He must've been six feet one or two and, bulked up in his ski gear, he looked all the more massive.

And strong.

And formidable.

At his side stood a black-and-white long-haired dog, some kind of spaniel mix, hackles stiff and raised. Its head was down, dark menacing eyes sparking with distrust.

"Is that dog going to attack me?"

"Not unless you come at it with the crutch."

She considered putting the metal crutch down, but hearing the dog growl, decided against it.

"Just control him."

"Not an animal lover?" His face was still hidden by the ski mask, but something registered in his movement, the easy manner as he turned to the dog. Amusement? Cruelty?

"Not if the animal is acting as if it wants to tear out my throat."

"Harley? Hear that? Stand down."

The dog growled.

"Great control."

"Sit!" he said sharply and the dog placed his back end on the plank floorboards. But he didn't let Jillian out of his sight.

"Better?" he asked.

Was he joking? Really? This whole situation was something out of a bad dream. For all she knew he could be a psycho of the worst kind, a killer. Hadn't Ted Bundy, a notorious sexual predator and serial killer, been considered charming, good-looking and intelligent? Wasn't one of the first things neighbors said about some of the worst murderers in history, "But he was such a nice guy"? Oh, there were killers who were outwardly crazy, or secretive or so weird that their psychosis was evident to those close to them from a young age, but the victims, those who didn't know the killer intimately from childhood, thought only they were "odd" or "loners." But that didn't always hold true. And in this case she wasn't about to trust her "savior," not yet anyway.

"So I'm Sleeping Beauty, he or she"—Jillian pointed the rubber tip of her crutch at the spaniel mix—"is Harley." The dog growled again. "So, that leaves you."

"I'm Zane MacGregor, and, for the record, Harley's a he."

"How long have I been here, MacGregor?" she demanded.

"Three days."

"Three days?" she repeated, horrified. She'd known, of course, that time had passed. But three days? She'd lost *seventy-two hours* of her life?

"Storms have been rolling in ever since. Roads are impassable. Electricity out. It's a mess."

She was stunned, still trying to piece together what had happened, while MacGregor took off his ski cap and mask and unwound a scarf that covered his neck. His hair, black, glossy and curling slightly, stuck up in weird-looking tufts, and three or maybe four days' growth of whiskers covered what she thought was a tight, strong jaw. His eyes, beneath thick dark brows, were an intense shade of gray. "You plannin' on smackin' me with that?" he asked, nodding toward the crutch.

"Maybe."

One of his thick eyebrows cocked, as if the idea was insane, as if he could rip the damned thing from her hands before she got in a blow. "Hear that, Harley? She's going to try and whack me."

The dog cocked his head, waiting for another command. One side of his face was black, the other white, his coat mottled and rough.

"Watch out, she might have it in for you, too," MacGregor warned the dog as he walked to the fire, pulled the screen away and, on one knee, tossed in a few pieces of wood. Flames crackled and licked at the moss. The dog didn't move. "How are you feeling?" he asked, looking over his shoulder. "I didn't expect you to be up."

"I needed to use the bathroom. And I feel like hell. I think I should be in a hospital."

"I know you should."

"Then why—?"

"Couldn't get you to one. Believe me, I wanted to." He glanced over his shoulder. "If you haven't noticed,

I'm not really set up here as a hospital ward." His gaze moved from her face to lower and she felt suddenly naked. He hitched his chin at her ankle. "You should be in bed."

"Sounds like I've been in bed a while."

"But you need to lie down, keep the ankle elevated, protect your ribs."

"So now you're a doctor?"

He grabbed a poker from a nearby stand and pushed the pieces of fir around until he was satisfied and the room was brighter, gold shadows moving against the walls. "Medic. First Gulf War. When I got out, I became an EMT for a while."

"But you gave it up?"

He slid her a glance. "Until three days ago." He seemed slightly irritated, but she didn't care. For all she knew he was a lying dog. He then flashed her a smile that was surprisingly engaging. His teeth weren't perfect, just the slightest bit crooked, enough to give him character, which, she thought, was probably an illusion.

Don't trust him. Do not!

"Harley," he said. "Let's have dinner."

The Lab mix, who had seemed so ferocious only minutes earlier, jumped to his feet and started prancing and heading to the kitchen, all the while keeping his head turned so that he could watch MacGregor as the big man walked through the archway. "Hungry?"

Harley gave out a loud, excited bark.

So much for the murderous guard dog.

"I thought so," MacGregor said as Jillian inched along the table until she could see through the doorway and watch as he found a bag of dry dog food in the cupboard. He rattled the bag and Harley went into an exhilarated spin.

"What do you do, starve him?"

"Hardly." MacGregor measured food into one of the

two stainless-steel bowls that were on the floor by the back door, bowls she hadn't noticed when she'd first explored the kitchen. "But don't ask him. He'd eat twenty-four seven if I let him."

Jillian made her way to the archway separating the rooms and brought the conversation back to information she wanted, information she needed. "So you brought me here because it was closer than a hospital or clinic. That means the accident happened nearby?"

"About a mile and a half or two miles west." As the dog gobbled down his kiblets, MacGregor folded the top of the sack of dog food over itself, creased it carefully and returned it to the shelf, which was as neat as if he expected an inspection from his commanding officer. "The nearest town is Grizzly Falls. About ten miles in the other direction. Unfortunately I haven't been able to get out that far." He bent down and picked up Harley's water dish, then tossed out what remained in the bottom of the bowl and refilled it at the sink. "Trust me, I've tried."

"How could you possibly travel that far in the snow?"

"The same way I brought you here. By snowmobile."

That she believed. She had a few splintered, jarring memories of the ride.

"So you live here," she said. "In the middle of nowhere."

He replaced the bowl on the floor. "I think a lot of Montanans might take offense to that."

"You know what I mean."

"Yep. You're talking about God's country."

He was making light of the situation? When she was injured, trapped here with him and his damned dog, while a serial killer was on the loose and a blizzard raged outside?

He snagged a towel hanging from the stove and dried his hands. "I'm serious, you should lie down."

Though she was tired, her face, chest and ankle all dull aches, she wasn't ready to be shepherded back into the bedroom, not until she learned more. "I have a few questions first."

"Shoot."

The single word caused her heart to drop, but she tried to keep focused despite the pain in her body, despite the fact that this stranger and his dog rattled her, made her nervous. "This place"—she motioned toward the interior with her free hand, nearly dropping the damned knife in the process but somehow holding onto the hilt, keeping the blade tucked up her sleeve—"is too far from a hospital, or clinic or any kind of civilization."

"You wrecked in a pretty isolated part of the country."

"Speaking of which," she said, "I think my tire was shot."

His head snapped up and his face was instantly tense. "Shot?"

The dog had finished eating and he also lifted his head, sensing the change in atmosphere, the sudden tension in his master. Harley turned intelligent, suspicious eyes in her direction.

Maybe she shouldn't have told him; if he was the serial killer, she'd be better off playing dumb. But it was too late to call the words back. "I heard a rifle crack just a second before I lost control. It sounded like someone shot something—my tire, I think—because then the car went over the cliff and I kinda blacked out. . . ."

MacGregor's jaw became rock hard, he tossed the towel onto the counter. "You're sure about that?"

"No, I'm not sure. That's the trouble. I'm not sure of anything." Tamping down her fear, her urge to break down all together, she added, "And the truth of the matter is, I don't know if I can trust you. I don't know you from Adam and I end up here alone with you . . . or does anyone else live with you?"

"Harley."

"Well . . . great." She paused, then decided if she was in for a penny, she was in for a pound. "I think I remember that several women were killed up here. It made the news in Seattle."

He nodded, a muscle working in his jaw.

Had she hit a nerve with him? Above the throbbing in her ankle and chest and the headache returning behind her eyes, she wasn't as sharp as she should be, couldn't read the unspoken innuendoes. Was he angry? Or afraid? A little of both?

"I haven't been into town in a few days, obviously," he said, making his way into the living area again, the dog on his heels. She moved out of the archway as quickly as possible and was surprised when Harley passed without so much as looking at her. "All communication has been out, but yeah, there have been women found out in the wilds, tied up to trees, I believe. Their cars were located separately, wrecked, a distance from where the bodies were discovered."

Fear skittered down her spine and inside she was suddenly as cold as death. Her fingers, clenched around the hidden knife, began to sweat, and her heart was trip-hammering out of control. What did she know about this man?

Nothing but what he's told you.

It could be a pack of lies.

It could be the truth.

But he's all you've got, Jillian.

Be he saint or sinner, he's all you've got.

"Were their tires shot out?" she asked, her voice a whisper that seemed to echo off the rafters high overhead.

He shook his head, but his skin had paled slightly

and she couldn't tell if he was telling the truth or lying through his teeth. "I don't know. But maybe. The police always hold back details, in case some nutcase claims responsibility." His eyes darkened a bit, his nostrils flaring. He rubbed his chin as he walked to the windows and glared through the panes. "To weed the goats from the sheep."

"The sheep being a killer in this case?" she asked, barely able to force the words past her teeth.

"Yeah. I guess so." He was dead serious when he asked her, "Do you think you were targeted by this guy?"

"I don't know." How much could she tell this man, a virtual stranger?

He still looked through the window, his eyes thinning, as if he were trying to see further into the blizzard, catch a view beyond the pale. "Why the hell were you driving up on that ridge in the storm?"

"Why were you?" she responded.

He turned quickly, but his expression was hard as ever. "I was trying to find an alternate way to town for supplies. I was on my snowmobile and the storm was getting worse, but I did hear something." He shook his head and rubbed a hand around his neck as he let out his breath and walked to the fire.

He's hiding something, Jillian sensed, and her skin prickled in dread. *He's playing the same kind of cat-and-mouse game with you as you are with him.*

She felt her heart drop.

"I thought . . . I mean, it was hard to hear because the engine on my Arctic Cat is pretty loud, but I thought I heard a rifle shot. Didn't sound like a car backfiring." His eyes found hers and she saw something in their gray depths, something dark and secret. She remembered someone near her car at the accident, a dark figure hovering nearby.

He walked to the fire again, his legs blocking the view of the flames, causing the room to darken. To shrink. While the wind never let up. Just kept shrieking.

"Okay," she said quietly, not wanting to irritate him. "So you heard the shot, then what?"

For a second he didn't answer and the soft hiss of the fire slipped through the room. "Then," he finally said, "there was the sound of the crash, breaking limbs, groaning metal, someone screaming."

Her throat turned to sand. Memories of the car's horrific spin and plunge through the gaping white canyon cut through her mind. "Yes," she said hoarsely.

He came a little closer, closing the distance between them. "Do you think you were a target?" he asked again.

She wanted to lie, but didn't dare. He was too close. Her fingers squeezed around the crutch handle as well as the knife. "I . . . yeah, I think so."

"And who would be out in the middle of the worst storm in a decade, lying in wait with a rifle, ready for target practice?"

She tensed inside. Wondered if she were talking to the very man who had taken aim at her, a sharpshooter who had intentionally shot at her.

"Tell me, Jillian," he insisted, near enough now that she could feel the heat of his body, see the pores of his skin, notice the cruel turn of his lips. "Who do you think would want to kill you?"

Chapter Eleven

MacGregor's question hung in the air between them while the dog, at last having given up bristling all over, turned in a circle in front of the hearth before settling onto a rag rug near the heat.

Her heart was pounding.

He was so damned close.

She thought about whipping out the knife, of telling him to back off, but she didn't, not yet. Best to hold the weapon in reserve, she thought.

"I have no idea who would want to kill me," she stated.

"Really?" MacGregor didn't bother to hide his disbelief, but he backed up a couple of steps, giving her some space, allowing her to let out her breath and hear something more than the pounding of her heart in her eardrums. "You don't have any enemies?"

"None that would want to murder me."

"You're certain of that?"

"Yes." But was she? Dear God, the man was making her paranoid.

"Someone took a shot at you." He unzipped his coat and slid his arms out of the sleeves, as if he'd finally warmed up. Something jangled in his pocket. Coins? Keys? A metal dog whistle?

"Or they were taking potshots at cars. I don't think it was intentional. At least, not at me."

"No?" Again, he was openly sarcastic and she felt a dread as cold and sharp as the icicles hanging from the eaves of this cabin.

Just who the hell was he?

It could be that he's part of some kind of elaborate plot to kidnap or even kill you, and so far it's working, isn't it? She reined in her thoughts in a hurry. She'd never been one to believe in conspiracy theories and wasn't about to start now.

But Aaron had been.

He'd always been certain someone, probably some kind of government agent, had been out to get him. He'd believed that John F. Kennedy had been killed by a group affiliated with Russia, Castro or the mafia, and he had been certain that D. B. Cooper, the skyjacker who had jumped out of a plane in the Northwest in the early seventies, had received help and somehow miraculously survived. Jillian, though, had always been a realist.

Until now.

Until she was trapped by a snowstorm with a stranger in the wilds of Montana.

Until she might possibly be the victim of a killer in this frigid killing ground. Had this man shot out her tire then "rescued" her, only to eventually murder her? It took all her restraint not to slide a glance toward his gun cabinet, though she wondered what kind of rifles were locked inside.

She clasped her hands together tightly. "You think someone was trying to kill me? Me, personally?"

"I don't know." He threw his jacket over the back of the couch and bent down to unlace his boots. "Do you?"

"I pissed off some people in my life, like I said. My sister, for sure. But not enough for anyone to want to kill me." She watched as he kicked off a boot, nudging the heel of one with the toe of the other, then unzipped his ski pants, beneath which he was wearing jeans. The Goretex-looking outer layer of pants wound up beside the jacket. Now, at least, he looked thirty pounds lighter, but still big and strong enough to be intimidating.

"You should lie down," MacGregor said, shoving a hand through his hair. "Elevate the ankle."

It was true enough; her whole leg was aching now and she was tired from balancing herself against the table with her crutch. But the thought of going back into the bedroom, lying on the cot alone while listening to the wind howl, her mind spinning with questions, her imagination running wild with what he was doing, didn't cut it.

"I think I'll just sit here." She pointed to the ancient chair and ottoman. Without waiting for him to answer, she hitched her way to the chair and sank down.

"How about I get us each something to drink?"

"Like what?" She settled into the chair and kept her knife in her sleeve. She wasn't about to relax. Not yet.

Harley climbed to his feet and trotted, toenails clicking, into the kitchen after MacGregor. Through the archway, he said, "I've got coffee . . . and . . ." She heard him rooting around in the cupboards, doors opening and closing with soft thuds. "Well . . . no tea . . . but I do have some packets of instant soup. Or whiskey. That's about what we're down to. Whiskey over snow. We've got lots of that. Kind of an alcoholic snow cone."

Was he kidding? "I think I'll pass on the frozen drink," she called toward the open doorway, but her stomach rumbled at the mere mention of food. How long had she gone without eating? Hell, she couldn't remember her last meal.

He returned with a coffeepot that he set in the glowing coals of the fire. "This'll take a while to heat," he explained as his dog, with a hard last glare and snarl at Jillian, turned several circles before lying down on his rug again. His black-and-white head rested on his white paws as he stared at her.

"You never answered my question," he reminded her. "What the hell were you doing driving in the blizzard?"

He hung his ski wear on pegs near the fireplace, then turned to her. "In the middle of the worst storm to hit this part of the state in a decade?"

"I was headed to Missoula," she admitted after a moment.

"What's there?"

"Not what. Who. And the answer is, my ex-husband."

MacGregor considered it. "Maybe there's someone who might want to kill you."

"The divorce was amicable."

He skewered her with a disbelieving look. "Yeah, right. And so why were you risking life and limb, driving through the Bitterroots in a snowstorm, to visit your ex?"

"I . . . I needed to talk to him."

A dark eyebrow raised.

"A phone call wouldn't have worked. I needed to see his reaction."

"When you told him what?"

"When I asked him if he sent me pictures that are supposedly of my first husband. My *dead* first husband."

He sat back on his heels. "Your ex–second husband sent you pictures of your dead first husband?"

"Yes, well, I think so. It could be a wild goose chase. I thought he died on a hiking trip in South America."

"Your first husband . . . who's dead. You think. But

you've seen pictures of him, from your second husband."

"Or someone who could be Aaron's twin."

"There a third husband in there?"

"No," she answered dryly. "Just the two."

"But now you think husband one might still be
alive."

"I don't know. I had the pictures with me. They were
in my notebook case."

He walked to a built-in cupboard and withdrew her
purse and laptop carrying case, both of which he brought
to her chair and set next to the ottoman. Something about
seeing her things again nearly brought tears to her eyes.
It was as if she suddenly realized the desperation of her
situation, how far removed she was from her life. Clearing her throat, she refused to break down, but she had
to blink rapidly.

MacGregor asked, "Want me to get the photos out?"

"I assume you've already seen them."

He nodded, not denying a word of it, as he took another trip to the cupboard and returned with her suitcase and the tattered remains of her grandmother's
quilt.

Again her heart squeezed and she wondered if she'd
ever get home again.

"I did look through all your things. I was trying to figure out who you were and who I should call."

"You have a phone?"

"A cell. But it's not working. Neither is yours."

She didn't doubt him, but opened her purse with
one hand and scrounged for her phone, searching past
the lipstick tubes, pens, wallet, checkbook and—

"It would be easier if you dropped the knife."

Her head snapped up to find him staring at her. For
a split second she was certain he could see to the bottom of her soul. The filet knife felt suddenly heavy and

bulky. She swallowed hard. Noticed that the dog had closed his eyes and fallen asleep. "I—uh . . ."

"Just drop it from your sleeve. Or do you want me to take it from you?"

"No . . . uh . . ." Deliberately, she set the knife on a small scarred table that held a single kerosene lamp, a fishing magazine and two books on astronomy.

"So now why don't you start at the beginning?" he suggested.

How foolish she'd been to think she could trust him. And how ultimately dependent she was on him. She pulled out her cell phone and turned it on, hoping beyond hope that she would have service. Of course, she didn't. No connecting bars registered and the battery was nearly dead.

Just as he'd said. She felt more vulnerable than ever.

"I have tried to call out," he said. "Every damned day. That's why I leave sometimes. To try and find a signal."

She wondered about that. The times she'd thought she was alone, the hours when he'd been out of the cabin in the middle of a blizzard. It just hadn't made much sense.

"I don't get much service to begin with and I think some of the towers have been damaged by the storms."

"Great."

"I could have told you that the minute you woke up, but I figured you wouldn't believe me."

That much was right.

"So now," he prodded. "About your husband?"

Jillian sighed. She stared at him and time stretched. And then she decided to go for it, just tell him everything. She began with her marriage to Aaron, what had happened in Suriname, then a fast-forward through her second marriage to the weird messages and finally the photographs, which, of course, he'd recovered from her car, as they'd been tucked in a pocket of her

computer case. While she explained, he listened and
tended the water heating in a coffeepot on the coals of
the fire. He asked a few questions, but for the most part
just let her speak, his face grim and taut.

When she'd finished, he poured hot water into a cup
filled with instant coffee crystals and asked, "So now
you believe your first husband, Aaron, is alive."

"I think someone wants me to believe it."

"To lure you here?" he asked.

She took a sip of the coffee. The hot liquid slid down
her throat and hit her stomach hard. "I don't know,"
she admitted.

"But the man in the picture looks enough like him
that you came?"

"Yeah, I guess." She was shaking her head at her own
folly. "I know, it seems kinda crazy now." She shoved her
hair out of her eyes. "Or really crazy."

"Was the marriage to Aaron in trouble?"

"No!" she said with more passion than she'd intended.
"Well, I don't think so. I mean, he had no reason to disappear that I know of."

"Did he have bad debts?"

"We didn't owe more than we could pay."

"Did he have life insurance?"

"Yes, and it took a while, but they finally paid me.
That's how I bought my townhouse." Why in the world
was she confiding in him?

"And until you saw the pictures, you were convinced
he was dead. He didn't come after you for the money."

"This letter and the phone calls—they came out of
the blue. And now I think they all might have been a
wild goose chase."

"To lure you here," he said again, "so someone could
kill you?"

"That sounds . . . ridiculous, doesn't it?"

He shrugged, then rocked back on his heels and

frowned. "I'm a hunter. I was in the military. There are lots of ways to kill a person and do it quickly, maybe not even get caught, but shooting out a tire and hoping the car will free-fall into an icy ravine isn't a sure thing."

"As evidenced that I'm still here," she agreed.

"Right, and the killer knows you survived. Or, at least, I'm assuming he checked the car."

"Maybe not. He could've thought the job was finished."

"Or been frightened away by me."

"Why not just shoot you, too?"

"He might not have been able to get a shot off. And anyway, we can't assume you were the ultimate target. As you said, there've been other women killed around here. A couple of them, I think, and they, too, were forced off the road, like you, though I don't know all the details."

"We talked about the serial killer thing before," she reminded him, and tried to ignore the panic she felt rising inside. "Are you trying to say that this killer *knows* his victims, or at least enough intimate details of their lives to get them here?" Dear God, she couldn't believe the words that passed her lips and yet. . . . "Do you know the names of the other women?"

He shook his head. "No. Why? Do you think you might know them?"

She glanced nervously to the windows and the darkening landscape beyond. "I think I read one of their names, but it didn't ring any bells." She forced herself to look directly into his eyes. How did she know he wasn't the killer? That he wasn't toying with her? It didn't seem that way. In fact he seemed downright concerned.

She swallowed hard.

Could she trust this man?

Did she have a choice?

The answer was no.

Like it or not, she was stuck here, at least for a while. But she didn't have to stay. If she could get herself mobile, able to walk just a little, and the weather broke. He'd mentioned he had a snowmobile. She'd driven one before, while she and Aaron were on a ski trip to Colorado. If push came to shove, she could get it started and drive the damned thing to civilization, or another cabin, or any damned where.

She just needed a key.

Mason Rivers was a prick.

And a prick who was hiding something, Pescoli thought as she pulled into her driveway, cell phone at her ear. She'd just driven home through the blizzard to make sure the kids took everything they needed for the weekend visit with their father. Lights were on inside the house, but Jeremy's truck wasn't parked in its usual spot.

"My secretary said you were trying to reach me," Rivers said guardedly, after brief introductions.

No shit, Sherlock, Pescoli thought, but kept it to herself.

"You've heard about your ex-wife?" Regan hit the button on her garage door opener.

"I was out of town, but a colleague brought in the paper saying that her car had been found at the bottom of a canyon."

"That's right."

"Is she okay?" he asked as the garage door slowly opened.

"We don't know. We can't find her."

A pause, the silence cut by the grinding of the garage door and her Jeep's idling engine.

"We thought you might have an idea of where she

was going, or where she'd been." The truth of the matter was that the accident reconstruction team had spent hours on the ridge where Jillian's car had spun out. They could tell from which direction the car had careened down the hill, but because of the spin, couldn't discern which direction she'd been traveling. They had the clue of an empty coffee cup from the Chocolate Moose Café in Spruce Creek, and a waitress remembered Jillian, as she'd been one of the few customers taking anything "to go" that day. So, it seemed that she had been traveling toward Missoula rather than away from the town.

"You know, we were divorced two years ago and I'm remarried now. I don't keep in contact with Jill or her family."

"We thought she might be coming to see you."

"Why?"

"That's what we wanted to know."

"Look, I have no idea where she was going or why. As I said, I haven't had any contact with her since the divorce was finalized. Now, if there's nothing further, I have a client waiting in my office."

"Just let us know if you think of anything."

"There's nothing to think about, Detective." He hung up and Regan was left with a bad feeling. She pulled into the garage, hit the remote so the door would crank down, then climbed out of the car and made her way into her house, where Cisco greeted her with wild tail wagging, excited yips and tight little circles of enthusiasm. She had only half an hour, then she had to be back at the department for a Friday afternoon meeting before she worked late into the night. Overtime. This year it would pay for Christmas.

The dog was still going out of what little he had for a mind.

"Cisco! Shut up!" Bianca yelled from her bedroom.

The TV was blaring in the living room, tuned into some reality show about twenty-somethings being overly dramatic about the minutiae of their lives, all while dressed in nearly nothing. Lots of tanned, toned flesh, a few piercings visible, numerous tattoos, all peppered with tears, bad language and raw, teen-type angst and emotion.

"Real life, my ass." Pescoli picked up the remote, downed the volume and turned to the local news.

Once the decibel level was in the normal hearing range again, Pescoli stuck her head into her daughter's room. Painted a blinding pink when Bianca was ten, it was now covered in posters of the latest teen "hotties" from boy bands and movie stardom. Bianca was flopped over her unmade bed, cell phone glued to her ear.

"Where's your brother?" Regan asked.

Bianca's expression got all pissy. She mouthed, "I'm on the phone."

"Big deal. Hang up. You can call whoever it is back."

"What? Just a minute. My mom came in. No, it's okay—"

"Hang up, Bianca. Your dad will be here in twenty minutes."

Sending her mother a look meant to melt steel, Bianca said, "Look, I'll call ya back. I gotta go. . . . What? . . . Yeah, that's right. The warden needs me." She hung up and sent her mother a triumphant smirk.

"The 'warden' wants to know that you've got all your stuff packed up for the weekend and where your brother is."

"I'm ready to go."

"Got your homework?"

"I don't have to do homework at Lucky's," she said, invoking the name of her father, whom she hadn't called "Daddy" since the divorce. "Michelle says—"

Pescoli snatched the cell phone out of her daughter's hand.

"Hey!" Bianca cried as Pescoli snapped the phone closed.

"I don't care what Michelle says, or really what 'Lucky' says either. You take your homework and you get it done, or you and 'the warden,' we're going to have serious issues."

"We already do!" Bianca declared.

"Yeah, I know. So where's your brother?"

"Don't know."

"Sure you do. You got home somehow and I'm betting you didn't take the bus."

"Chris brought me."

"Your boyfriend brought you home? Didn't I tell you he wasn't allowed in the house when I wasn't here?"

"He dropped me off. Well, yeah, he came in and I gave him a jar of Jeremy's Gatorade, so sue me, call the sport drink cops!"

"I am the cops," Pescoli reminded her.

"He gave me an effin' ride home! You should be glad. Jeremy ditched me."

"For what?"

"I don't know and I don't really care. He said something about Lucky not being his real dad and him not having to go." She glared at her mother. "Give me back my phone."

"As soon as you're packed, and that includes your homework." Pescoli held tight to the cell. Fuming, she returned to the kitchen, let Cisco outside to do his business and checked his water. "Did you feed the dog?" she called over her shoulder and was met with seething, muted silence emanating from Bianca's room. Obviously she was being given the silent treatment. Well, good. It was way better than hearing the backtalk. As the terrier pawed at the door to be let in, Pescoli dialed her son's cell number, then opened the door. A blast of cold air followed the dog back inside.

Jeremy didn't pick up. But then he never did. Why should now be different from every other day? The kid was being a jerk. *And whose fault is that, huh? Who let him get away with murder as a kid because of guilt over Joe's death?* "Damn it all," she muttered, not leaving a message on voice mail and, instead, defaulting to texting, which she hated, but at least now her kid would read the message.

Get your butt home. Now. xoxo Mom

"That should do it, huh?" she said to the dog, and then, hearing Bianca making noises as if she were putting together an overnight bag, Pescoli poured herself a Diet Coke, added ice and sat down on the couch. Cisco, done with his meager meal of dried food, hopped onto the lumpy cushion beside her and waited as she petted his scruffy head. "Feeling ignored?" she asked the dog. "Join the club."

He hopped onto her lap, put his paws on her chest and licked her face.

"Okay, okay, enough already. I may be single, but I'm not this desperate."

"Oh, sick," Bianca said, walking out of her bedroom and carrying an overstuffed backpack.

"Grow a sense of humor," Pescoli suggested, and finally Bianca managed a smile.

"Okay, okay," she said. "Now, can I have—"

Pescoli tossed her daughter the precious cell phone. "You do have your homework with you?"

"Yeah." For once Bianca didn't roll her eyes or go into her irritating pouty, put-upon act. She even bent over and petted Cisco on his head. "So what're you doing this weekend?"

"There's a maniac killer on the loose."

"Oh, work?"

"Give the girl a gold star." Regan took a long swallow from her glass, then watched as the ice cubes clicked and danced in the dark liquid.

"Don't you get tired of it?"

"Mmm. Beats sitting at a desk nine to five. Or waiting tables. Did both of those before."

Bianca wrinkled her nose. "I don't know. You see some pretty gross stuff."

"Gross and totally demoralizing. Makes you wonder what's wrong with the entire human race."

"Then why do you do it?"

"Someone has to."

"But why you?"

"Because I'm good at my job." And the truth of the matter was, she loved it. Lived for it. She, in her own way, was as much a workaholic as Alvarez. They just went at it from different angles. She smiled at her daughter and gave her a hug. "I try not to let it get me down." She glanced at the muted television and saw an image of Ivor Hicks being interviewed on the screen. "Oh no."

"What?"

"Someone let the loonies out." Hearing the sound of a large truck's engine, Regan braced herself for the inevitable meeting with Lucky. Today, after dealing with tight-assed Mason Rivers, she wasn't in the mood to face her own ex. "Dad's here," she said, and Bianca visibly brightened. God, the kid loved her father. Which was probably for the best, but it still irritated Pescoli a bit.

Bianca threw her a look. "Are you going to tell him about Jeremy, or should I?"

"I'll handle it."

* * *

Jillian had heard MacGregor's keys jangling in his jacket pocket. All she had to do was fish them out when he was sleeping, right? But she kept her thoughts to herself and asked instead, "Do you live here year-round?"

"Sometimes."

"Doing what?"

He hesitated just a second and looked over her shoulder. "Fishing, hunting, white-water guide in the summer."

"And in the winter?"

"Mostly get ready for the summer. Sometimes someone wants to go snowshoeing or cross-country skiing." He rubbed the back of his neck. "Not recently, though. Not with the storms."

Her eyes narrowed. It sounded like BS to her. And this good-ole-country-boy act didn't wash either. "All winter long, you stay inside here, by yourself."

"I've got Harley."

At the mention of his name, the dog, with eyes still closed, thumped his tail against the rug.

"What about family? Wife? Kids?"

There was just a second's hesitation, a slight tightening of his lips, before he shook his head. "Just Harley. Short for Harlequin." He bent down and scratched the dog behind his ears. "And no, I didn't name him. Someone else did the honors."

"Who?"

"Harley came with the place. I bought it from a guy a couple of years ago. His bitch had a litter of pups. One died, he gave the other four away and this one stayed on with me." He winked at the dog, who stretched and let out a contented sigh. "So far, it's worked out."

"You never get lonely?"

One side of his mouth lifted. "Not enough to make me change my ways."

"You got family?"

"Not much."

"How much?" she asked, wondering about him.

"Two half-sisters. Younger."

"Your folks are dead?"

Again the slight hesitation, as if he were checking his lies, making sure he didn't slip up. "I haven't seen my mother in three years. Far as I know, she and husband number five . . . or is it six . . . I can't remember, don't care to, but the last I heard she was living outside of Phoenix somewhere."

"You don't see her."

"Nope. And it suits us both fine. My old man took off before I was born. Never married my mother. I figure that's why she kept trying."

"Did you ever meet him?"

"What is this? Twenty questions?"

"At least," she said, and he finally leaned back in his chair, eyeing her over the rim of a cup that had to be holding cold coffee.

"Okay, I met him once. When I was about eighteen. It didn't go well."

She shifted in the chair and pain ricocheted up her leg, causing her to suck in her breath.

"I told you to lie down," he said, placing his cup on the hearth and climbing to his feet. "If you don't want to go back into the bedroom, you can lie here on the couch, or on the recliner, where you can elevate your feet."

"Oh. Well."

He walked over to her chair, picked the knife off the small table and carried it to a small bureau positioned near the tattered old La-Z-Boy. "You wouldn't want to forget this," he said. He set the boning knife in reach of the chair.

"I don't need it."

"Of course you do. You don't know me. You don't trust me and you're stuck here. Now, come on." He crossed the room again and offered her the crutch. "You rest and I'll make us dinner."

"Dinner?"

"Stew and chili out of cans." His lips twisted upward. "Gourmet chili," he clarified, then helped her to her feet and walked her to the recliner. "Trust me. You'll love it."

That was the trouble. She couldn't let herself trust him. Not for a minute.

Chapter Twelve

Through the icy window, Regan saw Lucky's pickup roll up the lane to idle near the front walk.

And, of course, he wasn't alone in the black Dodge that was jacked up higher than normal.

In the passenger seat, appearing very cool and lofty in what looked to be designer sunglasses, sat his new wife, the oft-quoted Michelle.

Pescoli's guts tightened just a fraction. Though she told herself and the outside world that she was "way over" her ex, she still felt a pinch of tension every time she had to deal with him. And wifey.

Regan made a face. She and Michelle were worlds apart. For the most part, Michelle was pleasant enough, just not the sharpest tool in the shed, the kind of woman who expected a man to do everything for her, the type Regan didn't like and really didn't trust.

But there it was. Like it or not, Michelle, via Lucky and their children, was a part of her life.

Which was a real pisser.

She set her soft drink down, crossed the small living room to the front door and opened it just as Lucky began stomping snow off his boots on the minuscule area some builder had decided was an adequate front porch.

"Everybody ready?" Lucky asked, looking at her through the glass panels of the storm door with his Pescoli eyes. Deep set and hazel, almost blue, they were sexy as hell. As was Lucky. Tall and trim, with thick nearly blond hair and a bad-boy attitude that drove women wild, Luke Pescoli was one good-looking man. And a pain in the backside.

"Jeremy's not here. I don't know what his deal is."

"I told you," Bianca said, her softer side disappearing in her father's presence. "He's not coming."

"Any reason why not?"

"He said you're not his real dad."

"Like this is news," Lucky said. He sent his ex-wife a can-you-believe-this look. "Somethin' happen?"

Regan shook her head. "Not that I'm aware of, but who knows? He's seventeen, which he tells me all the time. He believes he's grown up and can do his own thing."

"He's deluded," Bianca chimed in from her bedroom.

Lucky, frowning beneath the brim of his black felt hat, asked, "You want me to set him straight?"

"Nah. I'll take care of it," Regan assured him. "I'll call you and let you know what he says."

He nodded as Bianca pushed her way through the door and headed to the king-cab truck. Michelle, all bright and cheery, was waving frantically, her beauty-pageant smile pinned to her face.

"How's the serial killer case goin'?" Lucky asked.

"It's going," she hedged. Lucky knew she couldn't talk about it.

"Well, don't let it get to you. I know how these things do. It's not personal."

"Isn't it? A psycho killing women in my backyard?"

She watched her daughter climb into the truck. "Sorry, Lucky, I take it personally. It's very personal."

He pulled a face. "Some things don't change."

"No. And they shouldn't!"

"Okay, okay. I give up, Officer!" He held up his hands and backed up a step in mock surrender and she almost laughed. Almost. "Didn't mean to step on a nerve," he said, squaring his hat on his head. "Let me know what's up with Jeremy."

"I will. And make sure Bianca does her homework. She's drowning in Algebra II and Global Studies. I even think she's struggling in English, which is easy for her."

"Really?" Lucky said. "We'll take care of it. Michelle was an A student."

A four-point from the woman who didn't believe in homework? Regan doubted it, but she kept that little insight to herself. "Good. She can tutor Bianca," Regan said, though her jaw was tight.

Somehow she managed to nod, smile and sketch out a wave that was meant to include her daughter, her ex-husband and his new wife. Closing the door, she felt an empty sensation that bothered her. She knew it was silly, but watching Bianca get swallowed into Lucky's new family took a toll on her. The fact that Bianca always threw what a good time she had at her father's place in Regan's face was also a major pain.

One she had to live with.

She glanced at the TV and was relieved to see that Ivor Hicks was no longer on the screen. God, couldn't anyone shut that fruitcake up? He would put the public into a panic, get the press all stirred up and probably play into the killer's hands. No doubt the pervert who got off on freezing women to death was getting off on all the publicity and attention.

Her good mood totally shattered, she clicked off the televison and headed downstairs. She tried Jeremy's cell one more time, listening as the connection went directly to voice mail while she tossed in a load of laundry. As the washer filled, she poked her head into Jeremy's room, the "den of iniquity," and wondered where her son was. Her gaze landed on a picture of Joe, tucked between a mess of CDs and video games on the bookcase. Joe Strand, her high school sweetheart, the man she'd given her virginity to, the man she'd married and the man, when things had gotten rocky, she'd cheated on. Yes, they'd been separated at the time, and yes, he, too, had carried on an affair, but she'd broken her marriage vows pretty damned willingly, almost as a way to get back at him.

That had been a long time ago. Hell, she hadn't even been out of college and then she'd gotten pregnant. With Joe's son. Jeremy.

Joe had questioned the kid's paternity, of course, until Jeremy had been born and was the spitting image of her estranged husband. It had taken a few months before they'd decided to give the marriage another chance.

And then Joe had the nerve to die.

To be killed in the line of duty and leave her a widow with a small child.

The worst part of it was that Joe hadn't ever given up the woman who had wrecked their marriage in the first place. He'd lied and said the affair was over, but he had never completely broken it off with a woman who had been one of Regan's high school friends.

Gina Walters, also married, had come to the funeral and bawled her eyes out, even leaving a white rose on the casket, while Pescoli had stood by and taken it, her young son's fingers clenched in her own.

"Bitch," she said now, ignoring the washing machine that threatened to rock wildly as she headed up the stairs. She made a quick sandwich of leftover ham,

Dijon mustard and dry bread, tossed a few scraps to Cisco and downed another Diet Coke before heading out the door.

It was nearing dark now and she was due back at the office, but as she hit the garage door button she wondered where the hell her son was.

"I think we're going to see a break in the weather," MacGregor said as he spooned a hot glop of some kind of chili into a bowl and handed it to her.

"When?"

"Soon."

"How soon?"

"That's the million-dollar question, isn't it?" He walked into the kitchen and rummaged in a drawer. Less than a minute later he returned, handed her a spoon, then walked back to the pot resting in the fire and scooped some of the chili into a second bowl. A pan of pre-mixed cornbread was "baking" in a cast-iron skillet half buried in the coals, the edges of the bread already singed.

"How do you know? You got a television hooked up to a generator somewhere? Or a direct line to the weather service?"

"It's just a feeling." He glanced out the window to the snowy landscape. Darkness was falling fast, long shadows stretching through the trees, making the cabin feel more isolated than ever.

"A feeling?" Cradling the bowl in one hand, she stirred the chili, its spicy steam warming her face. She was improving a little, the throb in her ankle lessening, the pain in her ribs muted unless she moved too quickly or laughed too hard. But she wasn't betting on "feelings."

"It's time. The storm should let up."

She looked out the window and shook her head, not

daring to believe in miracles, as the storm didn't show any signs of letting up, not to her. She took a bite. The chili, a brand she'd eaten dozens of times, was now fabulously delicious. She took another bite and watched MacGregor at the fire.

Using a work glove as a pot holder, he retrieved the cornbread from the fire and cut her a chunk with the very knife she'd stolen earlier. He dropped the large square into her bowl and she picked at the crusty top.

It was as delicious as the chili, but hot enough to keep her from eating too quickly. Which was probably good, as it was all she could do not to bolt down the food.

The smell of wood smoke and sizzling tomato sauce scented the air, while firelight played across the walls and the embers glowed red in the grate.

Even the dog was at peace, his dark, begging gaze never leaving MacGregor as he ate. If she let herself, she might just relax with this man. But she didn't know him at all. Everything he had told her in the past few hours could well be a lie.

"If the storm breaks like I think it will, I'll try to get out of here tomorrow."

"On a snowmobile?"

He shook his head. "I've got a four-wheel-drive."

"Then we could have gotten out of here at any time?"

He shook his head. "Don't think so. And I couldn't take a chance of being stuck with you laid up in a blizzard. I'm not even sure about tomorrow, but we'll give it a shot, as I said, if the storm breaks."

"And if not?"

"You really want to think about that?" He took a bite of cornbread while the dog, watching, licked his lips.

"Where will we go?"

"Grizzly Falls. They've got a small hospital. I'll leave you in the ER."

"And then tell the police about my car."

His face was shuttered. "I'll leave that to you."

"But you have to tell them where it is. I don't know the area."

"It's in September Creek, off Johnson Road, about six miles from the cutoff to Missoula. Think you can remember that?"

"Yeah," she said, but wondered at his change in attitude, the newfound tension in his shoulders. "What is it you have against the police?"

One side of his mouth twisted. "Nothing."

"Liar." She wasn't buying his denials. Something was bothering him.

His nostrils flared a bit. "It's not what I have against them so much as what they have against me," he said and stood suddenly. "Want a beer?"

"No." The last thing she needed was any kind of alcohol. She had to keep her wits about her. "Tell me," she said as he tossed on a parka and gloves, then disappeared through the kitchen. The dog was on his feet and took off after MacGregor as the back door opened and shut quickly. Harley whined and scratched for all of thirty seconds before the door opened again and MacGregor's voice asked, "Miss me, boy?" He laughed and she heard the sound of a cap being pried from a bottle. And then another. Seconds later he returned with two long-necked bottles in his hand. "I keep 'em in the garage, in a cooler, otherwise they'd freeze."

"Oh."

He set a bottle on the table next to her. "Thought you might change your mind."

"Don't think so."

"Then I'll finish it." He took a long swallow, set his bottle down and stripped off the parka before settling into his chair again.

"So you were dodging the question," she said as he

picked up his beer again. "What do the police have against you?"

He thought for a moment, staring at the label on his bottle of Coors, then rolling the long neck between his palms. The tension in his shoulders was evident.

"What happened, MacGregor?"

A muscle worked in his jaw and he took another long swallow before looking at her again with such intensity her heart nearly stopped.

"Believe me, Jillian, you don't want to know."

"Try me," she said, her voice a whisper, her nerves suddenly tight.

"Shit." He raked angry fingers through his hair and glared at the fire. Harley, sensing the shift in the atmosphere, whined.

"What did you do, MacGregor?" she asked, the cabin suddenly feeling more isolated than ever. Old timbers creaked. The glass in the windowpanes rattled loudly enough to be heard over the soft breath of the fire. "Why don't the police trust you?"

He hesitated and closed his eyes.

She steeled herself for the worst.

"I killed a man, Jillian. It happened a long time ago, but the truth of the matter is that the son of a bitch had it coming and I gave it to him." He took another swallow of his beer and the lines around his mouth were etched deep, showing white.

"It was an accident, right?"

"An accident." MacGregor snorted. "I don't know." He shook his head. "I didn't intend to kill him that night, but the truth of the matter is that for a few seconds—just long enough—I wanted that son of a bitch dead."

* * *

Alvarez finished her forty minutes on the elliptical machine, then concluded her workout with two circuits of weights, all the while listening to her iPod blasting out some of her favorite upbeat songs from the eighties. It was just after three when she'd showed up here, opting for a quick carton of yogurt and a workout for her lunch break, and was nearing four when she finished. Today was fairly quiet, the storm keeping everyone but the most dedicated at home.

Clicking off her headset, she walked toward the locker room, passing a row of treadmills occupied by a handful of people. One woman was reading a magazine, but the other stationary runners stared at a wall-mounted television, sweating, hearts racing, legs moving at different speeds, all going nowhere.

On the screen, Ivor-the-Idiot was prattling with great animation to a petite newswoman in a blue parka. Snow was falling, catching in Ivor's thick eyebrows and dusting the steps of the courthouse behind them. Over the whine of several treadmills, Alvarez couldn't hear much of what Ivor was saying, but it didn't matter. She got the message.

Her day, already far from stellar, took a nosedive. Couldn't that old coot keep his mouth shut?

Not on a dare. You know the old man wallows in all of the attention.

"Terrific," she muttered under her breath, then made her way down a hallway past a group of teenaged boys playing basketball in the gymnasium. Further on she passed a step-aerobics class consisting of a handful of diehards exercising to a trim dance teacher's instructions.

Alvarez grabbed a towel from a bin and stepped into the locker room, where she stripped off her sweaty workout clothes, then headed to the shower.

All the while, she thought about the case.

It was getting to her, like a lover who had turned

stalker. It kept her awake at night, nagged at her in the morning and throughout the day, even when she was supposed to be on her own time, relaxing or having "fun."

She lathered her body and laughed at herself.

Fun.

What the hell was that?

She was only thirty-three and she wasn't sure she remembered the last time she'd really let her hair down or kicked up her heels, or got down or whatever the hell you called it. Her life was her job.

Which was not only stupid.

It was pathetic.

She rinsed off, toweled dry and put on clean jeans, a black turtleneck and a down vest and checked her image in the mirror bolted to the inside of her locker. She was fit and pretty, no doubt about it, but her lips didn't pull into as quick a smile as they once had and her eyes sometimes looked haunted.

Where was the girl who had once liked shiny lipstick, hoop earrings, loud music and high heels? The freshman in high school with a perfect figure to go along with her perfect GPA?

Oh, her! Don't you remember? You left her nearly twenty years ago. And when you fled, you didn't look back at family, friends or the grinding poverty of Woodburn, Oregon.

Her stomach twisted and she had the insane urge to make the sign of the cross over her chest, a rite she'd abandoned and buried along with her poor Hispanic roots and her secret... the damned secret that haunted her to this day.

Knock it off!

Alvarez grabbed her bag and slammed the locker shut.

She didn't have time for reminiscing or wondering about the rocky path she'd taken that had ended here in Grizzly Falls, Montana. Far from her dreams. Far from what she'd planned for herself. Not that it mattered today. All she needed to concentrate on now was catching the twisted sicko who was terrorizing this part of the state.

The gym was located fifteen minutes from the sheriff's department, though the drive took her nearly half an hour, as the streets were tangled from bad weather. Several vehicles were abandoned on the roadside and a collision made the icy conditions more difficult. Alvarez stopped to see if she could help, but the city officers who had responded had the situation handled. There were no injuries aside from the bruised ego of a driver of a Land Rover that had slid into a Ford Taurus.

She cut through the heart of the city, the part that had been first settled, on the banks of the river. Christmas lights winked in store windows. Snow was piled high along the gutters; walkways carved out on the sidewalks. A few shoppers braved the elements and in front of the courthouse a band was assembling for a holiday concert at the base of a huge fir tree strung with clusters of white lights in the shape of snowflakes. One tuba player, dressed in a thick coat, earmuffs, gloves and boots, was blowing a few practice notes.

She drove along the plowed streets, electing to take the longer, less steep road to the upper part of the city, where the sheriff's department was housed. For the first time since joining the Pinewood County Sheriff's Department, Detective Selena Alvarez was late.

"Wait a second . . . let's back up," Jillian insisted, her heart tapping a drum. It was one thing to suspect that the man who had pulled her from the wreckage of her car wasn't what he seemed, but another thing for him to admit he was a killer. "Why did you want the man dead?"

"My business."

"I need to know," she said tautly, wishing she'd never given up the knife. She didn't think he would do her harm, otherwise why bring up the killing at all? But she was still nervous. "Why did you want him dead?"

MacGregor's lips whitened. "Because he was beating his wife to a pulp."

"What? Where?"

"I was in a bar in Denver. This guy is drunk and starts insulting his wife, pushing her around, and he gets kicked out of the bar. His wife goes with him. I leave a few minutes later and he's in the parking lot, has her on the asphalt and is wailing on her, beating and kicking at her." MacGregor leaned on the mantel, staring at the coals, and his face looked a dozen years older. "She was swearing and writhing and yelling about the baby. Begging him not to hurt the baby. Pleading with him. And he just kept kicking."

Jillian's jaw slackened in empathy.

"I saw red," he went on. "She's screaming and crying, and I jumped over the hood of a car and grabbed him. He threw a punch and I threw a better one. Knocked him to the ground."

Jillian barely breathed. She knew that MacGregor wasn't in the room with her any longer, that in his mind's eye, he was reliving the whole nightmare scene again.

"She was just lying there, shuddering in the snow and slush, blood everywhere. Her face was . . . hardly a face. Jesus, it was black and blue, cuts everywhere, her jaw and nose broken. And her jeans. She had on tight jeans and there was blood running down her legs. . . ." He drained his bottle of beer and the room went deathly quiet. When he spoke again, his voice was softer. "I remember . . . oh hell . . . I remember sirens and the air crackling and the blue-and-red flash of lights against the snow. Someone had called the police and they yelled at me to put my hands in the air and get down on the ground. I did and the next second some two-hundred-fifty-pound cop was on me, forcing my face into the slush and gravel, cuffing my hands behind my back." Frowning, he set his bottle on the mantel.

"They arrested you?"

"Yep."

"But just until everything was straightened out."

He turned to face her, his eyes dark, his lips curved in irony. "Nothing ever got straightened out. The guy died that night. Cracked his skull wide open. Intracranial hemorrhage, I think it's called. Bleeding in the brain." MacGregor sighed through his nose. "And the wife . . . her name was Margot, not that it matters. Margot claimed that I was the one who was beating her, that I tried to rape her, that her husband Ned was the hero."

"What?" Jillian whispered, horrified.

"Yeah." He shook his head. "The evidence proved otherwise. The toes of good old Ned's boots told the story, but the end result was that he was dead. If I hadn't stuck my neck out for Margot, he could have survived. The baby wouldn't have, regardless. Margot miscarried. But I was directly responsible for Ned Tomkins's death. At least that's what the coroner and judge decided. I pled down to a lesser charge and spent sixteen months in jail."

"That's terrible!"

"Margot blamed me for losing her husband and baby." He managed a humorless smile. "So much for being a good guy." He nodded toward her beer. "You still haven't touched it."

She ignored that. "Then what?"

"The upshot was that I got out and the last I heard, from one of the guards who knew her, Margot hooked up with another loser who beat the crap out of her, too." He walked to the gun closet, unlocked it with a key he kept in his jeans and pulled out a long-barreled rifle, then locked the cabinet again.

"What're you doing?" Jillian watched with sudden trepidation.

"Going out."

"Now?" What the hell was he thinking? After telling her he'd killed a man, he pulls out a rifle? Was he trying to freak her out?

"Before it gets dark." He found some shells in a drawer of the bookcase and carried his Winchester and pack of ammo to the pegs near the front door, grabbing his jacket. Stuffing his arms down the sleeves, he said, "I need to check the roads. If the storm really does break, maybe we'll be able to get out of here soon."

Jillian didn't dare believe it. But then, she had trouble believing a lot of things, maybe even MacGregor's latest story. Was it true? It sure seemed like it was. The pain etched across his face, the anger burning deep in his eyes—it all seemed real enough.

And, he hadn't done anything to hurt her.

It appeared, also, that he wanted to get rid of her as much as she wanted to leave.

And yet . . . he still put her on edge. Especially with a rifle in his hands.

Get over it, Jillian. If he'd wanted to hurt you, he would have done it by now.

"You're making me nervous."

He looked up, saw her staring at the rifle and nodded. Quickly he opened the door and set the gun on the porch. "Bad timing."

"Horrible timing."

"I just realized how dark it was getting. And there are cougars and bears in this neck of the woods, not that they would attack, but just to be safe." He flashed her a guileless smile as he pulled a pair of snowshoes from the spot where they hung over the door. As he stretched upward, his jacket and sweater moved upward and she caught a glimpse, as she had before, of taut, rock-hard muscles.

He caught her looking at him and she pulled her gaze away, picking up her beer and finally taking a sip as he left the snowshoes by the door, then walked through the kitchen. "I'd better leave you with some more wood."

Dutifully, he brought in more firewood and stacked it on the hearth. Then he strapped the snowshoes over his boots while Harley danced around his feet, ready for an adventure, but MacGregor shushed him. "You stay. I'll be back in a few minutes."

Harley started to whine, but MacGregor snapped his fingers. "None of that."

The dog quieted and sat, gaze focused on his master.

"Good boy." MacGregor pulled on a ski mask, cap and gloves. "You hold down the fort." He glanced over at Jillian and her breath nearly stopped in her lungs. Tall and looming, all in black. Was he the person she'd thought she'd seen while she'd been trapped in the car, the evil presence she'd sensed?

"I'll be back soon."

"And if you're not?"

"You'll survive. The rest of the beer's in the garage and there's enough canned food to keep you and Harley alive until the spring thaw."

"Comforting."

He smiled, walked out the door and shut it behind him with a thud, the catch clicking into place.

"At least you're still alive and almost well," she said aloud, and her voice seemed to echo a bit. Already the cabin seemed quieter, darker, lonelier. "Just your imagination," she reminded herself. She sipped from her bottle, though she really wasn't much of a beer drinker. "Give me a glass of Cabernet any day of the week," she said, and Harley, with his two-toned face, looked over at her and cocked his head. At least he wasn't growling and snarling and acting as if he would tear her limb from limb. No, he was planted near the door, staring at the panels, waiting for some indication MacGregor would return.

"Looks like it's just you and me," she said to him, wondering at her need to converse with the animal. Was it because the cabin seemed so quiet and desolate, so cut off from any kind of human contact?

She glanced out the window to the bitter cold and wondered when he'd return. Or *if* he'd return. She could be up here alone for days or weeks. She shuddered, suddenly cold to the marrow of her bones. Whether he was friend or foe, she wasn't sure. But she had to admit she felt better when Zane MacGregor was around.

Chapter Thirteen

In the task force room, most of the team had assembled by the time Alvarez entered. One uniformed officer sat manning the phones on a desk shoved in a corner near the windows. Even the typically tardy Pescoli was seated at the table with the sheriff and two FBI agents. As Alvarez took an empty chair next to Pescoli, Cort Brewster, the undersheriff, showed up, as did Detective Brett Gage, the chief criminal deputy.

"Something up?" Alvarez asked, but Pescoli shook her head, a whiff of cigarette smoke suggesting she was once again smoking. Not that it was a big surprise. From the day Alvarez had met Regan, she'd discovered that in times of great stress, Pescoli took up the habit again. In the time since they'd become partners, which was nearly two and a half years now, Pescoli had quit four times.

"Since it's nearly the weekend and some of you will be officially off duty, whatever that means around here," Halden said, "we thought we should bring each other up to speed. It looks like Wendy Ito's Prius has been found in a ravine about four miles west of town."

He walked to the map and pointed to a spot in Star Fire
Canyon, about three miles from where Ito's body was
discovered. "An officer has secured the scene. The car
looks the same as the others, wrecked and pried open,
tire shot out, only this car was nearly buried in a foot of
snow. We'll all be rolling out there in a couple of minutes."

"Who found the car?" Alvarez asked.

Gage interjected, "Bob Simms. Lives up the road.
Looking for firewood during a break in the storm."

"Or setting traps," Pescoli said with a scowl. "Simms
thinks it's still the eighteen hundreds and he can do
whatever the hell he wants. Kills and traps whatever he
can without permits. Sells pelts on the black market.
You name it."

Gage agreed. Around forty, whip thin, with a prominent nose, glasses and brown hair starting to show the
first evidence of gray, the chief criminal deputy snorted.
"Hell, he's an anarchist."

"With a dead wife and half a dozen boys running
wild. All those kids have been in trouble with the law,"
Grayson reminded.

"That's the trouble—they don't believe in government or the law. I'm surprised Simms took the trouble
to call it in."

Pescoli said, "Even anarchists have consciences."

Gage snorted. "At least he found the car and not another body."

"Yet," Agent Chandler said. Today she was in
government-issued outerwear, her blond ponytail sticking out of the back of a navy baseball hat, her jacket unzipped to show off a navy blue sweater. "We're still looking
for Jillian Rivers. Something we've got to consider is the
timing of the deaths. Because of the frozen conditions
of the corpses, it's tough to pinpoint, but it looks like our

guy tries to kill them around the twentieth of the month. September for Charleton, October for Salvadore, November for Ito, and now, December for Rivers. The dates are a little off, and we're basing this on when the women were reported missing and when the ME guesses they died. They all went missing around the middle of the month, killed what appears to be a few days later, found later still. So, Jillian Rivers might already be dead."

"Jesus," Brewster said, and tossed his pen onto the table in disgust.

Chandler didn't miss a beat. "It could be that the stars carved over the victims' heads and on the notes have something to do with timing. Where a star might be positioned in the sky during the time of abduction."

"Or death," Halden added.

Chandler nodded. "Maybe our guy is into stargazing or astronomy or astrology."

Alvarez frowned. She'd thought of the night sky, of course. She'd also thought about witchcraft, or devil worship, or anything to do with the dark arts. Stars meant a lot of different things to different people.

"He could just be jerking our chain," Brewster said. "Maybe the stars are for decoration."

"They're part of his MO," Chandler disagreed. She traced her finger over the stars on each of the notes, which had been blown up and put near the pictures of the victims. "He's too precise. See how perfectly the initials are written, almost as if he traced them? If you put the pages one atop the other, you'll see that the letters remain in exactly the same positions, but the star moves. I'm willing to bet he's on some kind of astronomical calendar."

"Hey, isn't the twentieth when the astrological sign switches? Around the twentieth of the month, the signs of the zodiac change," Pescoli offered. "Though I think it varies a little; I'm not really into it. If it means anything."

"I don't like the word 'zodiac,' not when we're talking about serial killers," Grayson said.

"Jesus, no," Brewster agreed. "That bastard terrorized San Francisco during, what? The sixties or seventies? I remember my mother talking about it. She had a sister in the Bay Area at the time and was worried sick."

"Made a movie out of it," Alvarez said.

Pescoli nodded. "Never caught, was he?"

"Never." Chandler's face grew even more taut, the sharp angles of her cheekbones and chin prominent. "But Zodiac would be too old to be our guy, if he were alive, which I doubt."

"Could be a copycat. Someone who knows about the original. The killings are different, yeah," Pescoli said, "but the Zodiac's name might have been inspiration. And he plans the murders meticulously."

Alvarez had a mental image of a man with a pen, sitting at a desk, carefully creating his notes, all the while plotting the death of the woman he had captured, a woman probably bound and caged, locked in a dark, airless room, a frightened, injured woman who couldn't comprehend the extent of her jailor's depravity.

A killer who planned out his victim's capture and death in minute detail, all around the position of the stars in the heavens.

"These killings are way different from Zodiac's. Let's go check on Ito's car, unless you have anything else," Grayson said. Chandler and Halden discussed tips that had come in, none of which had developed into a true lead, then concluded the meeting.

Alvarez was left cold inside. Just the mention of the Zodiac killer chilled her to the bone. The monster had been on a rampage, picking out his victims, sometimes disabling cars. One woman had nearly been decapitated, others were shot at point-blank range, sometimes trophies were taken and the police were forever being taunted.

And he was never caught. Never.

Grayson scooted his chair back and gave a short whistle to his dog, a black Lab named Sturgis who rarely left his side. The dog, a reject from the K-9 unit, had been with Grayson for a couple of years, ever since the department had decided not to "hire" him. They'd been inseparable ever since and Alvarez had wondered if the Lab was some kind of replacement for the wife who had dumped him. Usually the retriever stayed in Grayson's office, but today, he'd been allowed into the task force room and now trotted happily, tail wagging, at the sheriff's boot heels. They disappeared into his office as Alvarez and Pescoli headed for the side door to the parking lot.

She walked with Pescoli outside to the parking lot and tucked her hair into a stocking cap. A sharp wind was blowing, dusk descending rapidly, and it was cold as hell. Already Pescoli's Jeep was collecting ice on its windshield.

"Cheery little meeting," Pescoli said, unlocking her Jeep and climbing behind the wheel while Alvarez slid into the passenger side.

"Yeah, a real upper."

They discussed the case as Pescoli flipped on the heater and wipers, driving away from the town, toward the hills. "Merry Christmas," Pescoli said under her breath as she reached in the console for her pack of cigarettes, cracking the window. "Mind if I smoke?"

"Yeah, but it's not gonna stop you, is it?"

"Sure it will. For a while." Pescoli dropped the cigarette into her near-empty pack, which she tucked back into the console. Meanwhile, the police band crackled, officers talking to each other while they drove through the foothills. She didn't light up until she'd driven to Star Fire Canyon, near the area where the car was discovered, and parked as close as possible.

This time there was no safe way down to the bottom of the ravine, though two deputies and a firefighter rappelled down the side of the sheer hillside to the narrow creek bed below.

"How the hell did Bob Simms find the car?" Alvarez asked.

"He patrols all the woods around here. Doesn't matter what the weather," Deputy Pete Watershed said.

"He must be half mountain goat." Pescoli drew hard on her filter-tip and stared down the embankment. "Hell, that's a drop."

"He wears snowshoes or cross-country skis."

"Doesn't matter, the man's a damned mountain goat."

Alvarez eyed the surrounding area, looking for the spot in the road where the Prius was hit.

As if reading her thoughts, Watershed pointed up to the next ridge. "We think the car was shot up there. It's a little off the beaten track if she were returning to Spokane, but when it's clearer weather there's a ridge across the canyon. From there a shooter with a sniper rifle might be able to make the shot. If conditions were right."

Alvarez squinted against the falling flakes and coming darkness, trying to understand what madness would consume a person and make him lie in wait in the bitter cold. She imagined seconds ticking off before he took aim and fired, blowing out the tires of his victim's vehicle.

None of the victims' phone records had helped. The friends who'd left messages on their cell phones, MySpace pages and other computer lists—none had yielded any

clues. The three victims had nothing in common aside
from the fact that they'd been stalked, abducted, then
abandoned, naked, tied to trees, to die alone.

Deep in her jacket, Alvarez shivered, her thoughts
turning to Jillian Rivers. Was she even still alive?

Jillian used the time that MacGregor was out of the
cabin to snoop. She didn't know anything about him, so
this was her chance. She maneuvered around the cabin
with one crutch, ignoring the pain as she carefully
searched through drawers and cupboards, looking for
some clue as to his identity, his life, his past. She felt a
little guilty, as if she were a trespasser, but all she had to
do to allay the sense of wrongdoing was remind herself
that he'd brought her here. She was his guest, and prisoner.

From the books in the bookcase she gleaned that he
was interested in hunting, fishing, astronomy, backpacking, survival in the wilderness, first aid and medicine. In drawers, he had maps that covered the states of
Montana, Idaho, Washington and Wyoming. Topographical maps, road maps, forest service maps, even
satellite maps.

But there wasn't a framed photograph in the place;
not on the mantel, walls, bookcase or tables. Not one
single snapshot. It was as if he kept the images of his life
hidden, even from himself.

"How odd," she said under her breath, then wondered if she was wrong. Dead wrong. This cabin might
just be his mountain retreat, his second home.

His lair, her mind taunted, as if he were the serial
killer she'd heard something about. Rationally, she'd
pretty much dismissed the idea, but irrationally, on a
purely gut level, she reminded herself to tread lightly,

to be on the alert, to remember that she didn't know anything about her savior except what he told her.

It could all be a pack of lies.

It took a little effort, but she managed to feed the fire, tossing a couple of chunks of fir into the grate and not hurting her ribs too much. As the flames rose, crackling hungrily, she replaced the screen. Using her crutch, she hobbled past the table to the far side of the room. She'd just reached the bookcase and was going to examine some of the titles when she felt it—that sensation that someone was watching her. She froze and turned, glancing around the empty room. No one was inside, and even the dog had curled up by the door, content to wait, eyelids closed.

No one is watching you.

She glanced up to the ceiling, searching, ridiculously, for a hidden camera.

"You're getting paranoid," she told herself but couldn't keep her pulse from racing, her heart from beating a little faster. Using her crutch, she made her way to the windows. It was getting close to dark, twilight shadowing the rugged hills, and she had to squint to see into the shadows.

Snow was falling, but slowly, and she thought there might be a chance that the sky would soon clear. In her mind she prioritized the tasks of returning to civilization. First get to the hospital, then call her mother and Emily, her neighbor, about her cat. She'd have to deal with the insurance company about the car, check her phone messages to see if anyone had work for her and . . . and . . . She froze, thinking that she would still have to track down Aaron, if he were truly alive.

And if not? What if this is a wild goose chase? What if someone lured you here just to shoot at your car and cause the accident? What if Zane MacGregor is a part of the "accident"? What if everything that's happened to you is scripted?

"Oh, shut up!" she said so loudly Harley lifted his head and let out a startled little woof. She felt like an idiot. "Sorry," she said, but couldn't shake the feeling that someone was watching her, a pair of malevolent eyes glaring at her with hatred from the twilight shadows.

She edged away from the window. Whoever had shot at her car had used a high-powered rifle, and even though the overhang of the roof was low, Jillian was backlit by the soft, warm glow of the fire and lanterns. Someone who forced a car over a ledge wouldn't think twice about shattering a window.

And then there was MacGregor.

With his rifle.

She licked her lips and eased away from the light so that she, too, was hidden in partial darkness.

Who are you, you bastard?

And what do you want with me?

Her fingers tightened over the handle of her crutch as she thought of the reason she'd shown up here.

Her first husband.

Supposedly dead.

From deep in the cabin she glared through the window, trying to locate the source of her fear. *Okay, you prick, how the hell are you connected with Aaron?*

Pescoli was eyeball deep in reports. Lab reports, notes on the victims' relatives and friends and cell phone bills. She'd read each of the women's backgrounds until she felt that she knew them as well as their siblings did. All of the victims, it turned out, had traces of Valium in their systems, so Pescoli figured the guy who'd held them had restrained them all with drugs, probably tranquilizers and pain pills. The FBI was already all over the local distributors, hoping to find a link to where the killer could have gotten the drugs.

The trouble was, each of the victims had prescriptions. Legal prescriptions for anxiety, pain and sleep.

Her back was beginning to ache a bit; she'd never been one to sit for hours on end. She just had too much restless energy and had to keep moving. She never would have been able to handle a desk job. As it was, the time she spent at her desk, reading through files and clicking on the damned mouse of her computer, was enough to drive her crazy.

She walked down a hallway and saw, for the first time in days, a sliver of late-afternoon sunlight shining through the windows, bright rays cutting through the clouds, which were collecting again. For a few seconds, the light was nearly blinding as it bounced off the thick drifts of snow piled outside around the parking lot and the yard where the flagpole stood. Old Glory moved slightly in the breeze, the State of Montana's flag, too, billowing a bit, gold fringe glinting in the sun.

Thank God for the tiny break in the weather, even if it was predicted to be short-lived.

Now, if there was only a break in the case.

She walked to the kitchen, poured herself a cup of "Joelle's Special Blend," according to the note left on the counter, and headed back to her desk.

Taking a sip as she sat in her chair, she thought the coffee tasted the same as it did every day. "Special blend, my ass," she whispered, setting the cup down and scanning the lists of friends and relatives of the three women one last time. None matched, nor did towns where they lived, schools they attended . . . anything. As far as she could tell, the women didn't know each other. But they were all targeted by one guy who had connections with each one; she was sure of it.

Her cell phone rang and she recognized her son's number on the ID. She let it ring twice and reined in the urge to answer with "Where the hell are you?" Instead, she picked up and said neutrally, "Detective Pescoli."

"You called me?"

"Yeah, Jer, I did. You're supposed to be with your fa—with Lucky this weekend."

"I didn't want to go."

"Why?"

"It's boring over there."

"And?" she prodded, twisting her desk chair around so that she couldn't see her computer monitor or the notes spread over her desk.

"He's not my real dad."

"He raised you."

"Part of the time, cuz he had to," Jeremy shot back indignantly.

"Look, Jeremy, this is part of the deal. You know it and I know it. You spend every other weekend with Lucky."

"It's your deal, not mine," he said. "I didn't get any say in it."

"I guess I need to remind you that you're the kid."

"I'm almost eighteen."

She winced. Hadn't she uttered the same words with the same passion to her own parents? "This might come as a big surprise to you, but just being eighteen doesn't mean you get to do anything you want."

"I'll be an adult then!"

If only.

"Jer, the rules won't change just because you're another day older. Eighteen shmeighteen. I think it just means that legally I can kick you out of the house."

"What?" His shock waves radiated through the airwaves. "Kick me out? Great, Mom, real supportive."

She wasn't going to be lured into that argument. "Well, for the moment, you're not eighteen and you need to hustle your butt over to your stepfather's place."

"But I was going to stay with Ryan tonight. Play video games."

"Take it up with Lucky."

"Way to pass the ball, Mom."

"I gotta go. If I don't hear from your stepdad that you made it over there or worked things out, there will be hell to pay."

"Aren't you tough?"

"Yeah, Jer, I am. Love you!" She hung up then, before she could hear another word of protest. The truth of the matter was that she could collar a suspect in a restraining hold, cuff him, toss him into the back of her rig, take all kinds of verbal abuse and put it right back at the damned perp, but when it came to her kids, hell, she was a wimp. A stupid, crazy-about-them, died-in-the-wool wuss and it pissed her off. She cradled the phone in her hands for a second, thinking about calling her son back and starting over with a cooler head. Instead she gritted her teeth, reminded herself that if she were on the outside looking in, if one of her friends were dealing with their rebellious teens, she would have told her friend to hang up.

"Sorry, Jer," she said and twirled her chair around to see the image of Wendy Ito's corpse stare back at her. "What the hell happened to you?" she asked the eerie photo. "Who did this?"

Whoever had shot out the tire had to have been a helluva marksman, one who could hide and wait, with his sniper rifle at the ready, and be able to fire off a shot in perfect timing to hit the vehicle dead-on. She had been going over lists of ex-military sharpshooters, winners of marksmen competitions, members of the local gun clubs and hunting associations. The lists were long, but so far she hadn't found anyone with obvious ties to any of the three victims.

"Who are you?" she muttered, feeling the urge for a cigarette. She settled on a stick of nicotine gum instead, telling herself she had to quit again, or at least cut back. She was up to half a pack a day and that could escalate in a hurry if she didn't nip it in the bud.

Her cell phone beeped again and she caught a glimpse of the incoming number. Her heart did a stupid little flip and she remembered the last time she'd seen him, lying across the bed in the motel room. "Pescoli," she said in a soft voice.

"Busy?" His voice was husky and rough and just the sound of it made her think of sex. Ridiculous.

"What do you think?"

"I think all work and no play makes Regan a . . ."

"Dull girl?"

"I was going to say bitchy."

"Bitchy? Isn't that sweet?" she said sarcastically. "And I love you, too."

"I know," he said, even though she'd been teasing.

"Get over yourself."

"I thought we could get together."

"With lines like that, how could a girl resist?"

"Okay, I take it back. You're never bitchy."

"Liar," she said, but smiled. He had that ability. To burrow beneath her thick skin and get to her. It was damned irritating. He wasn't right for her. She knew it and he knew it; in fact, he'd said as much. But then there was that chemistry thing that couldn't be denied. They made each other laugh, had fun together and were good in bed. In fact, even Lucky paled as a lover, and though Pescoli hated to admit it, Lucky had been damned good.

But now he was second best. Second to Nate. The outdoorsman.

"So, let's get together."

"I'm pretty booked."

"I'm just talkin' about a drink after work."

"Just a drink?" she asked, knowing better.

"Well . . . we'll see."

She wasn't that easily conned, but she felt a little zing of anticipation slipping through her bloodstream. "It's never just a drink, now is it?"

She envisioned his slow grin, a crooked slash of white teeth against his tanned skin. "No, Regan, you got me there. With you, it's never just a drink." His chuckle was low and knowing. "Give me a call when you get off."

She thought about saying something dirty to his "get off" line, but bit her tongue. No reason to appear crass, even if her retort was clever. He hung up, and Pescoli tried to tell herself that she wasn't interested, that he was just no good for her, that she wouldn't call him or meet him in one of their favorite bars . . . but she knew it was a lie.

She'd meet him. She couldn't help herself.

He was like a damned cocaine habit.

One she wasn't going to give up any time soon.

The bitch wouldn't stop moving.

Even after nearly an hour.

In that time the weather had changed again, moving from clear sky in patches to storm clouds gathering, looking more fierce than ever.

Jesus, it was cold.

And Jillian Rivers wouldn't stand still.

She would come to the window, appearing as a ghostly shadow, nearly close enough to catch in the gun sight, but then, almost as if she knew there was danger, she'd slip back into the interior of the cabin, making the shot tricky.

What to do?

Take a chance?

Shoot wildly?

But then there was the risk of missing, of warning her. Even though the point was not to kill her. Not yet. Just wound her a little more. Incapacitate her.

But it was better to wait.

The bitch was going to slip up.

And shooting her hadn't been part of the plan.

No . . . there was still time.

In this case, patience was truly a virtue.

Chapter Fourteen

Jillian glanced at the clock in the bookcase. Battery powered with an old-fashioned dial face, it clicked off the seconds of her life. She didn't know what day it was, but she was pretty damned sure of the time and MacGregor had been gone over an hour.

Her old paranoia kept taunting her. . . .

What if he doesn't come back for you?

What if this is part of his plan?

She looked to the door, where the dog was waiting patiently. No way would he leave old Harley. No, he would be back. Unless he was hurt. Oh Lord, she didn't want to go there. She kept searching through the cabin, searching for clues as to who he was, where they were. There were maps of the area on the walls but they didn't mean much to her. Forestry service maps, topographical maps of a mountainous terrain.

She hitched her way over to the gun cabinet and pulled on the handle, but he'd locked the damned thing. Out of habit? To hide something from her? "No, idiot, so you couldn't turn a gun on him when he returned." She thought of the eerie sensation she had that someone or something was hiding in the shadows outside and her skin crawled. She knew how to use a rifle; Grandpa Jim had made certain of that when she was still in her teens. He'd taken her out and shown her the kick of a .22, the damage it could inflict to targets, helped her learn to sight the rifle as well. She wasn't a crack shot, but she could hold her own.

She tried the door to the gun cabinet again.

It didn't budge.

"I guess it's back to filet knives," she said to the dog, who actually gave his tail a couple of thumps on the floor. Which was somewhat encouraging. The beast was warming to her. She poked around in a closet, found more hunting gear, a few clothes and, on an upper shelf, under a couple of hats, a few board games that seemed to have been there since the seventies.

If things got bad enough, she and MacGregor, if he ever returned, could play Chinese checkers.

"Great." She hadn't found anything exactly illuminating, nothing that would give her any insight into the man who had rescued her. *Or captured you.* She pushed that stupid idea aside. He didn't want her here; he'd made that abundantly clear.

But he could be a liar.

"Yeah, right, well, aren't we all?"

Defending him now?

Rather than have this discussion with herself and admit she really was going crazy, she kept searching through MacGregor's things. She glanced up to the loft. A room she couldn't ascend to. What was up there? If she reversed as far as possible and ended up standing at the fire, her back to the grate and door leading to the room where her cot was placed, she could see the upper half of the room, but not what was in it.

Did he use it for an attic? A storage area? A den? Guest room? What? It was in shadow and, as far as she knew, he'd never climbed the ladder. *But you're not certain, are you? You slept for days, or were nearly comatose, right? You were stuck in the smaller room, not knowing anything.*

She checked the bookcase one more time and picked up what looked like an empty vase, a rough ceramic replica of a worn cowboy boot. She looked inside. It was empty aside from two photographs. So, here were some snapshots. Good.

"In for a penny, in for a pound," she told herself when she felt renewed hesitation at prying into his personal possessions. Dusty and wedged tightly into the hollowed boot, the pictures had obviously been left untouched for months.

The first was a photo of a baby swaddled in a blue blanket. A boy. His son?

The second was of a woman in jeans, her long blond hair tied into a ponytail that had fallen over one shoulder, a toddler balanced on one outstretched hip. It was summer, leaves green, steep mountains rising in the distance behind her and the boy, a shadow cast by the photographer indicating it was late afternoon.

Hadn't he said he wasn't married? That he didn't have children? Could this be a nephew? She stared at the woman and decided this was not his sister.

No way.

In her heart she knew she was staring at Zane MacGregor's son and girlfriend or wife. She bit her lip and felt betrayed.

So he lied.

So what?

Did you really think he would pour his heart out to you?

Staring at the woman in the photograph, she felt a little sizzle of jealousy stream through her. Ridiculous! But true. There was something in the woman's confident smile, the easy way she balanced her son, the almost cocky turn of her head. As if she and the photographer had a special connection, one that set them apart from the world.

For the love of God, Jillian, you're making a big deal out of a couple of photographs! What do you care?

What indeed?

She reminded herself that she barely knew the man. So why did she feel a tiny sense of betrayal? Of disappointment? It wasn't as if she cared a fig about MacGregor.

Jillian glanced at the boy one last time. His coloring was like that of the woman, but there was a resemblance to the man who had pulled her from the wreckage of her car.

Or so she thought.

She stuffed the pictures back into their hiding place and made her way into the kitchen and bathroom, searching. But she didn't notice anything unusual. When she faced the kitchen window to the rear of the cabin, she saw only encroaching darkness and swirling snow.

Was there movement beneath the snow-laden bow of a pine tree near what appeared to be a woodshed? A dark figure pressed against the trunk of the tree?

No way. Her mind was just playing games with her.

Right?

She swallowed hard and tried to melt into the shadows. She hadn't carried a light with her into the kitchen and she wasn't backlit, but she still felt as if she were being watched, as if unseen eyes were following her every move.

You're paranoid, her mind insisted as the wind picked up again, whistling through the rafters and howling outside. She stared through the icy glass, but the movement, if she'd seen it, was gone. Probably a tree branch shuddering in the wind. Nothing more.

But she was left with a cold fear in the middle of her gut, and when she heard a thud at the front of the cabin and the dog let out a quick bark, she nearly screamed.

"Jillian?" MacGregor's voice boomed through the cabin and she didn't know whether to feel relief or fear.

Get a grip, she told herself. "In here." Using the crutch, she slipped through the doorway and found him unlacing his boots. "So, how was it out there?"

"Not good."

Her heart sank.

"So your storm radar wasn't up to snuff."

He snorted, stepped out of his boots and started peeling off his clothes. "I still think the storm is going to break, but there are trees down on the road, buried deep, too heavy for me to move. I'll have to try and tear through the trunks and branches with my chain saw. But that will take a while." He glanced over at her and appeared to note her disappointment. "I was hoping we could get out, too, but I'll have to take the snowmobile to the places where the road is blocked. Then I can cut the trees up and remove them piece by piece." His gaze found hers and held. "It'll take time and good weather."

"So we might be up here for *months*?"

"Hopefully not *that* long. Days, certainly. A week, well, maybe. But hopefully not any longer than that."

"I'll go stir-crazy," she said.

"You and me both."

Harley was dancing at his feet, so he hung up his jacket and leaned down to scratch the dog behind his ears. "Miss me?" he asked, and though he was petting the dog he glanced up at her.

"Me?"

He lifted a shoulder.

"It's isolated up here."

"Didn't answer my question."

Leaning a shoulder against the door jamb, she said, "Probably about as much as you missed me."

One side of his mouth twitched a bit and his eyes gleamed. "That much, huh?"

"Yeah. That much." She inched into the room and tried not to notice the angle of his beard-shadowed jaw or how dark his pupils had become or that his hair was long enough to curl at his collar and over his ears. She pretended that the cabin didn't seem intimate with its glowing fire and kerosene lanterns. She couldn't even go there. Wouldn't.

To think that her situation was the slightest bit romantic was just plain insane. She'd heard of women who took a chance on a man they barely knew, even going home and sleeping with that intriguing stranger. Jillian had never fallen into that trap, never been intrigued enough to tumble into a stranger's arms or so fascinated by potential danger to throw caution to the wind. She knew she was brave and had more courage than some women, but she wasn't foolhardy.

Or hadn't been until this moment in time.

The only explanation was that being caught up here alone with a man for so many days had addled her brain, clouded her thinking. That had to be it.

She could *not* be attracted to Zane MacGregor.

Not on a dare.

"So," she said and hated that her voice sounded husky. Clearing her throat, she moved to stand behind the couch as MacGregor put his gloves and ski cap on the mantel to warm. "How about an educated guess. When do you think we can get out of here?"

"If I could predict that, I'd sell myself to the weather service and make a fortune."

"Terrific," she muttered, and hiked her way to her chair, where she sat down. "Well, then, if you can't predict the future, maybe you can tell me about your past."

"Maybe," he said, but she caught the hesitation in his gaze, the tiny tensing of the corners of his eyes.

"When you were outside, were you ever in the back of the house or . . . I don't know . . ." She felt more than a little embarrassed. "I had this 'feeling,' I guess you'd call it, that someone was outside, watching the house."

His expression turned hard and she felt more than a little drip of fear in her blood.

"Did the dog react?"

"No . . . I thought it might be you. Standing outside and staring at the house?"

"I'll go check it out."

"No, it was probably nothing, I don't want you to. . . ."

"To what, Jillian?"

"I don't know. Maybe I'm just paranoid."

"Well, we're about to find out."

He threw on his outerwear again and reached for his boots.

"You don't have to go out and—"

"Of course I do," he said, and stepped into his boots. "You were in a car that wrecked because someone shot out your tire. At least, that's what we think." His jaw was set. "I'm going to check out what's going on." He whistled to the dog. "Harley, come." Then he thought again, reached into his pocket and tossed her a small key ring. "You know how to use a gun?"

"Yes."

"Good. The ammo's in the closet. Lock the door behind me." With that he and the dog were out the door.

Jillian didn't waste a second. She threw the deadbolt, then walked directly to the gun closet, pulled out a .22, found the right shells and loaded the chamber. Then she waited in the dark, the barrel of the gun aimed at the main entrance, every muscle stretched tight.

She listened hard, half-expecting to hear the crack

of a rifle, but all she heard was the ever-present rush of the wind, the creak of old timbers and the ticking of the clock.

On her computer screen, Pescoli placed one map over the other—first the topographical, which she overlaid with the road map that had been marked with the cabins of known winter residents, then a third map of the locations where the victims and their cars had been found. She saved this new map and printed it out, hoping that it would give her new insight into the path of the killer.

Studying her new map didn't help. She even marked the homes of Ivor Hicks, Grace Perchant and Bob Simms, the people who had located the crime scenes.

Still no epiphanies.

Time to give up for the day. Or night.

It was late, nearly nine, and she still had the Jeremy issue to deal with.

As well as the Nate issue. She thought about calling him first, but decided she'd better deal with her son before she made any plans. Grabbing her purse with one hand, she dialed with her free hand and, of course, her call was thrown directly into his voice-mail box, which just happened to be full.

So she couldn't leave a message.

"Clever, Jeremy," she said, knowing full well her son had somehow filled the damned thing so she couldn't leave a message. "Real clever." She settled back into her desk chair and muttered, "Oh, Jer, you are soooo toast." Switching her phone to text mode, she typed him a quick message that told him in no uncertain terms to meet her at home.

Then she signed out, barely noticing the gold letters looping along one of the bare green walls. "Merry

Christmas" had been swagged in the area near the door
and below it, in silver letters, "Happy New Year." The
tape was coming loose and the letters were on the verge
of falling, but Pescoli didn't have time to mess with
them. Besides, it looked like this was Joelle Fisher's attempt to "brighten this old drab place up" or "bring in
a little holiday cheer," as she had said about half a million times in the last month. How she kept her job was
beyond Pescoli.

Walking through the doors to the parking lot she
found her Jeep with four new inches of snow on the
roof and hood. And more flakes fell by the minute,
adding yet another layer to the already-covered ground.
Yes, she lived in western Montana, but this winter was
like no other she remembered. Using her gloves, she
brushed her windshield clear, then climbed inside.

It was freezing.

Even in department-issue down jacket and ski pants,
she was cold to the bone. She switched on the ignition,
the Jeep's engine fired and she pushed the thermostat
control to the highest setting. Wheeling out of the lot,
she ignored her sudden craving for a cigarette, more
because she didn't want to try and shake out a Marlboro Light while wearing gloves. Not worth it.

By the time she turned onto the plowed streets, the
heater had kicked on and she flipped on the blower.
Wipers battling the falling snow, she drove into the hills
and the rural area where her little piece of property was
located. She paused for the mail at the roadside box,
then shifted down and the Jeep ground up the lane, the
beams of her headlights washing on the trunks of a
thick stand of pine and hemlock.

Jeremy's truck was parked in front of the house.

Well, that was a start.

She hit the button of the garage door opener and drove
into the small space. Less than a minute later, the door

was grinding down and she was stepping into the house, where Cisco was going out of his mind and the smell of microwave pizza permeated the kitchen. Jeremy's tools of the trade—pizza cutter, plate, over-sized Big Gulp cup and the box the frozen pizza came in—were scattered over a counter amid tomato sauce smudges.

"Hey! Jer! Come up here!" she yelled down the stairs as Cisco demanded attention, jumping onto the couch and ottoman. He yipped until she unzipped her coat and petted his wriggling, scruffy body. "Yeah, yeah, I love you, too," she said, her voice an octave higher than usual. "Yes, I do." She turned off the television and plugged in the Christmas tree, noting the scraggly thing needed more water. "Jeremy!" she called again as she walked to the kitchen, tossed his mess into the sink and filled a glass measuring cup with water. It took two trips to fill the tree's basin and she ignored the fact that there wasn't a single package under its limbs. This was the weekend she had planned to go shopping in Missoula, but between the storms and ongoing investigations, she'd probably have to resort to Plan B, whatever the hell that was.

Since there was no sound from the basement, she headed down the stairs to Jeremy's room. Cisco shot ahead of her, nearly tripping her. She found her son asleep on his bed, earbuds from his iPod jammed into his ears. Even so, she heard a thin stream of music. The kid seemed determined to make himself deaf by the time he was thirty. Geez, he could piss her off.

She stood in the doorway and looked at him. On his back, slightly snoring, this big lug of a kid appeared at peace, and a lump filled the back of her throat when she remembered bringing him home from the hospital and being terrified of having a son when she'd grown up in a family of four girls, her father being so terribly outnumbered he'd finally left. Well, that probably hadn't been the reason, but he'd taken off when Regan was eleven and had said something about not being able to live with "a house full of females." That was when she'd understood that the reason her parents had so many children was because her dad had been dead-set on a boy. It hadn't mattered that Regan, the baby, had excelled at sports. Her father never knew she had learned to shoot a rifle as well as a layup, or that she'd been such a tomboy she'd been called "gay" and "lesbo" from the time she knew what the terms meant.

Considering her choices in men, she thought now, maybe she should have thought about swinging the other way. But that would have been impossible. The truth of the matter was, she liked men, was turned on by them, especially the sexy bad asses. Not the criminals. No, they were just plain losers. But the players . . . yeah, she had a fondness for them. Or, as she sometimes admitted, an addiction.

Like Nate.

How stupid was that? Yet she couldn't wait to hook up with him.

However, first things first. She stepped across the threshold into Jeremy's room—a room that reeked of pizza and . . . something else? Oh damn, was the kid smoking weed? The smell was masked, but she was pretty certain she caught the scent of smoke and the musky sweet odor of marijuana.

"Damn it," she muttered. The kid needed a dad. Maybe that's why she'd tried so hard for Jeremy to accept Lucky—so he'd have a father, a male role model, something she'd missed as a kid. Too bad she'd picked such a loser.

She touched him on the toe. "Hey," she said, then when he didn't respond, gave his foot a shake hard enough to get his attention. He blinked his eyes open and all the peace she'd seen on his face seconds earlier disappeared.

"What the fu—" He caught himself just in time, and scooting into a sitting position, pulled out the earbuds. "Geez, Mom, you scared the hell out of me!"

"I thought we needed to talk."

He rolled his eyes. "You *always* think we need to talk."

"Why don't you want to go to Lucky's?" she asked, and when he opened his mouth, she held up her hand, palm out. "Give me a real reason."

His face was a cloud of frustration. "It's boring there."

"Yes, yes, it's boring here, too. And by the way, the next time you make yourself dinner, clean up."

"Oh God, Mom."

"Have you been smoking weed?"

He started. "What the hell are you talking about?"

"I smell it, Jer. Remember, I'm trained."

"Fuck!"

"Watch the mouth."

"No, it's not weed. Mom, I swear, I've never done any drugs. None."

She didn't say a word because she wanted to believe him, but she worked for the sheriff's department. She knew how prevalent everything from ecstasy to meth was. "You haven't experimented?"

"I've been where they have stuff, yeah, and don't ask me who cuz I won't tell you, but I haven't used."

God, how she wanted to believe him. "So the weed I smell?"

"A friend came over. I told him not to do it here. He left." Jeremy narrowed angry eyes at her. "I won't rat him out."

"I'm a cop."

"I don't care."

Regan hesitated, then said, "Call Lucky, tell him what the deal is. I think he planned to take you and your sister Christmas shopping tomorrow."

Jeremy flopped back on his bed. "Save me."

"I know, a fate worse than death."

"Have you ever been to the mall with Michelle and Bianca?" He was shaking his head violently. "It takes *forever*. Nu-uh, I'm not doin' it."

"Then call Lucky and straighten it out with him." She was tired of arguing. "And figure out how you're going to get your sister a present."

"Just Bianca?"

"And your loving mother, of course." She glanced at the picture of Joe on the shelf. "And Jer?"

"Yeah?" He was already reaching for his phone.

"Just for the record, I miss your dad, too."

"Then why do you go out with all those losers?"

Oh Jesus. "I go out because he's gone."

"And so you married Lucky?"

"Well . . . yeah, I was in love with him."

"He's not like Dad."

"No, you're right, but he has his good qualities." She held up a hand to cut off further discussion. "Let's not get into trashing him, okay? He is what he is and what he is, is Bianca's father and your stepfather. Give the man a little respect."

"You don't like him and you hate Michelle."

"I don't care enough about her to hate her. And anyway, we're a family, okay? Maybe not the traditional *Leave It to Beaver* type of family, but a family, warts and all."

"Leave it to *what*?"

"You've never seen . . . or heard of . . . ? It's a sitcom from the fifties or sixties about a family that . . . oh, never mind—"

His grin said it all. "Okay, smarty, so ya got me," she said, realizing he had been pulling her leg.

"And you call yourself a detective?"

"Pinewood County's finest."

"Poor Pinewood," he said, but the twinkle in his eyes returned.

Regan felt a moment of parental pleasure, fleeting as it was bound to be. "I'm going out for a while. When I get home, will you be here?"

"I told you, I'm going over to Ryan's." He looked up at her. "He's got some E and—"

"Don't joke with me about it."

"Okay, okay." He shrugged as Cisco tried to find a place to lie down between his long legs. "We're not doing any drugs. We're just going to play video games."

"What about Heidi?" she asked, bringing up Jeremy's on-again, off-again girlfriend. A sticky situation, since Heidi was one of Cort Brewster, the undersheriff's, daughters.

"Eh. We broke up." He shrugged as if it didn't matter and he, at least, didn't seem heartbroken. This time.

"Okay. I'll see you later. Call Lucky."

He held up his cell phone and his eyebrows arched in reproach. "I'm on it, Mom. Got it." He waved at her with the hand holding his phone. "See ya. And be careful."

"What?"

Jeremy's grin stretched wide. Full of the devil, he suddenly looked a lot like his father. "Hey, I'm just sayin' what you always tell me when I go out."

"Smart ass," she muttered under her breath but headed up the stairs feeling slightly better. Jer had his struggles, but didn't they all?

She left him at the house, and as she drove onto the county road, she clicked on her cell phone to call Nate. Tonight was suddenly looking up.

As long as another dead body or wrecked car wasn't discovered.

Chapter Fifteen

Jillian heard the sound of boots on the front porch and she tensed, training the barrel of her gun on the doorway.

A few seconds later the lock clicked, the door opened and MacGregor stepped inside. Beside him, bounding joyfully, Harley swept past his long legs. Stopping at the fireplace grate, the spaniel shook his long coat, sending drops of water onto the fire and causing the embers to sizzle angrily.

Jillian's heart did a stupid little flip at the sight of MacGregor as he secured the cabin again, throwing the deadbolt back into its locked position.

"You okay?" he asked as he ripped off his ski cap. His dark hair stuck up in awkward spikes, but he didn't notice.

"I guess."

"Then maybe you should point the gun somewhere else." He motioned a gloved finger at the muzzle of her rifle, which, of course, was still aimed at the door.

"Sorry." She lowered the rifle, watching as he unzipped and shrugged out of his jacket, then hung it on a peg near the door. He was wearing a thick, bulky sweater, but even so, she noticed how fluidly his muscles worked as he moved around the cabin. He was earthy and male and . . . off limits. Why the hell did she even notice? She'd heard of captives who had become enamored with their abductors, who had even imagined themselves falling in love with the only person they were allowed to see, and she'd always thought the whole concept was ludicrous. But here, cut off from the world, the threat of danger at the door, she found herself attracted to this rugged man of few words and a very dark past.

What a crock!

Get over yourself.

She dragged her gaze away from the intensity of his. "What did you find out there?"

"I'm not sure." His thick eyebrows pulled together and he double-checked that the door was locked.

"What do you mean?"

"I think I saw some kind of disturbance in the snow. Most likely tracks." He shoved one hand through his hair, only messing the dark waves further. All the while he never let go of his rifle. "Looks like someone used a pine bough to scrape over the tracks. That might work in dirt or sand or dust. Not snow. Certainly not deep snow." He took a position in front of the fire, warming the back of his legs. "And it would only work if whoever was outside wore snowshoes. Boots sink too deep." Silhouetted by the firelight, he thought hard, his jaw sliding to one side as he scratched his chin. "But I didn't catch him. The way I figure it, I took off out the back and didn't find the front tracks for a while, until I doubled back. Since it was snowing pretty hard, I really don't know what was going on out there, but nothing I feel good about."

Panic streamed through Jillian's blood. All the fears

she'd tried so hard to allay suddenly came into hard, sharp focus. "So what're we going to do?"

"Nothin' to do but wait it out," he said, as if he'd considered the limited alternatives. "We'll lock all the doors and keep the guns ready, and the minute there's a break in the weather and the roads are clear, we're outta here."

"You make it sound like we're in some bad movie from the fifties and the zombies are lurking in the woods."

He didn't so much as crack a smile. "Whatever's out there isn't dead."

"You're worried?"

"Cautious." He looked at her intently, with eyes that darkened in the half light. "Just . . . cautious."

"I'm worried." She didn't add that she was scared to death; he probably figured that already.

He nodded and glanced out the window to the darkness that had gathered. "Why don't you try and sleep? I'll stand guard."

"You think you need to?"

"Maybe not. But as I said, cautious. And I need you as strong as possible. The only way we're going to get out of here is if you're as strong as possible."

"I couldn't sleep even if I tried."

One side of his mouth lifted in that disarming grin she found so damned charming. "Try. You can stay in here if you want or the bedroom."

"Here will be fine," she said reluctantly, then worked her way to the couch, where she dropped down on the lumpy pillows.

He settled into the chair with the ottoman and turned down the lanterns.

The wind sighed low and long, a branch beating against one side of the house. The fire hissed quietly, while Jillian's nerves were strung tight as bowstrings.

She thought about what she'd discovered about Mac-Gregor this afternoon, the bits and pieces of his life she'd been able to ferret out, and she nearly mentioned the pictures of the boy, but stopped herself.

This wasn't the time to admit that she'd been prying, searching through his things. Though he probably expected it, and she was dying to know more about him, she decided to hold her tongue.

For now.

She was alone in the mountains, being guarded by a stranger with a high-powered rifle, while outside, hidden somewhere in the shadows, was a twisted killer. And it wasn't MacGregor. If he'd wanted to harm her, he would have done it by now. She had to trust him.

Had to.

There was no other choice.

Selena threw in the towel for the day. Or the night. She'd testified in court earlier, then returned to the sheriff's department and worked long past the time she should have gone home. Now the offices and cubicles for the detectives were eerily quiet, most everyone having left hours earlier.

The calm before the storm, she thought as she grabbed her purse and pushed back her chair. The lights had been turned down and her footsteps, in the boots she'd worn to the courthouse, rang loudly on the stairs. The whole place was kind of empty and eerie. Alvarez usually liked working alone in the office, late at night, when the phones didn't ring and the buzz of conversation, the laughter, and angry outbursts from suspects didn't bother her, but tonight was different.

Maybe it had been testifying in court. She'd been on the witness stand only a few minutes, explaining how a five-year-old had been killed in a hit-and-run accident by a drunk driver. But the mother's tortured, tear-streaked face, her guilt for having taken her eyes off her son for just a second, had gotten to her. And on the other side of the courtroom sat the defendant, a boy of no more than twenty, scared and remorseful and guilty as sin of being drunk, leaving the scene of an accident, being a minor in possession of alcohol and on and on.

So many lives ruined.

She walked outside and hit a button on her keyless remote to unlock her rig, a department-issued Jeep not unlike Pescoli's, snow covering the roof and hood.

Using a scraper she kept in the pocket inside the door, she brushed the snow free from the windshield and climbed behind the steering wheel. It had been a long day. A long week. Hell, it had been a long few months since the body of Theresa Charleton, the single schoolteacher from Boise, had been found. That had been the start, clear back at the end of September. Her body hadn't been in the forest long; there'd been minimal decomposition and animal activity when they found it. And ever since, her brother Lyle Wilson had been calling, demanding answers.

"If only," Alvarez said as she started her SUV and pulled out of the lonely parking lot, where only a few vehicles remained. She angled down a side street before connecting to the main artery that cut down the hillside to the heart of Old Grizzly, the part of the town that was first settled. Where the brick courthouse was flanked by narrow streets lined with offices and shops that had been built over a hundred years earlier. Located nearly five hundred feet below the hill where the sheriff's offices and jail sat, this part of town had been built on the banks of the Grizzly River, just below the falls. It had originally been inhabited by miners and loggers, an old sawmill downriver giving testament to the boom of the early 1900s.

Rather than head straight to her empty apartment, she found a parking space on the street near Wild Wills, one of her favorite haunts and a place she knew she could get a decent meal. She climbed out of the SUV and felt a coldness on the back of her neck, a premonition of someone staring at her.

She turned and saw a man across the narrow street. Wearing a thick parka, his face hidden in shadow, he sent one final glance her way and ambled off toward the river.

Your cop radar is on overload, she told herself as he disappeared around the corner, and she decided there was no reason to give chase. Her stomach rumbled, reminding her that she hadn't eaten since a carton of yogurt and an apple that were supposed to be lunch.

Adjusting the strap of her purse, she walked through the cold night air to the restaurant.

Wild Wills, sporting an 1880s western/wilderness theme, was decorated with rough plank walls, hanging wagon-wheel chandeliers and the mounted heads of moose, deer, elk, big-horned sheep and antelope, all with glassy fixed eyes staring down at the patrons. A stuffed grizzly bear, his mouth open in a perpetual bared-tooth growl, greeted the customers as it stood on hind legs near the front door. He'd been dubbed "Grizz" by the townspeople and the owners had always decorated him with the seasons. The huge, shaggy bear had been known to wear a red, white and blue top hat reminiscent of Uncle Sam on the Fourth of July, a small flag wedged between his sharp claws, and last Halloween, he'd been outfitted in one of those freaky masks from the *Scream* movies, which had somehow been pinned over his face and gaping snout. His props had been a chain saw and witches' caldron . . . kind of mixed signals, but hey, it had been Halloween.

Personally, Alvarez had always found it weird and disturbing, but she'd kept her opinions to herself, and today, as she shoved open the glass doors, she found Grizz decorated to the max, glittery angel wings appearing out of his back, matching halo propped over his head, a necklace of colored lights strung around his furry neck.

All the while, his glittery glass eyes glowered in rage and his lips pulled back to expose his wide mouth and sharp teeth, despite the open book of Christmas carols tucked into his outstretched paws.

Like, oh yeah, he was trilling away on "Silent Night," the page to which the book had been opened. Well, all wasn't calm tonight, nor was it bright, she thought as she walked through the foyer to the main dining hall, where the decor only got worse.

As she headed to the back of the large room, she passed tables and booths filled with patrons and guarded by hundred-year-old dead herbivorous animals staring down at her, all their antlers dressed in winking lights or draped in tinsel.

It was damned freaky.

Welcome to Grizzly Falls, she thought, struggling out of her jacket and realizing that some of the customers were gazing at her, questions in their eyes for the cop who was trying and failing to find a maniac.

Ignoring the garish display on the walls and the customers, who turned back to their meals, she settled into a booth near the back. She sat facing the door, a cop habit she couldn't shake. She just couldn't stand it if she couldn't see who was entering or leaving a restaurant.

Sandi, the owner-waitress, came by. In her hands

were two steaming coffeepots. "You want coffee? Or somethin' stronger? The drink special tonight is what we call a Wild Christmas."

"I hate to ask." The last drink special had been known as a Wild Will Hiccup and had been a god-awful blend of whiskeys.

"Eggnog, cream de cacao, a splash of cola and a shot of Wild Turkey." One of Sandi's eyebrows lifted over the rims of her jeweled glasses. "You can have another kind of whiskey if you want. We use Wild Turkey because of the name."

"I think I'll stick with decaf," Alvarez said, turning up one of the cups on her table and watching the warm stream of dark liquid flow.

"Any luck gettin' that psycho?" Sandi asked. She was a tall woman with a long, gaunt face and eyes darkened with heavy liner and, today, probably in a nod to the season, glittery green eye shadow. She had once been married to William Aldridge, for whom the establishment had been named, but Will and she had divorced, or so rumor had it. Will had ended up with his favorite pickup, the RV, a hunting cabin and a twenty-year-younger-than-Sandi girlfriend, and Sandi had become full owner of Wild Wills, expanding the bland fare to include exotic dishes created from local trout and venison. She lived in an apartment upstairs and was at the restaurant 24-7, or so it seemed. Sandi also hadn't been able to hide her satisfaction when she'd heard Will's younger girlfriend had "dumped his sorry ass." She'd confided this little morsel of information to anyone who had sat in the faux-leather booths and café chairs in the past two years.

"We're working on it."

"Well, speed it up, will ya? It's got everybody in town nervous as hell. No one's talkin' about this blasted weather, uh-uh. Nope. It's all about the Bitterroot Killer. That's what Manny over at the *Reporter* calls him.."

Alvarez had seen the article written by Manny Douglas of the *Mountain Reporter*, Grizzly Falls's answer to the *L.A. Times*. "We'll get him," she said.

"I have faith." But it was a lie. Alvarez saw the nervousness in the edge of Sandi's glossy-red lips as she slid a menu across the table. "The special is buffalo steak with a wild huckleberry reduction and red potatoes or rice pilaf. It comes with a house salad of spinach, green apples and hazelnuts or a cup of cream of broccoli soup."

A man at a nearby table held up his empty drink glass and Sandi scurried off toward the bar in search of another Wild Christmas or something about as palatable.

Selena glanced around the room, where normal citizens, some with shopping bags, were clustered around tables or stuffed into booths. She listened to bits of conversation over the soft music, country-western ballads whispering through the speakers that battled with the loud thrum of the furnace and hiss of the fryer whenever the doors to the kitchen opened. As upscale as Sandi wanted to make the place, most of the patrons ordered steaks, burgers and fresh-cut fries or onion rings.

". . . what kind of a monster would do it? My goodness. This was such a nice town," a woman wearing a gray wig and large gold cross around her neck said to the man seated opposite her. Their meal finished, they were lingering over two cups of coffee and sharing a slice of coconut cake.

". . . if ya ask me, we should get ourselves a posse goin', search the hills ourselves." The man, waiting for his new drink, was already a little flushed and full of Old West bluster. "We all got guns around here. Maybe

it's time to take justice into our own hands. . . . Damned
police . . . Aaah, thank ya, dear," he said to Sandi as she
deposited the fresh glass onto the table in front of him.
He picked it up and nodded. "These are real good. Real
good."

"I heard they were tortured and tied to trees with
some kind of weird Satanic symbol cut into the bark."
Another woman, wearing a hand-quilted jacket and
dour expression and seated at a table not far from Alvarez's, was leaning over the remains of her buffalo
steak special and stage-whispering to her friend.

"Who would think, here, in Grizzly Falls?" her companion replied with the kind of relish that meant she
was savoring every tidbit of gossip cast her way.

Alvarez turned her attention away.

Who indeed?

For years, she'd hoped to be part of an investigation
of a major case, one that would get her juices flowing,
one that would offer some recognition, one that might
even garner national attention.

But not this one. Not a case where women were held,
probably tortured, then, when the sicko was finished
playing with them, left naked in the woods.

She ordered trout almondine with risotto and spinach
salad, and though she tried, she couldn't take her mind
off the case and the victims. Theresa Charleton had been
left around the twentieth of September, near the cusp of
the astrological signs, just as Chandler had pointed out.
Nina Salvadore a month later, then Wendy Ito and now
Jillian Rivers.

Was the killer really a Zodiac copycat?

Or something else? She glanced around the room
and noted the normal-looking people out for dinner or
drinks. Grizzly Falls had its share of nutcases, but now,
did they have a twisted killer?

He had to know the area. He had to know his victims.

He had to keep them somewhere close by. In a lair of sorts—a cabin, a cave, a basement, a barn, a shed, a damned attic—but hidden away.

And right under your damned nose.

Everyone was working nearly 'round the clock, but still, it was almost as if they were spinning their wheels, getting nowhere in a big hurry.

Pescoli was working on the maps, the FBI was checking files and creating a profile. Alvarez had calls into missing persons departments throughout Montana and the surrounding states. People of interest were being interviewed and re-interviewed. Everyone was going over notes and talking to friends and family, people in the area who might have seen something. The public had been alerted, the sheriff's department asking for citizens to report anything they deemed suspicious. Men, dogs, four-wheel-drive units and helicopters had been searching for more victims or abandoned wrecked vehicles or any damned piece of evidence they could find whenever the weather allowed.

All in all, it was frustrating.

There weren't enough leads and certainly not enough hours in the day.

So much for the glory of a major case, she thought as a sizzling platter was placed in front of her and a country Christmas carol sung by Wynonna Judd filtered through the speakers. So far they had no idea who was wreaking terror on this usually sleepy little Montana town.

She picked up a knife and looked at her plate, where a rainbow trout, head attached, seemed to stare up at her. Everywhere, it seemed, eyes were watching her. The man in the parka outside the restaurant, the other patrons here at Wild Wills, the heads of dead animals mounted high on the walls, the unseen eyes on the street outside and now, even her damned food.

Ah, well. She stared the trout down and cut into it, slicing out a flaky bite.

Bon appetit.

It's time for the next phase.

As I stare at her. I know.

The woman is healing well enough. With little assistance she can walk on her own, make her way through the snow. I think about that, how I will rope her and prod her. She'll try to curse me, of course, as well as herself, but she'll not be able to do anything but what I wish.

As I sit in the cabin, the fire crackling and warm, I'm keyed up and anxious to get rid of her. Keeping her much longer will only up my chances of being detected. The police, as ever, are clueless, but that could change.

I must not underestimate them.

Besides, my note is ready, the letters perfect, the position of the star precise. But then, of course it is: I made the letters as soon as I determined whom the women I would sacrifice would be. And the star alignment—that was preordained.

My nerves are jangled, my mind already playing ahead to the time when she realizes that I've duped her, that I'm not setting her free after all.

That moment—when they realize I have ultimate power over their fate, when I notice not only fear, but a bit of wary resignation in their faces—that is the sweetest moment of all. Nearly orgasmic.

Soon, I tell myself. Only a few more hours.

But I'm tired of pretending, playing a character that is foreign to me.

Flirting.

Laughing.

Appearing easygoing and affable.

It wears on me.

Right now she's sleeping, unaware of what is about to happen, so I have time. And though she doesn't trust me completely, she's accepted that I am her only lifeline; she has no one else to save her.

I saw the change tonight.

And now I can move forward.

The snowmobile is loaded.

Ready.

And the heavens are in agreement. Aren't the stars in perfect position? Oh yes.

Isn't the storm breaking? At least for a while?

There should be just enough time before the next arctic blast bears down on these mountains. Not only for one, but for two. I smile when I think how that will confound the stupid cops. They won't know what to do.

Not that they ever do.

Seeing her asleep on the couch, fire reflecting on her face, I feel just the bit of a tug on my heartstrings, but I won't go there. To feel any kind of emotion would only complicate matters and I could make mistakes.

I could want her.

I could even take the chance of making love to her . . . she's already considering it; I saw it in her eyes today. Yes, she's still frightened, but a little thrilled and beginning to depend upon me.

That's unacceptable.

I walk to the kitchen, where it's cold, the fire in the cooking stove long dead.

I pour myself a drink.

Neat.

Walking back to the doorway into the living room, looking at her, I take a sip.

The warmth of the whiskey trails down my throat and slowly eases into my bloodstream.

I swirl my drink and have another long, warming

swallow. The whiskey calms me and yet heightens my anticipation. I watch her as she lies so innocently.

Like a lamb to the slaughter.

Oh, I could easily start the seduction. Kiss her on that little bend of her neck, let my fingers trail lower, exploring as I hear her take in a swift little breath of anticipation laced with fear.

Almost eagerly, she would let me strip her. And I will, but she'll be expecting more. She'll want my fingers to push her legs apart, to tease her. She'll even hope that I'll lower my head and kiss her there, even caress her with my tongue. Her nipples will harden and she'll moan with desire.

Just like the others.

In the end they all want it.

To feel what it is to have a man dominate them completely. Oh, they, if given the chance, would protest it to their friends, but the truth of the matter is that every one of them wanted me to love them, to fill them, to hold their breasts firmly and press their butts up against my cock. They longed to feel the hardness, the maleness of my erection and wriggle against it. They ached to pant with desire, desire tinged with just enough terror to be erotic. They all hoped I would caress and touch them intimately, strain over their smooth backs, even nip at their necks, to draw just a hint of blood as I stiffened and came inside them, their buttocks and abdomen tightening in reaction, their pussies hot and wet.

Empty, soulless cunts.

As if I would degrade myself.

It would be too easy.

And without meaning.

I study my drink, swirling the amber liquid, before draining the glass and knowing that, at last, the time has come.

It is time for this one to go.

Another is already waiting.

For the dawn.

At the other cabin.

She, too, is about to meet her fate.

She, too, wonders if she can trust me.

If I will have my way with her.

If she will let me.

Smiling to myself, knowing all about them, I take another long swallow.

Silly, stupid girls.

Chapter Sixteen

Where am I?

Jillian's eyes flew open and for a second she was confused. Wrapped in a sleeping bag on an old couch in some kind of cold cabin. . . .

Her mind cleared and in an instant she snapped back to the bizarre reality of her plight. Her neck ached from sleeping in the wrong position and her ribs pained her a little, but when she moved her ankle, it felt slightly better.

The first light of dawn seeped through the windows, casting the furniture in soft, muted shadows.

But MacGregor wasn't in his chair.

She twisted to look over the back of the couch and saw him standing near the large window by the front door. He was staring through the glass panes, his silhouette in dark relief, the sharp angles of his face evident. Bladed cheekbones, a hard, square jaw, eyes cut deep into his head, razor-thin lips set in a hard, uncompromising line.

He stood just to the side of the glass panes, as if he

were being careful to position himself away from direct
viewpoint, so from his vantage point he had a view of
the exterior but no one looking in would see him.

"'Mornin','" he drawled, sliding a glance in her direction. Some of the tension left his face. "You slept hard."

"Did I?"

"Snored," he said.

"Sorry."

"It wasn't that bad." But the corners of his lips relaxed a bit.

"What're you looking for?"

"Whatever's out there. The storm let up last night."

"You hear something? See anything?"

"Nothing I shouldn't." But his gaze returned to the
window. "It's clear enough that I figure this is our shot.
We might just get out of here."

"Really?" She hardly dared believe him as she pulled
herself into a sitting position, wincing a little from the
pain in her ribs.

"We'll see. How're you feeling?"

"Compared to what?"

His lips twitched. "To normal."

"Oh, well." She shook her head. "Not there yet. But I
think I'm good enough to ride a snowmobile, if that's
what you're talking about. I mean, I've got a serious
case of cabin fever." She thought about her mother,
who had to be worried sick about her. Even her sister,
Dusti, was probably wondering what happened to her.
And then there was her cat, left for days with the neighbor. And her work. She pushed herself into an upright
position and onto her feet too quickly. Pain ricocheted
through her ankle. Sucking her breath through her
teeth, she almost yelped. "Damn it all to hell!"

In three swift strides he crossed the room and
grabbed her, a strong arm quickly around her shoul-

ders for support, his body rigid and stiff, a brace. "Hey," he said softly, his breath warm against the back of her head. "You okay?"

From his rug near the fire, Harley lifted his head and gave off a soft, disturbed "woof."

"No," she snapped, her patience dissolving in an instant. She was angry at herself and her damned body and the fact that she was noticing how decidedly male he was. A tiny bit of her mind reminded her it had been a long while since she'd been this close to a man, felt a male touch. "No, I'm not okay with being stuck here in the middle of no-damned-where with a sprained ankle, cracked ribs, bruises up the wazoo. Trapped in a cabin without electricity or phones with a stranger I know nothing, and I mean *nothing*, about." From the corner of her eye she noticed Harley starting to rouse. "Not to mention a dog who hates me."

"I don't think Harley hates—"

She turned so that she could look him squarely in his flinty eyes. "Oh, and let's not forget we think there might be a maniac on the loose, one who shot my car and forced me off the road. So, no, I'm not okay. Not even close to anything resembling okay. In fact, I'm definitely *not* okay at all."

"All right," he said, but a flash of amusement registered in his eyes.

"You're mocking me?"

"What? No."

"You think it's funny?"

"Wouldn't dream of it." He was dead serious again, all humor erased.

"Good. Then let's figure out how to get out of here." She shifted a little, trying to put a bit of space between their bodies.

"I'm working on it."

"Then work faster, would you?" she said, hearing the sting in her words.

"Doing what I can."

"Oh hell." She tried to calm down, but the truth of the matter was that she couldn't. "Sorry to be such a bitch. I'm sick to my back teeth of lying down and just being cooped up here and playing the poor, injured victim. It is *not* my style and . . . Oh, for the love of God," she said, trying to ignore the fact that his breath was ruffling her hair and she could actually smell the maleness of him. How stupid was that? "It's . . . it's just that I've got to do *something*, no, make that *anything*, to get out of here!" It was a struggle to ignore how steel-strong his forearm was, or that his scent was surprisingly clean and subtly male. She turned angry eyes up on him, as if it were his fault he was so sexual in a dark, almost frightening, way. "I'm going nuts. Completely loco. I . . . I have to get out of here! Today!"

One side of his mouth curved in that sexy, disarming smile she didn't dare trust.

And in that moment she realized just how bad she must look. She hadn't showered in days, her face was still bruised, though she was lucky that she hadn't lost any teeth or broken her jaw. Well, lucky was relative, she supposed, but it was really ironic that when she looked her worst she found this stranger so ridiculously attractive. Which was just plain idiotic on her part.

Angry with herself and her female fantasies—fantasies that were certainly running amok—she pushed herself away from him. Once they weren't touching, all sense of intimacy between them vanished, she balanced on her crutch and tried to pull herself together. She had to stay focused. They both did.

Yawning, Harley climbed to his feet, stretched and trotted over to MacGregor's side.

"Time to go out?" MacGregor patted the dog's head, then, with a final look at the ever-lightening landscape through the large window, said, "Come on, then. Out the back." He snagged his jacket from its hook, then walked to the kitchen, the spaniel trotting eagerly behind him.

Watching as he disappeared through the archway separating the kitchen from the living area, Jillian tamped down her temper. She had woken up on the wrong side of the bed, or, in this case, the couch. It wasn't his fault that she'd been in the accident.

Not his fault. . . .

Then whose?

She shook her head. No one she knew. If MacGregor were a killer bent on hurting her, he would have done it already. True, there was no reason to restrain her, as she couldn't walk far on her own, but he hadn't so much as hurled a harsh word at her or even done anything that suggested he wanted to harm her. He'd left her with a loaded gun, hadn't he?

She wondered about him, this person who had taken another man's life. Why had he chosen to live here all alone? Who was the boy in the picture? Did he have a wife? A fiancé? A girlfriend tucked away somewhere? Or was he one of those true loners who didn't need the companionship of other people, a mountain man?

Sighing, Jillian made her way to the bathroom. A bucket was filled with water, so she was able to use the toilet despite the fact that the pump wasn't working. Each night, MacGregor filled several buckets with snow and dragged them into the house so that the snow would melt and they would have water to drink and use to cook and wash. Hot water was at a premium, heated in a pot on the woodstove or a kettle nestled in the coals of the fireplace. But with that water he'd cooked everything from instant oatmeal to pre-packaged soup and dehydrated casseroles. He'd even managed to bake cornbread in the oven of the woodstove. It had been burned around the edges, but Jillian had been so hungry, she'd devoured two thick slabs.

Despite their isolation MacGregor had been prepared and they hadn't gone hungry. But still, the cabin was a long shot from a five-star hotel, or even a one-star hotel, for that matter.

Jillian glanced longingly at the tub shower and imagined how it would feel to have hot water cascading over her sore muscles or streaming through her hair as she shampooed it.

Now that would be pure heaven.

She imagined herself up to her neck in warm, scented water, candles burning, her skin soft with fragrant bath oil. She would close her eyes and . . . MacGregor would take a cloth and gently bathe her, his fingers grazing her skin, touching her breasts and lower, until her nipples would pucker and her breath would get lost deep in her throat as he worked over her slick skin. . . .

She made a sound of frustration low in her throat.

What was she thinking?

Cabin fever was addling her brain, making her dream of sex with a virtual stranger.

Angry with herself, she hitched back to the kitchen, found a saucepan and dipped a little water from the pot simmering on the stove. Balancing the pan carefully, she returned to the adjoining bathroom, mixed a little cold water from a bucket into the hot water, then, using a cloth, washed her face, hands, then the parts of her body that felt the worst. Her hair would have to wait, though she did run a little water through it, using a bit of soap to work up a small lather, then rinsing it as best she could. A salon shampoo it wasn't, but she felt better having clean hair. She finger-combed the tangles and found a brush to separate the strands.

"Bitterroot beauty at its finest," she told her reflection, where bruises still lingered beneath her skin.

Opening the door, she found MacGregor and the dog in the kitchen. He must've been there a while, as he was dressed only in his sweater and jeans, his jacket nowhere in sight.

"Someone cleaned up," he observed.

"About time, don't you think?"

He nodded. "You look good."

She nearly laughed. "Compared to what? Quasimoto or Jabba the Hut or Mr. Hyde? Are you kidding?"

"Not kidding, especially compared to what you looked like when I found you in the car, after the accident."

"Not a high standard, MacGregor."

"Maybe not, but really, you look . . . a whole lot better. Now, I thought you could use some coffee," he said as calmly as if they were an old married couple with nothing to do but read the newspaper together.

"Sounds like heaven." As she heard herself, she inwardly cringed. Dear God, was she actually flirting with him? What in the world was wrong with her?

"You'd better reserve judgment until you've had a taste." Opening a cupboard near the stove, he found a plastic tub of dark ground coffee. "Pre-roasted, pre-ground and vacuum-sealed," he explained. "Can't beat Folgers, no matter what the boutique shops would like you to think." He looked at the coffeemaker, sitting uselessly on a scarred wooden counter. "Since we've got no power, we're going to have to do this the old-fashioned way."

"Sounds perfect," Jillian said as his eyes caught hers. Her breath caught in her throat at the mysteries deep in his eyes.

I'm in trouble, she thought, but she wasn't afraid.

* * *

Her cell phone rang as Alvarez locked the door to her Jeep and headed into the office. One glance at the digital readout and she braced herself as her mother's number appeared on the screen. She thought about not answering, but that would only put off the inevitable.

"Good morning, Mom." Carrying her laptop in one hand and feeling the bite of the wind, she hurried toward the brick building.

"Hi, honey."

Despite the phone at her ear, Selena found her mind skipping ahead to her work day. At least it wasn't snowing, and overnight, the plows had made significant progress on the roads. Maybe the helicopters could fly today, get airborne and survey the surrounding area. Maybe, just maybe, today was the day the case would break wide open.

Then again . . .

"You're working today, aren't you?"

Alvarez didn't answer.

"*Dios*, Selena. It's not even eight in the morning. On a Sunday. The Sunday before Christmas. You should be in bed or getting ready for mass."

"I don't work by the clock, you know that." She shouldered her way into the building, nodding to the single clerk from the night shift who was manning the front desk.

"You work too much."

"So you say."

"So *everyone* says. Your brother Estevan, he's a policeman, decorated, and he says you don't have to work the hours you do."

In Alvarez's opinion Estevan was lazy, but she wouldn't say so to her mother. "What's up, Mom?" she asked as she made her way to her cubicle and flipped the switch on her desk lamp.

"I was hoping that you'd changed your mind. That you were coming home for Christmas."

In her mind's eye Selena flashed on "home": the two-storied house four blocks off Highway 99 in Woodburn, Oregon, where she'd grown up with five brothers and two sisters. The three girls had shared one small room under the eaves of the sloped roof. The boys had been spread out, three in the room across the hall, the two eldest in separate rooms in the basement. Her parents had been on the main floor. The house had been noisy and crowded, and for the first fourteen years of her life, a haven.

And later, hell.

But at Christmas, the house had been decorated with lights on every eave and gutter, a hand-painted life-sized creche displayed in the front yard, a live tree filling the space in front of the living room window, her aunt Biatriz pounding out carols on the piano while her grandmother and mother cooked traditional Mexican fare along with a turkey dinner. Everything from mashed potatoes and roast beef to steamed tamales.

"I'm sorry," Alvarez lied as she sat in her desk chair, "I can't get away."

"It's Christmas, *niña.*"

"I know, Mom, but we've got a serial killer on the loose here. I thought it would have made the papers there."

"But you must get a day off."

"Not this year."

"You're telling me that no one's going away for the holidays? I don't believe it."

"I just can't this year. Give my love to everyone," Alvarez said, refusing to let her mother guilt her into it.

"You always put up the piñata for the little ones."

"Not this year. But Lydia, she'll do it." Alvarez did feel a little pang of regret when she thought of her younger sister. Lydia, she would miss, and maybe Eduardo. Maybe. "I'll call and talk to everyone."

"From where? What will you be doing?"

God only knows. "I'll be with friends." Again a lie. She didn't have any plans for the day. She figured she'd work here, be paid overtime and celebrate at home in her pajamas with a movie and bowl of popcorn. That alone sounded like heaven, even if she had no one to sit beside her.

"You need your family, Selena," her mother cautioned.

"Of course I do. I love you, Mom, but I really have to go."

"God be with you, child," Juanita said, and whispered a quick prayer in Spanish before hanging up.

"Guilt trip, guilt trip, guilt trip," Alvarez told herself as she fired up her computer and clicked onto the images of the dead women and the letters left with their bodies. Using a computer program, she aligned the letters one over the other and saved the positions of the stars. What if this guy were trying to tell them something not only from the precise letters, but from the stars, as well?

Once she'd placed the stars on one screen, she used a computer program to help her identify which constellation, if any, the stars could be a part of. Unfortunately there were dozens of potential constellations.

"Because we don't have enough data," she thought, wincing inside. The more victims, the more clues left behind. Eventually, if the stars were part of an astrological grouping, they would be identified, just like, given enough letters in the message, the police would be able to figure out what the killer was trying to say.

Given enough time, enough letters and enough dead women.

"Damn," she muttered, pushing her chair back from the desk. It was all so sick. For the first time since walking into the nearly deserted room, she heard the sound of music drifting from the speakers. The notes of "Let It Snow" wafted around her and she almost laughed at the absurdity of the situation as she heard Bing Crosby's voice croon the final words of the song.

She glanced through the windows to the white parking lot. Yeah, the weather outside was sure as hell frightful, but there wasn't anything the least bit cozy or warm about being in the office at Christmastime.

Balanced against the counter, Jillian observed MacGregor as he went through the motions of making coffee "the old-fashioned way." He started by tossing some ground coffee into a lined basket that he balanced over the glass pot from the coffeemaker. Then he grabbed a tiny saucepan, dipped it into the hot water in the pot on the stove, and poured slowly streaming scalding water through the ground beans and filter.

Within seconds, dark liquid dripped into the waiting pot.

"Camp coffee," she said as the scent of brewing coffee filled the room.

He glanced over his shoulder at her, a spark of humor in his eyes. "I do this on the trail a lot. It impresses all the city women."

"Of course it does," she said, and couldn't help but smile. "*I'm* impressed."

He chuckled and for the first time she saw a different side to this intense man. When all the water had soaked through the grounds, he poured them each a cup. "I've got sugar and powdered creamer."

"I'm good with black. Cheers," she said, and clicked the edge of her chipped mug to his.

"Here's lookin' at ya."

The tension of the last few days seemed to evaporate for a few minutes. Even Harley, who had been ever-watchful, relaxed in a ball on the kitchen rag rug and closed his eyes. "I think he's accepting me," she said of the dog, and bent down to pet his scruffy head. The dog opened tired eyes and yawned, but didn't growl or pull away.

"He's really just a lover," MacGregor said, then, as if noticing her balancing on her crutch, added, "let's go into the other room. I'll carry this for you." He took the cup from her hand and followed her into the main living area of the cabin.

"Did you check outside again when you took out the dog?"

He nodded. "Nothing to indicate anyone was out there."

"You're sure?" she asked, and stared for a second through the icy panes. The storm had abated, the snow in thick drifts, even having blown onto the porch.

"I'm not sure of anything. If someone was there last night, the snow would have covered their tracks. But yeah, I think we're alone."

Which didn't mean she should be comforted, she reminded herself. She had to trust him. Damn but she *wanted* to trust him, but she still had to be wary. Harley, toenails clicking on the hardwood and stone, returned to the living room and his spot near the hearth.

MacGregor handed her back the mug of coffee and she cradled it in both hands, its warmth seeping through her skin and into her bones. She propped her foot on the coffee table.

He nodded toward her bound ankle. "It's not broken."

"So you said."

Their eyes locked as she remembered the one-sided conversation when she'd feigned sleep.

"So you were awake," he prodded.

"Yeah." She saw no reason to lie now; he knew the truth.

"I thought so." He took a long sip, but his gaze, over the rim of his cup, never left her. "But you did a pretty good job of faking sleep."

"Years of practice as a teenager." She cringed inwardly as she remembered how many times she'd sneaked out while pretending to be asleep. She'd pushed the car out of the driveway and cruised around with her friends. It had been foolish and stupid, and her older, uptight, do-everything-by-the-book sister, Dusti, had never stopped reminding her of what an idiot she'd been.

"A rebel?"

"Or just a moron. Take your pick."

He grinned and she found herself warming to him all the more. Maybe they did have something in common, a rebellious streak that couldn't quite be tamed. "You left me the crutch," she said, bringing the conversation back to the here and now, where the fire crackled, the dog snored and the warm scent of coffee permeated the room.

"So you could get up if you woke. I knew the ankle wouldn't support you and I keep a set of crutches in case anyone gets hurt on one of my expeditions. Just until I can get them to a clinic or hospital or call for help."

"Speaking of which, have you tried to call out lately?"

He sent her a you've-got-to-be-kidding look. "What do you think?"

That's the problem, I don't know what to think.

As if reading her thoughts, he walked to his jacket and unsnapped a pocket.

"Here." Retrieving a small phone, he pushed a button to turn it on and tossed it to her. She caught it with her good hand.

"Give it a try. As I said, cell service is spotty here at best, and the battery's low, but if you can get through, more power to you."

She held the phone as if it were a ticket to heaven, but as the tiny cell turned on, a picture of Harley on the screen, she saw the lack of service, and try as she might, no pushing of any buttons worked. "Dead as a doornail," she admitted, and tossed the useless piece of technology back to him.

"Your family is probably going out of their minds with worry."

She nodded slowly, thinking of her mother. Linnette, when she finally figured out Jillian was missing, would be on the phone to the city, county and state cops. Only after having already called the FBI. But, of course, her mother probably didn't know she was missing. Yet. A fact she decided to keep to herself. There was just no reason to tip off MacGregor that no one was looking for her. Better to let him think there was a national search going on.

"As soon as we can establish some kind of communication or are able to get out of here, we'll call them."

"*I'll* call them."

"However you want to do it." Again the smile, though this time there was the tiniest bit of hardness to it.

She thought of the photographs she'd found in the boot vase, the snapshots of a blond boy. "So, while you were out earlier, I did a little looking around."

One dark eyebrow cocked, encouraging her.

"You don't have any pictures displayed around here."

"The way I like it."

"What about your family?"

"I thought I told you. I'm not close to them."

"But there is a boy you care about," she said, deciding it was time to get to the bottom of some of her questions. "I found a couple of pictures of a little boy, over there, in the bookcase." She pointed to the spot where the vase sat.

MacGregor's lips thinned and, beneath the shadow of his beard, white lines bracketed his mouth.

"You know the boy I'm talking about."

He hesitated, then gave a slight nod. Raw emotion crossed his features and a muscle jumped at the edge of his jaw. "His name was David," he said, his voice low. "He was my son."

She waited, wishing she hadn't brought it up, hearing the "was" for what it meant.

"He's dead."

"I'm sorry," she said.

"You didn't know him."

"I mean, I'm sorry for your pain. You said you weren't married . . . that you didn't have . . ."

"I'm not and I don't. My wife and son are dead. Killed in a head-on collision, one of those freak things. No one was drinking, no one really knows what happened, but for some reason, maybe she was distracted, Callie's car crossed the center line and went right into the path of a semi."

"Oh God."

"I was supposed to drive them to the school open house that night, but I was too busy, caught up in work, so I called and told her I'd meet them there. I'm supposed to take solace in the fact that they died instantly. Like that's some consolation. Anyway, it happened a long time ago and I don't like talking about it or thinking about it."

"That's why you don't display any pictures."

"Yeah." He was reaching for his jacket.

"And you became a hermit."

"Not quite." Checking his pockets, he walked to the door.

"I'm sorry."

"So you said."

"I know, but—"

"Let's get back to what's happening here and now. In your snooping, did you find your things?"

"My things?"

He walked past her to the large bookcase, opened a lower cupboard drawer and pulled out a familiar-looking overnight bag.

How had she missed it earlier? She'd thought she'd gone through every cupboard, but then, she had been woozy. At the sight of her bag, she had the insane urge to break down completely, which was just plain stupid. She'd barely thought about the suitcase until now, which surely was a testament to her unclear mental state. It was nuts, but her nerves were strung tight, her body ached and she looked and felt like hell. Seeing the overnight case she'd packed days ago brought into sharp focus the fact that her real life was light years away, as well as the undeniable fact that she might never be a part of that life again.

"I thought you might want to change clothes," he said as he placed the bag near her.

She cleared her throat. "That would be nice."

"I'm not sure you can get any pants over your ankle."

"I'll see."

He hesitated. "Do you need some help? I could—"

"No!" Her reaction was swift, her voice louder than she'd intended. "Sorry. No, I think I can handle it myself."

His eyes narrowed slightly. "You know, I think I should change my diagnosis. You're getting around pretty well for having cracked ribs. There's a chance, if you're lucky, you might just have bruised them. Trust me, they would still hurt like hell."

"Believe me, they do."

"But if they were cracked, you wouldn't be able to move like you do."

"Good." It didn't matter if they were cracked or broken, they still pained her. "If you don't mind, would you just carry my bag into the bedroom?"

He did as she asked, and she climbed to her feet and eased into the bedroom, where she closed the door and, with more trouble than she thought possible, changed her underwear and bra and slid cautiously into a heavy-necked sweater. Her ribs ached with each movement, but she was determined to get through the ordeal. Her jeans were a little more difficult, but she did have one pair of boot-cuts that were slightly too big and she managed to pull them over the bulge of tape around her ankle.

Afterward, she even slapped on some lipstick and a bit of mascara and, using the small mirror over a beat-up bureau, surveyed her image. It was better, although her skin was still greenish and scraped, her eyes sunken.

Half an hour later she emerged, returning to the living room, where the fire was crackling loudly and Mac-Gregor was stacking more wood on the hearth. The pile was now nearly three feet high.

She knew why.

"You're leaving," she said, realizing he was trying to make it easy for her to keep the cabin warm while he was gone. A black pot simmered on the coals and packets of dried soup and oatmeal were stacked on a table near the fireplace.

"If I don't go now, I might not get another chance. I'm determined to find a way to get you out of here. If I can make a phone call, I'll do that. If I have to saw through some of the trees to open up the roads, then I'll be a little longer. In any event, I should be back in a few hours. At least before dusk."

The thought of being in the cabin alone, just sitting and waiting, was difficult. But she didn't have any choice.

"I'm leaving Harley with you, and there's the gun in the closet."

She nodded.

He walked back to the spot where she was still standing, balanced on her crutch. "I'll be back before you know it," he said, and then, to her surprise, he brushed the barest of kisses against her cheek. "Hang tough."

Chapter Seventeen

Help me!

Oh God, please, someone help me!

Rona struggled, fighting the cold, battling the constricting rope that lashed her to the tree, but the more she squirmed, the tighter her binds cut into her flesh. She tried to scream, to yell, to let someone know what he was doing, but the gag, more like a damned muzzle, held back her voice and the only sounds she heard were muffled cries, the frantic beating of her heart, the rush of the wind and her mind screaming at her that she'd been a fool. A fool of the worst order.

How could she have trusted him, this monster who was binding her to the rough bark of a tree? He'd slid her clothes off and she hadn't resisted. Had he drugged her? Had she been paralyzed with fear? Or had she felt so desperate and alone that she longed for his attention?

Oh God, she'd been an idiot, letting him skim off her clothes, allowing him to kiss her skin and then, when she was caught in an instant between temptation and fear, slip the noose around her neck. Only then did she realize how deadly was his trap.

Please, God, help me, she prayed, tears falling from her eyes as the frigid snow, hard with crystals, bit at her skin, causing it to pimple with the cold.

Surely he didn't mean to leave her here.

This had to be a test, that was all.

She heard him grunt as he pulled on the restraints and her back was yanked hard against the rough bark of this solitary fir tree. In front of her was a meadow, now covered in snow. She blinked hard, trying to dislodge the white flakes, hoping to see a way out of this horrible, freezing situation.

"Let me go! Don't do this. Please, please!" she cried, but her words were mute and dull, nearly unintelligible. And they were falling on deaf ears.

He'd known he was going to kill her.

All along.

And yet she'd believed him when he'd said he would take her to safety, that as soon as the storm lifted he would get her to a hospital or find a phone and call 911. Or . . .

And you fell for it. You dumb little fool!

She began to cry again, tears streaming from her eyes, blurring her vision and tracking down her icy cheeks. God, she was cold. Colder than she'd ever been in her life. Her bare nipples felt raw and puckered and there was no source of heat in her body. Even her blood felt sluggish and thick, and for the first time her feet began to go numb.

Frostbite.

Exposure.

Killed by Mother Nature and her own stupidity.

If only Connor was here . . . he would help her . . . *Connor, oh love, what . . . what have I done?* Blackness pulled at her consciousness and she tried to stay awake, to take one last look at the bastard's handsome face, but her thoughts were leaving her and she thought she saw

Connor standing before her, whispering that she'd only gotten what she'd deserved . . . then there was someone else . . . a woman . . . "Mom?" she said to the apparition because, really, her mother had been dead for nearly three years . . . but . . .

The darkness came again, swallowing her and she was vaguely aware of the sound of pounding. As if someone were knocking on the door. "I'll get it, Mama," she said, though no words escaped her lips and her mouth tasted bad. "I'll get it. . . ."

Pescoli glanced down at her paperwork and stifled a yawn. What she wouldn't give for a hit of nicotine to sharpen her focus.

"Son of a bitch!" Sheriff Grayson stormed out of his office, swearing a blue streak.

Every muscle around Pescoli's spine went rigid and her stomach clenched tight as her fists. It was Saturday afternoon, the skies had cleared in the last few hours and several of the detectives had come into the office to catch up on paperwork or go over their notes. She tossed her pen aside and pushed away from her desk. "Let me guess," she said, already knowing the answer. "Someone found another DB in the forest?"

"Yep," Grayson said, his face muscles taut, his jaw rigid with barely suppressed rage. He was already stuffing his arms through his jacket, his sidearm visible in its shoulder holster. "We didn't get the bastard soon enough."

"What?" Brewster, who had heard the conversation through the open door to his office, strode into the hallway, his jacket in hand. "Are you shittin' me?"

"Wouldn't do it," Grayson said as the undersheriff reached him.

"Well, fuck!" Cort Brewster's ruddy face flushed in

fury as he tugged his jacket over his sidearm. "That god-damned cocksucker."

Alvarez, whose cubicle was on the other side of the partition from Pescoli's, was already stuffing her hair into a cap as she hurried down the hallway between the desks to catch up with the rest of the little posse.

Through the open door of Grayson's office, Sturgis poked his head into the hallway and gave a nervous little bark.

"Stay!" Grayson ordered as his dog started to put a paw outside the office. In a gentler voice, Grayson said, "I'll be back soon, boy."

With a dejected look, the Lab turned around and, casting a final woebegone glance over his shoulder, eased back into the office, where a dog bed filled with cedar shavings was tucked not far from a heat register.

Pescoli grabbed her jacket, purse and pistol. "Jillian Rivers?" she asked as she followed the sheriff.

Grayson nodded sharply. "Looks like the bastard got to her. Same MO."

"Poor woman." Pescoli couldn't imagine the terror that must've been the victim's companion as she was forced to walk naked through the forest and, unable to fight, was bound to a tree to face the elements. "Who found her?"

"A couple out hiking called it in. They found her in a clearing up near Cougar Pass. A dead woman roped to a tree, just like the others. Scared them spitless." Grayson's eyes were haunted, guilt and frustration evident in the lines around the corners of his mouth. "We were just too damned late to save her."

No one tried platitudes.

As they strode through the building, their boots treading heavy on the flooring, he said to Brewster,

"Call the state police. See if they can put up some helicopters to view the surrounding area, take pictures, see what they can come up with before a new storm hits."

Pescoli added, "Have them make note of any cabins where smoke is rising from the chimneys. They're out of power up in that area, and if our killer is around, he'll need some kind of heat."

"He might have a generator."

"Then he's buying fuel for it somewhere, propane or diesel, and lots of it."

"We've already got calls into distributors in a hundred-mile radius," Alvarez said.

"Then have choppers look for disturbances in the snow. See if it's melted around any of the cabins that are supposed to be vacant. Generators give off exhaust and heat and noise. Maybe someone's heard one running that shouldn't be. And let's bring out the dogs. Maybe they can finally get a hit or lead us to where the bastard is." Grayson shoved open the glass door so hard, it banged against the building.

The sun was nearly blinding. Beams dazzled and bounced off the mantle of white, while the chain on the flagpole clanged in the wind that caused the Stars and Stripes to wave. Clumps of snow shuddered and fell from branches of trees planted near the parking lot.

Pescoli unlocked her Jeep and slid behind the wheel while Alvarez climbed into the passenger side. Regan was battling a slight hangover from one too many margaritas and not much sleep. Since Jeremy spent the night at his friend's house, Pescoli had spent a lot of hours with Nate.

All of them worth it.

That man had a way of turning her inside out. Of course they'd ended up in bed; they always did. And though the lovemaking put a smile on Pescoli's face, there was sometimes a hangover to dim the glow. This

morning she didn't have time to remember the way
Nate's muscular legs stretched out over hers, or how he
grabbed the cheeks of her butt as he pulled her close to
him. At least not now. Her concentration had to be
sharp and on the damned murders.

She slid a pair of sunglasses onto her nose and, following Grayson's rig, drove out of the lot and into the
hills.

"Did you have a chance to see the paper today?" Alvarez asked as they drove past the "Welcome to Grizzly
Falls" sign on the north end of town.

"Something interesting?"

"You might say, and the reason Grayson's on a tear."

"Something more than finding dead women lashed
to trees in his jurisdiction?"

"Someone leaked details to the press."

"What?" Pescoli couldn't believe it. "*What* details?
They already reported that the cars had been wrecked,
probably shot at."

"Now they know about the notes. Not all the details,
but that the victims were tied to trees, a star carved over
their heads. Before, there wasn't any mention of the
notes."

Pescoli's fingers tightened over the wheel and the headache at the base of her neck began to throb. One of the
advantages the sheriff's department had was knowing
the true nature of the crimes, of keeping details out of the
press, so they could sort out the real culprit from the
nutcases who wanted their fifteen minutes of fame. Up
in this neck of the woods, there were plenty of idiots
who might want a bit of notoriety by claiming participation in the killings.

"Who talked?"

Alvarez snorted. "Unknown at this time. But my
money's on Ivor Hicks. That guy can't keep his mouth
shut."

"I know we can't get through to Ivor, but maybe his family can."

"He's only got a son, and I think Bill tries to keep his distance from the old man. Wouldn't you?"

"I'd move away," Pescoli said.

"Would you?" Alvarez shook her head. "People stay where they want to. Near family, even if it's not that great."

Pescoli thought about it. She was still in the same town as her ex. Maybe Alvarez had a point. Or did she? "You moved."

"Yeah, well, the job opportunities where I grew up were limited."

"Not like here in Grizzly Falls." Pescoli turned off the main road and started along the uphill grade leading into the mountains.

Alvarez didn't respond, but that didn't surprise Pescoli. Her partner was always touchy whenever her family was mentioned. She'd never discussed it with Pescoli, but it was obvious there was bad blood in that family. Real bad.

"So someone's got to keep Ivor from spouting off to the press."

"If it was Ivor."

"Who else?" Pescoli asked.

"Now there's an interesting question," Alvarez stated. "Who else indeed? Anyway, the point is, someone did the honors and Grayson is *not* amused."

"I'll bet." Pescoli kept the sheriff's Suburban in sight while half-listening to the police-band conversation crackling over the hum of the Jeep's engine as it climbed the steep mountain road, tires digging into the sanded, packed snow. Tree trunks, flanking the side of the road, were obscured by mounds of ice and snow that had been tossed to the side by the heavy blades of the plows that worked these hills.

They passed no cars as the convoy of vehicles headed to the latest killing ground.

Pescoli tried to picture this part of Cougar Pass, about fifteen miles out of town. It was accessible only by an old mining road, which was buried in snow but protected enough that they would be able to trudge the hundred yards to the spot where the body had been left.

"We're gonna need boots and shovels today," she said. "This guy sure likes distant locales."

Tramping through drifts of snow that rose above her knees, Alvarez thought of her siblings, how, years ago, they had all prayed for a huge snowstorm, a snow day. Unfortunately, it didn't happen too often in Woodburn, Oregon.

Field agents from the FBI arrived as she was signing in at the crime scene, which had been secured by Pete Watershed, the first detective to arrive. As a group, they made their way down the snowy road and saw, as the hiking couple had reported, a dead woman strapped to a tree. The people who'd called 911 were huddled in their SUV and agreed to wait to be interviewed by the detectives.

"God have mercy," Alvarez said, and made the sign of the cross over her chest. A professed woman of science, she always fell back on the religion of her youth when she was faced with the darkest parts of human depravity.

Selena Alvarez believed in God, maybe not as deeply as her grandmother Rosarita had wished, but she believed and made no excuses for it. At times she'd gotten sideways glances from Brewster and Watershed but ignored them. Pescoli, at least, had never commented or acted like anything was out of the ordinary.

Now, as she stared at the body of the dead woman, she needed the tiniest connection to her faith, though reassurance was fleeting as she stood in the bitter cold and stared at the dead, naked woman roped to a solitary fir tree. She was petite and Caucasian, though her skin was tinged blue. Her short blond hair hung in frozen strands. Her head, covered with snow, tilted forward. Bruises were evident on her body, the heavy ropes having cut into her skin.

"Sweet Jesus," Brett Gage whispered, his expression grim.

"Not pretty, is it?" Pescoli was serious as she studied the gruesome scene. "God, I'd love to nail the psycho who did this."

Stephanie Chandler eyed the tracks in the snow. "Maybe we'll catch a break this time. Maybe the dogs can pick up a scent."

"Let's hope," Alvarez whispered. So far, the search-and-rescue dogs had proved useless, but today the weather was clearer, as were visible tracks leading to and from the clearing on the far side of the woods. "What's over there?"

"No access road, at least not one that's used, but there was a private lane leading to a mining operation that hasn't been in use for decades." Gage had pulled out a map and was folding it so that he could view the area where they were located.

"Any of the buildings left?" Alvarez asked.

Gage shook his head. "Don't know."

"One way to find out."

"I'll go," Gage offered. Giving the tracks wide berth so as not to disturb any piece of evidence, he started toward the stand of pines at the far edge of the clearing, the area from where the tracks appeared.

"The guy wouldn't be so stupid as to be nearby." Alvarez was sure.

"Really?" Pescoli viewed her partner through amber-colored sunglasses. "Everyone makes mistakes. Even psychos."

True enough, Alvarez thought.

"Not this guy." Stephanie Chandler was standing a few feet away, her blond hair tucked into a navy blue FBI hat, her gaze taking in every inch of the crime scene. "He's too precise. He's worked this out in his head a million times. No mistakes."

Pescoli didn't back down. "They make mistakes. It's what trips them up. So you'd better hope our guy isn't flawless or we're in for a world of hurt."

Chandler said, "They only make mistakes when they're pressured. We haven't been able to do that with this guy."

"Yet," Pescoli said. "We will."

"We'd better." Chandler was eyeing the surrounding woods.

"I don't think she's been dead long," Watershed said. "The body's warmer than the others and no snow is covering the tracks. Maybe the dogs can come up with something." He squinted, his gaze following Gage and the broken path in the snow, the killer's trail. "He went out the same way he went in."

"Just like before," Alvarez noted.

The crime scene team arrived and got down to business, collecting any kind of evidence from the body and surrounding area, taking pictures of the scene and victim from all angles, searching for anything the killer might have left behind.

"She's not Jillian Rivers," Alvarez said abruptly.

Pescoli nodded. "She doesn't look like the picture on her driver's license. The physical description's all wrong. Rivers is around five seven and weighs around a hundred and thirty and this woman couldn't be more than five one or two, barely tips the scale at a hundred pounds."

Alvarez braced herself as she studied the corpse. "Rivers has hazel eyes and long dark brown hair; this one's blond. Could have been dyed and cut, I suppose, but I don't think so. Looks natural." The victim's pubic hair was a dark shade of blond and her dead, sightless eyes were bright blue. "Eye color is wrong, too. And check out the note."

WAR T   SC   I N

"If our theory is right, then Jillian Rivers's initials should be somewhere in the message. There's an R, which could be for Rivers, but no J. Instead we've got an A." Alvarez shook her head. "This isn't right, unless he's changed his MO."

"No way," Chandler said, shaking her head as she studied the scene from twenty feet away. "He wouldn't. He's toying with us, yes, but trying to tell us something. He wants us to figure out what it is, so he can prove how smart he is."

Alvarez watched as Mikhail, a forensic technician, removed the note with tweezers, gently placing it in a plastic bag, and held it out to her. "Did you want a closer look?"

"Thanks." She pinched the edge of the bag and stepped away from the woman's frozen body, grateful for the chance to turn her back on the gruesome death scene. Although she had learned to hide it, especially on the job, Selena Alvarez struggled when it came time to process violent crime scenes. Especially crimes against women. Her cross to bear, as her grandmother Rosarita would say.

She liked to think that turmoil gave her the edge when it came to catching a psycho like this, a man who made a game out of killing.

The bastard.

It was also the reason she'd avoided employment in forensics. Much as she appreciated the science of it, she couldn't stomach it. Now, as the crime scene unit did their job, carefully bagging the woman's frozen hands, checking her body, combing the lone fir tree and the surrounding area, Alvarez stared at the most recent note, determined to work the case from this angle. Whether it was meant to be unscrambled, translated or decoded, she wasn't sure, but she sure as hell was going to spend some time trying to figure it out.

It was like finding a needle in a haystack.

Pescoli frowned as she eyed the rugged terrain that surrounded the latest crime scene. Mountains, ravines, frozen creek beds, curving rim roads. They'd been searching that area for Jillian Rivers, to no avail. Now the search would be on for this woman's vehicle.

If the weather held.

A goddamned needle in a haystack.

She thought about the topographical maps at the office. Maybe she could use her computer program and come up with potential sites for the next killing ground.

There were dozens of small meadows in these mountains and it would take forever to search them all out, but what choice did they have?

"At least we know Jillian Rivers isn't dead and we missed her. There's no J on the note. All the initials have bodies attached," Alvarez pointed out.

"Yeah, but it doesn't mean she's safe. He might have her ready to go," Pescoli said.

Alvarez stepped closer to the tracks. "True, but he was here in the past few hours. These are fresh, not covered in snow, and the weather's been clear only a few hours."

"Not much consolation there. The prick could be doing Jillian Rivers now for all we know," Pescoli said.

The *whomp, whomp, whomp* of helicopter rotor blades could be heard approaching. Already, it seemed, the state police were going airborne to search the area. Good, Pescoli thought, they might be able to see something from the air that would take days of good weather and a lot of luck to see on the ground.

"What the hell does the note mean?" Pescoli asked, staring over her partner's shoulder at the latest note.

"Beats me." Brewster glowered at the block letters and weird star.

"How about 'WAR TO SCIENCE'?" Watershed asked. "Maybe this guy's a religious nut. Maybe this is a sacrifice, some kind of rite."

"Satanic rite," Pescoli added.

"Could be 'WART SCIENCE.' " Although his face was red from the cold, Pete Watershed wasn't about to give up. "Or 'WAR OF THE SCIENTISTS' or even 'WARY OF THIS COIN.' "

"Then where would Jillian Rivers's initials fit in?" Alvarez asked. "I mean, assuming she's next." She glanced up at Pescoli. "The psycho must still have her."

"Son of a bitch," Pescoli whispered. "This guy just won't give up."

"Or . . . 'WAR OF THE SCHOOL INSTITUTIONS' . . . Hell, if that's the case, we got a whole lot more victims." Watershed was worried, scratching his jaw.

"Of course he won't give up." Stephanie Chandler walked the perimeter of the crime scene. "He can't. He lives for this." She read the note at a distance. "If anything, he'll escalate. We need to be looking for a missing person with the initials AR or RA in her early twenties. Who found this body again?" She turned her attention to Sheriff Grayson, who was standing twenty feet from the lone fir tree, hands stuffed in his pockets, lips flat against his teeth, as he eyed the dead woman.

"Eldon and Mischa York, who were out hiking. They have a summer cabin out here and came for a week. Their story is that they'd been cooped up with the storm and took advantage of the break in the weather to get a little exercise. The good news is that they saw the scene and all the footprints and hightailed it back to their cabin, climbed in their four-wheel-drive and drove to a spot where they had cell phone service, then called 911." Grayson finally turned his attention to the FBI agent. "Both of 'em are waiting in their rig, if you want to talk to them." He motioned a gloved hand toward the access road, where all the vehicles from the sheriff's department and crime lab were clustered around the Yorks' SUV.

"We will," Chandler said as the noise from the helicopter rotors sliced through the silence.

"Looks like we got lucky this time. We might get an actual cast out of the boot prints, something we can use," Alvarez said.

"Not lucky enough for the victim," Grayson muttered, and walked away, his gloved hands fisted, his jaw rock-hard. "Whoever the hell she is, she didn't make it." He glanced up at the sky as a helicopter appeared above the timberline, hovering over a sheer, rocky ridge covered with ice and snow.

The chopper moved in, coming in low, skimming the tops of trees surrounding the open space. It wasn't the police search-and-rescue chopper they'd all expected. A blue call sign announced that it belonged to a local news station, and a cameraman, his huge lens trained on the clearing, was leaning as far as he dared out of the noisy aircraft.

Pescoli wanted to wave the news copter away. "Looks like we've got company."

"Wouldn't ya know?" Grayson muttered between tight teeth. "Just when I thought things couldn't get worse, the damned press decides to show up."

"It was bound to happen sooner or later," Agent Chandler said, squinting up at the chopper. "Maybe we can use the footage to our advantage. See what else they locate and make a public statement. Use the news crew, rather than be used by them."

"Did you just say screw the news crew?" Brewster asked, an amused glint in his eye.

Chandler nodded. "Close enough."

Pescoli glanced up at the helicopter hanging in the crisp mountain air. Chandler had a point; the news copter would give them free aerial support.

"Go for it," Grayson told the FBI agent. "KBIT is all yours."

Jillian thought she would go out of her ever-lovin' mind. She stared out at the expanse of snow sparkling in the sunlight and knew this was her chance to finally get out of here.

And go where?

How?

She had to wait for him. MacGregor had talked about it and had left with a chain saw hours before. She'd watched as he'd driven off on the snowmobile, hearing the big engine roar, but once the sound from the Arctic Cat faded, she'd waited, hoping to hear the grind of saw teeth biting through wood.

No such luck.

The dog, having finally accepted her, was curled up near the door again, the fire stoked. Jillian had tried to get into several of the books she'd found but couldn't. She was too jangled. Too wired. Too anxious to get out of here. Time was moving along, and if she wanted to find out if Aaron were really alive—or just get back to her real life!—she couldn't be waylaid any longer.

So what about MacGregor? Are you just going to leave him here?

"Of course," she bit out. The man was nothing to her. Yeah, she found him a little bit intriguing, but she chalked that up to being alone with him in this isolated canyon. She knew of Stockholm Syndrome, how a hostage came to trust, even depend upon, her abductor; how once rescued she wouldn't turn on the very person who kidnapped her.

Was that what this was? The root of all her fantasizing?

She remembered his lips brushing her cheek.

So he kissed her. Big deal.

So he was attractive. Who cared?

So he was mysterious. Then run the other way!

Adding wood to the fire, she listened hard, hoping to hear the roar of the snowmobile, but no sound broke the silence of the cabin. She dug in her bag and fiddled with her cell phone, trying it in every corner of the house, but just when she thought she might get a signal, the screen would flash and show "no service."

"Great," she muttered to the dog, walking to the windows and wishing MacGregor would return. She still didn't hear the growl of a chain saw ripping through fallen trees, nor the buzz of an approaching snowmobile.

As she gazed out the window she wondered exactly where she was. He had a stack of maps on the table, so she flipped through them before selecting one that she thought encompassed the area.

She saw roads and rivers and towns, including Grizzly Falls and Spruce Creek, both of which rang bells in her mind. She noticed Missoula and stared at the letters, thinking of Mason and how she was certain he was the one who had lured her to Montana.

But did that make sense?

Why would Mason want her to come here?

Why would he want to kill her?

There had, at one time, been life insurance, of course. A policy worth several hundred thousand dollars that Mason had insisted upon, but she didn't even know if the policy was in existence any longer.

And the voice on the phone. Had it been Mason, disguising himself? Whispering so that she couldn't identify him?

Why now?

As far as she knew, he was happily married to his new trophy wife. So why dredge up Aaron now? He'd been presumed dead so long Jillian barely remembered what he looked like. She searched a stack of astrological charts and maps on the table and found the envelope with the pictures that were supposedly of her dead husband. Holding the images under the light of a kerosene lantern, she studied the man carefully, trying to remember.

Was he Aaron?

Maybe. There was the beard and sunglasses and baseball cap pulled low over his eyes partially obscuring his face. And the extra weight, while Aaron had always been trim.

But ten years had passed. A decade. She'd remarried and divorced in that time. And now, if he were alive, Aaron would be just a few months shy of forty.

Frowning, she wondered if the man in the photo was Aaron or an imposter. Even more likely, was he an unsuspecting target? A man whose resemblance to her dead husband had prompted the photographer to snap the pictures. These weren't posed shots, but pictures of him on the street, walking into a store, near a sidewalk where cars were parked on a snowy street.

"Who are you? Just who the hell are you?" she whispered to the picture, and at the sound of her voice the dog climbed to his feet, metal ID tags jangling on his collar. With a glance at her, he walked to the front door, where he whined loudly and scratched.

"Need to go out?" she asked, with a glance outside.

Where the hell was MacGregor?

Gone. Not coming back. Maybe someone, whoever you thought was outside the other night, attacked him.

Now she was being ridiculous, letting her paranoia get the better of her.

Harley whined loudly.

"Yeah, yeah, I know. Hold onto your horses." She hitched to the gun cupboard and, feeling a little foolish, grabbed the loaded rifle with her free hand. She didn't like the idea of having to use the weapon, but knew she could if threatened. Grandpa Jim had seen to that.

She whistled to the dog. "Come on, Harley, you know the drill. Out the back." Using her crutch, she hobbled to the back door and opened it and the dog shot out before she had second thoughts and worried that letting Harley outside was a mistake. What if the damned dog took off after MacGregor?

Got lost.

He's a dog, for God's sake.

He's home. He won't stay out in the cold for long.

He just needs to get out, stretch his legs, urinate a few times.

"Stick around, please," she muttered, and watched as he lifted his leg on the trunk of a small tree near the back of the garage. He ambled through the chest-high snow, seeming to find joy in breaking a trail through the icy powder.

Jillian, in the doorjamb, felt the cold air and shivered. She was about to go inside when she saw Harley, now out in the middle of a clearing near the back, stop suddenly, ears cocked forward.

She almost called out to him but held her tongue.

Something in the dog's intense gaze gave her pause. Her fingers flexed over the handle of the crutch.

Nose in the air, hair bristling on the scruff of his neck, Harley stared intently into the woods.

Sweet Jesus.

Panic spurted through Jillian's blood.

She hoisted the rifle to her shoulder.

Don't be paranoid.

The dog growled low in his throat and lowered his head, his tail, too, moving downward.

This was no good.

She'd been around dogs enough to know when they sensed danger.

Harley started moving through the heavy snow, breaking a trail toward a thick copse of pines, where his gaze was centered.

Heart in her throat, rifle aimed at the spot where the dog seemed to be staring, a place on the other side of the pine trees, she stayed close to the building and whistled to the dog, just as she'd heard MacGregor do a dozen times.

The spaniel's ears didn't even flick as he advanced, moving awkwardly through the shoulder-deep snow.

"Harley!" she commanded, eyeing him through the sight of the rifle. "Come."

Was the dog crazy? He was nearly buried.

Still the damned spaniel ignored her. He slipped beneath the first sagging, snow-laden branch of a Ponderosa.

"Damn!" she said under her breath as she clicked off the safety.

The day was clear and still. Sunlight reflecting on the ice, nearly blinding. Not a breath of wind. No birds calling. Just the sound of her own anxious breathing.

She squinted hard. Strained to hear the slightest noise.

"Come back," she mouthed, hoping the dog could hear her.

Don't freak out. The dog could have seen a squirrel.

Or a deer.

Or a wolf. You read recently where the gray wolf has made a comeback in Montana.

And they travel in packs.

Could tear a domestic dog to bits.

All the spit dried in her mouth.

She'd never in her life been afraid of wild animals, had always thought humans were far more deadly, but now . . . "Harley, get back here!" she yelled, her one booted foot a little unsteady, the other toes bare in the cold air. "Harley! Come!" Heart thumping wildly she lowered her rifle and made her way to the edge of the porch, eyeing the broken snow where the dog had disappeared.

"Harley!" she called again, her voice echoing off the mountains.

Bam!

A rifle cracked loudly.

"Oh God!"

The dog yelped in pain.

"Harley!" Jillian yelled, her heart clutching. Oh God, now what? She had to go after the poor animal. "Harley!" He could still be alive!

She stepped off the porch before remembering two steps had been buried in the drifts. The rubber tip of her crutch slipped a little, but she steadied herself, then plowed forward along the half-broken path the dog had created.

Who would shoot him?

A hunter mistaking him for a wolf or coyote?

Or . . . someone who had been lying in wait?

Someone with a dark, deadly purpose.

Someone who had shot out the tire of her car. . . .

Oh God. She forced the gun to her shoulder, licked her lips nervously and, ignoring the cold, pushed onward. She didn't say a word, listened hard to hear the sound of the dog whining, footsteps or whispered voices—but nothing disturbed the quietude.

At the edge of the copse, she leaned forward, ducking under a branch, a sharp, shooting pain cutting through her abdomen and ribs. *This is nuts, Jillian. Go back. What can you do for the poor animal if you do find him? Carry him back to the house? How?*

Gritting her teeth, she kept moving forward, trying to be as silent as possible, her heart drumming wildly as she followed the path where, beneath the trees, the snow wasn't as deep. She heard the tiniest gurgle of a creek, probably nearly frozen, and over that, the distant reverberations of an engine.

MacGregor's snowmobile?

Oh please.

Using the barrel of her rifle to push aside low-hanging branches, she heard the dog's whine . . . he was still alive! And MacGregor was coming. The roar of the snowmobile's engine was getting closer . . . or was it?

Come on, MacGregor, get the hell back here.

She stepped around an outcropping of rock and saw the dog, a patch of black and white on the snowy ground. And more. Stains of bright red where blood was matting his coat and seeping from his body into the pristine whiteness of the forest floor.

"Oh, Harley," she said as he lifted his head. "Oh no, I'm so . . ."

He wasn't looking at her.

But at a spot just over her shoulder.

She took one step forward.

His lips pulled back into a hard growl, exposing sharp teeth. From the corner of her eye, Jillian caught a glimpse of movement, a flash.

Fingers tight over the gunstock, she swung.

But it was too late. Her attacker was upon her back, forcing her onto the frozen ground. Jillian squirmed as the sickening sweet smell of a chemical stung her nostrils. There was a flash of a dark, gloved hand mashing into her face, a bare span of scarred wrist catching her eye as the damp rag was forced over her nose and mouth.

Turning her panic to sweet oblivion.

Chapter Eighteen

Crack!

The sound of a rifle's report ricocheted through the canyons. MacGregor slowed his snowmobile and let the engine idle as he listened.

Had the sound come from the direction of his cabin? Jillian?

Had she shot the rifle he'd left her?

Or was it someone else?

Hunters?

He felt dread as he hit the gas and headed out toward his home in the mountains. He could be mistaken. The cabin was miles away and it would take him nearly half an hour to reach it.

Don't let your imagination run wild, he told himself, but couldn't shake the sensation that something was wrong. The roads near his place were still impassable for even the toughest SUV, snow having drifted deep into crevices and ravines, but once down the mountain a mile and a half, the roads were clearer, with packed snow and sand giving tires some purchase. If he found a way to haul Jillian on a sled pulled by the snowmobile, he could get her out. Or, better yet, he could take the Arctic Cat into town and get help.

The thought wasn't pleasant. He'd spent the past ten years of his life avoiding the police, but he might not have a choice. Time was running out; another storm was projected.

He pushed on the throttle and with a roar the Cat took off, skis sliding easily over the snow. Mentally beating himself up, he second-guessed himself about leaving her.

What had been the choice?

He'd wondered what to do with her, hadn't liked the fact that he was getting used to having her around, that he felt an attraction to her that was just plain stupid. He'd sworn off women long ago; didn't need one. Didn't want one.

Then he'd found her trapped in the car, passing out, nearly frozen, and he'd had no choice but to put her in a makeshift sling on poles that he then tied to his rig to drag her to the cabin. He'd gone back for her things, tried to contact the authorities, but then, because the storm had raged so wildly, locked himself in his house with her.

That had been a mistake.

Taking care of her while she slept. Washing and dressing her wounds, warming her body and giving her dry clothes, seeing her naked, all had been his undoing. It wasn't as if he hadn't professionally tended women before, but this one . . .

He guided the snowmobile through the trees and down a hill to the frozen creek bed, now covered in two feet of powder. This was the shortest way back to the cabin, though not the safest, as the terrain was steep and rocky. A few of the boulders peeked through the wide expanse of white.

Sunlight sparkled on the snow, glinting through his

tinted goggles. The whole world was shaded in tones of sepia, and so pristine, so isolated, it seemed he was on an uninhabited landscape, like something out of a science-fiction movie.

Trees rushed by as the Arctic Cat strained around a final bend, its engine growling, the drive belt pulling the snowmobile over a final ridge, skis sliding over the icy terrain. He saw the cabin far below this crest. Black smoke curled lazily from the chimney and he felt a little better.

Everything was fine.

It had to be.

He was just rattled because he'd driven to September Creek, to the spot where her mangled Subaru had ended up. The car was long gone, all evidence of it lost in two feet of new snow, but bits of yellow-and-black crime scene tape still caught on a few trees. The police had found her vehicle and were, no doubt, looking for her.

It was time to take her into town.

One way or another.

If he had to rig up the damned sling again.

People would be worried, search parties assembled, the police on alert.

Somehow he would find a way of hauling her into town.

As long as she was all right.

He hit the throttle and tore down the hill, dread chasing after him, a sixth sense telling him that things weren't as he'd left them.

"The pilot of the chopper thinks he might have found the car," Grayson said as he clicked off his phone.

Glad for the lead, Pescoli trudged back to her rig, leaving the crime scene investigators to go over every inch of the clearing. Pescoli knew they wouldn't find anything, but protocol had to be followed.

The dogs had already come up with zero, the broken trail in the snow leading again to an old mining road, one that hadn't been in use in thirty or forty years. But this guy, the killer, knew all the local roads, every nook and cranny.

A local guy.

Maybe someone she knew? Someone she saw down at Wild Wills having a drink or two, or maybe one of those rabid fathers who coached soccer? She'd met more than her share when Bianca was playing and had watched several of the dads and moms, for that matter, look as if they were going to have an aneurism after what they considered an unfair call against their kid's team. Then there were always the elders in the local church, the scions of virtue who had a dark undercurrent of evil running beneath their benevolent exterior. Or could the killer be someone she'd booked for a misdemeanor or lesser crime? Perhaps someone with a history of violence?

Deep in thought, Regan climbed behind the wheel of her Jeep. They had already gone through the lists of local men who had been arrested for violent acts, assault, armed robbery and the like over the past five years. They'd pulled in a few men accused of wife battery as well as military marksmen and local hunting experts, but everyone they'd interviewed had come out clean.

Unless they missed something.

Alvarez closed the door to the passenger side and Pescoli wheeled her rig around, following the sheriff's four-wheel-drive Suburban and thinking.

"Why can't we find this guy?" Alvarez asked, staring out the windshield as Pescoli adjusted the defroster.

"We will."

"Yeah, but when? How many other women have to freeze to death?" She was angry as she pulled out her cell phone and dialed. "Yeah, this is Alvarez. Any luck?" A pause. "I know it's the weekend, Marcia, but we've got an unidentified dead woman." Another long pause. "That's right, A and R." She rattled off a description of the dead woman and Pescoli's stomach tightened. "I'll bet you dollars to donuts *someone's* missing her. Check statewide, and if that doesn't work, northwest. What? Canada? No, not yet. I know we're close to the border, but so far all the victims are U.S. citizens. Mmm . . . yeah, okay. Call me if you find out anything." She hung up as they reached a mountain road that wound down toward the town.

"All the victims and cars were found within a ten-mile radius," Pescoli said.

"Square that. What do you get? A hundred square miles of mountains, canyons, cliffs and rivers. Rough territory."

"And someone who knows it well." Pescoli reached for her cigarettes and ignored the sharp look she got from her partner. "My rig," she said.

"My lungs."

"You know, you should loosen up a bit."

"I don't work out, eat right and do yoga so that you can pollute my respiratory system."

"Give it a rest," Pescoli said, but didn't light up. She could wait until they were back at the station in the parking lot. Besides, she didn't have the habit that bad. It was just to help her think. . . .

Her phone rang about the same time the sheriff's lights and sirens flipped on. She answered. "Pescoli."

"We've got another one."

"What?"

Alvarez's head spun toward her, the unspoken question in her eyes.

Grayson said, "Looks like another woman tied to a

tree, up near Broken Pine Lodge. The KBIT helicopter found her. I've already sent Van Droz up there; she's the closest road deputy on the road. She should beat us there and secure the scene."

"Great," Pescoli said, more worried than ever.

"Another victim?" Alvarez asked.

"Yeah." Pescoli was nodding, keeping up both conversations, the one with her partner and the one over the phone.

"Is this guy escalating or what?" Alvarez asked, loud enough that Grayson heard her.

"Looks like," he responded.

"Found by the news copter," Pescoli clarified, shifting down.

"That's what I said," the sheriff said impatiently. "Film at eleven."

MacGregor stepped into the cabin.

The interior was as still as death, the fire low, a feeling of abandonment in the air. "Jillian?" he called, looking through the few empty rooms, panic slowly inching up his spine.

She was gone.

Plain and simple.

The rifle he'd left with her was gone, and her crutch was missing.

Along with the dog.

"Harley?" His boots rang hollowly against the old floorboards as he walked through the kitchen to the back porch. The uneasy feeling that had been with him ever since hearing the rifle's report less than an hour earlier increased. He walked to the front porch and whistled long and low, half expecting the black-and-white spaniel to come bounding through the drifts.

Nothing.

"Hell."

Quickly, he walked through the house to the back porch and cupping his hands around his mouth, yelled, "Jillian? Harley?" His own voice echoed through the canyons and he grabbed his rifle and walked the length of the porch. A path was broken in the snow and it led toward the woods.

"Son of a bitch." What was she thinking? Escaping on foot while she was still laid up?

Maybe she'd been forced.

That thought chilled him to the bone and he replayed the gunshot in his mind.

But the prints in the snow were only of the dog and the crutch and her good boot. No others. There was a chance the dog had taken off after MacGregor, or after a marauding racoon or deer. Jillian might have followed.

Damn, fool woman, he thought, but broke into a trot, following the trail of footsteps, leaning down beneath the overhang of branches as he flushed a rabbit through the undergrowth.

"Harley!" he yelled, whistling. Why would the dog take off?

A pitiful whine whistled through the pines and MacGregor's blood turned to ice.

Heart thudding, he threw the bolt on his rifle, ready to shoot as he rounded a large boulder and saw his dog, lying on his side in the snow, black-and-white fur matted and stained red. Too much blood had pooled beneath him. Even so, the spaniel gazed up at him, whined and gave one feeble thump of his tail. "Hang on, buddy," he said, stripping off his jacket and tearing out the lining. He moved the dog onto his jacket and tied the sleeve over his back leg, where a bullet hole gaped. "Son of a bitch," he muttered through clenched teeth. "Son of a goddamned bitch."

Kneeling beside Harley, he noticed the tracks. Not just Jillian's but a second set, decidedly larger, heading east, in the direction of an old abandoned sawmill that was over two miles away.

There was no way Jillian could hobble that far.

He hated to abandon the dog but he had no choice.

Jillian Rivers's life was at stake.

Rifle held in a death grip, defying the cold, following the tracks, Zane MacGregor took off at a dead run.

He only hoped he wasn't too late.

"Jesus H. Christ!" Brewster stared at the woman who'd been lashed to the tree and looked as if he were about to throw up. Pescoli and Alvarez hurried forward. The scene was nearly identical to the last one, except the naked woman had been cut down from a solitary white pine tree in a small alpine meadow. She was lying on a jacket, her eyes glassy and vacant as they stared upward. Bruises covered her body and her lips were chapped. Deputy Trilby Van Droz worked over her, squatting in the mashed snow around the tree.

Van Droz, hearing them approach, looked up and yelled, "She's alive. I've already called for an ambulance."

"Alive," Pescoli repeated, as overhead, marring the clear blue sky, a news-crew helicopter hovered, a cameraman hanging out a window while filming the scene.

"Damned fool idiots," Grayson said, waving them off. "Someone call KBIT and tell them to clear the airspace in case a rescue copter has to land."

Brewster was on his walkie-talkie, calling back to the department offices, relaying orders.

"At least they found her," Alvarez said. "I'll be in charge of the crime scene sheet." The area had to be roped off and protected. Everyone who showed up here had to sign in.

Grayson scribbled his name. "Is she conscious?" he yelled.

"No. But I found a pulse and she's breathing." Van Droz was performing first aid, trying to keep the victim warm, just as the sound of a siren cut through the still mountain air.

Pescoli signed into the crime scene and, trying not to disturb any of the evidence, hurried to the victim's side, where she knelt in the snow and tried to help. "Is she Jillian Rivers?"

"Don't know."

"No," Watershed said from somewhere over her right shoulder. He was standing back, eyeing the message nailed to the gnarled bark of the pine. "The letters aren't right."

Pescoli glanced up and caught a glimpse of the weird message.

Sure enough, Jillian Rivers's initials weren't written down. There was the R from the last note but no J.

Now the note read:

WAR   T   HE   SC   I   N

"What the hell does that mean?" Watershed whispered.

Trilby Van Droz was still on her knees at the victim's side, Pescoli beside her. The sheriff ordered Brett Gage, the chief criminal deputy, to follow the trail broken in the snow. He, along with a deputy in charge of the dogs, took off toward the east end of the clearing.

"How the hell would someone get in here?" Grayson asked as the ambulance's siren screamed louder.

Pescoli rubbed the woman's wrist. "Can you hear me?" she asked. From the corner of her eyes, she saw the ambulance slide to a stop in the old, snow-covered parking lot of the dilapidated lodge. "What's your name? Who did this to you?"

"She's unresponsive," Deputy Van Droz said. "I haven't been able to get a word out of her."

Two EMTs, carrying their equipment, hurried toward the woman lying in the snow. With one quick examination the shorter of the two rescue workers, a black woman with a no-nonsense look on her face, whipped out a two-way and called for a chopper. "We need to get her out of here," she said, giving the helicopter directions, then hanging up. "It'll take too long to drive her back to the hospital." Her dark eyes moved back to the victim as she told the detectives, "Chopper on its way. Should be here in five. So all of you just back the hell up and let us work!"

The detectives and FBI agents took a few steps backward, while the woman and her partner, a tall man still in his twenties, worked quickly, monitoring the victim's vital signs, administering oxygen, covering her and tending to her. In the distance, the sound of a helicopter's rotors sliced through the air.

"The scene's been destroyed," Chandler said, frowning, her gaze traveling over the mashed snow and solitary tree.

"It's like the others," Pescoli said.

"But there may be evidence buried here." Chandler's gaze scanned the trodden-down snow and the poor woman who lay motionless on the gurney.

"The crime scene investigators will figure that out," Pescoli said as the rescue helicopter came into view and the news chopper flew to a spot higher in the sky, never quite giving up its vantage point.

"War to the scientists," Watershed said.

"What?" Pescoli frowned.

"The note."

"We can figure that out later," she snapped, uninterested in the stupid clues the killer had left behind. Now they had a victim who was alive, one they could save, one who could potentially name her attacker.

To hell with the damned note.

"Did that copter happen to find the car?" Chandler asked as a basket was lowered. "We're still missing two cars, assuming this person isn't Jillian Rivers."

"She's not," Pescoli said as she noted the victim's tiny nose and wide mouth. Her hair was short and streaked with shades of blond, a widow's peak was evident, and her eyes were a brown so intense they were nearly black. She was tall and thin, probably five nine or ten, so gaunt her ribs showed, her feet at least a size nine. Pescoli remembered the pictures she'd seen of Jillian Rivers. Even if Rivers lost weight, cut and dyed her hair and wore dark contacts, she wouldn't resemble either woman they'd found today.

"So where the hell is she? Why do we have her car and not this woman's or the Jane Doe we found up at Cougar Pass?" Agent Chandler asked, her eyebrows knit in frustration, her breath fogging in the cold air.

"We'll find her," Halden, her partner, said. He was the calmer of the two, though he, too, was irritated, his mouth set and grim, his eyes scanning the surrounding area, where the dilapidated, graying buildings of what had once been a profitable hunting lodge were partially hidden by snow-laden trees and rocky hills. It was desolate up here, the whole area looking decrepit and forgotten, a testament to death.

The victim was transferred to the rescue basket and winched skyward as the helicopter started moving, heading back to Grizzly Falls, just as the crime scene team arrived.

"How the hell did he get them to two different places, miles apart?" Chandler muttered angrily.

"One at a time. First the victim at Cougar Pass and now this Jane Doe."

"Her initials being HE or EH, if the pattern remains the same."

"It is," Chandler said. "He's just escalating."

"Not just escalating," Pescoli said. "So far he's duplicating. He's not killing closer together; it's like he's doing a two-for-the-price-of-one thing. Two women in one day." She was worried as she stared at the note and the tree to which the victim had been lashed. Traces of blood were visible on the bark, and drops of red dotted the snow. Whoever this woman was, she had struggled and fought.

"What the hell does that mean?" Grayson asked.

"I don't know." Stephanie Chandler was shaking her head. "We need to find out who these women are."

"I've already called in both sets of initials to Missing Persons on the walkie," Alvarez said. She was still standing near the entrance to the crime scene, making certain everyone was signing in as she waited for the crime scene team to arrive. "They're checking."

"Call dispatch. Have them bring in every available detective," Sheriff Grayson said. "And I don't want to hear any complaints about it being Sunday or a few days before Christmas or even that their kid has the flu. I want every available road deputy at the department when we get back into town. Overtime's no problem. Screw the damned budget. Are the cell phone towers working again?"

"Not all of them, not yet," Watershed said. "Just like the electricity. It's spotty."

A muscle worked in the sheriff's jaw and his lips were flat beneath his moustache. He lifted his hat from his head, and staring at the pine tree, the would-be death scene, he raked stiff, gloved fingers through his hair. "I hate this son of a bitch," he muttered under his breath.

Pescoli silently agreed. She prayed that they had found this victim in time. That EH or HE or whoever she was would live. And not just survive. Oh no. Pescoli hoped that the woman would be able to name her attacker and testify against him at the prick's trial.

Yeah, that's what she wanted, Pescoli thought as she shaded her eyes against the lowering sun and watched the helicopter disappear over the craggy summit of the mountain.

It would serve the bastard right.

Detective Gage returned with the dogs and the bad news that the trail had gone cold, ending up at a lower parking lot for the old lodge where tire tracks led away. The crime scene team would take tire and footprint casts, which were tricky but not impossible in the snow. With Snow Print Wax sprayed onto the tracks several times and followed by the dental stone impression material, clear casts could be created. Once the impression material hardened, experts would make duplicate prints and study them, trying to figure out the make and imperfections in the tire tread and boot prints. Methodically, experts would go through the painstaking process of finding out who had bought those particular tires in a hundred-mile radius of the area and start comparing the tread, vehicle by vehicle.

It could take weeks. Or longer. Assuming they were able to get a good, clear print.

At that moment, the sheriff's cell phone beeped. "Looks like we got service up here again," he said, and answered, his expression darkening as he listened. "Yeah . . . right . . . good. Send the chopper up. Use one from the state police if you have to, but check out the area. See if there's any sign of activity. Tracks. Smoke from a chimney. Noise or exhaust from a generator. Any damned thing! Yeah . . . yeah . . . I know. Get back to me."

He hung up and said, "It looks like we might have caught a break. Jillian Rivers's cell phone company called. They got a ping off her phone and pinpointed it to a tower up on Star Ridge."

"That's wicked country up there," Watershed said.

"Yeah, well, what else is new?" Grayson was already headed back to his Suburban. "The crime scene team can handle this. Let's go."

Pescoli didn't waste a second. Finally, it seemed, they'd caught a break. She felt a surge of satisfaction. *We're going to get you, you bastard.*

Look at them!

Police officers crawling over the "crime scene" like ants on an anthill. Hurrying this way, scurrying that. Not having a clue that I'm here, in the warmth of the bar, sipping a drink of fine Kentucky whiskey as I blend in with the rest of the patrons, the men and women who have stopped in for a drink after work to share conversation, even laughter, and shake off the bitter cold of winter, here in the lower part of the town, in a century-old building overlooking the river.

As one, we stare at the old television mounted over the colored bottles glistening in front of the mirror.

The bar is glossy wood, reflecting the lights overhead, holding up a half dozen sets of elbows of men who've come inside after a day's labor. There are women, too, but most of them are seated at the tables near the fire, where real logs are blazing in a massive stone fireplace that was built over a hundred years earlier, when miners and loggers in cork boots trod on these old plank floors. From the kitchen, the scents of grilled onions and burgers seep through the open doorway, accompanied by the sizzle of the deep-fat fryer.

I, like the other customers, am shaking my head at the senseless horror playing out on the screen.

"I can't believe it could happen here. Right outside Grizzly Falls," one sawmill worker says. While he stares up at the images on the flickering television screen, some faint Christmas carol can be heard over the buzz of the patrons. What is it? Oh yeah. "God Rest Ye Merry Gentlemen."

As if that's possible in Grizzly Falls tonight.

The guy next to me isn't small. In fact, his belly is so big it swings up to the bar, seemingly independent of him, as he settles onto a stool. Grease shows around his fingernails, bits of sawdust cling to the long hairs that grow from the back of his neck, hairs that should have been shaved away from his unruly beard.

"The world's changed," I say, frowning as if I, too, am aghast at the horror being shown to us via the airwaves. The simpleton thinks I'm agreeing.

"This used to be a safe place."

"Didn't it?"

"No more, I guess. Hey!" Crooking one fat finger, he signals to Nadine, the barkeep.

"The usual, Dell?" she asks, sliding a coaster to him and pretending that his ordering her around doesn't bother her. But she slides me a glance. We both know Dell Blight's a pig.

"Yeah. A Bud."

She's already got a chilled glass under the spigot of a hidden keg. "This is just so horrible. What kind of monster would leave those women out in the forest?" Nadine asks, and looks at my near-empty shot glass. "Another?" She lifts her gaze a bit and our eyes hold for the briefest of seconds.

I nod, return her smile, pretend I don't really understand what she's offering.

"You'd think the sheriff could nail this fucker," Big

Belly Blight says with a knowing nod. He believes if he were the sheriff, he'd have "the fucker" behind bars already. "What the hell do we elect him for?"

"Grayson's doing a good job. And they might just catch the guy." Nadine obviously isn't in the mood to take any crap from the likes of Dell Blight. "This woman"—she hooks her thumb toward the television—"she didn't die."

What? Every muscle in my body freezes. "Is that so?" I ask, as if I'm really concerned. Nadine must have her information wrong. The woman is dead. Hannah is dead. She has to be!

"That's what they're sayin'," Nadine assures both me and Dell. "I'd turn up the sound, but, you know, Farley, he likes the volume down so we can enjoy the music." She makes a sour face. "It's Christmas, y'know."

I nod, grinning, but deep down I feel not only fear but a little spark of anger. Nadine has to be wrong. Dead wrong. *Calm down. Take control.* I lift my glass to my lips, as if to sip, but instead take a deep breath, tamp down my fear.

"I heard about the latest victim surviving. A bit ago, when I was out back on my break. It was all over the radio," Nadine assures us with the eager anticipation of one imparting fresh gossip. "They found two women today. One's dead, but this one, the one the news crew located, she's alive. In some kind of coma, but alive."

"Will she make it?" I ask, feigning concern for the stupid bitch who was supposed to expire. What the hell was wrong with her? I left her to succumb to the elements, but, obviously Hannah is stronger than she looks. *Fool. Damned superior fool. You let your ego get the better of your good sense.*

"Who knows if she'll survive?" Nadine touches my hand then. A caress, where her thumb trails down the back of mine.

"*Two* women? They found two? Holy cripes!" Beer Belly Dell shakes his balding head and the scent of fresh sawdust wafts my way. "I don't get how this guy gets off. They say the women haven't been raped. No sexual activity whatsoever. The guy's probably a queer."

I smile, as if I agree, but the man's an idiot. Of course an imbecile like Dell Blight can't understand. His brain is probably the size of a walnut.

But still I'm bothered. Is it possible? Is Hannah alive? Her living would make things difficult.

"Nah," Ole Olson, the round little guy in the dirty baseball cap sitting next to Dell, pipes up. "He ain't no queer. If he was, he'd be haulin' men up there and tyin' 'em up and doin' weird shit to 'em. More'n likely he got no balls at all."

"What do y'mean, no balls? Like a woman?"

"Like no balls. He's been neutered, he's . . . he's one of them . . . them . . ." Ole snaps his thick fingers. "One of them U-nuts."

"U-nuts?" Dell repeats with a snort, then takes a long drink. "You mean like U-bolts?"

"I think he means eunuch," I say, then wish I hadn't even opened my mouth. What would these cretins know?

"What the hell is a fuckin' U-nick?" Dell's face is screwed up like he'd just smelled week-old dead fish.

"That's just it, they can't fuck cuz they got no balls," Ole says.

"Enough!" Nadine shakes her head as she scoops up a couple of empty glasses and drops them into a sink. Quick as a rattler striking, she slides the tips across the bar with her polished fingernails and stuffs the bills into the pocket of her apron. She glances up at the television screen, where a reporter is standing in front of the local hospital.

"I hope she survives," she whispers.

"Who?" Ole, true to character, missed a vital part of the earlier conversation.

"The woman they found in the forest, the one who didn't die." Nadine is starting to get pissed.

"She's seen that psycho," Ole says, catching on.

I feel an unlikely chill. My face was exposed. She knows my touch, can recognize me.

"Yep. She'll nail his ass in court." Nadine nods, stiff red-blond hair unmoving.

Dell snorts before draining his glass and wiggling the empty as a signal for another. "He's got to be caught first, and my money says that Sheriff Numb-Nuts won't come close."

I take a drink to hide my smile.

"Oh, Grayson will catch him all right." Coming to Grayson's defense, Nadine looks to me for support.

I lift a noncommittal shoulder that says *Maybe*, though I think *Don't count on it*.

"He will!" Nadine is certain as she snaps a clean towel from a stack under the counter. "You just wait and see." She swabs the bar with a vengeance.

"Humph. Not by countin' on the likes of crazy Ivor Hicks. Shit, that nutcase found a body and claimed the aliens sent him there," Ole says.

"That Crypton, he's one smart sergeant," Dell corrects.

"It's Crytor, moron. And he's a fuckin' general. Get it right. An orange reptile and a fuckin' general."

They both laugh uproariously.

"The old man hallucinates," Nadine says quickly, and looks at me, embarrassed. She doesn't like the way the conversation has turned. The crazy old man's a regular, too, when he's not on the wagon. "Give Ivor a break, will ya? And for God's sake, have some faith in Sheriff Grayson. He's doing a great job."

I finish the first drink and wait as she places a fresh glass and coaster in front of me.

"Great job, my ass." Dell isn't cutting Grayson any breaks. "Why hasn't this piece of shit been brought in? Huh? How hard could it be to track a killer in the god-damned snow? What the hell are those tracking dogs for? Hell, do you know what it costs for one of them? Sheeeeiiiiit."

"Grayson will get the guy," Nadine insists, with a look at me, as if she and I, the two of us, have a secret. As if we co-conspirators realize that Big Belly is an oaf and we, of far superior intellect, have the good sense to trust Sheriff Dan Grayson.

"What's he waitin' for?" Big Belly Dell is staring up at the television, where the cameraman in the chopper zooms in on Grayson's worried, hard face.

"Grayson's an asshole," a voice from my other side af-firms. "I went to school with him. He don't know up from damned sideways. Hey, Nadine, how about an-other?"

"Whiskey sour is it, Ed?" she asks, and flashes him a grin meant to tease the biggest tip possible from Ed's slim wallet. Nadine knows how to work the crowd. She's flirty and sassy enough to keep the men interested. On the skinny side, smelling of cigarettes, she nonetheless has teeth that always show a brilliant white behind lips always glossed to a fine peach shine. And her blouse is always buttoned low enough to allow the regulars a glimpse of the tops of her breasts. She wears low-cut jeans with a silvery belt that dangles low and offers just a hint of skin and the tease of a tattoo peeking above her waistband. Turquoise and pink swirls rise up her backbone, widening visibly before dipping suggestively below the denim and giving a man a hard-on just think-ing about what naughty splay of colors might be caress-ing her buttocks.

I hear the men speculate.

"I think it's a butterfly," one bearded young man once said.

"No way. It's like some kind of Chinese symbol," his compatriot argued.

Another said, "I've got it on good account that it's humming birds, a whole flock of 'em, some peering out from between her butt cheeks."

This caused some raucous laughter but none of the simpletons had the faintest idea of the intricacies that really lay beneath her clothes, that sexy, wild series of waves that undulate around her hips as she slowly undresses.

Few have had the privilege of actually seeing her lying naked, butt up, hips tilted, suggesting she wants to rut like a mare in heat, those pink-tinged waves offering a warm, wet sea for me to thrust into.

I look at her and she catches the glance.

Doesn't say a word.

But she knows.

I take a long pull from my drink and suck in ice cubes, cracking them between my teeth, as I turn my attention back to the television screen, where now the sheriff, hanging up his phone, begins striding away from the crime scene.

That's not right.

Another mistake. You made another mistake!

I won't think of it, but I can feel my nerves tighten as I see the detectives rushing to their vehicles. I zero in on Regan Pescoli, that bitch of a woman. Beautiful and rough. Tough as nails.

Or so she thinks.

I feel my eyes narrow upon her as the fantasy unwinds in my mind. . . . *Get ready*, I think, but her time has not yet come.

I have others . . . one not yet discovered.

Or am I wrong?

Is that possible?

Why are the cops hurrying away from the scene, running to their vehicles, lights on their SUVs flashing red and blue as they peel out of the lot of the old lodge.

Where the hell are they going?

My heart nearly stops.

I crack an ice cube so loudly, Dell slides a glance my way.

"Jesus, you got jaws of steel or what?"

I laugh. "'Course I do," I say, trying to appear calm, attempting to hide my agitation, as on the screen the posse drives away and deep inside fear threatens to consume me. I couldn't have erred again. Couldn't have.

"See what I mean? A real asshole," Dell says, looking upward at the television. "Grayson's useless."

Of course he is.

I calm.

Tamp down my momentary fear.

As Burl Ives's voice starts to sing "A Holly, Jolly Christmas" from hidden speakers, my gaze meets Nadine's and we share a secretive smile.

The kind exchanged by secret lovers.

Holly, jolly, my ass.

Chapter Nineteen

Jillian had never been so cold in her life.

Teeth chattering, mind numb with fear, she struggled to free herself, to slip through the bonds. Her mind was sluggish and dull, but she forced herself to think, to find a way to extricate herself from the rope that held her fast to the tree.

The sick smell of ether still clung to her nostrils and she coughed and spat as her mind began to clear. Vaguely she recalled being attacked as she tried to save the dog, of having a rag held over her nose and mouth as she flailed wildly, fighting for a breath of air, feeling her good leg wobble and battling the darkness that encroached upon her vision and dragged her under.

Then her thoughts were scattered and vague. She remembered nothing clearly and the memories she did have were dull, mainly sensations. She sensed she was being dragged, that whoever had attacked her was laboring, having trouble breathing, and obviously hadn't planned on having to carry her. But other than that, she remembered little.

Shivering, she forced her eyes open. Daylight was

fading, shadows lengthening, and she was just so cold, her skin covered in goosebumps, her flesh feeling as if it were ice.

Help me!

The thought stuck in her mind and she forced the words over her lips. "Help, oh please help!" she screamed, but her voice was raw and tight, the sound no louder than a whisper. She blinked and tried to look into the forest, into the encroaching darkness.

This, she was certain, was how the others had died, though she remembered little of the details. That information hadn't been big news in Seattle.

Oh God, Seattle.

Home.

The townhouse with its narrow stairs, small decks and warm, soft calico cat. Her throat tightened and tears formed in her eyes. And she thought of Zane MacGregor, the man who had saved her from freezing to death in her car, all his efforts wasted. Her throat thickened as she remembered him. Dear Lord, how had she mistrusted him? Why hadn't she gone with her instincts and gotten closer to him? Touched him? Kissed him? Now she would never get the chance. Now, aside from that chaste brush of his lips against her cheek, she'd never know his touch.

Fool! She nearly sobbed as the tears tracked from her eyes only to freeze against her skin.

Oh for God's sake, Jillian, what're ya doin' sniveling and giving up? For the love of God, don't feel sorry for yourself. Do something! Save yourself, honey. Show what you're made of! Grandpa Jim's voice echoed through her brain, though he'd been dead for years and she doubted, rationally, that his spirit was wandering through the snow-shrouded forests of these hills.

"Help!" she yelled with more force, and looked down at the ropes surrounding her. She'd been tied at the waist first, secured against the cedar tree, her wrists lashed in front of her. Then her shoulders and legs had been bound so tightly that the rough fibers of the rope cut deep into her skin, making every movement even more painful.

Her ribs still ached and her damned ankle throbbed.

You won't have to worry about that much longer, though, if your body goes numb.

Great.

Her mind was clearing, the ether wearing off, the urge to spit and cough lessening.

Come on, Jillian. Somehow you have to untie the ropes. Work on your wrists. Get your hands free.

But her fingers were unresponsive, unable to grab the ends of the knots. Nor could she reach them with her mouth, as her shoulders were so tightly lashed. She thought about the person who'd brought her here, a strong, determined individual hell-bent on destroying her.

Why?

And why harm the dog?

Jillian's stomach roiled when she thought how Harley, poor innocent pup, had given up his life for her. Why the hell would someone hurt MacGregor's dog? Fury spurted through her blood, and if she ever got the chance, she'd beat the living tar out of the person who had done this.

Perverted, twisted sicko!

Angrier now, her head clearer, Jillian shook her body, trying to force the shoulder lashings lower so she could dip her head, but try as she might, she managed only to chafe her already raw skin.

It was useless!

So you're just going to give up? Freeze to death without a fight? Her grandfather's voice mocked her and she thought of the tough old man who had been so kind and loving. God, she missed him. And now, facing death, she missed her crazy, busybody of a mother and even her supercilious sister. Dusti could be such a pain in the neck, but she was still her damned sister.

And then there was Mason, her ex. Had he lured her to this part of Montana, taunting her with information about Aaron, with pictures of her first husband? Pictures that somehow jogged an obscure recollection? Mason had accused her of still loving her first husband, even long after they were married. Her "mental infidelity," as Mason had called it, had been a major crack in the foundation of their marriage and she'd never been able to convince him that she was over Aaron, that though his body had never been found, she'd buried him and his memory forever.

Had it been a lie?

Trembling with the cold, she didn't know the answer to her feelings for her supposedly dead husband, but she saw no reason for Mason to bring it all up now. He'd remarried, had claimed to be happy, was "getting on with his life." So why would he now, long after they were divorced, try to draw her back to Montana, shoot out her tire and leave her here for dead?

That just didn't make sense.

But then, nothing did.

Again she began to cry, and again she sniffed back the stupid tears.

Setting her back teeth down hard, she struggled again, then heard the sound of someone running, hard. She looked up, half-expecting her tormentor to reappear. Instead, racing wildly through the trees was Zane Mac-Gregor.

Her heart soared at the sight of him, wearing nothing but a sweater and jeans. He carried a rifle in one hand and didn't falter one step as he broke from the woods to the clearing and the solitary tree to which she was bound.

"Jillian! Oh God!" He covered the snow-crusted ground in an instant.

Her voice squeaked and tears rained from her eyes.

"What the hell happened?" he asked, but was already reaching into his pocket, withdrawing a jackknife and sawing through the thick rope. "Who did this?"

"I don't know. I didn't see him."

"Son of a bitch," he muttered, a muscle in his jaw jumping. "Sick bastard." The ropes around her shoulders gave way and she sank against him as he sliced through the cords binding her wrists. "Are you all right?"

"Ye–e-ss."

He gave her an impassioned look that turned her insides to liquid. Then he cut through the ropes that held her hips to the tree, stripped off his sweater and forced it over her head. Her arms were lost in its sleeves, the hem barely covering her buttocks. "I'm getting you out of here."

She was still fighting tears of relief that seemed hellbent to track from her eyes though she cleared her throat and refused, absolutely refused, to allow herself to sob. "How?"

"I'll carry you."

"Oh no, you can't—"

"Watch me." With one arm, he lifted her off her feet and she sucked in her breath as pain shot through her ribs.

"Sorry," he started to apologize. "I didn't mean to—"

She kissed him. Without hesitation. Pressing her frozen mouth to his and wrapping her arms around his neck. His lips were warm and hard, the arms around her tightening as he kissed her back.

Eagerly.

Hungrily.

It felt so good to let go and kiss him. Despite the

bruises on her body, the emotional horror she'd been through, the harrowing, near-death experience, she reveled in his touch, in the feeling of being alive again.

His fingers were strong and supple, their warmth permeating the oversized sweater, and in her mind's eye she saw herself making love to him. Soon. She would be lying across his bed, the fire crackling on the hearth, desire pounding through her brain as need coursed through her bloodstream. She envisioned him as he came to her, his skin taut over hard muscles, his pupils dilated with the night, his hands and mouth insistent as he loved her.

Even now she felt it—that need to connect, the desire to lose herself completely to this man whom she barely knew, this stranger who had saved her twice.

She moaned when his tongue slipped between her teeth. Her fingers tangled in his hair as she held his face fast to hers, her mouth opening for him, her entire body trembling more from desire than the cold.

And yet they were alone in the forest, only the snow-crusted pines and hemlocks as tall sentinels.

Dear God, she wanted him. As crazy as it was, as cold as she was, as frightened as she was, she wanted him. He shifted a bit, breaking the kiss. "I have to get you to a hospital," he said, his voice husky.

"MacGregor, I—"

"Shh."

She just clung to him, burying her face in his neck and believing for the first time since she woke up naked and bound to the tree that she might actually live.

And then she remembered.

The dog!

"Oh God," she whispered, her heart tearing at the image in her mind, a picture of Harley lying in the snow, blood crusting on his mottled fur. "Harley. He—"

"I know," MacGregor said quickly, the corners of his mouth hard and set. "I found him."

Tears welled in her eyes. "Is he—?"

"Still alive. Or at least he was half an hour ago." He looked at the tree again and hitched his chin toward a marking hewn from the bark. It was smaller than a man's palm and positioned around six feet from the ground, obviously having been whittled over her head while she was tied to the tree.

"What the hell is that?"

"I don't know."

"A star?" His eyebrows slammed together and worry clouded his eyes. Somewhere, from the surrounding forest, an owl let out its lonely call.

Jillian, still clinging to MacGregor, felt the tiniest breath of wind play against the back of her neck. "Why would anyone cut a star or any kind of symbol into the trunk of that tree?"

"It's a calling card. Whoever tied you up wanted the world to know that it's his handiwork."

"Sweet Jesus," she whispered as the realization that she was in the hands of a demented killer suddenly hit home.

"It's fresh. He did it today. After binding you to the tree."

"I don't know. I don't remember." She stared at the crude symbol, and though the day was still bright, the snow blindingly white in the sunlight, she felt a darkness hidden in the trees, an evil concealed but present in the icy forest.

"You have slivers in your hair." He pulled a bit of wood out and she nearly threw up. The thought of the monster working over her as she was slumped against the ropes, of him taking the time to carve out a symbol as she was helpless, drugged and naked, made her sick.

A man who would go to so much trouble wouldn't give up.

MacGregor must've felt it, too—the danger that lay in the surrounding thickets. His features hardened and his gaze scoured the surrounding woodland. "Let's get out of here," he said. He carried her to a stump, where he set her on her good foot, then turned so that his back was to her. "Wrap your legs around my waist and hold onto my neck."

"You can't carry me like . . ."

He stared at her so hard her thought dissipated and she let her voice trail off.

"I was in the war, Jillian. I've packed out soldiers and they were a helluva lot heavier than you. It was the desert, a hundred degrees, and I had a lot of equipment. You . . . here . . . a piece of cake."

"Yeah, right," she said, but didn't argue. She thought about the fact that she was naked from the hips down, and though she felt a flush of embarrassment, his stare convinced her that they had no choice. "I should try to walk."

"You should climb the hell on my back so we can get out of here now," he said, "before whoever did this to you decides to come back."

"Come back? No," she said.

"Seems pretty determined to me."

She didn't want to believe it, couldn't let herself think that the monster who had debased her and left her to suffer and die in the wilderness would still be stalking her. But she stared at the forest with new eyes, with a new fear. What if, even now, the psycho was watching them through binoculars or sighting her through a rifle.

Her throat went dry and fear, cold as the air surrounding them, burrowed deep into her heart. Who would be doing this to her? Trying to kill her, but doing it slowly. Ritualistically. "Is this . . . this being tied to a tree and left, the way the serial killer does it?"

"After he shoots out the tires of their cars. I think so. At least I read of a couple of women it happened to, but that was before the last spate of storms knocked out all the phone lines and electricity."

"You think me and the other women were targeted for a reason?"

"I'd bet on it."

She studied the horizon, searching for a dark figure lurking on the ridge, a sparkle of reflection off field glasses or a rifle's sight. Was someone even now aiming at the back of her head or the spot between her shoulder blades?

"So, we'd better not go back to the cabin." He was thinking aloud as he walked into the forest from the clearing.

"Why not?"

"He could be waiting for us."

"He thinks I'm dead."

"Does he?" MacGregor wasn't convinced. "What makes you so sure that he isn't watching us now?"

"The fact that we're still alive. He's got two guns that we know of, the one he used on Harley and the one you left for me, which he took. If he was still around, he would have picked you off before you cut me loose."

"But if he figures out you didn't die, he'll be back," MacGregor said, breathing with some difficulty. "When he couldn't get you in the wrecked car, he tracked you down."

"How?"

"Good question, but whoever this guy is, he's damned determined." He cast a glance over his shoulder. "Are you still betting on your ex?"

"Not if this guy is a serial killer."

He shifted her again and she tried not to think about

her bare thighs surrounding his waist, the way she jostled against him. It was all too bizarre, like something out of a weird, disjointed dream—the frigid cold, being half-dressed and carried, a killer potentially watching them after having tied her to a tree. "Not Mason," she said at length. "It doesn't make sense."

"Not the serial killer type?"

"No." Mason Rivers was a lot of things, some of them not good. He was greedy and a cheat, an attorney who could bend the rules to his way of thinking, but a cold-blooded murderer? No way.

"Hold on." He hiked her body up higher and she bit back the urge to cry out.

Walking briskly, trudging through the knee-deep snow and beginning to sweat despite the frigid temperature, MacGregor said, "Tell you what. I'll leave you near the cabin, then check it out. If it's safe, I'll carry you there and then I'll get Harley."

Her heart twisted at the thought of the dog. "I'm so sorry."

"Don't write him off yet. He's tougher than he looks."

But she didn't believe it. The dog had been shot so badly he couldn't move, then had been cruelly left to bleed and die in the snow.

"That twisted son of a bitch," she whispered, her fingers curling into fists.

"Tell me what happened." MacGregor was breathing hard now, sweat trickling down his neck as he trudged on.

"I could try to walk."

"I'm okay."

"But—"

"Just tell me what happened," he said tersely. "How you ended up tied to the tree without a stitch on."

"Okay." As he hauled her down a short hill and across a frozen stream, Jillian began with her fears, how she'd been waiting for MacGregor at the cabin as the hours had passed, how she'd worried that he wasn't returning, that something had happened to him, how she'd let the dog out to relieve himself before realizing she'd made a mistake.

"I was watching him and then Harley took off. I followed, but with my damned ankle and using a crutch, there was no way I could keep up with him. He took off through a thicket and I followed and then . . . and then . . . oh God, I heard a gunshot and this horrible, painful yelp. It was awful," she said, replaying the horrible scene in her mind. "I found him and he was just lying in the snow. . . . Oh dear God, it was so awful," she whispered, her teeth chattering.

"And you didn't see the guy?" MacGregor said, trudging onward, through the play of sunlight and shadow, and heading, she assumed, toward the cabin.

"I don't remember anything after coming upon the dog. I . . . I don't know what happened to my clothes or my crutch or the rifle. He jumped me from behind, put a rag soaked in something—I think maybe ether—over my face. The next thing I knew I woke up naked and tied to the tree."

"Where did the bastard go?"

"I don't know," she said. "As I said, I was out." She shuddered and he held her closer, his body warmth seeping through the T-shirt he still wore and the bulky sweater covering her body.

"Did you recognize anything about him?"

"I didn't see him." And that was the God's honest truth. He'd jumped her from behind and . . .

A noise caught her attention.

"What's that?" she asked, looking up through the ice-

laden canopy of naked branches just as she recognized
the *whomp, whomp, whomp* of a helicopter's rotor
whirring in the distance.

"Maybe help," he said, looking up, squinting into the
heavens. His lips tightened a fraction just as a rescue
copter appeared over the sharp crest of the surrounding mountains.

"Oh God, you're right!" Her heart soared and her
throat closed. Rescue! Finally!

Still holding her with one arm, Zane waved frantically, trying to get the pilot's attention. "What did I tell
ya?" he said with more than a touch of irony. "The Cav-
alry is finally on its way!"

MacGregor sat in the uncomfortable chair in the interrogation room and, while the two investigators peppered him with questions, stared at the large one-way
mirror through which he knew the sheriff, district attorney and probably a host of other cops were watching
his reactions. He could invoke his right to a lawyer; hell,
they were expecting it as they videotaped the interview,
but he had nothing to hide.

He picked his way through the minefield of questions, answering honestly but not giving up any extra information in the cinder-block room, where the acrid
scent of ammonia couldn't quite hide the smells of
body odor, vomit and desperation. Fluorescent tubes offered a buzzing, jittery light. Mounted in one corner
was a camera, its lens focused on the small table, where
a half-filled ashtray sat in one corner and a thick manila
file with notes jotted across it and papers stuffed inside
lay, like a coiled snake, silent and deadly, ready to strike
in a split second.

". . . so you expect us to believe that in the middle of
one of the worst blizzards in the last decade, you just

came across Jillian Rivers's car and saved her?" the
taller detective, Pescoli, asked. Her eyebrows were
raised in wonder, her expression total disbelief.

"I heard the sound of the rifle report," he said again.
"That's why I found her. And there was a break in the
weather, a small one, but a break."

The other detective, a quieter, calmer woman with
shiny black hair knotted at the base of her neck and
eyes that were an intense, unreadable brown, was listening. Something in her demeanor suggested that she believed him, or that at least enough of his rendition of
the events was believable to have her doubt him as a suspect.

He'd told them the entire story. Once the helicopter
had rescued Jillian and he, too, had been hauled into
the chopper, he'd been handcuffed and brought to the
sheriff's department while Jillian was taken to a hospital. Here, in this dull, windowless room with its flat gray
walls and cement floor, he'd been offered a folding
chair at a simple table and the cuffs had been removed
as he'd given his statement. At first he'd been spitting
mad, demanding his freedom, insisting that someone
find his dog, cursing the fact that no one seemed to believe that he'd actually saved Jillian Rivers rather than
tried to harm her.

But this woman, Alvarez, had told him they'd found
his dog, alive, and she was beginning to buy into some of
what he was telling her. It had been hours since the helicopter had touched down, a long time since he'd been
hauled in here and they'd begun interrogating him.

The room was cold but he'd been given another one
of his shirts, one brought from his cabin, which, he
knew, had been turned inside out while the detectives
had looked for evidence, clues that he'd been involved
not only in Jillian Rivers's abduction but the murders of
several other women.

Pictures of corpses had been laid on the table in front of him, photos of battered, dead women, all of whom had been lashed to trees and left in the elements to die.

"You've never met any of these women before?" he was asked for about the twentieth time.

"No."

"You don't recognize them?"

"No."

He held Pescoli's gaze. "I've never seen any of them before in my life."

Pissed, she walked away from him and rotated her neck a bit, as if she, too, were weary of this discussion that was going nowhere.

"You have a record," she said, leaning against the wall and crossing her arms under her chest.

"That's right."

"And we're not talking about speeding tickets. You killed a man in Denver. Did time."

MacGregor didn't say anything. Didn't have to. They had his file, knew all about the charges.

"So you're not a stranger to murder."

It wasn't a question. He didn't rise to the bait. The charge had been manslaughter. Big difference. They both knew it. He wondered what time it was but resisted the urge to check his watch. They'd been at it long enough that he'd told them not only how he'd found Jillian but what had transpired in the ensuing days. He figured everything he told them would be confirmed by his cabin or by Jillian herself. He'd already asked about her, and they'd responded with, "She's at the hospital under a doctor's care," but wouldn't give him any other information. The same was true of Harley. "He's alive. A vet is examining him," was all he got.

"You have books on astrology and astronomy," Alvarez said. Again, a statement.

"And you're a guide, know the area," Pescoli added, double-teaming him. "You've led expeditions to Cougar Pass?"

"Yes."

"And you've fished in September Creek?"

"Of course."

"Know about Broken Pine Lodge?" she asked, leaning closer, near enough that he smelled the faint scent of perfume laced with cigarette smoke.

"I'm a guide. I know the area."

"Including all the places the bodies and cars were found." She pulled a map from the file on the edge of the desk. Upon the familiar topography were red marks that he assumed were the areas in which they found the bodies and the cars. "You've been to all of these places, right?" She pointed out the marked areas.

"At one time or another, yes. But not recently."

They kept at it, asking him what he'd done this winter, specifically centering on the dates around the twentieth of each month. They asked what he could tell them about the significance of the stars carved into the boles of the trees and then they showed him copies of notes on white paper, notes with letters that meant nothing to him other than they seemed to progress—with each new victim, new letters, the initials of the dead woman, were inserted.

"So you're asking us to believe that you're not the Star-Crossed Killer. That's what the press has dubbed you."

"Ask Jillian Rivers," he suggested.

"We have. And you know what? She's not exactly backing you up."

He didn't flinch. Didn't believe this hard-nosed detective with her narrowed eyes. "In fact, she said there were times when you were gone for hours. *Hours.*" She closed the gap between herself and the table and pointed to the pictures of the dead women. "Enough time to get to your lair and prod your victim to her doom."

"My lair?" he repeated. "Are you kidding? *Lair?*"

"A cave or another cabin, maybe something like the old abandoned lodge, a mining shed, some place where you keep them."

She was fishing. Didn't have a case and she knew it, all the while hoping he'd get mad enough to blurt out some piece of critical information to lock him to the murders.

"So are you going to arrest me or what?" he asked, finally tired of the game. He was exhausted, mentally fatigued, and his bullshit meter hovered well over full. He'd said what he had to say.

"We're holding you."

He knew the law, knew this was within their rights. "Okay, but I'm done answering questions. I've given you my statement, so anything else you want to ask me will be with my attorney present. Garret Wilkes in Missoula. Give him a call." He stood then, half-expecting the bigger woman to order him back into his chair, but she didn't.

She looked as tired as he felt, and if she was any cop at all, she'd already figured out he was innocent.

"I want to see my dog and talk to Jillian."

Pescoli was having none of it. "Can't do it."

"Sure you can. As soon as you give up all this 'bad cop' act."

Pescoli's eyes flashed.

"I'll see what I can do," Alvarez said, stepping in before her partner did anything they'd both regret. She fished her handcuffs from her back pocket. "For now, though, Mr. MacGregor, you're going to have to spend the rest of the night in a holding cell. Compliments of Pinewood County."

Chapter Twenty

"I don't care what the doctor says, I need to be released and I need to be released now," Jillian insisted until a nurse shut her up by stuffing a thermometer under her tongue. Lying in the hospital bed, hooked up to an IV, nearly gagging on the damned thermometer, she plotted her escape. It was only a matter of going against her doctor's orders, and as far as she was concerned, she needed to get out now.

She'd never been one to sit idle, and lying around in a hospital bed was worse. The television was tuned in to some sitcom that should have died a death three seasons earlier, and there was noise from the outer hallway. The nurses' hub was just outside her door and conversation, along with the rattle of carts and whisper of footsteps, seeped in through her cracked door.

Her room was small but private, with a large window overlooking a nearly empty parking lot that had been plowed of snow. Security lights offered a smoky blue glow, and a few flakes were falling again, reminding Jillian how cold she'd been, how she'd nearly died from exposure and that she was lucky to be in a warm, lighted room in a clean bed.

If not for MacGregor, she could very easily be dead or dying in the frigid night. She shivered inwardly at the thought and decided she should be a little grateful instead of bitchy.

With a ping, the thermometer indicated it had found her internal temperature.

The nurse, a heavy woman of around fifty, was holding the base of the electronic thermometer and wasn't paying too much attention to any of Jillian's complaints. She recorded the temperature, removed the probe and, with the dexterity borne of years of service, shot the plastic sleeve off the probe and into a waiting trash can. "Ninety-eight point nine," she said without much enthusiasm. In fact, Nurse Claire Patterson seemed a little ragged around the edges, as if she'd been pulling a double shift. A trace of lipstick had faded, and if she'd been wearing any makeup it had rubbed off to show a reddish mask of rosacea.

"Not even ninety-nine," Jillian pointed out as Nurse Claire tightened the blood-pressure cuff over her arm. "Not elevated enough to keep me."

"I'll see what the doctor says but he wanted you overnight for observation." Her eyes didn't move from the dial on the cuff.

"I don't need 'observation.'" Her chest and ankle had been X-rayed, and she'd lucked out and was suffering only a sprained ankle, which a doctor had taped, not even placed in a cast. Her ribs turned out to be bruised. Miraculously, she'd suffered no fractures or broken bones, just as MacGregor had predicted. Good. Her ribs still hurt like hell, though, but if she were given a prescription for pain medication, she saw no reason she needed to be kept a prisoner in this small, rural hospital.

"BP's one ten over seventy-five. Normal," the nurse said with a nod of her head as she read Jillian's blood pressure. "Good." She marked the chart again. "I think the police want to talk to you."

"I already spoke with them."

Nurse Claire stopped to take her pulse, was satisfied with the count and wrote the information down. Then she looked up and her expression was kinder than it had been. "I know, but they want to interview you *again*."

As if Jillian were lying. Why didn't they believe her? Why did they treat MacGregor like a criminal?

"I already told them everything I know," she argued, her vow to not let her anger get the better of her tongue quickly forgotten. The police had questioned her in the helicopter and when she'd first arrived at the hospital, but her doctor had intervened.

"I'm sure you did." Claire's gaze touched Jillian's. "I'll talk to Dr. Haas and see what I can do about getting you released, but I doubt he'll agree."

Terrific, Jillian thought as she watched the nurse head to the door. She grabbed the television remote from the tray next to her bed and muted a commercial for home-baked pizza. *Home.* How long had it been since she had curled up in her favorite overstuffed chair, absently petting Marilyn while eating popcorn and watching some schmaltzy old movie?

She'd already called her mother and Linnie had cried on the telephone. "I knew they'd found you; they called earlier. But . . . but, oh Jillian, I was so afraid that I'd lost you forever, that you'd been abducted by that crazed madman and I would never see you, hear your voice again." Her mother had started sobbing and tears had tracked from Jillian's eyes, as well.

"I'm okay."

"But what you've gone through. With that madman."

"Oh no, Mom, you've got it all wrong. I was safe most of the time." She'd spent nearly half an hour trying to convince her mother that Zane MacGregor was not the killer. When Linnie had asked about who had abducted her and left her in the forest, Jillian had told her mother exactly what she'd told the police—that she had no idea who had tried to murder her.

Linnie hadn't been convinced but her sobs had stopped abruptly. "I'll take the next flight to Missoula and rent a car and—"

"No, Mom!" Jillian had cut her off. "I'll be home in a day or two and I'll call you with a new cell phone number."

"But after your ordeal—"

"I'm fine. The doctors are treating me and nothing's broken and I'll be able to drive home as soon as the roads are clear."

"You're injured! I should be with you." And then Jillian had understood. Her mother wanted not only to help her, but also to share in some of the bizarre limelight of the case. Already reporters had tried to call her room.

"I'm okay, Mom. Really. Don't come. Just call Dusti and tell her I'm fine, and anyone else who asks."

"Well, of course!" Linnie was never more in her element than when she had a task to complete. "And what about the newspapers and the television reporters here? I've already had a call."

"Really?" Jillian was floored. "How did they find out about me?"

"I've no idea."

"Tell you what, Mom, you handle them. Okay? Can you do that?"

"Of course!"

"Great, that would be good. And I've got another favor."

"Shoot," her mother said eagerly.

"Would you call Emily Hardy and explain, then pick up my cat and take care of her until I get back?"

"Oh, of course, honey. Consider it done!" Linnie loved nothing better than having a mission.

"Thanks, Mom. I'll call you in a while, once I get a cell phone. Then I'll let you know when I'll be back."

"If you're sure you don't need me—"

"I'm fine, but I need you to handle these things for me." She gave her mother the number of the hospital. "I'm in three twenty-three."

"Got it," her mother said.

"Thanks. I'll call soon."

"Thank God you're okay! And don't you worry about the press. I'll handle them."

I bet.

"I had planned to visit your sister for the holidays," she'd said. "Why don't you join us? I can board the cat and you could meet me there."

"I don't think so. Isn't Christmas in . . . what? Three days?" Jillian couldn't imagine spending time with her sister's family in San Diego. She loved her nieces—they were both pistols and gave Dusti a run for her money—but she didn't doubt for a second that her older sister would be uptight about making Christmas "perfect" and in so doing ruining all the fun of the holidays. Not to mention Drew the Drip. God, he was a bore. A tall, good-looking man who worked sixty hours a week. In his spare time he played golf, smoked cigars with "the boys" and talked forever about the stock market. He could drive Jillian up the wall. He'd been pressuring Dusti into getting pregnant again in hopes of fathering a son.

Yeah, Christmas with the Bellamys sounded like a blast.

Jillian had decided to pass.

"Yes. I'm leaving on the twenty-fourth. I'll . . . I'll figure out something for your cat."

"Emily might keep her longer."

"I'll check," Linnie said with relief.

"Okay. Give Reece and Carrie my love. Tell them Aunt Jillie hopes to see them soon."

"Of course! And, as I said, I'll take care of the reporters, don't you worry about a thing. We'll celebrate when we both get home. After the New Year. I'll . . . I'll throw a party."

"Oh, don't, please." She thought of one of Linnie's overdone gala events and shuddered. Too much to think about.

"Whatever you want," Linnie said, her tone a little wounded.

Jillian wasn't going to pick up the guilt card her mother was playing. She loved her mother, yes, but there was no denying the woman was a piece of work. Instead she wrapped up the conversation and plotted how to get herself free of the hospital. She didn't have time to loll around. Someone seemed hell-bent on killing her, and her savior, Zane MacGregor, was locked up. They'd strapped him into handcuffs, for God's sake. Her car was wrecked, her cell phone was confiscated and someone was trying to convince her that her first husband was still alive.

Scratching at her wrist where the tape from the IV was pulling, she tried to think about the future, what she would do when she was released. In the past ten days her life had changed irrevocably. She still didn't know if Aaron was alive or not, she had no idea who had tried to kill her, and then there was Zane MacGregor, whom she ridiculously felt she was falling for.

Falling for? You barely know the man. The police think he might be involved in your abduction. Ten days trapped in a cabin does not a love story make. This is crazy. It has to be the Vicadin talking.

But, the truth was, ever since she'd been "rescued" by the police, her thoughts had been with MacGregor and his dog, one being interviewed by the local cops, the other under a veterinarian's care. At least Harley had survived the gunshot—one of the few bits of good news from today.

She edged toward the precipice of the bed, trying to see into the corridor. The door to her room was ajar and over the rustle of footsteps and ding of an elevator she heard bits of disjointed conversations.

One high-pitched voice was worried about a patient in room 314, afraid that the antibiotics wouldn't halt his pneumonia. She was wondering where the hell the doctor was.

Another voice, a male voice, was talking on the phone, trying to give someone on the other end information about dosages of medications.

A third was gossiping, and Jillian had to set her jaw as she was the subject of the conversation.

". . . just like the others, I guess. Not a stitch on and tied to a tree. Can you believe it?"

The response was muted; Jillian couldn't catch it.

"I know, it's beyond weird to think a serial killer is around, like, here, in Grizzly Falls. Why here? I keep telling Jason it's the middle of nowhere, so who would think a psycho would end up here? . . . What? Oh, I don't think so. Someone we know? God, wouldn't that be the creepiest. I mean, we've got our share of village idiots. Oh, that's not P.C. I mean we've got more than our share of 'local color,' what with Ivor Hicks thinking he was abducted by aliens."

"Abducted, and he still gets orders from them," the other woman said, and Jillian recognized Nurse Claire's nasal tone. "Don't forget Grace Perchant, who found one of the cars. She's the gal who's always seeing ghosts."

"Spirits. Like she's got a direct line to the ghost world."

"Oh, sure. If you ask me, that Grace is already in another world."

They chuckled together as a phone rang, interrupting their conversation.

Great, Jillian thought, more anxious than ever to get out of the hospital. She'd been in her room only a few hours, but already the four walls were beginning to close in on her.

She tried to convince herself she should stay. A voice in her head reminded her of the fact that she wasn't a hundred percent yet. *What's wrong with letting someone else take care of you? Why can't you relax, sleep in a warm bed, let the doctors and nurses monitor your injuries? Then you can pull yourself together, think about leaving in the morning or even later, after you've slept and eaten breakfast, had a shower and put everything into perspective. Then you can figure out what you're going to do.*

So far her care here at Pinewood General had been good. She'd been served a dinner of broiled chicken, green beans, some kind of squash, a dinner roll and a cup of fruited Jell-O. Not exactly five-star restaurant fare, but not bad. And an aide had bathed her with warm rags that had felt like heaven, though she still couldn't wait for a long, hot shower.

So what's the rush?

Are you going to start looking for Aaron again?

Or are you going back to Seattle?

Closing her eyes, she couldn't decide. And then there was MacGregor. She couldn't just leave him or Harley. . . . Dear Lord, she was a mental case!

What about the police? You're not done with them yet.

She groaned at the thought of another interview.

The last thing she wanted to do was talk to the police again. She'd already given her statement and suffered through an interview with not only two female detectives, but also a team of agents from the FBI, all of whom seemed to think that she was a victim and that Zane MacGregor was the twisted sicko who had been terrorizing this area of the Bitterroot Mountains.

Jillian knew better now.

Ever since he'd cut her away from that solitary cedar tree and carried her to safety, she'd trusted him. Zane MacGregor meant her no harm, and now, from what she understood, he was in jail, trying to explain himself.

Her conversations with the police had been tedious and tense. First she'd undergone questioning from the two female detectives from the Pinewood Sheriff's Department, Regan Pescoli and her partner, the quieter Selena Alvarez. That interview had been before a fun Q and A with the FBI.

It seemed that everyone associated with the police wanted to hang MacGregor for the recent spate of killings. They clearly wanted answers—a solution—and they were hell-bent on pinning the blame on someone, someone like MacGregor.

Jillian had made it clear that she wasn't buying into any of their theories against the man she insisted had saved her. The cops had been irritated with her that she had been more concerned with Zane MacGregor's fate and his dog's health than she was about trying to nail him as a serial killer.

"That's ridiculous," she'd told them, unable to hide her anger as Alvarez had taken notes and taped the conversation on a small recorder. Petite, with sharp features and hair black enough to shine blue under the fluorescent lights, she seemed the more serious, less explosive of the two.

The taller detective, Pescoli, had stood near the doorway, as if giving herself and Jillian a little space. Tanned and slightly freckled, though it was the dead of winter, she'd obviously spent lots of time outdoors. But under the fluorescent glow of the hospital lights, Pescoli had appeared dead on her feet, dark smudges showing under her eyes, curly red-brown hair surrounding an angular, uncompromising face. She seemed intense. Driven. Angry.

"MacGregor didn't try to hurt me," Jillian argued. "He saved me, for God's sake. You saw him carrying me away from the tree where I . . . where I'd been tied and left. If it weren't for Zane MacGregor, I'd be dead!"

The cops were unmoved. "But if you didn't see your attacker, how do you know it wasn't him?" Pescoli had folded her arms over her chest, almost defying Jillian to lie to her.

"I just know," she asserted. "I got the sense that the person who jumped me from behind wasn't as tall as MacGregor or as heavy."

Alvarez had stepped in. "But you really didn't catch a glimpse of his face or any identifying marks?"

"No."

"Did you see his hands?"

"I saw nothing. Just . . . black gloves. I felt the weight of him as he forced me to the ground. He pressed a rag over my face and I fought but couldn't push him off. I passed out."

Pescoli nodded. "But it's true that MacGregor had been gone for several hours, right? You didn't really know where he was."

"He left me with a rifle. Not a move I'd expect if he were just going to kill me."

They didn't respond.

Jillian added, "He damned well didn't shoot his own pet!"

Calmly Pescoli said, "He's done time for murder."

"Manslaughter," Jillian corrected, irritated beyond belief. This was nuts! "He told me all about it."

"Did he?" Pescoli hadn't bothered to hide her skepticism as she'd walked closer to stand near the side of Jillian's elevated bed. "All you heard was his side."

"True. And I believe him." She'd met the bigger cop's stare. "I want to see him."

"He's in custody," Pescoli said.

"For what? My God, didn't I just tell you? The man saved my life!" Jillian had understood why they'd considered MacGregor a suspect, but to actually hear the words from the detectives made it so much more real, so much more painful.

The softer-spoken detective, Alvarez, suggested, "Why don't you just tell us what happened from the beginning? Why were you in Montana in the first place? You're from Seattle, right?"

So Jillian told them everything she could remember, from the time in Seattle when she'd received the phone calls from an anonymous caller about Aaron to when she received the pictures of the man who was supposed to be her dead husband. She explained what she remembered of her car accident and the rescue, then of waking up in Zane MacGregor's cabin. She didn't hold back. She was convinced that MacGregor had saved her life. She believed she'd seen someone else lurking in the trees on the day of the accident and later MacGregor had found evidence that someone had been watching the cabin. MacGregor had not only offered her a loaded rifle but he'd also left her with the dog to guard her.

Pescoli and Alvarez interrupted her a few times, but for the most part, they listened as she explained that Zane MacGregor had been as desperate as she to find a way out of the cabin and into town. He'd been worried about her, had wanted to get her to a doctor.

She had been convinced the truth would only help MacGregor. But she'd been wrong.

After the interview, she realized that the more she tried to assure Pescoli and Alvarez that Zane MacGregor was innocent, the less they had believed her.

Which was downright infuriating.

The good news, if there was any, was that they'd brought her things to her. The suitcase with her clothes, as well as her purse with her wallet, ID and credit cards. They were still "processing" her bags, whatever that meant. The only item missing was her cell phone, which, Alvarez had explained, they wanted to hold on to for "a day or so." It bugged the hell out of Jillian not to have the phone. In the cell's memory were stored all of the phone numbers of her friends, family and business associates, as well as text and voice messages she'd saved.

Assured that they would release the cell phone "as soon as possible," they'd asked a few more questions and thanked her, as if to end the interview. Alvarez had clicked off the recorder and Pescoli was one step from the door.

"Wait a minute," Jillian had called, and both women stopped in their tracks. "I just want to say again that Zane MacGregor never did anything that would indicate he wanted me dead and he had ample opportunity. I was unconscious, unable to walk on my own, nearly immobile with my bruised ribs. If he wanted me dead, believe me, I would be."

The cops didn't say a word and she couldn't help but add, "I know you've got a serious problem on your hands with this serial killer. You have to find him. But keep looking. You've got the wrong man."

Alvarez met her gaze. "We're checking into all possibilities, Ms. Rivers. MacGregor is only one person of interest."

"But I told you—" she started, then read something

she didn't like in the smaller woman's eyes. Though she had been trying to hide it, Detective Selena Alvarez, the one detective she'd trusted, hadn't believed her story, or at least not all of it.

"Oh my God," Jillian had whispered, aghast. "You think . . . you think what? That I'm lying? Or . . . or that I'm confused or that I've fallen for my abductor?" Her heart sank as the two women stood in front of the doorway, blocking her view of the nurses' station.

"Right now, Ms. Rivers," Pescoli said, "we're not sure what to think."

"I'm telling you, it's not MacGregor."

"Duly noted. Thanks." Pescoli, obviously irritated, stepped out of the room.

"We might have more questions later," Alvarez said and took the time to return to Jillian's bedside. "If you think of anything else, or have questions of your own, please call." She left her card on the table near Jillian's water glass. "This," she added, tapping the card with a slim finger, "has my direct line at the sheriff's office, as well as my cell. Thanks again."

And then she left, walking briskly to catch up with her partner.

Jillian had picked up the card and slipped it into her wallet. She'd thought she'd been finished with questions but she'd been wrong.

Within the next hour the FBI had sent agents Halden and Chandler to double-team Jillian one more time. As if she'd remember something new.

They'd gone over the same information but were a little more reserved and held back their emotions better than the local cops had.

Not that Jillian had liked them much better.

Stephanie Chandler, tall, blond and athletic, without so much of a hint of a smile in her blue eyes, had led the interview, while her partner, with his slight southern drawl and easy smile, had come up with a few questions of his own. Of the two, Craig Halden had seemed vastly more relaxed and approachable. But Jillian had suspected the good ol' boy charm was an act and she was damned tired of answering questions.

"Okay," she'd finally said, her eyes focused on Chandler. "I've already said everything I know to Detectives Pescoli and Alvarez. You can check with them. It's all on tape." She shifted in the bed, her IV tugging on her wrist, the bedclothes starting to wrinkle.

Halden, as if he agreed with her, had nodded thoughtfully. He'd offered the kind of aw-shucks grin meant to put her at ease. The country-boy smile had only had the opposite effect and ratcheted up her anxiety level. "Yeah," he said. "We know. This is just routine."

"I wouldn't think there is anything routine about a serial-killer investigation," Jillian countered, and for the first time saw a twitch in his partner's arched eyebrows. Despite her cool façade, Stephanie Chandler was an intelligent woman who didn't miss a trick.

Which wasn't surprising. The woman was an FBI agent, after all.

So Jillian had felt a little outgunned and unnerved. In the span of her lifetime, Jillian had never considered the police the enemy. Sure, she worried about speeding tickets whenever she was being followed by a police cruiser, but her uncle had been an Oregon State police officer and one of her cousins was with the Reno, Nevada, police department. Aside from a few drinks before she was twenty-one, experimenting with pot a total of twice and inadvertently running a red light or pushing the pedal to the metal on the freeway, Jillian had never broken the law.

The only time she'd had the slightest inclination to think the authorities might not be looking out for her best interests had been in Suriname when Aaron had gone missing. Maybe it had been the language barrier, or a natural distrust of foreign police fostered by the news and movies or her own prejudices. Whatever the reason, Jillian had doubted that the men in power in that remote area of the jungle were on the up-and-up.

"The thing is," Jillian told the federal agents, "the only reason I was in Montana in the first place was because of the pictures I was sent, the phone calls I received, all indicating that my first husband, Aaron Caruso, was alive."

"Caruso as in Robinson Crusoe?"

"Spelled differently," Chandler said.

So they had already checked. "You've looked into it," Jillian said.

Chandler nodded. "When your car was located, we started searching for you."

"And digging into my personal life."

Chandler didn't crack a smile. "We wanted to find you."

Halden said, "But we just found the photographs at the cabin today. We'll analyze them."

"I'll get them back?"

"Eventually."

"I need them."

Chandler nodded again. "So do we. Now, tell us. Who do you think called you?"

"I don't know."

"You didn't recognize the voice?"

"No, it was a whisper and caller ID didn't come up with a name or number." She looked from one agent to the other. "And I don't know who sent me the pictures. The postmark on the envelope was Missoula, so I was going to confront my ex-husband, as he lives there."

"Mason Rivers?"

"Yes, he's an attorney, excuse me, a partner in the law firm of Olsen, Nye and Rivers," she'd said, but had the feeling they already knew this information as well. "We were divorced two years ago."

"When was the last time you saw him?" Halden asked.

"Just a few days after the divorce was final. We exchanged the final things we had of each other's. It was all very . . . civil."

"And since then?"

"Nothing. I wasn't invited to the wedding." Jillian felt a twisted smile curve her lips. "Sherice, that's Mason's new wife, she's not a big fan."

"Of yours?"

"Of any woman Mason remotely showed an interest in. That goes double for ex-wives."

Halden chuckled, but Chandler didn't react.

They asked a few more questions, then, satisfied for the moment, concluded the interview and took their leave.

Jillian had been left alone, hooked up to an IV she didn't think she needed, her vital signs monitored by one nurse after another.

The feeling that lingered after the FBI agents left made her uncomfortable. She sensed the detectives and agents were trying to trip her up so she would incriminate MacGregor. And that just wasn't right.

And then her mind circled to her own circumstances. Why had someone lured her to Montana in an effort to kill her? After the second attempt on her life, she was damned certain, as the police were, that she had become the target of a serial killer.

How did that fit?

Who hated her so much?

Who hated the other women?

She glanced up at the muted television, noticing that the local news was on the air. There, on the screen, was her own face, the photo from her driver's license.

"Oh God," she whispered as she turned the sound on. A reporter dressed in a blue parka, snow falling around her, currently stood in front of the emergency room doors of this very hospital. Brunette and serious, a gust of wind ruffling her hood, she explained about Jillian's abduction.

The image on the screen changed quickly to an aerial shot of a snow-covered clearing surrounded by forested hills. Near the edge of the snowy glen was a lone cedar tree.

Jillian started shivering when she recognized the area. The snow around the tree was trodden and mashed, and ropes lay like dark snakes on the white ground.

Her stomach roiled as she stared at the lengths of nylon that had cut into her skin.

Deputies from the sheriff's department were examining the roped-off scene as a camera from a helicopter recorded the whole tableau.

Jillian told herself to turn the damned television off, to stop looking at the place where she'd nearly died, but the images held a macabre fascination for her.

Even tucked in the warmth of the hospital bedding, she quivered. Her memories were vivid. Visceral. She remembered waking up tied to the rough bark, her flesh so cold it stung, the nylon rope digging into her skin like teeth.

She remembered the dark, gloved hands mashing that chemical-soaked rag into her face. And the glimmer of a scar on the wrist. Or was that her own wrist? She checked her arms, looking for a crescent-shaped scar. Nothing. Was it a memory? Or part of a nightmare?

Think, Jillian, think, she told herself as the screen switched again to the anchor desk, and then, to her horror, they listed the names and photographs of the women who hadn't survived the maniac's attack—pic-

tures of vital, smiling women. Jillian thought she might
be sick as the voiceover continued and yet another victim's smiling face filled the screen.

"... and as an update, the other victim who survived
the killer's attack, still unidentified, is listed in critical
condition at a hospital in Missoula. The victim, we've
learned, has not regained consciousness at the time of
this report. . . ."

Another woman survived?

Riveted, Jillian watched the rest of the newscast,
much of which was devoted to reporting on the "Star-
Crossed Killer" and his targets. She learned of the victims, of how they had endured the same fate as she,
stripped of clothing and tied to a tree, where a star had
been cut over their heads.

She clicked off the television and glanced out the
window again to the night, where snow was falling
rapidly, millions of tiny flakes visible as they danced in
the light from the security cameras.

Even now, the killer could be outside.

Waiting.

The soft strains of music filtered in from the hallway,
an instrumental rendition of "Silent Night."

She was exhausted and, deep down, frightened. Yes,
she'd survived, but how did she know the killer wouldn't
try again? She thought of Zane MacGregor, now behind
bars, and of Harley, still alive but suffering . . . all because some whacko wanted her dead.

Why?

Who?

*What unknown enemy had she made? One determined to
take her life?*

Back to the same old questions.

She thought of Aaron and their marriage, how at
times it had been strained and distant. There had been

incidents when he'd seemed to not be in the same room with her.

Jillian yawned, fighting exhaustion. Aaron hadn't liked living in Seattle. A wanderer at heart, he'd wanted to get away from the gloom of the city, go somewhere with more seasons. He'd always brought up moving east, over the mountains. . . .

All of her bones seemed to ache and she realized how truly spent she was. She could barely keep her eyes open and figured the hospital staff had slipped some kind of sedative into her IV.

Well, fine.

For tonight, she'd stop worrying about the danger that lurked outside the windows in the darkness. Maybe she could forget that something deadly and intent waited for her. Tonight she would stay in the hospital, warm and safe.

But come the morning, she was outta here.

As she started to doze off, the words to the Christmas carol slipped through her mind.

"Silent night, holy night."

Uncomfortable, she drifted off to sleep.

Chapter Twenty-One

"MacGregor's not our guy," Pescoli ground out as she parked her rig at Shorty's, an all-night diner on the main drag not far from the sheriff's department. Shorty, a cook for a mining company back before the turn of the twentieth century, had established the restaurant and, though he was long dead, his name, in flickering neon, had been indelibly etched on the landscape. A huge sign had been planted near the highway sometime in the last century.

"I thought you were convinced he was good for it."

Pescoli spit her wad of tasteless gum into a wrapper and tossed it into the ashtray. Rather than hear Alvarez bitch about her smoking, she'd found a pack of nicotine gum in her purse, popped a stick into her mouth and chewed it for the last hour or so as if her life depended on it. "I was hoping." She cut the engine and threw open the door of her Jeep, nearly hitting the side of a King Cab truck that was parked cockeyed in the lot. "I *wanted* him to be good for it." She locked the rig and trudged through the snow that was swirling down from the dark heavens. Would the storms ever abate long enough to give them a break?

"Me, too," Alvarez admitted.

Shorty's was long and low with a slightly pitched roof that was now thick with snow. Icicles dripped from the eaves and, in honor of the season, a leering, winking Santa had been propped on the roofline near one of the original smokestacks. Not so jolly, this Saint Nick. To Pescoli he looked like a pervert in a red suit and fake beard, a creepy old guy whose image had been captured on a plywood easel.

She shoved open a double set of glass doors and stepped into the "dining" area of the establishment. A wave of heat smelling of fried foods hit her hard in the face. For the most part, the open room with worn floor tiles was empty. It was too late for the dinner crowd and those patrons who remained had migrated to the sports bar that was attached via a short hallway where a vintage cigarette machine, circa 1960, still stood guard beneath "space age" dangling lights.

This was one of her regular hangouts, so just inside the door Pescoli plucked a couple of plastic-encased menus from the empty podium then walked to the back of the seating area. After taking off her jacket, gloves and hat and tossing them onto one of the faux-leather bench seats of a booth, she slid in beside them. Alvarez, too, stripped off her outerwear, but she took the time to stuff her gloves and hat into the pockets of her jacket, then hung everything on a peg attached to the side of the booth. They sat across from each other, Alvarez, as always, in a position where she could eye the front door.

They were both in lousy moods, disgusted that they were back at square one on the case, and Pescoli was looking for comfort food. She'd forgo the booze for the night, because, though officially she was off duty, she was still working the case. Everyone was. But that didn't mean she couldn't have fried food and calories galore.

They had found nothing in MacGregor's cabin to indicate he'd held any of the victims captive. Aside from the fact that he'd "rescued" Jillian Rivers and kept her with him during the storms, the only other evidence against him—and it wasn't anything worthwhile—was the fact that he had some maps of the area as well as a collection of astrology books.

It did seem as if he hadn't intended to harm Jillian Rivers, that he had in fact pulled her from harm, not once, but twice.

Which only made their job harder.

Stomach rumbling, Pescoli glanced over the menu she'd read weekly ever since the place opened and settled on a Reuben sandwich. Tonight she needed comfort food, so she changed from her usual side salad to fries, and traded her default drink of Diet Coke for a "Shorty's famous" black-and-white milkshake, which was a decadent confection of hot fudge, chocolate syrup, vanilla ice cream and crushed Oreo cookies. As the waitress Lillian had always said, "Only one way to describe the black-and-white: to die for."

Which was probably true considering the amounts of sugar, fat, and every other edible sin imaginable chocked into it.

To hell with it.

Tonight she didn't care.

Lillian appeared without a notepad. In her seventies, she was as sharp as she had been fifty years earlier, never so much as writing an order down, never making a mistake.

"You two are in here late," she observed.

Regan made a face. "Long day."

"Yeah. It was all over the TV and we had some news guys from outta town. Big van with a satellite dish, parked right over there near the Bull and Bear, just off main street."

"I know where it is," Pescoli said. She knew Rod Larimer, the B&B's innkeeper. A guy who looked like he enjoyed the breakfast part of the B&B too much, Rod loved any publicity the town could garner, was all for developing the hell out of Grizzly Falls.

"Man alive, what a day!" Lillian said, then asked slyly, "you any closer to getting that guy?"

"All the time," Pescoli said breezily, and Alvarez almost smiled.

"Three women in one day! Scares the living crap outta me, let me tell you. And I ain't the only one. I hear the customers talking, don't ya know, and everyone's pretty wigged out. We're all counting on you to kill that son of a bitch or lock him up and cut off his balls."

Lillian was nothing if not opinionated.

"I think they outlawed castration a few years back," Alvarez said dryly.

"Big mistake, if ya ask me. That's the trouble, ain't it? No one asks. Now, what can I getcha?"

Alvarez ordered a cup of lentil soup, a lettuce-wedge salad with lite bleu cheese dressing and an iced tea with extra lemon.

Was she kidding?

After a day like today?

Pescoli didn't understand it, but Alvarez never seemed to give in to pressure. She didn't smoke, barely drank, stayed clear of most men and stuck to her damned diet and exercise regimen like Super Glue.

Well, Pescoli wasn't bashful. She ordered up a heart attack and sent Lillian off grinning.

"It's worse than just MacGregor not being the doer," Alvarez said once the drinks had been delivered and Lillian had disappeared behind the swinging doors to the kitchen. They were alone in the restaurant aside from a single guy reading the paper in the far corner and some antsy teenagers sucking down sodas, eating fries and blowing straw wrappers at each other.

Thankfully the background music wasn't, for once, Christmas carols. Instead the strains of "Hotel California" could be heard over the fan of the furnace and the clink of dishes from the kitchen.

Alvarez swirled her tea with a long-handled spoon while watching the lemon slices dance around the ice cubes in her drink. "I hate to say it, but I think we've got a copycat."

Damn it all to hell. Pescoli had come up with the same irritating conclusion on her own, but she'd tried to talk herself out of it. Didn't want to believe it. "I'm listening. Why?"

"First of all, there was no note left at the scene where Jillian Rivers was found. I thought maybe MacGregor had second thoughts about killing her and had somehow destroyed the note when he went back for her, but that just doesn't work." Alvarez tested the drink, sipping through a plastic straw. "The star carved into the tree was different. Six-pointed, not five."

Pescoli decided to play devil's advocate. She plucked the cherry from her milkshake. "So maybe he was interrupted. Didn't have time to post the note."

"Still doesn't explain the star. Huh-uh. Something's up."

"It could be he's evolving. They do that." She dropped the red maraschino into her mouth.

Alvarez lifted a shoulder. "He's escalating. That much is given. But evolving?" She shook her head.

"Well, then he's panicking. That's why he's dumping the girls so fast. He's scared."

"Why?"

"Maybe we're closer than we think." Pescoli took a

long swallow of the sweet drink and nearly gave herself an ice-cream headache.

Alvarez snorted. "We're close to nothing. Nothing. Nada. Zero. Zilch."

"Could be he doesn't know that."

"Still . . . three in one day, after a pattern of one a month?" Lines of frustration showing around her lips, Alvarez shook her head and took a sip of her tea. "Nope, I'm not buying it. What does he think we know? What would it be that scares him? How could we be closer?"

Pescoli grunted. "Does the guy have a damned harem, or what? Three women, well, maybe two, if Jillian Rivers is out of the mix, both of whom we think were held hostage for a while before being dumped in the forest. How many more does he have stashed away?"

Alvarez looked up at her with horror. "Oh God . . . you think he's got others?"

"I hope not. God, I hope not."

Lillian swept through the doors from the kitchen about the same time one of the teenagers was opening his table's saltshaker. "Hey, there! Cut that out." The boy, a pimple-faced kid in a stocking cap pulled low over his eyes, froze. "I mean it." Lillian's thin lips were pursed in anger and her eyes flashed fire from behind eyeglasses rimmed in tiger stripes. The kid, flushing so that his acne was even redder than before, dropped the saltshaker, and it fell, spilling its contents across the table.

"Sorry," he muttered with a look to his friends. They all scrambled out of the booth and into the night.

"Little twerps." Lillian deposited Regan's and Selena's food on the table. "Who needs 'em? I'll clean that up and be back, if you need anything. Darn fool kids probably didn't even leave a tip!"

The man reading the paper held up his cup for another shot of coffee, and Lillian, in her ire, swept past.

"Be right with ya," she said, intent on cleaning up the spilled salt.

Alvarez cautiously spread a little dressing onto her lettuce wedge. "I guess we'll know more when we ID the victims."

Pescoli nibbled a crispy, thick fry. Fried heaven. "Missing Persons is working on that."

"Yeah, along with the FBI and agencies in the surrounding states."

"You'd think we'd find their cars." She snagged a catsup bottle from the end of the table and squirted a large pool on one side of her plate.

"Maybe they were grabbed another way."

"Doubt it." Pescoli took a long drink from her milkshake. "At least now we have two witnesses, though Jillian Rivers can't remember anything about the guy. Maybe when EH or HE wakes up she can ID him."

"*If* she wakes up."

"Oh hell, she'd better. She's our only witness. So far, since Ms. Rivers thinks Zane MacGregor is her knight in shining armor—"

"Face it, Pescoli, he might just be. Not all men are losers," Alvarez said, blowing over her steaming cup of soup, sending the scent of warm spices drifting across the table.

Though Alvarez hadn't mentioned Regan's love life specifically, it felt like a barb. Alvarez had made no bones about the fact that she thought Pescoli wasn't particular enough in her choices in men. Well, hell, she was probably right. Not that it was any of her damned business.

"MacGregor might have saved her," Alvarez said.

"But from whom?"

"That's the million-dollar question."

"Only part of the question." As she was picking up half her grilled sandwich, some of the sauerkraut fell onto her plate where the sauce was already dripping. She didn't care. "The other part is, who's the original killer, the guy with all the notches on his grisly belt?" Taking a large bite, she barely tasted the blend of corned beef, Swiss cheese, kraut and secret sauce the chef piled on rye bread. Instead, she felt that old rage, the anger she tried to keep tamped down in order to maintain her perspective, her cool. Tonight, considering the number of terrorized and murdered women piling up, it just wasn't happening. Her brain was moving too quickly and she was scared to death that the surviving victim found up at the abandoned lodge might die before she could identify her attacker.

Pescoli worked through her sandwich half, then munched on the pickle that came with the meal. There were just too many inconsistencies in this case. For one thing, the ropes were all wrong. All of them had been twisted-fiber rope—but the one used for Jillian Rivers was nylon and braided. "Unless our guy's run out of sisal, or he's trying to throw us off or just screwing with us, you're right, we've got ourselves a bonafide nutcase of a copycat. Who would want to do that?" She stared for a second at an aluminum tree spinning under a pink spotlight, moving in the opposite direction of the refrigerated pie case revolving on the counter. "And why Jillian Rivers? Simple bad luck? She was the next car through and he wanted to jump in on the action?"

"Or was she selected by the copycat for some reason?"

"A lot of questions with no answers."

Alvarez sighed and said, "I hate to admit it, but I'm with Chandler on this one. I peg the first killer as someone who likes to toy with us, show us how much smarter he is. He keeps things the same so we *know* it's him. Jillian Rivers is an anomaly. It's not just the rope that makes her a different kind of victim. No one else was

332 *Lisa Jackson*

ever drugged with ether, right? Or carried to the killing ground?" She stirred her soup. "Uh-uh. They were all marched naked to the place where they were killed, urged along with a knife or some other weapon sharp enough to make razor-like slits in their skin. And the footprints in the snow show only one set going in and out at the spot we found Jillian Rivers. Her footprints weren't there."

"She said she was carried. And there were MacGregor's prints."

"Aside from his. The other prints were smaller than his size twelves and the first killer's elevens. These are more like eights or nines, not a huge guy."

"One with a hard-on for Jillian Rivers."

"Right. Another woman with no known enemies."

"Oh, she's got enemies, at least one, maybe two."

"Who?" Alvarez asked, eyebrows lifting in interest.

"She's divorced, isn't she? Believe me. She's got enemies."

"Some divorces are amicable."

Pescoli snorted before taking another bite. "Spoken like a woman who's never been married. And here's the thing. I don't like her ex. I talked to Mason Rivers. He's just a little too slick for me." She dug into the rest of her sandwich and Alvarez polished off most of her soup as they lapsed into silence.

Pescoli couldn't help thinking of the woman lying comatose in a hospital bed in Missoula. That victim, identified with the initials E and H, was key to the case, so important she was under round-the-clock police guard, even in the hospital. Jillian Rivers, too, had a guard in the hospital, though Pescoli begrudgingly believed Alvarez's theory, that Ms. Rivers was the victim of a very determined copycat killer. A nutcase? One seeking his own sick notoriety, or something else, something more personal?

Pushing her half-eaten salad aside, Alvarez voiced her own concerns. "It doesn't look good for the woman we found at Broken Pine. The doctors don't have a lot of hope."

"I know," Pescoli said. She left a quarter of her sandwich, but polished off her milkshake as a middle-aged couple walked into the restaurant and found a private booth. They looked like they'd been married for twenty years and were still in love. Hard to believe. She tossed her napkin onto her plate and set the empty milkshake glass near the edge of the table.

"It's not like we're going to learn anything new from the dead one we found up at Cougar Pass," Pescoli said. "I'd bet dollars to donuts that we'll get the same information we did off the other victims: no epithelial transfer from the killer, nothing under the vic's fingernails, no sign of sexual attack or semen."

"Don't be so optimistic."

"She'll probably have a few broken bones courtesy of the car 'accident.'" Pescoli made air quotes as she reached for her wallet. "There will also be some bruising and contusions consistent with the accident, and evidence that she was prodded with a knife, along with burns from the ropes that bound her."

Lillian appeared. "Anything else? We've got a killer coconut creme pie tonight, only a couple pieces left. Oops. Did I say that? *Killer* creme pie? No pun intended."

"Think I'll pass," Pescoli said, and Alvarez, true to her nature and her damned diet regimen, shook her head. Just once Pescoli would love to see her partner cut loose. Have a Long Island iced tea or give in to the urge for a donut or brownie left by Joelle in the break room at the office. Or, better yet, start dating.

They squared up, each paying for her share of the meal and leaving Lillian a decent tip, before donning jackets, hats and gloves again as notes from an old Gordon Lightfoot tune swirled around them.

Outside it was cold and dark, the snow coming down fast enough that half an inch had piled on the Jeep. Pescoli felt the urge for a cigarette but pushed it aside as she squeezed into her side of the rig and noted that the King Cab truck hadn't moved. So it didn't belong to the teenagers. Nor the couple that had shown up. Maybe the guy reading the paper in the corner?

Who was he anyway?

No one she recognized. She slid behind the wheel and glanced in her rearview mirror. Sure enough, the guy who had been reading and drinking coffee was still at his table, but he was looking up, out the window, and for the briefest of seconds Pescoli thought his gaze found hers.

Ridiculous!

Her cop radar was working overtime.

"What did you think about the single guy in the diner?"

"Why? Are you looking for a date?" Alvarez snapped her seat belt into place as Regan fired the engine.

"Very funny. Really, what did you think?"

"Single. Maybe waiting for someone. He kept looking at the door."

"He pay any attention to us?" Pescoli hit the wipers and they began scraping off the snow that had collected on the windshield.

"A little. Nothing serious."

"You sure?" She turned the fan onto high and hit the button on the dash labeled DEFROST.

"Yeah. Why?" Alvarez asked, and looked over her shoulder to the restaurant, but the guy had turned his attention to his paper again. Lillian was sauntering up with a carafe of coffee, and Pescoli was suddenly uneasy, though the exchange, as Lillian poured more coffee into his cup, seemed routine. Innocent.

Still . . .

"Don't know. But he bothers me. Run the plates of the vehicles in the lot, would you?"

"Sure." That was a simple matter, as the computer was hooked up inside Pescoli's rig. "But I think this case is getting to you."

"It's getting to all of us." Pescoli pulled out of the tight parking space and shoved her Jeep into drive. The lot was relatively empty, the traffic thin, and the damned snow just kept falling from the sky, covering the parking lots and the streets where tire tracks were visible.

Alvarez checked the system for a few minutes and said, "None of the vehicles were stolen; plates match up. The Buick belongs to Lillian Marsden, the King Cab to a Thomas Cohen, the Toyota to Ernesto Hernandez and the Taurus to—"

"Okay, okay, I get it. I'm being paranoid."

Alvarez shrugged. "Look, I'm going to call Chandler even though it's late. The woman never sleeps. I think we're gonna have to release MacGregor. I'll call Grayson in the morning."

"Fine," Pescoli bit out. She was angry that they'd probably wasted their time. Unless the crime scene people found anything of interest up at MacGregor's cabin, which hadn't happened as yet.

She was nearly back at the office, where Alvarez's car was parked, when her cell phone rang. With a glance, she noticed that the call was coming from the Pinewood Sheriff's Department. "Guess we're not off duty."

"Maybe there's a break in the case."

She answered, "Pescoli."

"Pescoli, this is Rule."

Kyan Rule was a road deputy, a tall black man with

the build of an NBA forward and a crooked smile of white teeth that caused many a female heart to flutter. Pescoli herself wasn't immune to the man's serious charms.

"What's up?" she asked as they passed a snowplow heading in the opposite direction.

"Bad news." For the first time she noticed the sober tone in his deep voice.

"Oh hell, what now? Don't tell me there's another victim." From the corner of her eye she saw Alvarez turn to look at her.

"No. It's your son."

The hospital stood starkly in the night, rising above the surrounding clinics and linked parking lots that serviced the medical community of Grizzly Falls. Small in comparison to the complexes in bigger cities, Pinewood General Hospital was still one of the largest buildings in the city. From its position on the bluff, the hospital overlooked the older part of the town and the river far below. The sheriff's department was less than three miles away.

Tonight, with snow falling steadily, the hospital lights were muted but still visible in the darkness. Among the rows of empty spaces in the snowy parking lot was a cruiser from the Pinewood County Sheriff's Department, which indicated, just as an earlier newscast had stated, that she was still a patient and under guard.

The damned woman just wouldn't die!

And time was running out.

Her room was on the third floor.

Her guard, not the sharpest tool in the shed, sometimes wandered down to the cafeteria for a fresh cup of coffee or a snack. Once in a while he walked to the public restroom to take a leak. Other times he flirted with some of the young nurses. But he was there, nonetheless.

A presence.

So contact couldn't be made tonight.

But come the morning, only a few hours off, when the hospital staff shifts were changing and the damned guard was getting replaced, then there would be a chance.

If not to kill, then to lure once again . . .

Away from this place.

To a new killing ground.

Chapter Twenty-Two

"My son?" Pescoli repeated.

Her heart nearly dropped out of her chest.

With suddenly shaking hands she guided the Jeep onto the side street leading to the cluster of county buildings where the sheriff's department was located, high on Boxer Bluff.

"Jeremy?" she whispered, flashing on blood-chilling images of his body in a mangled car that had slid off an icy embankment, or on a respirator in a hospital gasping for life. Oh dear God, what would she do if she lost him?

"He's all right," Rule assured her. He'd barely paused in the conversation, but in the span of a heartbeat, Regan Pescoli had faced her worst fears—the fear that every time she came upon an accident scene, one of her children would be trapped in the car, covered in blood, skin the gray of death. "But he's been arrested."

"Arrested?" she repeated, letting out her breath. Thank God he was alive. Unhurt. "For what?"

"MIP," Rule said. "He's pretty wasted. We sent him to

the juvenile facility but he's yelling that he wants you to bail him out."

In an instant, her deepest fears turned to anger. "He was drinking?"

"He and three others. One of them is Brewster's daughter."

She wheeled with controlled fury into the parking lot, her tires sliding just a bit. "Don't tell me: Heidi." Brewster's youngest. His baby. His pampered princess. Even though he'd made no bones about "trying for a son" before his wife got pregnant with his last two girls, Heidi, the youngest, had become the apple of his eye.

"That's the one."

Regan swore beneath her breath. "She's only fifteen."

"Exactly what Brewster's saying."

Regan could almost hear the undersheriff spouting off about her no-good, useless son. "And not all he's saying, I'm guessing."

"Uh . . . no . . ."

Things were going rapidly from bad to worse. She threw her Jeep into park. "I'll be right in. I'm here. In the parking lot."

"Good."

She hung up, hit the steering wheel with her fist and swore a blue streak.

"Trouble?" Alvarez asked mildly as Pescoli cut the engine.

"Big trouble. But at least my son's not dead. Yet. Not until I personally throttle that kid!" She'd gone from scared to death to furious in less than two seconds. She tried to remind herself how she'd feel if the call had been about her son being zipped into a body bag. Worse yet, what if not only Jeremy, but also Heidi and whomever they were with, and maybe some innocent

driver heading in the opposite direction, had been
killed? "How in God's name could he be so stupid?"

"He's a teenager."

"He's an idiot. I mean, it's not like he doesn't know
what's up. I've told him over and over again . . .
preached to him about drinking and driving and . . . no
matter what I say it seems to go in one ear and out the
other."

"Jeremy's a good kid."

"Who's in a lot of trouble." She was shaking her
head, and inside, her guts were quivering. It was hard to
believe her reaction, even to herself, as hard-nosed a
cop as she was. She'd witnessed horrific crimes, seen
charred, bludgeoned and butchered bodies, and was always able to keep her emotional distance from the victims, to keep a level head while solving a crime. But
when it came to her own kids, she was just a damned
wuss, a mother bear who would do anything to protect
her cubs. "Geez, Jer," she said, as if her son was in the
car.

"Take a breath," Alvarez suggested as Pescoli threw
open the driver's door and a blast of cold air swept into
the Jeep.

But Pescoli was having none of it. Ignoring the snow
falling all around her, she charged toward the sheriff's
office.

If she could, she'd spit nails.

Dead on her feet, Alvarez followed her partner inside. She gave Pescoli some space and headed instead
to the task force room, where one of the deputies, a junior detective named Zoller, was handling all the incoming calls.

"How's it going?" Alvarez asked.

The junior detective lifted a shoulder. "Lots of action

earlier, after the newscasts about the current victims, but they've dwindled to nothing." She climbed out of her chair and stretched, a phone bud still in her ear. All of five feet two, Zoller was fit and trim, a thirty-year-old who ran marathons, mentored teens struggling with school and worked her ass off for the department. "A call came in an hour ago from an upset parent. Seems his kids had snuck out to go sledding up at Timber Junction, and in one of their runs, guess what they came across?"

"Oh God, another dead body," Alvarez guessed, thinking the worst.

Zoller shook her head, springy curls shivering around her small, elfin face. "No, thank God. A wrecked car. Four-year-old Ford Explorer. Beck O'Day has already been to the scene and roped it off. Waiting for the crime scene technicians, who are going up there to see if there's any evidence. They can't wait until morning light with all the snow falling."

"No body?"

"None."

"Same MO as the others?"

"O'Day hasn't reported back in, but she was going to check the tires, see if they've been shot. I do know this: she called in the plates and the SUV is registered to C. Randall Jones of Billings, Montana. The C stands for Coolidge, like the president."

Alvarez snorted. "No wonder he uses an initial."

"Better than Polk."

"Why do I think he wasn't at the wheel?" She thought of the two unidentified women they'd found earlier in the day. One dead. One hanging on by a thread. Both victims. "Jones . . . none of the notes had a J in them. If our theory is right, the driver wasn't his wife or daughter or mother."

"Not married. No kids. I'm waiting for a callback. An

officer from the Montana State Police was going to visit him."

"Good." If it weren't for the horrendous nature of the crimes, the police would have waited until the morning to contact him. As it was, time was of the essence and C. Randall would have to get out of bed to answer the door. "Anything else?"

"A list from Missing Persons of people with the initials we found on the notes. These are Caucasian women within the age group we're looking for who have gone missing in the past two months in a thousand-mile radius within the United States."

"Amazing what computers can do," Alvarez said as Zoller handed her the short printout. Only a few names appeared: Helena Estavez, Elle Holden and Hannah Estes for the women with the initials EH or HE, and Roberta Artez, Roxanne Anderson, Rona Anders, Annabelle Rollins and Alicia Rhodes for the others. Two of the women, Helena Estavez and Roxanne Anderson, had been crossed off the list. "Why are these two off?" she asked.

"Anderson's driver's license photo was way off from our victim, and Estavez showed up at home earlier tonight. The family called the Idaho State Police but her name hadn't been taken out of the computer."

"And it was verified that she returned?"

"Yeah, an Idaho State Trooper called half an hour ago."

"Where are the other pictures?"

"I'm waiting for them. They're supposed to be e-mailed to me, but with the holiday people are a little slow to respond. So far none have come in, but it should be soon."

Unbuttoning her coat, Alvarez studied the list as Zoller made her way back to the desk, where a laptop computer, phone, legal pad and can of Pepsi were at the ready.

"Rona Anders," Alvarez said aloud. "It says she's from Billings, Montana?"

"That's right."

"But not the same address as where the SUV was registered, so she's not living with the owner of the Explorer."

"Doesn't mean she didn't borrow his car."

"No, it doesn't," Alvarez thought aloud as she glanced out the window to the snowy night. If she were going to be traveling through the mountains and didn't have a four-wheel-drive vehicle, she might borrow a friend's.

"We'll know soon enough," Zoller said, and settled back into her chair. She picked up her drink while Alvarez walked over to the maps on the wall, eyeing the terrain, noticing where new pushpins had been placed on the map. All the victims and cars were confined to a circle with a ten-mile radius. Jillian Rivers, too, had been found in that area, her car located within the boundaries of the imaginary circle.

So what was in the middle?

She stared at the map and found its center, a spot not far from what was left of Broken Pine Lodge, where they'd found the victim who'd survived, and only a quarter of a mile away from Star Fire Canyon, where Wendy Ito's Prius with its vanity plates had been discovered. But that area was uninhabited, for the most part. Mesa Ridge, a flat-topped mountain, was the biggest attraction in the area for hikers in the summer months and snowshoers and cross-country skiers in the winter.

She narrowed her gaze on that mountaintop and wondered why there was something about it that bothered her.

She heard Zoller typing on her computer. "Hey," she said, "looks like the first of the pictures is coming through. Your Jane Doe in the hospital? Her name is

Hannah Estes and she lives in Butte. Got her address here."

"Good. I'll call the hospital and we'll try to find out what she was doing in the Bitterroots in the middle of a storm, while you keep on looking for her friends and family."

"This might be the break we're looking for," Zoller said, already making a call.

"Let's hope," Alvarez said, without much enthusiasm. The map of the Montana wilderness was flattened in front of her on the wall, a daunting picture of rough terrain where a smart killer was hiding. "Let's hope."

Pescoli shouldered her way through the main doors of the sheriff's department and waved at the guard. The linked rooms were quiet, only a few officers working the graveyard shift. One operator manned the phones in the task force room and only a few bits of conversation wafted through the cubicles. A bedraggled man, hands cuffed, feet in shackles, was clicking his way to a chair near a deputy's desk. Ashen-faced, hair matted, jeans showing bloodstains, the guy looked strung out on something. He sat down and nearly missed the chair as she passed by.

Merry Christmas, she thought, unbuttoning her coat as she found Deputy Kyan Rule making himself at home in her cubicle. He was waiting for her, one leg tossed over the edge of her desk, big hands clasped over his knee.

"I'm not going over and getting Jeremy out of lockup," she said.

"I was afraid that would be your attitude."

"It's not an 'attitude'; it's a fact."

"Hey! You can't arrest me!" The strung-out guy was finally cluing into the fact that he was in trouble. Funny, he must not have gotten it when he was handcuffed and shackled.

Rule sent the guy a look and said to Pescoli, "Let's go where there's a little more privacy." He climbed from the desk and they walked down the short hallway to the back of the building.

Thankfully, the kitchen was empty. She threw her coat and hat onto a table and pushed her hair out of her eyes. "And for the record, I'm not phoning my son either. Not tonight."

"You sure about that?" Rule didn't seem to believe her new tough-love act.

"You bet. He can't think that just because he's the son of a cop, he gets special privileges. If anything, he's got to work harder to walk the straight and narrow."

"You never screwed up when you were a kid?"

"Never."

"Bullshit."

"Okay, right," she admitted with a shrug as they paced the kitchen, where the wastebasket was overflowing and chairs were pushed cockeyed from the tables. "But now's not the time to confide in my son and tell him about my mistakes. That can come later." She walked to a counter in the adjoining room, the one with the only window. Through the tiny pane and across the yard she had a view of the juvenile detention center. Most of the county buildings, aside from the courthouse, were located up here on Boxer Hill and the juvenile center was no exception. It was a long, low, sand-colored brick building with wide lawns now white and crusty with snow, the lights within glowing warm against a frozen night.

Her heart ached and her first instinct was to run as fast as she could across the frozen parking lot and snowy lawn, burst through the doors and demand to see her son. She would love to haul him out of there and make the whole scene disappear. Grateful that he was alive and, from all accounts, uninjured, she would like nothing better than to close her eyes and wish it all away.

Oh, Joe, she thought, conjuring up a mental picture of her first husband, Jeremy's father. *If only you were here. . . .*

Pescoli caught herself. Found her fingers gripping the edge of the counter so tightly her knuckles bleached through her skin.

"You all right?" Rule asked, his baritone voice cutting into her thoughts. He was a good man. Kind but tough. Big-hearted but strong as steel. His dark eyes assessed her, and for just a heartbeat, she second-guessed herself. Her instinct to get Jeremy out of the detention center, to talk to the officer who'd brought him in, to some way use her status and influence to erase the fact that he'd broken the law, came up to the surface.

She gritted her teeth.

She had to let him sit and stew in his own juices. He needed time to think about his mistake, to come up with an alternative way of dealing with his problems. He was too old to automatically think his mother was his fail-safe, that she would do anything to get him out of any trouble he got himself into. Especially when it came to breaking the law. And with all of the statistics about teenagers and alcohol, drugs and driving . . .

No, he had to learn the difference between right and wrong and to stand on his own feet now. However, as she wandered into a separate dining space and stared through the glass, she saw two people emerge from the squatty building that housed the juvenile facility. A tall man was walking rapidly. At his side, far enough away so that he couldn't touch her, was a small woman, nearly running to keep up with him. Her blond hair was loose and free, catching in the light of the security lamps. The scarf around her neck billowing behind her, her arms were wrapped around her dark coat as she ran. No, not a woman. Make that a girl.

Heidi Brewster.

Pescoli's stomach twisted as she recognized the under-sheriff as he unlocked his rig. Brewster seemed to have no qualms about using his influence to get his kid released.

"You sure you don't want to go over there, get Jeremy out and then give him the talkin'-to of his life?" Rule asked from the other room, where she saw him lifting the coffeepot off its warming burner. Only a thin bit of sludge was visible at the bottom of the glass carafe. "Then you could ground his ass for . . . uh, I dunno, maybe six or seven years?"

He was trying to lighten the mood. Pescoli's gut wouldn't let her laugh. "I don't think it hurts Jeremy to chill out and think about what he's done."

Rule carried the dirty coffeepot to the sink and squirted a stream of dishwashing soap into it. Swishing the soap around, he flipped on the faucet.

"You think differently?" Pescoli returned to the kitchen and stood in the wide archway separating the two areas.

Rule lifted a muscular shoulder. "Jeremy doesn't have the easiest path. Dad dead. Mom working round the clock as a homicide dick. Stepdad who took a hike and hooked up with a new woman." Soapy water was cascading out of the pot. He turned off the tap and let the carafe soak in the sink. "It's a tough row to hoe, Regan," he said, using her first name, as they really were friends. "I know. I've been there. My old man was a cop. My mom, she died when I was born. I had three step-mamas and none of them cared a lick about me or my older sister. So, I'm just sayin' it's not easy for your boy."

Sighing, she shook her head. A few strands of hair fell into her eyes as the clock mounted above the sink

ticked off the seconds of her life. "Nothing is, Rule."
God, she needed a shower and about twenty-four hours
of sleep. Make that forty-eight hours. Or seventy-two.
She was exhausted deep into her bones. "I'm going
home. Let him sleep it off. Besides, I've got a dog who
probably has had an accident in the house and a daughter who may have already heard about her brother."

"She with Lucky?"

"Yeah."

"Maybe you need a little time for yourself," he suggested, and she realized he was probably talking about
Nate.

It seemed everyone in the department knew she was
involved with Nate Santana. Why did people have such
a hard-on for him? Some called him a drifter just because he hadn't lived his whole damned life in Pinewood
County. And she figured that a lot of people resented
Nate because he worked for Brady Long, the richest man
in Pinewood County. Brady was local legend, even if he
was considered to be the black sheep of the Longs, a
family made rich from their copper mines.

Right now a tangle with Nate would be the perfect
de-stresser. But not tonight.

Not when attacks from a serial killer were escalating,
her son was locked up and she was too tired to think
straight.

Stepping a little closer to her, he draped a steadying
arm around her shoulders, then gave her a squeeze.
"Y'know, Pescoli," he said, his voice low and familiar.
"You don't always have to be so damned tough."

"No?" she said, forcing a lightness in her tone she
didn't feel. "Then who would take care of your sorry
ass, hmm? All you wimps in the department might have
to start carrying your own damned weight."

He laughed, squeezed her again, then let his arm
drop as the old refrigerator in the corner hummed to

life. "Okay, I've said what I had to. Now I'm going out on the road again. Catch me some speeders."

"Thanks, Rule."

"You take it easy, Pescoli." He turned and walked out of the kitchen and she let her gaze wander back to the window in the adjoining room.

Rule's footsteps rang down the hallway.

Pescoli returned to the small room and pressed her face to the window. Through the bulletproof glass, she noticed Cort Brewster's pickup driving out of the lot near the juvenile center. Inside the truck, huddled against the passenger door, putting as much distance as she could between herself and her father, was Heidi.

Good.

Brewster could blame Jeremy all he wanted, and it was true, Jer was older, should have known better, could be accused of leading the younger, more innocent girl down the wrong path, but Heidi Brewster, apple of her father's eye, wasn't entirely innocent. Fifteen or not, Heidi Brewster, in Pescoli's estimation, was no angel.

Alvarez was about to leave the building.

The clock on the wall was inching past one in the morning and she was dead tired.

She'd spent the last hour reading anagrams, playing with programs trying to figure out how the letters on the notes went together to make any sense.

WAR   T HE   SC   I N

She tried filling in the blanks and came up with nothing that made any sense: "WAR OF THE SCREAM-ING"? "WAR TO THE SCHOOLS IN . . ."? Or maybe "WAR" didn't start the note. Maybe it was gobbledy-gook.

What a nightmare.

When the phone rang, Zoller caught it before it jangled for the second time. Alvarez watched as she began making notes and typing on her computer all at once. Her eyes brightened and she looked up to signal Alvarez.

"Okay, I got it. . . . Yeah, repeat that address again. . . . Good. Thanks." Zoller hung up. "Rona Anders is our Jane Doe in the morgue. This C. Randall is an attorney who lives in Bozeman and Rona is his fiancée, a grad student at Montana State. According to the trooper, the guy was devastated at the news, had been holding out hope that she wasn't one of the women who'd been abducted. She was on her way to visit her folks in Bend, Oregon, for the holidays. When she didn't show up, they filed a separate missing persons report, just like C. Randall did here in Bozeman. I'm sure we have both of them, just hadn't sorted through them yet. At first the parents weren't concerned, and since she and her fiancé had a major fight, she'd told her folks she might take a detour up the Idaho panhandle, give herself time to think."

"How long has she been missing?"

"Her fiancé saw her last Tuesday. I don't know about anyone else." Zoller's usually animated face had gone somber and Alvarez felt that same old despair she always did in the face of a young person's death and their family's grief. "The OSP are on their way to the parents' house in Bend now."

"I'll tell Grayson and Pescoli," she said. "Why don't you contact the FBI agents?"

"I will."

Alvarez walked out of the task room, but didn't hunt down her partner. It was late; the news would wait until morning.

Chapter Twenty-Three

MacGregor wanted to crawl out of his own skin.

Sitting in a holding cell, staring through the bars, reminded him too much of the time he'd spent locked up for that mess in Denver. The place smelled bad, that particular blend of piss, body odor and despair MacGregor hated. He'd sworn he'd never go through the particular hell of incarceration again.

But he'd been wrong. Here he was, sitting on his butt in the Pinewood County Jail, waiting to find out if he'd be charged with some crime. Attempted murder? Kidnapping? Resisting arrest? Oh hell, who knew? The more important question was: Why?

Why the hell was he here, staring through bars and across a hallway to a series of like cells, some of them inhabited by drunks, derelicts and drug dealers? Because, just like before, once again, he'd done what he thought best to save a woman. And it had backfired. Big-time. The cops actually thought he was the maniac who had been terrorizing this area of the Bitterroot Mountains.

"I want my lawyer," he said to the guard who opened the door at the far end of the cell block, where the floors gleamed as if freshly polished but couldn't hide the ground-in dirt visible under coats of wax and the walls, once blindingly white, had grown dingy. "And I want him now."

"It's five thirty in the morning." The guy, a big lug of a man whose nametag read "A. Schwartz," obviously wasn't in the mood to help. With hair buzzed close to the skin, big ears and the thick neck of someone who had once played football, Schwartz was a man who didn't want any grief.

Other prisoners who had been quiet now began to stir, to come to the edges of their pens and press their noses through the bars. Like dogs in a kennel.

MacGregor wasn't going to back down. "I don't care what time it is. I've been here all night and I want to talk to my lawyer, or believe me, I'll have your job."

"Yeah, right."

"Garret Wilkes. In Missoula. He's independent."

"And I would care *why?*" the guard asked. "Oh, that's right, you think I should be worried about my job."

"Wilkes is a personal friend of the sheriff."

"*Now* I'm shakin' in my boots."

"Get him for me. His number is on my cell, which someone here has. It'll save you looking it up in the phone book."

"We're not exactly keepin' lawyers' hours, y'know? So why don't you all just cool your jets?" He motioned to MacGregor and to the rest of the men who were locked up.

"Either you get me my damned lawyer, give me a phone so I can do it or you charge me, right here and now."

"Yeah, yeah." The big guy's smile was patient, but there was an edge to it, too, something just a little ophidian. As if he might enjoy being a bully. As if he was actually waiting for the chance.

MacGregor had done his bit, answered all their questions, but he'd had it. He'd played by the rules, even managed to get a little sleep, all the while his mind filled with images of Jillian tied to the tree and his dog bleeding in the snow. Some bastard was out to harm those he loved and he'd had it. Loved? Oh hell, he didn't love Jillian Rivers. She was really just a pain in his backside. But he didn't like the fact that not only was someone determined to leave her in the cold to freeze to death, but this person was using him as a scapegoat. Worse yet, the bastard had shot his dog.

He ground his teeth.

He'd had it with being patient and waiting for the authorities to release him. No more. He wanted to know about Jillian and Harley and no heavyset cretin of a jailor with a bad haircut and snaky smile was going to push him around.

"If I were you, I wouldn't get so riled up," Schwartz advised. "But then if I were you, I wouldn't be behind bars in the first place. That's the difference between us, MacGregor. I'm on the outside and you're fuckin' locked up."

"Hey, I want out, too!" a thin reedy voice called from a cell closer to the door.

"In the morning, Ivor."

"It is the morning," the voice responded.

"It ain't even light out. I mean *later* in the morning." Schwartz rolled his eyes at MacGregor, as if they were suddenly buddies.

"It will be too late."

Schwartz chuckled and shook his head, his bald pate shining under the bright lights overhead. "Why is that, Ivor? Is Krypton gonna invade or somethin'?"

Through the bars, MacGregor caught a glimpse of a small wiry man with a thick shock of white hair on the other side of the aisle separating the cages. He had a scrawny neck, stretched thin, and owlish glasses that made his eyes appear bulbous and oversized for his face.

"Is that what's gonna happen?" Schwartz taunted again, enjoying himself, as he ran his nightstick along the bars, the noise reverberating. "Is the lizard king gonna come down from outer space and devour all us poor little earthlings?"

"Not the lizard king, you moron," Ivor said indignantly. "That was Jim Morrison. He said so hisself. Don't you know nuthin'?"

"The 'Light My Fire' guy? Before my time, old man."

Ivor Hicks was incensed. "And his name isn't Krypton! You'd better be careful." Ivor wagged a bony finger through the bars. "It really pisses him off when people get it wrong. It's General Crytor, of the Reptilian Army."

"You're a freakin' lunatic, Hicks. You know that?"

"Crytor hears all!" Veins pulsed in Ivor's head.

Again the locks on the door clanked as it opened and Detective Alvarez strode into the hallway.

In a second Schwartz stopped his childish antics. "Hey," he said, his demeanor sliding from antagonism into interest as the petite detective dared enter his domain.

"We're releasing MacGregor," she said without preamble.

"What?" Clearly A. Schwartz didn't like this turn of events. "When?"

"Right now." She made her way to MacGregor's cell, and if she noticed Schwartz or any of the inmates' gazes following her, checking out her ass as she passed, she didn't show it. "Unlock him."

"Does the sheriff know about this?"

She shot the jailor a disdainful glance. "And the DA. And anyone else who needs to." As she looked at Mac-Gregor through the bars, it was obvious to him that she wasn't any happier about his release than Schwartz was. "We contacted your lawyer and you can sign for and pick up your things at the front desk."

"What about Pescoli?" Schwartz asked. "She ain't gonna like this, let me tell you." But he was fiddling with his keys. "Oh, that's right, she's got her own problems, doesn't she? Her stupid-ass kid got himself picked up."

The glare Alvarez sent the idiot jailor this time was blistering, filled with unspoken warnings.

The big oaf didn't take the message. "That kid's a real prick, if you ask me."

"No one did," she said tightly.

He blurted on, "If the undersheriff doesn't keep his daughter away from him, Brewster might find out that he's gonna be a granddaddy."

"Shut up, Schwartz, and unlock the door."

"Oooh. Okay. Whatever you say, Detective."

Her lips were thin, her hair pulled back and gleaming beneath the harsh lights, her eyes angry and dark. If looks could kill, A. Schwartz would be a dead man several times over right now. As it was, the big guy with the creases in the back of his neck didn't seem to notice her mood as he took his time with his keys, finally unlocked the door and slid it open. "Guess you're a free man, MacGregor," Schwartz said, suddenly all seething smiles.

MacGregor didn't answer, just headed to the main door.

"How about me?" another voice called from one of the cells.

"Your wife gonna bail you out, Dobbs?"

"She left me. Can you believe that?" he slurred, and MacGregor recognized the man who created chain saw and metal art and sold it on the highway. Trees, stumps, garbage cans, hubcaps, soda cans or whatever, it was all an artist's palette to Gordon Dobbs. "Right after

Thanksgivin'!" A big bear of a man, he seemed about to fall as he clung to the bars. "Married twelve years and Wilma just up and leaves me. . . ."

"Go figure," Schwartz said, then, under his breath, to Alvarez whispered, "it fuckin' must be Christmas, cuz we got enough nuts in here tonight to make our own special fruitcake! All we need to make it official is Grace Perchant, the damned crackpot who sees ghosts, and Alma Shepherd, with her divining switch, and we got ourselves a real interesting party in here."

"You need a ride?" Alvarez asked as they walked to the front together.

"No."

MacGregor collected the few things he'd had with him when he'd been arrested and pushed his way out of the jail. It was over a two-mile walk to the hospital where Jillian was, but he'd make it. Once there he'd call a friend who owed him one helluva favor.

Flipping the collar of his jacket up, he decided it was time to call in his long-overdue marker.

"So that's the deal, Jeremy," Pescoli said as her son, pale and wan, looking sicker than death, gave her the silent treatment. "You're grounded until I say differently, and in the meantime, you'll just go to school and go out and get that job you've been talking about. Football season's over. You're not involved in another sport and all this hanging-out is just no good."

He stared out the passenger side of her Jeep and doodled on the condensation on the window. With one shoulder effectively shunning her, he acted fascinated by the figure eights he drew over and over again as the miles slid beneath her wheels.

The snow had stopped sometime in the early morning, the eastern sky showing streaks of pink and purple as dawn slid over the land.

Since her son was intent on playing the passive-aggressive card, she flipped on the radio only to hear a newscaster reporting on the series of murders in the area.

Jeremy snorted and she shut the radio off.

"You know, we could discuss this," she said, her fingers tight over the wheel as she drove into the foothills toward their house.

He shrugged.

"I'm not able to ignore this, Jer. Underage drinking? What were you thinking?"

Silence. He was furious that she'd let him sit it out at the juvenile center while his friends had been picked up.

"I thought you needed to cool your jets," she added, keeping her mouth shut about the fact that she, too, had spent a lousy night, barely sleeping a wink, afer feeding Cisco, letting him outside, then allowing him to sleep in her bed with her. At six thirty this morning she'd showered, dressed and driven into town to pick up her kid. All in all, Jeremy had sat in juvie for about six hours. Long enough to make a point, not enough to do any permanent damage.

"Everyone else's parents came," he finally charged as she turned off the main road and slowed for the bridge spanning the small creek that bordered her property.

"I came."

He snorted. "*They* came last night."

"I was working."

"Heidi's dad is the undersheriff. Kind of an important job. More important than yours. He came right away." Jeremy's eyes, so like Joe's, glared at her, and her heart nearly broke as she recognized his hurt, his anger and, beyond the resentment, a bit of hatred.

"I can't speak to how he raises his kid, but I can tell you that you'll probably be blamed for this. Even if Heidi admits to being a part of it, you're older, a boy, and Cort Brewster will see you as the guilty party."

"Maybe it was my fault."

"Maybe it was. Where did you get the alcohol?"

Jeremy's lips tightened before he lapsed into stony silence again. She pulled into the driveway and gave him a look. "We'll talk about this later. When I get home. But I'm serious. You start looking for a job, you stay home and take care of your dog, you get your grades up to where they should be and then we'll figure out just how long you're going to be grounded."

"I'll be eighteen in—"

"You want to move out?" She cut him off. "To find an apartment on your own? Maybe with some buddies? You think you can afford rent and electricity and gas and *cable* television?" Pescoli tried to keep her anger from boiling over. She didn't bother with the garage door, just parked in front of the small house where she'd first taught her son how to tie his shoes and memorize the Boy Scout creed or whatever it was, the place where he'd gone fishing in the creek in the backyard and where he'd stepped on a nest of yellow jackets when he was only six and been covered in red welts. His little chin had trembled but he'd tried hard not to cry. In some respects he was right, he wasn't that little boy any longer. Hadn't been for a long, long time. "You can make dinner," she said. "Take out something from the freezer. There're chicken pieces—thighs and legs, I think."

He stared at her as if she'd just landed on a spaceship from another universe.

"Well, if you're going to move out in a few months, you'd better learn how to cook. Eating out all the time is too expensive."

"I'm not cooking!"

"Sure you are. Grandma's recipe cards are in a box in the cupboard by the stove; you know where. Pick out a recipe; you like the one with the rice and condensed soup. I think we have all the ingredients and there should be something for a salad. Make enough for three. Bianca will be back for dinner."

"Are you out of your effin' mind? I'm not cooking any—"

"And clean the kitchen when you're done."

"I'm not your fu—slave!" he said as he leapt out of the car.

"For a second I thought you were going to say 'wife.'"

"Oh God, Mom, you are so sick!" He slammed the door shut.

"Probably," she muttered as she backed into the turn out of the driveway, watching as he unlocked the door and stomped his way inside. She shoved the gearshift into drive and pushed aside the guilt that suggested she was running out on him, the feeling that her place was home, that she should try and talk things out. But the reality was that they both needed time to cool off. That if she did stay at the house, if her job didn't demand her to be back at the office, he would just hole up in his room and refuse to talk to her, and she, angry, would cook and clean with a vengeance, rattling pots and dishes and stomping loudly to let him know she was upset, too.

"Height of maturity," she said, and reached for her pack of cigarettes. At the end of the lane she lit up and decided she'd quit again. As soon as this case was solved, she'd smoke her last one and this time she would never pick up the habit again.

Never.

At least she hoped not.

* * *

MacGregor explained what he wanted. It took a while, but Chilcoate listened, all the while smoking a cigarette and gazing out the window of his two-bedroom cabin. The window was opened just a bit, a small crack allowing in some of the cold air, which battled with the heat from a gas fireplace on the opposite wall. The living area was furnished with a few secondhand chairs, a love seat and a beat-up leather recliner that was positioned to face a huge television screen hung on the opposite wall.

The larger bedroom was his office, one set up with the finest state-of-the-art computer, radio and television equipment. The smaller of the two bedrooms held a double bed with a faded camouflage comforter and a dresser with the same decals he'd stuck on it as a child.

Downstairs, behind shelves used to store anything from wine to old files and clothes never to be worn again, was a secret room, one only a handful of people knew about. Behind that fake wall was a long, narrow space filled with the most sophisticated electronic equipment known to man.

Chilcoate was a computer hacker.

And a damned good one.

He'd learned from the best: the government.

It wasn't a surprise to MacGregor. The kid had been an electronic genius from the get-go, something that hadn't gone unnoticed by MIT and a few others. The trouble was, at the time, Chilcoate had been a screw-off and had blown his scholarship to Stanford and been kicked out.

Hence the stint in the army, and the rest was history.

MacGregor and Chilcoate had been childhood buddies and still were. They knew each other's secrets and MacGregor had bailed out Chilcoate from one sticky situation after another over the years, everything from helping him through a DUI and getting into AA to opening his own door to the man after a bad marriage and worse divorce.

So now Chilcoate owed him.

And MacGregor expected to collect on the man's knowledge—knowledge gained from a dozen years in the military working with electronic surveillance before opting out. He'd spent a few more years with the FBI before giving up his government jobs and going freelance. With the Feds there had been too much red tape. Too many meetings. Too much regimentation for a wild-ass Montana boy with a natural-born rebellious streak that, try as he might, he just couldn't tame.

Now he lived in the foothills of the Bitterroots, not far from where he and MacGregor had spent idyllic childhoods fishing, hiking, hunting, camping under the stars, unaware of the twisted paths their lives would take.

His full name was Tydeus Melville Chilcoate. His Mensa-member single mother had been influenced by all things Greek and had a thing for Captain Ahab and anything written by Herman Melville, hence the heavy name. Unimpressed, Chilcoate went by his last name. It was just easier.

"Is that all you want?" he asked MacGregor as he walked to the kitchen sink, turned on the tap and doused the remains of his smoke. The cigarette hissed and smoldered for a second before he tossed the wet butt into the trash can near the slider door. "A truck, a cell phone and me to hack into a person's private account on the Internet?"

"For starters. I also want you to look after Harley."

Chilcoate grunted his assent. "Let's go downstairs," he said and led the way down a narrow stairway.

MacGregor had made three calls from the first pay

phone he'd come across. One was to the hospital, where he was assured Jillian Rivers was in stable condition, though the hospital would give him no further information. The second was to Jordan Eagle, the veterinarian at the clinic on Fourth Street. Jordan, who he'd known for years, had talked to him personally and assured him that Harley would live, though there was a chance that the dog might lose his back right leg. "He lost a lot of blood and there's quite a bit of tissue damage, a torn tendon, but he's lucky in that the bullet didn't hit his spine or go through his other leg." MacGregor had listened quietly, the receiver held in a death grip, his back to the cold wind. He'd barely noticed, so intent was he on the phone conversation. "Worst-case scenario: I'll have to amputate. Best: a partial recovery. I won't kid you, Zane, he won't be the same, but I think he'll live a full, good life. Lots of dogs get around great on three legs."

MacGregor's stomach had roiled, bile rising in his throat when he thought of the bastard who had sighted a rifle on his dog and, with malicious intent, pulled the trigger. This was no accident. To Jordan, he'd said, "Do the best you can. I'm on my way."

"He's gonna live, Zane. But don't rush over here. He's still out of it from the anesthesia."

"Thanks." He'd hung up and sworn a blue streak at the son of a bitch who had tried to kill his dog and then left Jillian for dead. At least Harley knew Jordan, as she was an old friend of MacGregor's, a woman he'd once dated, a woman who had, briefly, shared his bed. Had he loved her? No. Nor had she loved him. Not in any way other than being lonely friends. They both had realized the mistake and ended the affair amicably. Sex always changed things, but in their case, their friendship had only deepened.

It was, however, the singular time that had happened

in his life. He thought about Jillian and knew, deep in his gut, if they ever made love, the course of his life would change forever. She affected him in a way that bothered him, a complicated way he'd rather avoid.

Even more than Callie, the woman he'd once loved and married. He felt a pang of regret thinking of his wife and child, so long gone, but he couldn't dwell on the past. That never helped.

But it could serve as a reminder that with love came the chance of heartache.

Not that he was in love with Jillian Rivers.

Far from it.

But she'd gotten to him.

No doubt about it.

That woman had burrowed her way under his skin.

The third call was to Chilcoate and they'd agreed to meet at the diner up the street. Zane had walked the three blocks, ordered two cups of coffee to go and, collecting the steaming drinks, then strode into the parking lot, where a few early risers had parked their rigs.

Within minutes Chilcoate had arrived in an old army Jeep, and they'd hauled ass up to his cabin, a rough-hewn log building complete with running water, electricity and a basement few people knew about.

During the ride up a winding road, MacGregor had told Chilcoate as much of his story as he thought advisable, including how he'd found Jillian in her wrecked car at the bottom of a ravine and how, after healing, she'd been abducted and left in the forest, while his dog had been shot.

Chilcoate had listened, asking few questions, then had led the way into his cabin. Now MacGregor followed him into a dusty basement, where they dodged old ductwork, made their way past broken furniture and a rusted-out barbecue, passing hidden cameras tucked into the shadowy cobwebs of the crossbeams. At the back wall, Chilcoate stepped into an alcove ostensibly built for firewood and hit a switch. The back wall swung open and an array of computers, monitors, photographic equipment, radios and cameras was revealed.

"Okay, then," Chilcoate said, smiling, as he sat at a desk chair that rolled the length of a twenty-foot table. "Let's get to work."

Jillian felt the heat from the fire.

Outside the winter raged, snow blowing against the windows, ice hanging in glittering shards from the roof. But inside the cabin was warm. Hot. Blood pounded through her veins as she stared into the eyes of a stranger, a lover.

"MacGregor," she whispered as his hands skimmed over her body, finger pads stroking her bare skin, brushing over her rib cage and the bend of her waist, as they lay face-to-face upon the wide couch.

God, she wanted him. Ached for him. And yet she knew this was wrong. So very wrong.

There was danger.

Evil.

Lurking in the dark corners of the room, unseen eyes watched with the same hunger and passion that, at this moment, ran through her veins. She caught a glimpse of something, a piece of glass reflecting the room, but the image was distorted, in grainy black and white, a photo with a bus and a man . . . no, not just a man. Aaron. Her husband. So why was she here, with this stranger?

Aaron ran to catch the bus, his legs moving.

He's running away from you, Jillian. He's . . . he's . . .

As he charged forward, flagging the bus, his clothes ripped away and his exposed body was shriveled, the flesh decaying.

She gasped and he turned, looking over his shoulder, smiling widely as his face became a skull and the mirror on the bus flashed numbers and letters that she couldn't see.

He'd dead. Aaron's dead. Your husband died in South America.

No, not Aaron. Mason. Mason is my husband. Or was he?

The skeleton face grinned in wicked glee before stepping in front of the bus.

She cringed. Shrank away from the image. Screamed in silent horror.

In a second the image faded and she was again in the cabin, lying naked with a man, feeling the heat of his body. He held her tight and kissed the crook of her neck. Instantly her blood turned to liquid fire and her fear was replaced by desire, hot, wanton, undeniable desire.

She looked into the eyes of the man holding her, this sexy stranger, who was caressing her, cradling her against him, pushing his hips against hers. His erection was thick and hard against her, rubbing against her abdomen, creating friction and a shameless need. Oh, to feel him inside her, to experience the ecstasy of his thrusts as he parted her legs and pushed deep inside.

But it was wrong. She didn't know him. Couldn't just foolishly make love to him. Yet she was quivering with want, perspiring with need. "MacGregor . . . I—I don't—"

"Shhh." His lips swept softly over hers and she moaned. "Don't think about anything." His voice was so low, so seductive, and his hands, oh Lord, his hands. Skimming her nipples, whispering across her abdomen, touching gently, exploring eagerly, probing into her flesh. She gasped as he caressed her, getting her ready, her body responding, juices flowing.

"This is wrong," she managed to say, though it was a whisper, as her lips barely moved.

He kissed her then. Hard. Urgently.

She felt all of his muscles strain as he pulled her up against him, and she couldn't help but wind her arms around his neck, kissing him back fervently. Eyes closed, she felt the hard wall of his chest, the delicious scratch of his hair against her flesh, the heat from his skin below.

Her own heart was pounding crazily, blood throbbing in her ears, her skin afire.

Don't do this, a voice in her head warned. *You don't even know him.*

But that was crazy. Of course she knew him. She understood him. It was as if they'd been searching for each other for years.

Do not do this, Jillian.

Oh, be quiet, she thought, and gave herself up to the sensations of his touch, the smell of his skin, the feel of his whiskers against her face, the salty taste of his lips upon hers, as he shifted, pulling her beneath him, pressing her body into the cushions with his, breathing hard and fast against her skin. His tongue flicked against her lips, pushing through to glide along her teeth.

With a groan she opened to him. His hands found her breasts, kneading the soft flesh, causing her nipples to pucker and her insides to melt. An ache, deep and primal, swirled deep between her legs, and she closed her mind to anything but making love to him.

What would it hurt, just this once?

She loved him, didn't she? Hadn't she known it from the minute she'd awoken in this very cabin? And his touch, oh Lord, what he was doing to her, what her mind was imagining. She wanted this, the fusion of their bodies, the blending of their souls.

Moist heat curled deep inside, and she caught her breath as he came to her, his hard body covered in

sweat, a sheen to his skin in the firelight. One mascu-
line hand cupped her buttocks, pulled her close, fingers digging into her skin.

She trembled.

Desire pumped through her body.

"Jillian," he said, gazing longingly at her. "Jillian."

She tried to answer.

Couldn't.

Her breath and voice were lost in this weird mix of
love and lust and fear. He was breathing faster now,
harder . . . or was that eager, excited panting her own
unchained breaths?

She swallowed hard and thought the sound might be
coming from another source.

A chill ran down her spine as she realized it might be
from something dark and hidden and observing.

Something rabid and excited.

Something, or someone, licking his tongue in anticipation.

Oh God . . .

"Jillian!"

What?

The voice . . . was it MacGregor's? Or was it resonat-
ing from the dark corners of the room?

Her heart stilled.

From somewhere in the distance a dog barked.

Harley?

She was suddenly outside in snowdrifts that reached
her knees. She thought she saw the dog loping easily
through the snow, as if following a broken path. She
tried to call to him, to run after him, but her legs were
leaden and he was moving so fast, a blur of white and
black, his tail streaking behind. His ears were cocked
forward as he leaped over a final snowbank and disappeared into a frigid thicket of pine and spruce.

No!

She felt the danger.

Tried to call out.

A rifle cracked.

The dog yelped in pain. "Harley!" she gasped, but again, her voice failed her, and Zane MacGregor, who had just been with her, was gone. She was freezing. She looked to the fire, where the dog, teeth bared, eyes glowing red from the reflection of the coals in the fire, lay, his coat matted in blood.

"Jillian!"

Someone was yanking on her hand. The demon in the corner? The monster who was watching her make love to MacGregor? The psychopath who had shot the dog?

Terror ripped through her.

She tried to scream.

Where the hell was MacGregor?

"Jillian! For the love of God, wake up!"

Her eyes flew open and she swept air into her lungs. In a second she realized she'd been dreaming and the images of the cabin withered away. She was still in the hospital, lying beneath wrinkled sheets, her heart pounding in fear. Outside a dog was barking, not crying in pain, and here, in the room, standing next to the bed, his big hand clasped over hers, his face a mask of concern, was Zane MacGregor.

The man to whom she'd just made mental love.

Chapter Twenty-Four

"Are you all right?" Zane asked, and she shook the cobwebs, as well as the fantasies, from her mind. She thought about her dream and how she'd imagined making love to him, and she felt herself blush.

It had to be the drugs. Whatever they were pumping into her body in terms of antibiotics and painkillers and sleeping medication had obviously caused her to lose contact with all reality.

"I'm fine . . . well, kind of." Scooting herself up in the bed, she tried not to think about the blue-gray of his eyes or the way she imagined his hands would feel on her body. For the love of God, they hadn't even really kissed, unless you counted that chaste little brush of his lips across her cheek, and here she was dreaming about stripping him of his clothes and making love to him in front of the fire.

But the dream had changed, turned into a nightmare.

"Harley," she said. "Is he all right?"

"Recovering. I stopped by there a few minutes ago.

There's still a chance he could lose a leg, but he'll survive."

"Thank God. I'm so sorry."

"It wasn't your fault."

"I shouldn't have let him out."

"And what? Let him pee all over the house? It's okay, Jillian. You're both alive. That's all that matters." For the first time, she noticed that his hand was still holding hers, his big, calloused fingers wrapped around hers.

As if he, too, recognized that he was touching her, he slowly released her hand and took a step back.

"You look like hell," she said softly.

"That's what a night in the Pinewood County Jail can do."

"Did you break out?"

He almost laughed. She saw it in his weary gaze. "Nah. They had to let me go. Lack of evidence. And it really pissed them off, just like I pissed off the guard who's at your door. He didn't want me to come inside, but I sweet-talked one of the nurses, who told him to back off."

"And he did?"

"A little."

She glanced past MacGregor to the door, where a short cop was glowering but not entering the room. He took one step over the threshold, and Jillian shook her head, glaring back at the man and letting him know in silent but no uncertain terms that he was to keep his distance.

"I need to get out of here," she said softly to MacGregor.

One side of his mouth lifted. "Cabin fever?"

"Hospital fever, but yeah."

"And do what? Go home?" he asked, his eyes narrowing just a fraction.

She shook her head. "I've got unfinished business."

She found the controls for the bed and pushed the button to raise the head of the bed until she was in a sitting position.

"What're you planning?"

"I'm going to find Aaron, if he's alive."

"You still think he is?"

"I don't know what to think. Maybe it's an elaborate scam to lure me over here; I don't know. I wanted to believe that I was a mistake, that this maniac killer you've got running around this part of the country hit the wrong car. But I've had to rethink that since the attack that put me here. This guy, whoever he is, wants me dead."

"Then you should let the police handle it."

She stared at him. Hard. "Would you?" When he didn't answer, she half-smiled. "Okay, I know the answer to that. And the police will probably want me to go somewhere safe and hide."

"Probably."

She shook her head. "How would you feel if someone tried to kill you twice? If they jumped you, stripped you and tied you to a damned tree?" She felt her blood burning through her veins again, anger and adrenalin spurring her on. "I know how to shoot a gun. I've had courses in self-defense. I'm no wimp—"

"And right now you're feeling angry and self-righteous and foolish," he said. "But you're right, I'd feel the same way. But even with all your qualifications, this guy's got something over you, something that you just can't fight."

"Yeah?"

"He's nuts, Jillian. A bonafide, dyed-in-the-wool psychopath. You can't begin to fathom the depths of depravity in his black soul, so leave the investigating to the cops. Let them do their job."

"Because they've done it so well? How many women are dead now? Four? Five?"

"Four dead, two in the hospital, counting you."

"Six victims." She began working on the IV, peeling off the tape. "And you know what? I have a feeling this guy's not done. So I'm not going to be a sitting duck here at the hospital, okay? I'm not pinning my hopes on Nurse Claire and the rent-a-cop out in the hallway being my first line of defense. Everyone knows I'm here; I saw it on a news broadcast. And I'm willing to bet that the reason I haven't gotten any calls from reporters is that the hospital is blocking them, and the police are checking them out. I think the smarter move is to just leave. Let the police say that I'm still here; I'm cool with that. But I can't just lie here and wait, hoping the guards will protect me."

"I could stay—"

"And you're going to tell me that you're not after this guy? That you don't intend to track down the guy who set you up?"

MacGregor frowned. "I won't lie to you, Jillian. That bastard is going to pay. But 'til he's caught, you need to be safe."

Jillian winced as she swung her legs over the side of the bed, her taped ankle visible beneath the hem of her short, unflattering hospital gown. She thought about telling him the truth about Aaron, about how the louse had stolen money from clients, people who had trusted him, and left her to deal with the victims of his fraud. Whether he'd really died in Suriname or faked his death, he'd set her up for a major, horrible and scandalizing fall. Between the police, the press and the victims of a pyramid scheme that she'd known nothing about, she was left to deal with the fallout and try to pick up the pieces of her life. It had taken her years to regain her reputation, and she couldn't deny that re-marrying and changing her name had held more than a little appeal, a fact that Mason had accused her of more often than once. If Aaron Caruso dared to be alive, she damned well wanted to see him.

Face to face.

But, of course, she hadn't confided in Zane MacGregor, at least not yet. It just wasn't an easy thing to admit that she'd been played for the ultimate schmuck—a fool in love.

She couldn't count the number of times she'd thought of what he'd done to her and looked in the mirror only to say, "Idiot," as she'd washed her face or brushed her teeth or combed her hair. It had taken years to bury all that anger and pain. However, upon learning that Aaron might be alive today, the old wounds had reopened, as if the scars had been slit, then burned with acid.

MacGregor said, "You can't leave, Jillian. It's unsafe."

"I don't think so," she said, feigning a smile she didn't feel. "Besides, I've got you to protect me."

"You're out of your mind." But he grinned, and it was a killer smile, the kind that melted her to the center of her heart.

"Not yet. But I will be totally nuts if I stay here a second longer, so don't argue with me, MacGregor, okay? It's just not gonna work."

On her way to the office, Pescoli stopped at the Safeway store for a cup of coffee and while she was inside she picked up a copy of the local paper and, from a revolving rack, some colorful gift bags and a couple of gift cards to stores, restaurants, even airlines. She plucked one for Bianca's favorite department store, another for an electronics superstore for Jeremy. She also picked up a couple of fast-food cards and one for gas for Jeremy. In a shopping mood, she found foil-wrapped candy in holiday bags and a couple of novels in the book section. Within twenty minutes some of her Christmas shopping was accomplished. Not too inspired, but the kids would be okay with it. And it was the best she could do.

She eyed the cigarettes, considered buying a pack and keeping up the habit just until the Star-Crossed Killer case was solved, then decided she might be ninety and in the lung cancer ward before that happened.

She could get through raising teenagers without nicotine. Or so she tried to convince herself.

At the checkout, she swiped her credit card to pay for her purchases and was denied. "What the hell?" she muttered, tried again, but the card didn't work.

By now two other people were behind her in the "under fifteen items" line. A third swipe of the card was no good. The checker, a girl of about nineteen with hair streaked purple and wearing a Santa hat held onto her head with a bobby pin, asked, "Do you want to call the credit card company?"

"No . . . wait." Pescoli, irritated and embarrassed, fished through her wallet, while the guy behind her, unshaven and wearing thick glasses, tried not to look pissy. He failed. She found her debit card and swiped it, wiping out a good portion of the money she'd set aside for the rest of the month.

A minute later the transaction was finished and she was over two hundred dollars poorer, but she did have a few paltry presents. "It's going to be a spiritual Christmas this year," she muttered under her breath as she climbed into her rig, fired up the engine and pulled out of the lot. It was still early, traffic sparse, and she was almost to the crest of Boxer Bluff and past the jail when the phone rang.

She picked up as she wheeled into the parking lot, which, in the past few hours, had been plowed. "Pescoli," she said, without checking caller ID.

"Hey, Regan." Lucky's voice was low and gravelly, a

combination of too many smokes and not enough sleep, if she guessed right. "Jeremy just called."

Pescoli yanked on the emergency brake. "Oh? And what did he have to say for himself?"

"He told me the story about how he and his friends had a few beers and got picked up, the whole nine yards." He yawned, and Pescoli imagined him standing in his boxers and a T-shirt that was tight over the shoulders— Lucky Pescoli's answer to pajamas. His hair would be rumpled, his jaw covered by a thick beard, his hazel eyes heavy with sleep.

The image used to turn her on.

No more.

"Did he also tell you that I let him sit all night in juvie?"

"Oh yeah."

"So why did he call you?"

There was a pause, then he got right down to it. "Jeremy wants to come and live with me and Michelle."

"You're kidding."

"That's what he says."

"And you believe him?" She was seeing red, her hand clenching the damned cell phone in a death grip. "He won't even stay with you for a weekend, Lucky! And now he wants to make a permanent arrangement?" What was all that talk about Lucky not being his real father just a few days ago?

"So he says."

" 'Cuz he's ticked off. That'll change." Another beat and she felt her own heart stutter. "Wait a second. You *want* this?" The world seemed off-kilter, tipping on its axis.

"Michelle and I have been talking."

"Leave your wife out of this. She's *not* the kids' mother."

"But I'm their dad. Bianca's my daughter and I've been the most significant male influence in Jeremy's life."

"Well, that explains his sudden bout of insanity!" she said, suddenly hot.

"Face it, Regan, you're always working."

"And you're on the road when you are working."

"Michelle can be there for them when I can't."

"Michelle's a kid herself! For the love of God, Lucky, you can't be serious!" She noticed movement in her rearview mirror, and her insides curdled a bit when she recognized Cort Brewster's pickup as the undersheriff parked in his designated spot.

"Maybe it's time for a change, Regan," Lucky said so calmly she wanted to reach right through the airwaves and shake some sense into him. "I'm married, more stable than you. Jeremy knows about the men—"

"Men?" she repeated, dumbstruck. Yes, she'd had a couple of boyfriends, none of whom had ever lived, or even shown up, at the house. No, she wasn't a virgin, but there had been more years than she'd like to remember when abstinence was her lifestyle. She'd lived the life of a nun.

In her mind's eye, she saw Nate, with his sexy, crooked, blindingly white smile and honed, muscular body. He was an outdoorsman, good with animals, and oh so good with her. Yeah, she was into him. Yeah, the sex was phenomenal. No, it hadn't messed her up with her kids. Nate never came first. The kids did.

But the job—now the job was demanding.

"Jeremy knows you're dating some drifter type."

"My private life, or lack thereof, is not relevant to this conversation. I take care of the kids, Lucky, and you know it."

"You work all the time."

"Except when I'm screwing my brains out with some

drifter, right? Now, you listen to me, Lucky. I was faithful to you from the time we met. You, on the other hand, didn't seem to realize what the term 'adultery' meant, so get off your high horse and leave my personal life out of this. I've tried like hell to get along with you because you are Bianca's father, but if push comes to shove, I'll take the kids from you."

"Michelle and I are more stable, more financially secure."

"And why is that? Because you owe me over seven thousand dollars in back child support and medical expenses? You know, I could use that money. The only reason I haven't taken you to court already is that I didn't want the kids to see us fight. I figured you'd be good for it anyway, that when college rolled around, you'd make it up to them. But now I'm not so sure. So take all your 'emotionally stable, financially secure' crap and shove it. Tell Jeremy, and Bianca, for that matter, the answer is no. Now I've got work to do—"

"Always. You've always got work to do."

"Someone has to pay the bills," she said, "and it sure as hell isn't going to be the kids' stable, secure father, is it?" In the rearview, she watched Cort Brewster walk across the lot to a back door. He didn't so much as glance in her direction, a bad sign, as they always waved or acknowledged each other. Again her guts tightened.

Lucky wasn't taking her attack lying down. "You know, Regan, Bianca's right. You really can be a bitch."

"That's hardly a news flash." But he'd wounded her. Bringing their daughter into the fight, hitting her where it hurt the most. But she wasn't about to buckle. "Just make sure the kids are both home tonight. Jeremy has chores, which, by the way, you could back me up on. He was picked up last night. He was in the wrong. And when you leave Bianca at the house, leave a check, too. At least a grand. No . . . make that two, and start the hell whittling that debt down or, trust me, I will take you to court. Merry Christmas!" She snapped off the phone and found herself shaking inside. No one on this earth could make her as crazy as Lucky Pescoli. Even his cute little wife wasn't as irritating. In fact, given spending an evening with either Michelle or Lucky, Pescoli would probably pick the bubblehead.

"Damn. Damn. Damn." She climbed out of the car and was still steaming as she marched through the wintry cold and into the back door of the building.

Alvarez had done her homework.

And something was off.

Really off, she thought as she drove into the parking lot of the station, spying the group of news reporters huddled near the front door, the vans parked in the visitors' lot.

The case had turned on its ear and the press knew all about it. They'd known that MacGregor had been held as a "person of interest," then released early this morning.

She pulled into the spot reserved for employees, then walked to a back door to avoid the cluster of reporters camped out near the front of the building. She was fighting a headache, and her nose was starting to run, but she'd be damned if she was going to fall victim to a cold virus now, a few days before Christmas, with this case still unsolved.

And just wait until the holiday.

For all the peace and goodwill of the season, there were always the family disputes and suicides and officers taking time off to be with their loved ones.

She could not afford to be less than a hundred percent. Not now. She had far too much to do.

Inside, the sheriff's office was a madhouse.

All calm shattered.

Everyone who could be was on duty.

Phones rang, people talked, boots scraped on the floor. Somewhere a copy machine was churning out pages, and through it all, barely discernible, was the sound of piped-in music, orchestral arrangements of Christmas classics.

Peeling off her jacket and hat, Selena found her cubicle, checked her e-mail and messages, then, still sniffing, walked into the break room, where she made herself a cup of hot tea. Her grandmother swore by tea with lemon and honey in it; her grandfather always supplemented the home remedy with a shot or two of whiskey or tequila, whatever was handy and out of Grandma Rosarita's watchful eye.

Still dunking the tea bag in her cup, she walked to Pescoli's desk.

Her partner was flipping through a thick stack of lab and autopsy reports, witness statements and notes she'd taken. "I can't believe MacGregor wasn't our killer," she groused. "Now we're back to square one."

"It happens," Alvarez said, sharing her partner's disappointment.

Pescoli rolled her chair back and shook her head. "I just hate being two steps behind this guy." She rubbed the nape of her neck.

"How'd it go with Jeremy?" Alvarez asked, tossing her tea bag into the plastic wastebasket at the corner of Pescoli's desk.

Pescoli's shoulders tightened. "He's not talking to me. But I think I'll live." With a glance toward the undersheriff's office she added, "So far, I haven't spoken to Cort. He's probably gonna want Jeremy run out of town on a rail or strung up by his balls."

"He's just a kid."

"A stupid kid." She threw up one hand. "For someone as smart as all get-out, he can be dumber than dirt."

"They all are sometimes. We all made major errors in judgment growing up."

Pescoli glanced up at her and squinted, as if she were trying to figure out what really made her partner tick. "I stole my dad's car and wrecked it. Three girls with me. We were all lucky no one was hurt. But there wasn't any booze or drugs involved. What about you?"

Alvarez didn't like where this was heading. Too personal. "The usual stuff. Cutting out of school, smoking behind the gym, sneaking out. It wasn't major, I guess, because I was pretty focused. But I think it's pretty normal." She didn't say that she'd trusted the wrong people, that one in particular had abused that trust and her life had never been the same.

"It's different when it's your own kids, y'know? You would lay down your life for them in a heartbeat, and the next second you want to throttle them. I'm gonna have to break the ice with Brewster, but not yet." She picked up a well-worn stack of papers, her eyes on Brewster's office.

Alvarez took an experimental sip of her tea. "Did you get the information Zoller retrieved on the vics?"

"Yep."

"I was going to call you last night," Alvarez started, but Pescoli waved her aside.

"It was a crazy night," she said dismissively. "But look at this. I've been doing a little research on Jillian Rivers, the victim who's different from the others. I double-checked her story, you know, about the ex-husband and the photos." She motioned to a stack of photographs, copies of the originals they'd found with Jillian Rivers's things at MacGregor's cabin.

Alvarez picked up the snapshots of the man walking across the street. The photograph was grainy and the man could have been the dead husband, she supposed, as she glanced at another shot, one of Aaron Caruso's driver's license, which was over ten years old. There was a resemblance, but nothing definite that she could see, no telltale ID marks like a tattoo or scar or even a mole in the same place.

"I googled Jillian Rivers aka Jillian Caruso, as well as her first husband, and I located newspaper articles from the towns where she lived."

"You've been busy."

"Got here early," Pescoli explained, again glancing toward Cort Brewster's closed door. "Anyway, it turns out that this husband she told us about, the first one, Aaron Caruso, he didn't just disappear. He disappeared with a whole lotta OPM."

"Other people's money?" Alvarez was about to drop the photos but stopped. "An embezzler? Scam artist?"

"Bingo. You got it. Look at this." She handed Alvarez several newspaper articles that she'd printed out, along with reports from an earlier investigation involving the SEC.

Selena placed her cup on the end of Pescoli's desk as she skimmed the articles. "So Caruso left his wife holding the bag."

"Only it was empty. Far as anyone can tell. At that time, there was no indication that she had any money. And he took half a million dollars, ten years ago."

Alvarez stared again at the photos. This guy in the old cap? He absconded with five-hundred grand? "None of the other victims had anything like this in their past."

"Another anomaly." Pescoli leaned back in her chair and tapped the ring finger of her right hand with her thumb. "Jillian Rivers is the victim who falls away from the usual MO. The killing site was only partially correct. The little open space in the forest and the single tree with her tied up naked—that was right. But that's about as far as it goes. The note left at the scene wasn't right, the star carved over her head wrong. The rope that bound her was different. The shoe size of the doer was smaller, the fact that he carried her rather than prodded her along in her bare feet another difference. This isn't an evolving MO. It's something else." She held Alvarez's gaze, squinting a little as she thought. "I bet whoever wants Jillian Rivers dead was just trying to throw us off. They're the copycat."

"So we need to go back to motive," Alvarez thought aloud.

"Exactly. I think we should find out who inherits if Ms. Rivers meets an untimely end. She's probably got some assets. Life insurance. Bank accounts. Retirement plans. Real estate. Whatever. Let's see if she has a will. She's got no kids, right?"

"Just a mother and a sister with a couple of kids."

"And an ex who's an attorney, lives in the state and might have drawn up her will while they were still married. If she hasn't changed it, then he could inherit. Maybe he got wind of the fact that she was going to rewrite it?"

"A big leap there," Alvarez pointed out. "Just because he's an ex—"

"Yeah, well, I go by the theory that the only good ex-husband is a dead ex-husband."

"What about the other victims?"

Pescoli scowled. "Therein lies the problem. Nina Salvadore had a small insurance policy on herself; the beneficiary was her kid. Theresa Charleton and Wendy Ito had no insurance and, as far as we can tell, their estates aren't worth much. Neither owned their homes and their cars are totaled. Theresa Charleton's Ford Eclipse isn't worth much now, and Wendy Ito still owed a lot of money on her Prius, so the bank will get the insurance proceeds to pay off the loan. Neither woman had a will, so whatever Charleton had will go to her husband, and Wendy Ito's estate, if there is anything, will go to her parents."

"We're still missing a car."

Pescoli nodded. "But when we find it, I'm betting it's emptied out. Just like the others."

"And all the heirs seem grief-riddled?"

"You got that right. If I get one more call from Lyle Wilson, I might just scream."

"Wilson? The brother of Theresa Charleton?"

"He seems to think that if he calls more often, we'll catch the killer sooner. Like we'd slack off if he didn't keep nudging us."

"He feels helpless and doesn't know what to do."

"Well, he can back the hell off, that's what he can do."

"You tell him that?" Alvarez took another long swallow of tea, the hot liquid soothing her throat.

"Not in so many words, no. But he got the message."

"I bet he did." Alvarez coughed, nearly spilling her tea.

"Hey, are you sick or something?"

"Nah, maybe a cold coming on."

"You've got to nip that in the bud." She opened a drawer to showcase an array of over-the-counter meds. "I've got anything you need . . . take the daytime non-drowsy stuff." She found a packet of cold tablets and a bottle of ibuprofen.

"This is like a drugstore," Alvarez said.

"Yeah, I know, but I can't afford to be sick." She tossed the packet to Alvarez, who caught it without slopping any of her tea. "Neither can you." She glanced at her watch. "Get ready, we've got a meeting in half an hour. The phone lines in the task force room have been going nuts, the Feds have been doing their own thing and Grayson's got to come up with a statement for the press."

"Sounds like fun," Alvarez muttered as she slid out the card of cold tablets and popped one from its blister pack. Usually she wasn't a fan of medication bought without a prescription, but today she was willing to try anything.

"Fun?" Pescoli glanced at her partner. "You really do need to get out more."

Chapter Twenty-Five

It took Jillian nearly two hours to secure her release from the hospital.

Dr. Haas, tall, reed-thin, with short silvery hair and deep crow's feet around his eyes, tried to intervene, to convince her that she needed more time to allow her system to recuperate, but she was having none of it.

"Fine." The doctor, thin lips pinched, nostrils slightly flared, finally acquiesced, albeit unwillingly, as MacGregor waited, leaning insouciantly against the wall, jean-clad hips resting on the edge of the counter that encased the sink. "I can't stop you." Haas handed her a prescription and signed the orders for her release. With a final disapproving glance, he swept out of the room, and Jillian, after hobbling to the bathroom, dressed with difficulty in the clothes that the sheriff's department had left for her. Shoes were a problem, as nothing fit over her wrapped ankle, but her boot-cut jeans were a godsend.

"I don't know how you think you're going to track down your dead husband and outrun a killer on crutches," MacGregor commented.

"One crutch," she corrected, "and remember, I have you, right?"

He inclined his head. "I think I've got as much at stake in this as you do. The sheriff's department and the FBI released me, but that doesn't mean I'm not still on their radar for this mess."

"And you're not willing to sit around and wait for them to catch the guy either."

"Nope." His face was grim. "Whoever he is, he set me up, too. Shot my dog. Left you out in the woods to die. Pointed the authorities in my direction. No, Jillian, I'm not going to wait for the detectives. They'd just as soon pin this on me and I wouldn't be the first innocent man locked away."

She knew he was thinking of the time he'd done in Colorado. "Good, then let's get out of here. I was thinking we should start in Missoula, since that's where the envelopes that I received were postmarked. That's where I was heading in the first place."

"Any place special?"

"Well, I was going to start with Mason, my ex. He's the only person I know there, I mean, the only one who has any axe to grind with me." She paused. Something wasn't right about the whole Missoula thing. She couldn't put her finger on it, but there was an idea tugging at the back of her mind, a notion that she couldn't quite grasp, a feeling that Missoula, Montana, was all wrong. Even a decoy. But that sensation faded in an instant, a wispy thought that escaped her.

MacGregor seemed to sense it. "What?"

"Nothing, just . . . I don't know. Missoula seems off somehow. As if whoever sent me the photographs *wanted* me to head there. I knew it before I left Seattle but I couldn't help myself." She tried to call back the image that escaped her. "I feel like if we go to Missoula, we're playing into his hands."

Frowning, MacGregor walked to the window and stared outside, where sunlight was beginning to melt some of the snow. "Have you got any other ideas?"

She shook her head. "Not really."

"Then for right now let's go somewhere private. Plan our next move without the chance of anyone overhearing. Somewhere out of town."

"What about Harley?"

"We'll stop by the veterinary clinic. I've already called Jordan. She's waiting."

"Jordan?"

"The vet." He picked up Jillian's travel case. "She's a friend of mine."

"A good friend?" she asked, more than curious. There was something in the tone of his voice that caused a bit of envy to run through her veins.

He glanced over his shoulder as he held the door to the room open. "Very good," he said as she hitched her way through with one crutch.

"Should I be jealous?"

His smile spread easily over his beard-darkened chin. "Very."

For the first time since meeting the two FBI agents, Alvarez finally understood what Craig Halden's role was in his partnership with Stephanie Chandler. Usually content to let his partner do most of the talking, he'd always hung in the background, making a few comments, but mostly watching from the sidelines. A good ol' country boy who was skating along on his job.

Not so.

Today the show was all Halden's, and his affable demeanor evaporated under the new, hard-nosed agent who was stepping up in the investigation. Not that Stephanie Chandler took a backseat; that wasn't her style. But today, when all hell was breaking out among the news people and the public, and the case against Zane MacGregor, who had been their only serious suspect, had broken down, Halden had stepped up.

He stood at the head of the long table in the task force room and brought everyone up to speed. The FBI, too, was convinced that MacGregor wasn't their man, that Jillian Rivers's abduction was the result of a personal attack against her, someone who was using the Star-Crossed Killer as a decoy. The psycho they were looking for was an organized, systematic serial killer. He wouldn't have made the mistakes that had occurred at the intended killing site of Jillian Rivers.

So now they had two killers and two cases, and their focus at the moment was on the Rivers woman.

Agents Halden and Chandler had studied the theory that Aaron Caruso, a scam artist who had bilked investors out of their savings, might still be alive, but again, there was no proof. The pictures and e-mail and voice messages may have been just a lure to get Jillian Rivers to Montana.

Trouble was, other than her ex-husband, Mason Rivers, who was in Spokane at the time of the shooting, Ms. Rivers had no known enemies.

"Could be someone pissed off about losing their nest egg," Watershed offered.

Chandler frowned. "Ten years is a long time to hold a grudge."

"Not if you need the money now," Pescoli said. She was seated at the table, wedged between Watershed and Alvarez, while the agents were walking back and forth in front of the geographical maps and pictures of the victims. "Not if you're suddenly desperate, your life is falling apart and you need a scapegoat."

"But murder?" Chandler asked. "Elaborate murder?"

"Could be the guy's been waiting for the opportunity

and then the Star-Crossed Killer comes along and he thinks he's got his ticket." Watershed glanced toward Grayson for support.

Grayson grimaced and rubbed his chin. "We should take a look at the victims of Caruso's scam, see if anyone lives in the area or within a hundred-mile radius."

"I'll do it," Zoller offered. For once she wasn't manning the phone and was seated at one end of the long table.

"Good."

"But that's just one side of the equation." Halden tapped a finger on the map of the area, the spot near MacGregor's cabin where Jillian Rivers had been found. "If our copycat is after Ms. Rivers for a reason, he won't kill anyone else."

"No, he'll go after her again," Alvarez said. "He's missed twice. He won't give up."

Halden nodded. "But our other guy, he won't give up either and he'll be looking for more victims if he doesn't have some already stashed away. Have we checked the missing persons in the area?"

Alvarez answered, "Checked within a hundred-mile radius. Since he crosses race barriers, I narrowed it down to women between twenty and forty missing in the last month." She walked to the map on the wall. "All of the shootings took place within ten miles of each other, so I tried to narrow the fields even further to women who were known, or thought by their families to have been passing through the area. Fortunately we have only five who meet all the criteria." She placed the five reports face up on the table, driver's license pictures included. "Any, all or none of them could be our next victim."

"God, I hate this," Pescoli said, scanning the pictures, and Alvarez agreed. The thought that some of these women might be in the killer's lair, already held, bound, tortured or heaven knew what else, bothered her deeply.

"We have to ID this guy," Chandler said, walking past each of the pictures. Her face was set and hard and, as thin as she was, she looked as if she'd lost weight since arriving in Grizzly Falls. "Has anyone been able to talk to the Jane Doe in the hospital?"

"No," Zoller said. "She's still unconscious, but we've identified her as Hannah Estes. Twenty-nine, a secretary for an insurance firm, divorced, no children. Lives in Butte with a roommate. Hannah's the registered owner of a Chevrolet Impala, which, too, is missing."

Cort Brewster added, "And the only living victim, the only person who can positively ID this prick."

The sheriff nodded. "Someone needs to go up to Missoula, be there when she wakes up."

"If she wakes up." Brewster stood then, put his hands in his pockets and shook his head. He made a big point of avoiding Pescoli's eyes, but she seemed to be ignoring him right back. Alvarez didn't blame her; they had more important issues to deal with. The pictures of the missing women, all potential victims of this maniac, called to her. Were any of them even now trapped in some windowless lair, being used as slaves or . . . ?

But not sex slaves. None of the bodies had shown any signs of vaginal trauma or sexual intercourse. What is this nutcase's game?

"Here's what we've got," Halden said. "I've been working on this." He laid down page after page of the stars left at the killing scenes, each traced onto tissue paper as thin as onion skins. "If you look closely, they all fit onto this—" He drew out another, heavier piece of paper from his briefcase, laid it flat and placed the stack of traced drawings over the image. Every star fit perfectly except one. "This is the star we found with Jillian

Rivers. Not only is it a different shape but it doesn't fit into the constellation."

"Which constellation?" Pescoli asked.

"Orion." Alvarez recognized the familiar outline. "The hunter."

She noticed Pescoli stiffen. "He thinks he's a hunter? Shooting out their tires, keeping them with him before he leaves them in the woods?"

"Maybe . . . ?" Alvarez looked to Halden.

"That part we don't get," the agent said. "If it was about hunting and killing, why not just shoot them when he has the chance?"

"So, if you scramble the letters, do they say something about hunting or Orion?" Alvarez suggested.

Halden pulled out a copy of the note and placed it on the table. The large block letters were visible to everyone:

WAR   **T HE**   **SC**   **I N**

"Not yet," he said.

"R, I, N." Alvarez frowned. "And the S and C and E could be part of 'CONSTELLATION.'"

"Or the H and N and T and E and R could be part of 'HUNTER.' We're only missing a U on that one," Watershed said, scratching at his beard stubble.

"It's all conjecture." Stephanie Chandler was terse. "The bureau's working on it."

Halden went on a little bit more about the stars and the letters, and the FBI agents agreed to go to Missoula and talk to Hannah Estes's doctors and family. Everyone was hoping she would awaken and make ID'ing the killer easier, but so far it wasn't happening. When the meeting broke up, Alvarez left the room worrying that they were no closer to arresting the killer than they had been when Theresa Charleton's body had been found months before.

She made her way out of the task force room and nearly ran into Joelle, who was carrying a platter of decorated sugar cookies: jolly Santa faces, snowmen with raisin eyes, holly wreaths decorated in gooey green frosting with tiny red hearts clustered to look like berries. "I thought everyone could use a little cheering up," she said.

"Thanks," Alvarez said, and grabbed a reindeer with a red heart nose that was much too large for his little head. Poor Rudolph looked like he was in serious need of rhinoplasty. Worse yet, the cookie crumbled in her fingers.

Joelle didn't notice as she passed the plate around to the officers exiting the room, then walked self-importantly down the hallway, high heels clicking, earrings bobbing, as she made her way to the kitchen, where she paused to brew coffee, then left the platter with its homemade sweets on the table.

"Merry Christmas," she breathed to them all as she hurried out the front door and somehow pushed her way through the crowd of reporters on the steps. Joelle wasn't part of the investigative team and therefore wasn't expected to come to work on her days off.

"What a case," Pescoli whispered, snapping off Santa's hat with her teeth.

"She's just spreading good cheer."

"In a serial-murder investigation?" Pescoli shook her head and made her way back to her desk.

"She means well," Alvarez offered.

"Have you ever wondered why people say that? 'She *means* well?' It implies that the person they're talking about is rude, self-involved or just plain oblivious to what's really going on, and I'm not so sure Joelle ever means well. I think it's an act, that deep down she's a mean-spirited bitch."

Alvarez lifted her brows. "You got up on the wrong side of . . . oh yeah, sorry." Of course Pescoli was snappy. She'd had a horrible night with her kid.

"I guess I have a date with destiny," Pescoli said, and as Alvarez watched, her partner finished her cookie and, visibly squaring her shoulders, walked across the hall and straight for the door of Cort Brewster's office.

The storm had abated a bit. MacGregor was at the wheel of a truck loaned to him by a friend, Jillian in the passenger seat. The roads were plowed, the pickup making good time in the scant traffic.

For once the sun's rays burned through the remaining clouds and Jillian felt better than she had in days. It had been long over a week since she'd woken up in MacGregor's cabin, and from that time forward, she'd always been laid up, in someone's care and feeling useless.

Today, however, she thought as the pickup's wide tires hummed across the wet pavement, she felt in control, able to determine her own destiny.

Well . . . somewhat. There were still the bruised ribs and sprained ankle to deal with, and the painkillers she was on not only took the edge off, but dulled her a bit.

She didn't care.

Finally she was free.

With the heat blasting into the cab and the radio turned to some country-western station that plucked Christmas classics from obscurity, MacGregor drove straight from the hospital's front doors, where a few newscasters had tried to get a statement from her, to the veterinary clinic a few miles away. He parked in an alley next to a dented Dumpster that had survived more than one unfortunate tangle with a car.

Fortunately she wasn't a big enough news item for the press to chase. With MacGregor's help and her single crutch, she was able to walk along a snow-covered concrete path, past a row of stiff arborvitae to the back door, where MacGregor rapped sharply with his knuckles. "She's doing this as a favor to me," he explained. "The clinic's officially closed."

"A favor?"

"Mmm." The door swung open and a petite woman who couldn't have weighed a hundred pounds ushered them inside, where the smells of animals and urine were faint and masked by the stronger odors of antiseptic and pine cleaner. Fluorescent lights illuminated rooms and hallways painted white to match a gleaming tile floor. MacGregor made quick introductions and Jordan Eagle shook her hand with fingers that were as strong as steel. "You're the woman who survived the attack," she said, her eyes assessing. Without any makeup, she was still beautiful, her skin smooth and coppery, her eyes surrounded by thick black lashes and perfect eyebrows. Her cheekbones were high and separated by a thin, straight nose. Full lips parted to expose white teeth that were only slightly crooked, just enough to add interest to her face. "You're lucky," she observed.

"Because of MacGregor."

Jordan's gaze skated to Zane. "I heard. So now you're a hero?"

He snorted derisively and sent Jillian a look meant to shut her up. "Hardly."

She didn't take the hint. "He saved my life," Jillian said flatly. "Twice." Jillian wanted everyone in Pinewood and the surrounding counties to know the facts, not the distorted truth that she suspected was grist for the local gossip mill. Not the facts twisted to make a case against him by the sheriff's department.

One of Jordan's arched brows quirked upward. "Well, how about that, MacGregor? I knew you always had it in you."

He shifted uncomfortably from one foot to the other. "How's Harley?"

"Groggy but okay. I was able to save the leg, but my guess is that he won't use it much. Maybe for balance. But when he runs, he'll probably tuck it up and gallop on three legs." She glanced up at MacGregor. "He'll be fine. Don't worry. The jackrabbits will have just as much to fear as they used to."

"Which wasn't all that much," MacGregor allowed. "He gives a good chase, but wouldn't know what to do with one if he caught it."

She laughed, her dark eyes crinkling at the corners. She was tanned, lithe, her black hair pulled into a ponytail that hung halfway to her waist. How she could wrestle an eighty-pound German shepherd or anxious foaling mare, Jillian couldn't understand. Nonetheless, if anything, Jordan Eagle, DVM, looked efficient.

"He's in here." She led them along a well-lit hallway to an examination room, then opened a door to a larger area, where Harley lay in a large crate. He looked through the grate with groggy eyes, but Jillian heard his tail thump a few times.

"Hey, buddy," MacGregor said, and opened the gate to pet his dog. Harley's tongue hung out of his mouth and the thumping increased in tempo for a second. "Is the doc takin' good care of you?"

Jillian felt as if her heart might crack. Even though she and the spaniel had started out mistrusting each other, she'd begun to care for the damned dog, and she felt terrible that he'd been attacked because of her.

"As I said, he's going to be fine. He's one tough dog," Jordan said when MacGregor straightened and Jillian took her turn petting the dog's head. Harley even managed to wag his tail for her, and she felt all the more pain, more responsibility.

"So you'll watch him?" MacGregor asked.

"Like a hawk," she said.

"Not an eagle?"

"Lame joke, MacGregor. Real lame."

Jillian agreed but couldn't help feeling another little twinge of jealousy at the easy banter between MacGregor and Jordan Eagle. It was ridiculous, but she was helpless to control it.

"I'll call and check in."

"Where're you going?" Jordan asked, glancing again at Jillian, as if she were suddenly aware that there might be something more than friendship between the woman on crutches and MacGregor.

"Not sure yet, but I'll call."

"I've heard that before."

"Seriously. I will."

Jordan paused in the doorway. "You'd better or I might just hold Harley for ransom."

MacGregor smiled as he helped Jillian into the truck. "Yeah, right, like you'd want him," he said, and walked to the driver's side. "Thanks, Jordan."

"Anytime." She smiled then, the curve of her lips wistful.

"She's in love with you," Jillian said as MacGregor jammed the truck into reverse and the vet disappeared into the clinic.

"Don't think so."

"Bull. You know it as much as I do."

"She's married."

"That's not what I said. Are you having an affair with her?"

"Nah." Once the pickup was in drive and moving forward, he steered the old rig onto the street, where sunlight was dancing on the wet pavement.

"But you did."

"A long time ago." He squinted against the glare. "Look in the glove box. See if you can find a pair of sunglasses."

"So what happened?" She rummaged through loose papers and old rags, and the manual for the truck. "Nothing."

MacGregor checked the visor and found a pair. "Can you clean these off?"

"Sure." She rubbed the dusty lenses with the hem of her sweater. "So what happened? With the lady vet?"

"The lady vet. She'd love that. It ran its course. She wanted something more than I was willing to give and she found somebody else."

"That simple."

A long dimple, filled with irony and a bit of regret, creased his cheek. "Well, nothing's that simple, but I figure you know that, since you've been married twice."

She wanted to ask more questions, to delve further, but he'd effectively shut her down. He was teasing her but also telling her to let it go. His past was his past. Had nothing to do with her. And yet . . . She shifted on the old bench seat and stared out a windshield that didn't look as if it had been cleaned since the millennium. Pockmarked, dusty, with streaks where the wipers had scraped across it, the glass had a crack that ran along the bottom of the pane.

"Where are we going?" she asked.

"I was thinking of Spruce Creek."

"What?" He was driving out of the city limits, the low-slung buildings of mini-malls passing by.

"You had coffee there, right? At some place called the Chocolate Moose Café?"

She was nodding. "I can barely remember it, but yeah, I think so. How did you know?"

"Because the detectives asked me if I'd been there or knew about the place. Did I have coffee there? Was I a regular? They didn't say why, but it had to be connected to you, and since it's on the way from Seattle to September Creek, where your car was found, I figured you'd been there."

"And you think the killer might have been, too?" she asked as he passed a slow-moving semi hauling cars that were dented and wrecked.

"It's as good a place to start as any, don't you think?"

"To tell you the truth, I don't know what to think. I'm not a detective or an investigator, but there's no reason to sit around here."

"Agreed."

"Okay," she said as he picked up speed and the town street gave way to a curvy mountain road lined with trees that were still drooping under the weight of snow. She'd never been afraid of adventure, had always welcomed a test, but taking off with no good plan to a destination she didn't know, with a man who at times frightened her and other times excited her, seemed a little crazy. Okay, a lot crazy.

She wanted to deny her attraction to him but it was just damned impossible. The truth of the matter was that she was attracted to Zane MacGregor. And it wasn't just a little, casual flirtation.

Unfortunately, she was beginning to fall for the man.

And that, she knew, was a problem.

A big problem.

Chapter Twenty-Six

"So what is it you want to say, Detective?"

Cort Brewster was sitting at his desk, a pile of paperwork in front of him, his pen in hand. He looked up as Pescoli walked into the room, and the expression on his face could have turned flesh to stone.

"I thought we should talk about last night. The kids."

He leaned back in his chair, so far that it squeaked. His face remained grim as he said, "Before you launch into all kinds of reasons or explanations or apologies or whatever it is you want to say, let's just get one thing clear. You and I have to work together. No matter what happens between your son and my daughter."

She felt a bit of relief, until he started clicking his pen.

"Even so, that does not excuse what happened last night, and I want you to know that I hold your son responsible."

Here we go.

"He's older, should know better and has no right dragging my girl along on some drunken joyride." All Brewster's calm faded away and his face infused with color. "She's only fifteen, for crying out loud, and as far as I'm concerned your boy is going nowhere, getting into trouble, sliding down one helluva slippery slope."

"You're blaming Jeremy," she said stonily.

"Hell yes, I'm blaming him. Those kids could have been killed or maimed or made vegetables for life. You and I see it every day, what happens when booze and kids and cars mix. Hell, even adults! They are lucky, so damned lucky, that nothing happened last night, Pescoli." His feet slammed to the ground, and he stood tall and angry behind the desk, a scant two-foot barrier between them. "You tell that boy of yours that I won't stand for this. Got it? If anything happens to my little girl I will hold your son personally responsible. I told her and I'm telling you, I want him to stay away from her."

Pescoli remained silent for a long moment. She'd known, of course, that Brewster would be mad, even blame Jeremy, but the hate in his eyes suggested that his feelings ran too deep to try to reason with him. Finally, she said, "Don't you think we should talk this out with the kids?"

"Are you insane? No. I laid down the law and I expect you to do the same." His thin lips flattened on themselves as he leaned across the desk. "You and me, we're different. We raise our kids differently. I'm a deacon in the church and have been married for twenty-two years to the same woman. I play by the rules of God and country."

"So do I," she said, but she saw that glint in his eye telling her he didn't believe her. "Look, Brewster, I may not be a cookie-baking soccer mom, but I teach my kids how to live their lives."

"Like yours?" he cut in.

She stiffened, realizing he was talking about her sex

life. "None of your business, Cort, and if you make it yours, I'll file a complaint. I came in here hoping to talk civilly about a problem we both share. I admit Jeremy is not blameless, but I think, in all fairness, no one put a gun to Heidi's head and dragged her out to the car or forced a can of Budweiser down her throat."

"For the love of God! You're out of your mind to think that—"

"That what? Your"—she made air quotes—" 'little girl' is partially to blame? How many kids do you have, Cort? Four, right? All girls? All perfect angels, is that what you want me to believe?"

He looked as if he might blow a gasket. A vein was throbbing in his temple, and at any minute she half-expected he might have a stroke, right there on the desk. "Your boy is the bad seed, Pescoli. You and I both know it. He doesn't have a decent father figure in his life and, from the way you've been . . ."

"Been what, Brewster?" He snapped his jaw shut and she felt her hands clench. "I thought we could discuss what had happened. You know, come up with a plan to set things right, guide the kids, but, apparently, that's not gonna happen. And you and I, we've got a problem, which isn't going to help either of us, since we have to work together."

"You are so out of line."

"Out of line," she repeated slowly, feeling the back of her neck grow hot. They glared at each other, and eventually Pescoli said tautly, "We've got ourselves one sicko here in Pinewood County, and we both know he's not about to stop killing until we catch him. So we'd better put aside our personal grudges and get on with it. You deal with your daughter and I'll handle my son."

"Amen."

Pescoli turned on her heel, stinging from his insinuations. *Bastard,* she thought, *holier-than-thou bastard.* God only knew what skeletons Cort Brewster had in his own damned closet.

The woman has to die. I thought she would expire on her own, that there wasn't the slimmest chance that she would survive, and yet she hangs on, by the tiniest of threads. Enough to worry me.

The police and the FBI aren't giving up, not that I expected them to, but I can't let this one mistake ruin everything. There is just too much yet to be accomplished!

So I'm taking a chance, my adrenaline whistling through my veins as I drive to the restaurant, my hands precise on the wheel. The plan is simple. Once I arrive, I'll put on hospital scrubs, colored contact lenses and a toupee. I will stuff my jowls with cotton and wear padding under my clothes. I have a set of false teeth that slip over my own. I've had them for years—bought long ago in California from a man who made costumes for the film industry before he fell victim to an ugly meth habit. He is long dead, but some of his costumes, including the oversized shoes I wear, are still a part of my arsenal of disguises.

It's a simple plan: slip into the hospital, cause a Code Blue to occur down the hall from Estes and, when all hell breaks loose, slip into her room and turn off the life support. She's too weak to be resuscitated. I've learned that much from reading between the lines in the news stories.

But I can't take a chance that she'll survive.

I just have to make sure the cop left to guard her is distracted.

If he won't leave his post, then he'll have to be disposed of, which I would like to avoid. He's not meant to die, not one of the chosen.

But if push comes to shove, well, so be it.

I drive to a restaurant and change in a stall in the bathroom. No one at Denny's really notices, as I've left a substantial tip for my piece of Christmas Cherry Pie and cup of coffee. By the time I am out the door, my table's been cleared and a couple of men in their seventies have slid into the booth.

Good.

I drive two blocks from the hospital and then walk briskly inside. There are a few reporters hovering near the front door, a cameraman smoking under the portico, but I pass unnoticed and the security, for all of the press about this case, seems remarkably lax.

No doubt a decision by the hospital administration to make things appear normal, to not disturb the other patients, to soothe concerned friends and relatives. I already know what floor she's on; I've learned this bit of information from drinking coffee and having lunch in the cafeteria and picking up bits of information. In each case, I appeared distraught, a worried husband or boyfriend. No doubt my image was caught on the security cameras, but again, thanks to my old meth-loving costume-making friend, my identity was hidden and I know where the cameras are, am able to turn my face away from those prying lenses.

Today I make my way to the second floor and the west wing. Now things are interesting. Yes, there is a guard posted at the woman's door, and the room itself is not isolated, but opens to the nurses' station. A tougher act than I'd anticipated.

But still easy enough.

I stroll into a room down a hallway and spy an old woman gasping for air, on a ventilator. I walk into the room and, as she stares at me with curious, worried eyes—this woman who is drugged and not entirely aware—I unhook her from the machine.

Before the monitors can react, I hurry down the hall, nearly tripping on an aide pushing a man in a wheelchair.

"Excuse me," I grunt.

"Hey—" the aide says as I round the corner, and there in the hallway is my salvation. Without a moment's hesitation, I pull the lever on the fire alarm.

Within a heartbeat, sirens and alarm bells are ringing crazily.

"Code Blue!"

"Room 212! Mrs. Bancroft!"

I hear the panic and smile as they all come running. I duck into a closet and strip off the lab coat and wig, then hurry back toward the fray. In the ensuing chaos, I work quickly, slipping into a suddenly unattended room, glancing down at the woman who had been my prisoner for nearly a week. This part of my mission isn't what I live for. The actual taking of life has little meaning. It's the gaining of their trust, making them feel love, knowing they will give themselves to me and I won't take what they offer—that's what appeals. The ultimate thrill is to see the despair and fear in their eyes when they realize that I've tricked them, that I am not a would-be lover but their ultimate doom.

So this yanking of a cord has no appeal. It's the diversion that's thrilling. Forcing the others into a panic mode, creating pandemonium—now that is a sweet, succulent drug, one I enjoy.

But I must not tarry.

Again I look at the weak, unconscious woman and wish for just a second she would open her eyes, catch a glimpse of me as I so easily take her life. If only I could witness that quick understanding, the first gasp of true, brutal fear.

It is not to be.

And time is running out.

"Sorry, Hannah," I say without conviction as the ventilator forces air into her lungs. "Sweet dreams."

With a quick, hard jerk, I pull the plug.

And then it's over.

Judging from Pescoli's expression, Alvarez concluded that her partner's discussion with the undersheriff didn't go well. She'd holed up at her desk for the rest of the morning, and only hours later, on her way back from the ladies' room, did she stop by Alvarez's cubicle. "Are you buying all this Orion and hunter crap?" Pescoli asked, blocking the opening to Alvarez's small desk area.

"It's the best we've got."

"Then what's with the letters? Why not just spell out 'Orion' or 'hunter'? Why the big puzzle?"

"Because that's what the guy is all about," Alvarez said. She'd manned the phones for a couple of hours, gone through all the notes from each of the crime scenes and autopsy reports and spoken to several of the victims' family members who had called in, hoping for closure, pushing the police into arresting the monster who was terrorizing the area and had killed their daughter or sister or niece.

"Let's get some lunch," Pescoli said, and slid a glance toward Cort Brewster's office. The department had quieted down since the morning meeting, and while the road deputies were patrolling, some of the detectives had headed home rather than put in for more overtime. Agents Chandler and Halden had left an hour earlier, but the sheriff and his dog were tucked into his office and Brewster, too, had given up his church duties and family life to stay near the center of the investigation.

"I'm with you."

Alvarez grabbed her jacket and sidearm, then followed her partner outside. Without a word she climbed into the passenger seat of the Jeep. Pescoli started the engine and put the rig into gear before Alvarez had fully closed her door.

"In a hurry?" Selena commented.

"Things are a little tense in there." Pescoli glanced in the rearview mirror at the office.

"They always are."

"I suppose."

"I take it things didn't go well with Brewster."

"Depends. On whether you mean crappy or really crappy. Take your pick. Wild Wills?"

Alvarez grunted an assent.

Pescoli drove to the restaurant, parked on the street, and together they walked inside, passing Grizz, the dead bear, still dressed in his angelic garb, long teeth bared, claws visible despite his fake wings and halo. "Can you believe this?" Pescoli asked, but strode into the dining area, where the after-church crowd had gathered. They found a table near the back, removed their jackets, and Alvarez took a chair with a view of the front door, while through the speakers a woman's voice warbled "Silver Bells."

"Is that Dolly Parton?" Pescoli asked.

"No."

"Whitney Houston?"

"No," Alvarez assured her partner as the song was drowned out by the rattling of a cart of dishes. "I don't know who she is but it's not Dolly or Whitney."

"You sure?"

"Absolutely."

"Doesn't matter, I'm about silver-belled, wished a merry Christmas and herald angeled out this season."

"Bah, humbug," Alvarez said as the scent of coffee mingled with the aromas of cinnamon and sizzling bacon. Alvarez's stomach rumbled and she realized how hungry she was.

"You know, I could use a beer. Or maybe a shot of Jack Daniels on the rocks." Pescoli looked tired. Her eyes were bloodshot and rimmed by dark circles that testified to too many sleepless nights.

Alvarez lifted a shoulder, but by the time Sandi came around, Pescoli had thought twice about it and ordered a Diet Coke, hamburger and curly fries. "Live a little," she advised Alvarez.

"I'm thinking more like 'live a little *longer*,'" Alvarez said, and ordered a spinach, apple and hazelnut salad with broiled chicken in lieu of bacon and hot tea with lemon in lieu of alcohol.

"Still fighting a cold?" Pescoli asked.

"I'll be all right."

"Whiskey might help."

"Couldn't hurt." But she stuck with tea, adding extra slices of lemon when Sandi delivered the drinks.

Pescoli sighed. "You know, you get pregnant and bring home a baby, this precious, innocent little bit of life whose whole future is in your hands, and you think, 'I'm gonna do everything right for this kid. I'm going to be the best damned mother he could want and his life is going to be perfect. I'll make sure of it.' He's little and sweet and inquisitive and crazy about you and . . ." She shook her head dolefully. "And then life happens to the kid. Little things like scraped knees and slivers and forgotten homework assignments. Then bigger things like being bullied on the playground and teased cuz his mother's a cop, and then really big things like losing his dad and suddenly gaining a stepdad and a sister and a divorce and . . . oh hell. Suddenly, and I mean it seems like that," she said, snapping her fingers, ". . . he's seventeen and in trouble. Big trouble." She leaned back in her chair and took a long swallow from her Diet Coke.

"But you don't regret your children."

"Not for a second."

"And you'd do it again."

"In a heartbeat." Pescoli nodded. "So what about you? Why no kids?"

"It just never happened," Alvarez lied, then added in all truthfulness, "I never found the right guy." That much was patently true. The boys she'd met in high school were unimpressive, and then there had been the "incident," as her mother had called it, though they both knew better. Alvarez didn't want to think about it now, what had happened to her when she was seventeen, just Jeremy's age, but it was always chasing after her, a ghost touching a cold finger against the back of her neck, a faint voice echoing in her ear.

You have a son. Somewhere. A boy you haven't seen since he was a few minutes old. . . .

"You still looking?"

"What?"

"For a husband. You're only thirty-two."

"Three. I'm thirty-three."

"Not exactly ancient."

"Well, yeah, but I have this job," Alvarez said, trying to lighten the heavy conversation. "It takes up a lot of time."

"That it does. And believe me, sometimes husbands are vastly overrated."

Sandi returned with their orders and they lapsed into silence, letting the buzz of conversation and the soft strains of music fill the gaps while they ate.

Alvarez was about half-finished with her salad, though her appetite had waned with talk of children and her headache was back, her nose still threatening to run, when a gust of cold air caused her to look up. Grace Perchant, dressed in some kind of medieval-looking tunic and long velvet coat, walked slowly from the foyer into the dining area. She was about to be seated, following Sandi toward a window booth, when she stopped suddenly.

"Uh-oh," Alvarez said. Grace, the woman who saw ghosts, communed with the dead and had found Jillian Rivers's Subaru while walking her wolf-dog, froze in her tracks.

Pescoli looked over her shoulder. "Oh Christ."

At that, Grace's head swiveled and her faded green eyes zeroed in on Pescoli.

"Great," she whispered, "just what we need," as Grace walked unerringly to their table.

Grace's usually calm expression had lost any trace of serenity as she laid a long-fingered hand over Pescoli's shoulder before the cop could pull away.

Pescoli scooted her chair back, out of Grace's reach, and instinctively reached for her sidearm, before she caught herself.

A couple with two kids at the next table stopped eating to stare.

"He knows about you," Grace whispered, those weird eyes fixed on something in the middle distance, on a point, Alvarez was certain, only she could see.

"Who?" Pescoli asked.

"The predator. He knows about you." Grace's words were murmured but loud enough to cause every hair on the back of Pescoli's neck to stand on end.

"What predator?" But she knew. Alvarez saw it in her eyes. They both knew.

"The one you seek."

"We seek a lot of predators."

"This one is different. This one is evil. . . ."

"They are all freakin' evil, Grace, but I figure you're talking about the whack job who leaves women in the friggin' blizzard. That the one?" Pescoli demanded, but her face, instead of turning red with rage, had whitened. "I sure as hell hope he does know about me, cuz I'm going to nail his ass."

"Don't listen to that, honey," the wife at the next table warned her son of about ten.

Grace was unmoved. "He's not afraid."

Pescoli gave her a long look. "The last time we met, I believe you told Alvarez, 'You'll find him.' What happened to that?"

Grace's gaze, that faint, watery green, slid to Alvarez, then back again to Pescoli. "I'm speaking to you now." Again she touched Pescoli's shoulder with her fingertips, and again Regan pulled away. "You, Detective, are in grave danger."

"It comes with the job, Grace," Pescoli said, brushing off the woman's warning, some of her color returning.

"Be careful."

"Yes, ma'am."

"Be more than careful. He's relentless. A hunter."

Alvarez snapped to attention. Hunter? She was out of her chair in an instant. "Come on, Grace, let's go outside and have a talk." She put a hold on the weird woman and escorted her into the vestibule, while patrons nearly fell out of their seats watching her. They moved past the glowering eyes of the grizzly bear done up in holiday attire and into an empty, dark room used for banquets. Pescoli was only a step behind.

Once away from the interested eyes of the patrons, Selena released Grace and said, "If you know this son of a bitch so well, why don't you save us all a lot of trouble and tell us who he is."

Grace frowned. Rubbed her arm as if wounded.

"There is no reason to get violent. I'm just warning you. Her." She slid Pescoli a confused glance.

"What's this about him being a hunter?" Alvarez asked.

"He hunts his prey." Grace's face had a wounded look to it, and she kept rubbing her arm, as if she couldn't believe the policewoman had been so angry with her for imparting her wisdom.

Alvarez wasn't backing down, wasn't buying into the frightened-deer routine. "So why are you warning Pescoli, singling her out?"

"When I walked into the dining area a few minutes ago, I sensed a disturbance in the atmosphere, heard a voice in my head."

"And what did that voice say?" Alvarez asked with extreme patience.

"Regan Elizabeth Pescoli."

Alvarez glanced at Pescoli, who nodded and swallowed hard. "You know my middle name?" she asked.

"Not until a few minutes ago."

"It's common knowledge," Alvarez heard herself saying, but Pescoli was shaking her head. "I use my maiden name for my middle name. Regan C. Pescoli. C for Connors. Not E for Elizabeth. I stopped that in grade school."

Alvarez felt a chill deep in her heart. Something was wrong here. Very wrong.

Pescoli stepped closer to the odd ghost whisperer of a woman. "How did you know what my middle name was, Grace? Have you seen my birth certificate?"

"It came to me. I can't explain any further. I just know that you're in danger, and instead of roughing me up and pushing me around, I would think that you'd thank me."

"Is there a problem in here?" Sandi strode into the

darkened banquet room and her pinched lips said it all. "I got me a room full of people trying to eat their lunch here after church and all, and then you go and make a scene." Her eyebrows were raised high over the frames of her glasses, her green eyelids stretching. "This might be called Wild Wills, but it's a family kind of restaurant. I've no use for any arrests or police shenanigans."

"It's all right, Sandi," Grace said with her usual calm. "I was just warning the detectives."

"Warning them?"

"Everything's under control," Alvarez assured Sandi, and she headed out of the banquet room to the register. "What do we owe you?"

"Just a sec. I'll get the tab!" Sandi was quick as a cat in retrieving her tickets, adding their bill and handing it to Alvarez.

"I assume I can leave now?" Grace asked Pescoli.

"You're free to go," Pescoli said. Grace sent her a strange look as she headed back to the dining area. If she noticed the interested gazes following her, she didn't show it, didn't so much as falter in her steps toward her table.

Alvarez retrieved their jackets and met up with Pescoli. "You owe me ten," she said, stuffing her arms down the sleeves of her down coat.

"I'll buy next time."

"You bet you will."

Together they walked outside. The wind was kicking down the street, smelling of the river, and Alvarez, yanking on her gloves, noticed the clouds beginning to roll in again.

She felt a chill, as much from the scene with Grace Perchant as the breeze plucking strands of hair from the knot at the base of her neck.

As one, she and Pescoli jaywalked to the Jeep. Once again the temperature seemed to be falling.

"Good thing you didn't smack Grace's face down in the middle of my catsup and fries," Pescoli said, as if to break the tension. "Now *that* would have been a scene." She unlocked her Cherokee and climbed inside.

"Sandi would have had a heart attack." Alvarez climbed into the passenger seat again and rubbed her hands together, trying to get warm. "What do you think about what she said?"

Pescoli checked her sideview mirror and fired up the engine. "About the hunter? God, who knows?"

"No, about you." Alvarez buckled up as the Jeep darted between two cars. "Her warning."

"Grace is a nut job."

"Yeah, I know, but . . ."

"But nothing, and don't give me any lip about having a smoke, okay? This is my last one." She pulled a final cigarette from her pack of Marlboro Lights, and for once Alvarez didn't make a sarcastic remark as she lit up, cracking the window, holding her filter tip just outside in an effort to draw out the smoke. Whether Regan Elizabeth Pescoli was admitting it or not, she was shaken up. Grace's predictions weren't always spot-on, but she had enough of a track record that it would make anyone worry.

"If the sicko comes after me, I'll be ready." She snorted. "How stupid would he be to target a cop?"

"Maybe he wants to make a point. Keep showing us how clever he is."

Regan drew hard on her cigarette, then shot a stream of smoke out of the corner of her mouth. "You know, if anyone wants to get back at me or put a hit on me, it's my ex. Lucky's making noise about taking the kids."

"Really?"

She snorted. "I should let him have 'em. It wouldn't last a month." She switched lanes and melded the Jeep

into the traffic heading up the hill to Boxer Bluff. Alvarez didn't like what had gone down in the restaurant
and was worried. She stared out the window, where
snow was falling rapidly again, and as the Jeep climbed
she caught a view of the falls, wild white water tumbling
over a ledge of rocks that had forced settlers to home-
stead on the lower banks nearly two hundred years earlier.

"Right now, Lucky's the fun parent," Pescoli went on.
"I'm the authoritarian." She slid a glance in Alvarez's direction. "I can't friggin' win for losin'."

A cell phone blasted. "It's mine," Alvarez said.

"This is Grayson," the sheriff said when she answered,
his voice low and disturbed. "Jillian Rivers checked herself out of the hospital here in town. In the company of
Zane MacGregor."

Alvarez groaned. "Is she nuts?"

"Nothing we can do. She doesn't want protection.
We think she's not the target of the serial, and my guess
is, she's going out of our jurisdiction. The Feds aren't
involved, since it's not a kidnapping or part of the ongoing serial-killer investigation."

"Great."

"It only gets better," Grayson assured her. "We just
got a call from Chandler up in Missoula. Hannah Estes
died this afternoon. Someone pulled her life support
before the Feds got up there."

Chapter Twenty-Seven

The problem with returning to Spruce Creek was that it was located in the wrong direction. North and west of Grizzly Falls, it was backtracking away from Missoula, where Jillian was certain all the answers to her questions lay.

Or was she?

She still had the feeling that she was missing something, a piece of important information that was right under her nose or locked deep in her damned subconscious. But she'd gone along with this plan, hoping she'd learn something in Spruce Creek, the last place she'd stopped before someone had decided to use her Subaru as skeet practice.

They drove into the small town and had no trouble locating the coffee shop/deli/diner where she'd stopped. MacGregor parked, and with Jillian still using the troublesome crutch, they made their way up a few steps and through ancient glass doors.

The Chocolate Moose Café wasn't anything to write home about. A once-upon-a-time post office and general store, it had been converted into a coffeehouse and diner, which now seemed to be in the middle of a major renovation. Part of the walls were painted a dusky blue, another part mustard yellow, the rest brick red, and Jillian wasn't certain if the colors were supposed to be complementary or if the owner had just run out of paint and scrounged around in the garage for whatever was left over.

But what the Chocolate Moose Café lacked in ambiance it made up for in enthusiasm, as there were moose replicas everywhere—all reigned over by a huge stuffed moose head hanging over a potbellied stove that no longer seemed to work. There were moose salt and pepper shakers, napkin holders, napkins, pot holders, and moose silhouettes in the plaid of the checked tablecloths and stenciled on the walls in the opposing colors of paint. Each chair had a moose head painted on its back and there was moose memorabilia for every kind of collector.

The word "overkill" sprang to mind.

They ordered sandwich wraps and coffee, then sat at a table wedged between a staircase and a bank of pane windows that looked out onto a rustic front porch. Outside planters, now filled with dirt and not much else, sat ready to be filled with colorful annuals once the weather turned.

"I do remember being here," Jillian said as she eyed the row of bar stools located at the counter that separated the baristas and kitchen staff from the dining area.

Today there were a smattering of patrons lounging over coffee and reading the paper, listening to music or using their laptops.

"Was anyone else here that you'd recognize?"

She shook her head. "I was in such a hurry, I just came in, used the restroom and grabbed a coffee drink to go. There were a few people, kind of like this, I guess, and I was behind a woman with a little girl of maybe five or so. They were bundled up in snow gear and the little girl was having trouble deciding what kind of muffin she wanted with her hot chocolate, but that's about it. I ordered my coffee, paid for it and worried a little about the weather."

"No one followed you?"

"Not that I noticed."

They talked and ate and even spoke to the same girl who had waited on Jillian before, who said, as she wiped the nozzle of the foam dispenser, that she'd answered the same questions from the police a while ago and re-membered nothing unusual about that day.

"Strike one," MacGregor said as he helped Jillian into the truck. They took off again, this time turning around, pointing the nose of the loaned truck south, with the full intention of continuing her original journey to Mis-soula. Using her cell phone, Jillian called her mother and left a message that she was out of the hospital. Then, finding the card Detective Alvarez had left her with in the hospital, she put in a call to the cop's cell phone.

Alvarez picked up on the second ring, and when Jil-lian explained where she was and what she was doing, the detective listened, then graciously gave her an up-date—sparing her the directives of what she should or shouldn't be doing that Jillian had half-expected. Zane drove on with a scowl on his face. He didn't trust the cops, any cops, and who could blame him? But Jillian was glad she'd placed the call. He just kept driving steadily southeast toward Missoula.

When Jillian hung up, she cradled the phone in her hand and said thoughtfully, "They don't think I'm a vic-tim of the Star-Crossed Killer."

Zane threw her a look. "What do you mean?"

"They think whoever did it is a copycat, that he lured me here and used the same MO to throw everyone off."

"What brought them to that?"

"I don't know." She relayed as much information as she'd learned, then said, "They're obviously not telling me everything but at least I'm not the target of some maniac."

"No? You're a target of someone. I suppose it might be better that you've got your own personal head case. At least there could be a motive that makes sense and leads us to him, rather than some random sicko picking off a group of women."

"That doesn't sound better. I really do have to find him, Zane. Going home won't help. He'll hunt me down."

MacGregor's jaw tightened. "That's what this trip is all about—hunting the hunter."

"So you're my personal bodyguard?" She half-smiled.

"Something like that." He slowed for a corner. "This all started with the e-mails and phone calls and pictures concerning your first husband. So it has to do with him, someone who knows him."

"Seems likely, doesn't it?"

"But you don't think it's your ex? The Rivers guy?"

"The only reason I thought Mason might know something about it is because of the postmarks, but no, I don't see any reason to think he's behind it. Originally, I was so determined to find out what happened, I was headed to Missoula and I was going to start with Mason."

"But now?"

"Now, I just don't get why he would be involved. I guess I've had more time to think about it, and there's really no reason for him to want me dead."

"What about his wife?"

"Well, she hates me. That's for sure. But I don't think she'd do anything to bring me closer to him. I think

Sherice would like it if I moved to Anchorage or Tokyo or Istanbul. The farther away, the better."

"She's afraid Mason still has feelings for you?"

"I don't know what she thinks. She's got . . . issues. But why try to kill me now? Why bring me to her with all this Aaron business? That doesn't make any sense."

"Then who else in Missoula?"

"No one that I can think of."

Her words hung in the air as he drove for a few miles. When they reached Grizzly Falls again, and after they'd filled the gas tank and cleaned the windshield, MacGregor pulled to the side of the attached convenience store and cut the engine.

"Maybe whoever is after you has set a trap and is trying to lure you to Missoula. He nailed you on your way there, so he anticipated the move. Now that you're out of the hospital, he'd expect you to do one of two things: return to Seattle or continue on to Missoula. Knowing you, which I have to assume he does, he'd know you wouldn't back down. Am I right?"

She lifted a shoulder and felt that little niggle of something teasing her brain, the same idea that had tugged at her after her dream in the hospital, only to disappear.

"What?"

"I . . . I agree . . . something about this is out of kilter. Well, lots about it is. But I feel that my brain isn't quite in full gear, that I'm missing something, something important." She thought hard as she stared out the windshield. "Something that's been in front of my face all the time."

He waited a few seconds, and she listened to the sound of traffic rushing by, the tick of the engine as it cooled, the hiss of air as someone filled his tires.

What was it?

And why did Missoula, the only destination that held one iota of sense, feel wrong?

Because whoever this is, whoever is trying to kill you, wouldn't be that careless. No way. Missoula is just the bait. Then what? If you don't follow the obvious lead, then where will you go? You can't return home; you can't allow yourself to be a sitting duck. Her stomach twisted as she thought about being left alone in the cold, without a stitch on, in the freezing temperatures . . . a copycat? Someone had used another twisted monster's plan to get back at her. That's why it was happening now, because whoever her personal nut job was, he was taking advantage of a serial killer's sick scheme.

And now he would stop at nothing to finish the job. She knew it. Sensed it. Her skin crawled at the thought.

MacGregor touched her lightly on the shoulder and she nearly jumped out of her seat.

"He's never going to stop," she said, scared and angry as hell. "Whoever tried to kill me won't back off."

"I agree. He's an opportunist," MacGregor said, and she nodded, glancing in the sideview mirrors, watching as a van pulled up to the pumps. A man in his early twenties with a scrubby beard and baseball cap pumped gas as his very pregnant woman of about the same age picked her way through the pumps to the store. The man glanced at their pickup and she froze.

Did he really need gas? Or had this couple been following them? The van had no side windows . . . and what about the pickup with the camper, facing the other way? That guy, too, a big man with a sour expression, had cast a look in their direction.

She shivered.

"Cold?"

"Scared, I think. No . . . more like paranoid." She kept her eye on the mirror, watching the twenty-something replacing the nozzle.

"Don't be."

The man walked into the convenience store and a

few seconds later returned with his pregnant woman and a sack filled to overflowing with chips. A few seconds later they were in the van and driving away, no longer appearing sinister.

Jillian shook her head. "I'm . . . I'm jumping at shadows and it pisses me off. You know, the creep really did a number on me. I was never one of those scaredy-cats who run around with Mace or have triple locks on their doors or rely on alarm systems and big dogs. I've just never been really frightened." She glanced at him. "Until now."

"You're not exactly locking yourself into a bunker and demanding police protection or changing your identity."

"No, but . . . it's unsettling."

"To say the least. But maybe we're going about this all wrong. What's happening now appears to have started a long time ago. With your first husband."

"You think this is really about him?"

"He was the reason you dropped everything and headed this way." He didn't say it, but the question hung between them: *Are you still in love with him, this man who left you? This con artist who may have faked his own death?*

And the answer was a hard, resounding *no*. Aaron Caruso was a scam artist and a user, a man she'd thought she'd loved years before but really hadn't known at all.

However, if he were alive, if he'd left her holding the bag, man oh man, did she want five minutes with the guy.

Even if he tried to kill you?

Her stomach plummeted. Why would he do that? Some old insurance policy? No way. Then he'd have to admit that he was alive. Once again, there just wasn't any reason for this.

"Tell me about Aaron," MacGregor said, twisting the

key in the ignition. With a rumble, the old engine ground to life. "You said a few things, but let's pick the man's life apart. I'll buy you a beer and you can spill your guts about your first husband." He hitched his chin toward a tavern on the other side of the street. Long and low-slung, built sometime in the twentieth century and sporting a faux-western front, it was called the Elbow Room. Its windows were stenciled with a family of happy sledding snowmen in top hats and red and white scarves, ringed in stenciled holly. Behind the snowmen, in pulsing blue, pink and yellow neon, beer signs beckoned.

"You really know how to treat a girl," she said as he drove around the gas station and sped across two lanes of traffic before finding a parking spot near the front door.

"Only the best for you."

"Oh, you charmer," she murmured, feeling her heart beat warm and deep. What was it with her? She always got involved with the wrong men, Aaron Caruso and Mason Rivers being two prime cases in point.

She decided to leave her damned crutch in the rig.

Leaning on MacGregor but walking better than she'd anticipated, she made her way through the scratched red door to the tavern, where peanuts covered the cement floor, a dart game was in session, a TV turned to some basketball game mounted over the bar. Only a few patrons were lounging in the Elbow Room today, so a waitress was Johnny-on-the spot to take their order, flipping out coasters like Frisbees, before Jillian had really settled into the booth.

She thought about the pain meds she was taking and, though she longed for a beer, decided to play it safe and keep her wits about her.

"How about a diet cola?" she told the girl.

"Lightweight," MacGregor teased.

"He's right. Make it with a slice of lime."

"Walkin' on the wild side."

The waitress, a middle-aged woman with over-permed hair and an expression that said she'd seen it all, nearly rolled her eyes. But within two minutes, their drinks and a bowl of party mix were deposited on the glossy faux-marble tabletop.

"Tell me about the first Mr. Jillian," he invited.

"God, he would have hated that." She laughed and pushed at the wedge of lime with a thin black straw. "I fell hard for Aaron," she admitted. "Too hard and way too fast. It was like the romance was turbocharged, at least in the beginning."

She told MacGregor everything she could remember about her first husband. How she'd thought she was in love. Crazy in love. Blindly in love. How they'd hiked and camped in exotic places. How the outdoors had been their home and wanderlust their way of life. Aaron had been a mountain climber, an extreme skier, an avid boater and a general adventurer. He'd thought the world was his home and wanted to see every inch of the planet, or so he'd said. That's how they'd ended up in South America.

Jillian and Aaron had planned to take the trip together and had been signed up as part of a tour group, but she'd taken ill right before their flight and Aaron, reluctantly, had gone alone but had been delayed and had missed connecting with the tour. When he'd reached Suriname, he'd gone off hiking by himself and disappeared.

Jillian had been devastated but had clung to hope for over a year that he'd return—even after learning that he'd embezzled half a million dollars from investors who had trusted him. She'd borne the brunt of the investors' wrath and the scrutiny from the SEC and insurance companies, the press and the victims. Everyone had assumed she was in on the plot and had inherited a fortune in life insurance, which hadn't been true at all. She'd slowly had to believe that the man she'd loved had been a crook, and she'd been sick over the betrayal.

"Do you know how that feels, to have everyone think you're a part of something so ugly?" she asked, then wished she could call the words back when she saw the flash of anger in his eyes and remembered his own history. "Sorry. Of course you do."

"Go on," he said, his jaw tight.

"There's not much left to tell. I went to Suriname to find him. I even got in the face of the local authorities, which was stupid. I think now I'm lucky that I wasn't arrested. But it didn't matter. After three months of getting nowhere, I came back to the states, and about two years after I'd reconciled myself to being a widow, his backpack was found by a couple of German hikers. They located it in the wilds of the high mountains. It was speculated that he'd taken a fall, dropped down to the bottom of a canyon covered in tall trees, his body hidden by the steep terrain and dense foliage. A search team was sent but he was never found." She drained her drink, leaving only ice and the bit of lime. "Eventually I had to accept that he was dead, that he'd died up there on that ridge, and, you know, I felt guilty for not being with him." She let out a derisive breath. "Even the insurance company finally paid me his life insurance benefits, which I used to pay off the investors, pennies on the dollar, but it was something. Then there were the attorneys." She offered him a twisted smile. "Let's just say I didn't end up a rich woman."

"Then a few years later, you married Mason Rivers."

She rolled her eyes. "Another great idea."

"Who lives in Missoula."

"Right."

MacGregor reached over and plucked the cell phone he'd given her from her jacket pocket. "What do ya say? Let's give him a call."

Deep in her cubicle, a bottle of water on her desk along with a cooling cup of tea, Alvarez stared at the computer monitor. Her throat was scratchy and dry, her nose running, but the symptoms of her impending cold or flu or whatever-the-hell-it-was-going-to-be were forgotten when she put the sentence together:

BEWARE THE SCORPION

Whatever that meant. She told herself it was probably wrong, but she got that little sizzle in her blood, the gut feeling telling her she'd stumbled onto something.

From the corner of her eye she noticed Pescoli, stuffing her arms through the sleeves of her jacket as she started for the exit. "Hey, look at this," Alvarez called, plucking a tissue from the box on her desk. She blew hard and tossed the tissue into an already-overflowing trash can as her partner backtracked.

"What?" Pescoli paused at the opening of Alvarez's tidy desk area as she slid her remaining arm into its sleeve, all the while looking at the screen. "Beware the scorpion?" she said, reading from the monitor. "What the hell does that mean? Oh hell . . ."

So her partner saw it, too. "All the letters we found at the crime scenes are in this message." Alvarez pointed to copies of the notes left by the killer, spread upon her desk. The most recent note was nearest her:

WAR   T HE   SC   I N

*   *   *

Regan shrugged so that her jacket settled over her shoulders. Her brow was furrowed.

"I noticed how the letters in the notes were spaced, like a fill-in-the-blanks. So I just put in the missing letters: **beWARe   T HE   SC orp IoN**."

"You think that's the message?" Pescoli asked carefully. "All the letters are there, in the right order, the initials from the victims' names, plus more than a few extra. Pretty crafty of you, but so what? He calls himself Scorpion?"

"Ever since hearing Halden's theory about Orion's belt, I've been doing research on the constellation and the mythology surrounding it." Sniffing, Alvarez pointed to Craig Halden's constellation charts, which were piled neatly next to a cup holding pens. "In Greek mythology, in some of the versions of the whole Orion story, it's said that Orion was killed by a scorpion, then cast into the sky."

"Those Greeks. Imaginative people." But Pescoli now eyed the screen like she was looking deep into a crystal ball for some sort of clue to her own murky future. "What does it mean? Beware of him? I think we got that."

"He's trying to tell us," Alvarez said. "If the stars on the notes left at the scenes and the ones carved into the tree trunks are all part of the Orion constellation, and the letters of the victims' names are meant to be part of this intricate note, then . . ."

"There are a lot of victims we haven't found or a lot more that have yet to be abducted." Pescoli sounded as tired as Alvarez felt.

"And Jillian Rivers isn't one, as we already thought. Just another confirmation that she's got her own private whack job."

"Who's still out there. I wish Jillian Rivers had stayed put."

"Yeah, right." Alvarez, too, didn't like the fact that Jillian had taken off from the hospital, and though she'd called and checked in, getting the news that she wasn't considered a victim of the Star-Crossed Killer, she was still in danger. Alvarez had told her as much. The police, however, couldn't stop her from leaving the county.

Pescoli shook her head. "Maybe your interpretation of the note is meaningless. It could be a mistake. The result of too many over-the-counter pills and a flu-addled brain."

"It's not the flu."

"Fine. Even so."

"I know it's not concrete. And I suppose other letters could be interjected, other phrases created. But I just have a feeling that this is what his message means."

"Okay." Pescoli crossed her arms. "So if your guess is right, that means he's already targeted future victims, right? He would need to kidnap women with initials that match the missing letters in the note."

"True. But it's not as if we can warn women within ten square miles. You can't really say, 'If your name begins with B or E, then get the hell out of Dodge.'"

"But we could look at missing persons reports and see if there are any victims whose initials match . . ." Pescoli glanced back at Alvarez's doodling, "B, E, E, O, R, P or O." She scrawled the letters in the margin, then grinned. "Beeorpo. Sounds like one of the aliens who abducted Ivor Hicks."

"Checking the initials against missing persons is not a bad idea," Alvarez said. It might help determine if her idea for the note was correct.

"Hey, wait." Regan's grin faded as she squinted at the letters she'd jotted down. "Did you know there's an R and a P in here?"

"I didn't notice."

Pescoli grunted. "No S or A, so I guess you're safe."

"It's just a theory," Alvarez said.

"This after crazy Grace Perchant sees ghosts dancing on my head." Raking her tumbled curls from her neck, Pescoli sighed. "Can this day get any worse? I'm outta here."

Alvarez felt deflated and picked up her teacup, only to realize the orange pekoe had gone stone cold. She set it back on the desk and tried not to feel discouraged. "It's not much," she admitted, and lunged for a Kleenex, snapping one in front of her nose just before she sneezed, "but it's something." She dabbed at her nostrils.

"Still, he hasn't told us jack shit," Regan zipped her jacket. "Even if your fill-in-the-blanks is right, we still have one big question. Who the hell is the scorpion?"

"Vodka tonic," I say to the waitress, who smiles at me, hoping for a big tip. "On the rocks." I'm antsy, waiting for the drink, watching the damned television screen, where there is footage of Jillian Rivers, the imposter, being sent to the hospital. The scene is a few days old but it's cut into a montage of other bits of film, pictures taken of the various "killing sites" and images of the victims with their names; Theresa Charleton, Nina Salvadore, Wendy Ito, Rona Anders, Hannah Estes and Jillian Rivers.

But they've got it wrong.

Again.

Fools!

Who is this imposter? He can't know what I do, can't copy my careful plans. Surely the police know there's a difference. Or do they? Is it something they are withholding from the press or are they just that damned moronic?

My drink is placed in front of me and I take a long,

calming sip, feeling the vodka slither down my throat before it coils in warm anticipation in my stomach . . . soothing. Soon, thankfully, it will seep into my bloodstream.

I'm angry that there's an imposter, taking over my work, no, *ruining* my purpose. What kind of idiot is fucking with my plan? Who is he? And why are the police fooled?

After all the time I've waited, perfecting every detail, now some moron comes in clumsily and erroneously, making a mess of things. I feel a headache coming on and take another drink, allowing a small ice cube to slide past my lips. Once it's in my mouth, I crush the damned thing with my teeth.

"Another?" the waitress, Taffy, says, surprised that I've already tossed back a drink I usually sip. She's new to this place, only been at the job a couple of months, but she recognizes me.

I nod, my gaze riveted to the screen.

Jillian Rivers has been released from the hospital, but she's giving no statement. Instead there is footage of some older woman . . . her mother! She looks as if she just came out of a beauty salon. She's blubbering about how happy she is that her daughter's safe, that she'd been so worried and blah, blah, blah.

Don't they understand?

Jillian Rivers is a fraud.

The person who left her in the forest is a fraud.

This is all wrong!

My fist clenches and the waitress, a tiny doe-eyed girl with a small . . . too small mouth that matches her breasts and hair twisted into an unkempt knot at her crown, eyes me warily.

Relax. Don't let anyone become suspicious.

"Isn't your drink okay?" Taffy asks, then sees that I'm utterly fascinated by the television.

"It's fine. Perfect." I relax my fingers, manage a smile.

"Oh. I get it."

I bet not. You nitwit. You don't get anything. Even the difference between a vodka tonic and a vodka collins.

"You're upset about that killer."

"It's worrisome."

"You bet it is. Me and Tony, that's my boyfriend, we're not taking no chances. We've got a sawed-off shotgun trip-wired to blast if anyone so much as touches the front door."

Tony and Taffy. How cute. "What about the back?"

"Ferdinand, that's our dog—he's part Doberman and part German shepherd—he's got that covered."

"Aren't you afraid you might injure a friend or someone from the family?"

Taffy, all of twenty-one, shakes her head and the topknot wiggles a bit. "*Every*body knows they've got to call us before they come over. If not . . . they take their chances."

"Well, I hope Granny doesn't forget and decides to pop in with some Christmas cookies," I say before I catch myself. It's the vodka talking and the waitress looks at me strangely. "Just kidding," I add with a laugh. "We're all a little nervous. Hey, I installed a peephole in my doors and nailed my windows shut."

"You didn't!"

"God's honest truth!" I raise my right hand and smile, though I'd love to reach across the bar and slap the bitch. "And," I add, "I sleep with a forty-four under my pillow. A Magnum."

"Loaded?"

"You bet. What would be the point if it wasn't?" I take another sip from my glass. "I'm not bluffing."

"No shit. I get it."

Again, no. You don't, you stupid bitch. You never will.

She picks up some half-empty glasses a few spots down on the bar and I take a little longer with the second drink. I have to be careful. I don't want to raise suspicion. Everyone in the area is being looked at warily. Friend to friend. Lover to lover. Mother to son.

Because they don't understand.

Will never.

Just like Taffy, they are all too damned stupid.

But this isn't a problem. In fact it might be working to my advantage. It's time to make a statement. A big one. Get the damned cops' attention. I stare up at the screen again, and this time there is footage of the sheriff's department at one of the scenes, taken from a distance. Most of them are visible: Sheriff Grayson, Pete Watershed . . . and the two detectives.

Again I crush some of the ice and enjoy the cold water that mixes with the warmth of the vodka.

On the screen, the quiet, dark-haired one—Alvarez—is looking over a snowy death scene, the one up at the abandoned lodge. She's got some Hispanic blood in her, not only her name and warm coppery skin tell me, but also that spark in her dark eyes, which convinces me she's complicated, holds her cards close to her vest, never lets anyone know what's really going on behind those dark, Latino eyes. Which is probably a lot. She's petite, fiery and, I suspect, has her own reasons for keeping people at arm's length.

Alvarez is smart and has the degrees to prove it. She's also sly and, deep down, I bet, ruthless. It's there in the jut of her jaw, the stretch of that beautiful skin over her sharp cheekbones.

A worthy adversary.

Then there's the other one. Regan Pescoli. My eyes examine her. She's another interesting woman; almost the opposite of her partner. Pescoli doesn't hold anything back. Her cards are firmly on the table and she's tapping them with a strong, determined finger, letting you know just where she stands. Athletic, larger than Al-rez, she's a bitch on wheels who has a family that's falling apart.

Poor thing.

Of course it's falling apart, you workaholic of a woman. What kind of mother are you? What kind of wife were you? You're a loser, Pescoli, and always will be.

But a beautiful one.

Strong, smart and oh so predictable.

Regan Pescoli is a woman who will take a while to break . . . but everyone has their breaking point.

I crack the ice and stare at her image before it is replaced by that of a reporter.

Detective Pescoli.

Get ready.

Your luck is just about to run out.

Chapter Twenty-Eight

Mason Rivers was under the radar.

Not at his office, of course. It *was* Sunday.

Not answering his cell.

Not at home. Nor was Sherice. Or if they were home, they weren't picking up.

At the very least, he was screening his calls, not answering an anonymous call from an unregistered cell phone.

"I struck out," Jillian admitted, sliding the phone into the pocket of her jacket again. "Same away message on his voice mail every time."

MacGregor studied what was left in his glass, a dark brew that looked, in Jillian's opinion, more like cold coffee with a smidgen of foam rather than beer. "And yet, he seems to be a part of this, whether intentional or not. Whoever attacked you knew that you would immediately think he was involved and propel yourself straight here."

She frowned as the waitress brought refills, eyed the untouched bowl of salty bits, then retreated to some hidden cavern behind the bar.

"So glad I'm so well trained." She leaned back against the booth and shifted a bit. Her ribs were healing but still pained her every so often. At least she could laugh now, could breathe. Coughing, though, that was still out.

"What is the away message?"

"Sorry, I'm out. Leave a message. I'll call back." She hesitated. "Except for the office. That one said, 'I'm out of town for a few days. If you need to reach me, leave a message with my secretary. . . .' " She thought back to the days of their marriage and how many times she'd listened to Mason's stock line. The message hadn't changed—nor had the inflection of his voice. Just then something shifted in her brain. A cold awareness cut her to the bone.

"What?"

"Mason and I had a place in Spokane—a place he got in the divorce. I don't know . . . that's the same message he left whenever he went out of town, and it reminded me of how he would escape to Spokane."

"What exactly are you thinking?"

"Mason has a license to practice law in Washington. Maybe he kept the place in Spokane."

"And so . . . ?"

Partial ideas, little bits of memory that had been digging at her, came together. "And it's probably nothing, but Spokane always held a fascination for Aaron, too . . . well, lots of places held a fascination for him, but I think I remember him mentioning it as one of the places he'd settle down in if he ever settled. Spokane or Bend, Oregon, or Colorado Springs . . . somewhere around Tahoe. But Spokane, that was one of the places. He and Mason share a connection there, I guess."

MacGregor was staring at her, letting her work through her thoughts. "You think Spokane's a key?"

She asked suddenly, "Do you have those pictures of

Aaron, the ones I was sent when I was in Seattle, the ones that started off this whole wild goose chase?"

"Copies," he reminded her. "The police still have the originals. They're in the truck. I'll go get them." Before she could say another word, he'd left the table and was striding past the beer signs reflecting on the fake snow sprayed upon the windows.

Now that she'd leapt to the conclusion that Spokane, not Missoula, should be her destination, Jillian was antsy, could scarcely wait the two minutes it took him to return and slide the pictures across the table.

She examined the grainy copies and shook her head. "I . . . I don't know. It's too dark in here."

"We can fix that. Right now." He motioned for the waitress, slapped some bills onto the table and helped Jillian outside. A couple of patrons looked up from their drinks for a second—a woman near the door and a guy at the bar who was huddled over his drink when not staring at the television screen.

Jillian felt his eyes on her, and when she looked over her shoulder, he turned his attention to his drink quickly, as if he were embarrassed about being caught ogling.

Or was it more than that?

She didn't wait to find out but walked as quickly as she could to the truck. Inside the cab, MacGregor found a flashlight and a magnifying glass.

"Who keeps a magnifying glass in their glove box?" she asked.

MacGregor cleaned the lens with his hot breath and his sleeve. "My friend, the one who loaned me this truck. He's a little . . ."

"Strange? Paranoid?"

"All of the above, and curious, too." He handed her the circular lens and she looked for any sign on the pictures that would give her a sense of where Aaron, or the man who looked like her long-lost husband, was when they were taken. But no street signs were visible, and the storefronts looked as flat and nondescript as a thousand strip malls across the country. "This could be Anywhere USA," she said. "Don't you think the police have done this?"

"Yes. And maybe they know something they aren't telling us. But unless they checked deep into Mason Rivers, they might not know about Spokane."

"I think he was just a consultant, not listed with any particular firm there. But I don't really know."

"Believe it or not, it hasn't been all that long since you were abducted, and they have a few other victims to check out as well, so I'm thinking the police will get there. Soon, if not already."

"Do you think we should call them with this information?"

MacGregor's jaw grew rock hard. "Probably. But you know how I feel about them. Let's just see if your ex is there. We need something more, something corroborating."

She looked over the pictures, inch by inch, but even the magnifying glass couldn't help her. "It's no use," she said. "I can't see anything. Whoever took this picture was careful."

"Everyone trips up."

"You'd think," she said, and then she noticed something in the picture, something unintentional. "There's something . . . in the mirror of the bus. It's just a smudge but it might be letters . . . a signpost or something? If I could just make it out. . . ."

MacGregor angled the flashlight and the magnifying glass.

The smudges became no clearer. "It's probably nothing," he said, but he snatched up his cell phone, dialed a number and said into the receiver, "have you looked at photograph number two, the one where the subject is crossing the street? Yeah . . . uh-huh. No, we couldn't either, but Jillian thought there might be something in the mirror on the bus. If you can enlarge that, see what it says and get back to me. Yeah? Well . . . that goes without saying. Back to even." He hung up and switched on the ignition.

"Chilcoate?" she asked. MacGregor had filled her in on the childhood friend who owed him, big-time.

"He's rapidly getting himself out of debt." MacGregor pulled out of the lot and headed toward the interstate. Though they were less than a hundred and fifty miles from Spokane, it would take some time getting there because of the weather. "There's a key in the glove box. Can you find it?"

She opened the box again, felt around and came up with a key.

"Open that panel on the passenger door," he instructed.

"What?"

"There, just beside your feet."

"Now what?" she asked, but fiddled with the key. A compartment opened and within it lay a small cache of weapons. Two pistols and a hunting knife. "This looks . . . illegal."

MacGregor smiled.

"You think we'll need them?"

He sent her a look and she was reminded all too quickly of freezing, being alone in the bitter cold. Naked. Tied to a tree. Knowing that she would die.

"Okay, I get the point."

"There's ammunition in there, too. Load up your weapon of choice, keep the knife, and load the second gun, then give it to me."

"Don't we need licenses . . . something? Okay, forget I asked that," she said, and pulled out the pistols.

"I assume you're game?"

She snorted and snapped the ammo clip into the first pistol, a Glock that was heavier than it looked. "If there's anything in Spokane, then let's find it."

"That's my girl." He gunned the engine and Jillian started loading the second gun.

His girl?

Oh hell.

Probably more than he knew.

Pescoli took a late lunch and cruised through the only stores in the old Flagstone Mall that would have anything either of her kids would like. It was snowing again. Nothing crazy. Not a blizzard. But with this winter, who knew how fierce the next storm might be, and though Missoula wasn't that far from home, she didn't want to be delayed too long.

Or too far from the case.

Since Hannah Estes had given up the ghost, with a little help, it seemed, from the FBI reports, they were in a holding pattern, waiting for something to happen, some clue to emerge. So far, nothing but theories.

She settled on a chain drugstore that carried everything from pantyhose to Pepto-Bismol, household cleaners to hush puppies. As requisite Christmas music piped cheerily through the store, she jostled with several other shoppers, searching for the perfect gifts. In desperation, she found a new toy in the shape of a Christmas elf for Cisco to tear to shreds, a makeup case and some hair "product" for Bianca, along with a couple of colors of hideous nail polish a salesgirl of about sixteen insisted were "tight," and a couple of DVDs and a CD case for Jeremy, though he'd probably hate both. She planned on putting a twenty-dollar bill in the makeup case and the same in the CD case. Lastly, she grabbed a board game for "the whole family." It wasn't a lot, but it would just have to do.

Satisfied that Christmas wasn't going to be a total disaster, Regan loaded up with a few groceries and headed home to talk to Jeremy. If he was in the mood. Well, even if he wasn't. She wasn't done with work for the day, not officially, so she'd have to return to town for a couple of hours, probably making it home for dinner after seven. By then Bianca would be back and they could actually have time together. She glanced at her watch. It was already after three, pushing four, so dinner might be closer to eight, but so be it.

Tonight they were going to eat together, without the television, iPods, cell phones or computers as distractions. Everyone around the table for the first time since . . . oh God . . . she couldn't remember when. Certainly not *last* Christmas.

Rotating the kinks out of her neck, she drove out of Missoula and through the snowy hills to her house. The weather was turning again, snow collecting on the road, her windshield wipers battling against the fluff. It was winters like this one that caused her to understand the people who had sand for lawns and decorated palm trees with colored lights for the holidays.

Jeremy's truck was parked in its usual spot, which made her feel a little better. The truth of the matter was that she'd been worried he would take off on her, think, "Screw this, Mom can't tell me what to do," and drive away to some unknown destination, so it was rewarding to see the snow piling up on his old truck's hood and roof.

She'd guided the Jeep into the garage and pushed the button to close the door when she first sensed that something was different. Not quite right. The whole place seemed quiet. *Too* quiet.

Why didn't she hear the dog clawing and yipping on the other side of the door?

She inhaled a long, careful breath.

Unzipping her pistol from her shoulder holster, she flipped off the safety. She wouldn't be stupid enough to shoot her own kids, even if they jumped out at her, but she had a feeling. . . . She opened the door slowly and the dark interior welcomed her coldly. No lights were lit on the Christmas tree, no candles burning, not a sound from within.

Her skin crawled, and in her mind's eye she saw the victims of the Star-Crossed Killer, all lashed to trees, their skin stiff and blue, their eyes open and sightless, frozen in their own terror.

She thought of Bianca, caught a glimpse of a picture of her that was framed and propped on the bookcase. She'd been seven, her front teeth too big for her face, other gaps visible in her bright, wide smile.

Don't let them be harmed, oh please.

And Jeremy. What would the brutal killer do with her son?

She swallowed back her fear, couldn't think that way. Any minute now her kids would leap out at her and scare her half to death. She was careful as she walked slowly from room to room . . . but even if the kids could keep quiet in their game of scare-the-liver-out-of-Mom, what about Cisco? The dog couldn't be kept quiet.

Oh God.

She heard something pounding, then realized it was the drumming of her own heart. She pushed open Bianca's door but it looked as if her daughter hadn't been home, and then the bathroom, too . . . but the dog? And Jeremy? Had he taken off with a friend? She stood in the hallway upstairs and dialed her son's number, half-expecting Jer's cell phone to start its weird ring tone from some rocker he loved.

Nothing.

She tried Bianca's.

Again, no answer, nor ringing within the house.

Her guts turned to water. Something had happened to them, to her precious babies.

Don't. Don't go there! Don't let your job make you paranoid. If they're not here, then they're with friends or their damned father. . . .

She started down the stairs, the steps squeaking under her weight. Well, now there was no reason to be quiet. "Jeremy?" she called. "Bianca?"

Nothing.

Only the creaking of old timbers settling, the gentle hum of the furnace and the rustle of the wind as it picked up to press against the house.

"Cisco! Come on, boy!"

The door to Jeremy's room was ajar, weird turquoise shadows playing upon the walls. Holding her breath, she nudged the door open and peeked inside. His lava lamp was glowing, the floating globules of oil, or whatever it was, casting the shifting colors of light.

No one inside.

Not even the dog. She saw the picture of Jeremy's father in its usual place and thought, *I'm sorry, Joe. I'm so sorry, but damn it, why did you have to die?*

Backing out of the room and up the stairs, she was standing in the kitchen when her own cell phone went off.

The kids!

Lucky's number showed on caller ID.

Her heart sank, and before she even said hello, she knew she was going to hear something she didn't want to. "Hi, Lucky. Don't tell me, the kids are with you."

"That's right."

"You took them?"

"You weren't there."

"I was working! We talked about this."

"Jeremy called. I came and got him." There was a long, pregnant pause and Pescoli half-collapsed against the archway into the kitchen because she knew, deep in her gut, she was going to hear bad news. She wasn't wrong.

"The kids, Michelle and I have been talking—"

You goddamned son of a bitch.

"—and we all agree that Jeremy and Bianca should live with us."

Her knees, always so steady, wanted to buckle as her darkest fears surrounded her. She backed into a small corner of her kitchen. "We all didn't agree. I have a vote in this. I'm their mother."

"But—"

"And the State of Montana. The court system, remember that? I have custody."

"Things change. At the time, yeah, I wasn't the best role model around, but now that Michelle and I are married—"

"Hey!" she cut in, anger burning through her, chasing away her despair. "Do *not* play the 'happily married' card with the Barbie doll, okay? Cuz I'm not buying it. She's too young to be the kids' mother."

"I just thought you'd want to know they were safe," he said, and there was that brittle, almost punishing tone to his voice, as if he enjoyed making her crazy. Well, he succeeded. Hadn't he time and time again while they were married? He could be devastatingly charming one second and as deadly as a viper the next.

"You can't even muster up child support and now you want to raise them? Get real."

"Well, about that. We'd have to turn that around. You would be paying me."

Whatever hope she'd had for having a civil relationship with him withered at that point. So that's what this was about. Money. Not that he didn't care for the kids in his own Lucky Pescoli kind of way, but it was the money that really motivated him. He'd always griped that she'd gotten a sweet deal in the divorce. It had always pissed him off, although it hadn't been true. She had ended up with the house because she'd bought him out, and she'd gotten the kids because she had been more steadily employed, but he hadn't wanted to look at the truth at the time. Now her steady demanding job was the weapon he was using against her. What a damned prick.

"I want the kids back here tonight."

"Not gonna happen."

"And what about Cisco? Did you take my dog, too?"

"Let's get one thing straight. I didn't 'take' my kids. They came because they wanted to, because their mother doesn't have time for them, because they want some stability in their lives."

"With you?" she asked, dumbfounded.

"And as for the dog, Cisco belongs to Jeremy, so yeah, he's here, too."

She glanced at the empty water and dog-food dishes on the floor and she felt a weird sadness, different from the pain of knowing the kids had picked their father and stepmother over her. She felt the sting of tears but wouldn't give in to them. "Pack the kids up, Lucky," she said, her teeth clenched, her lips barely moving. "Because I'm coming to get them. And that includes Cisco. I want my son. I want my daughter. I want my dog. And I'm coming to get them."

"Is that Mason's car?" MacGregor asked as he drove to the condominium Jillian's ex-husband had owned in Spokane. It was a four-storied brick building, one- and two-bedroom units on each of the floors, all accessed by a private entrance that required an electronic key. Parking spots were under the building, and Jillian and Zane were staring through the locked gates of the garage, which occupied the part of the ground level of the building not dedicated to shops and specialty boutiques.

Peering through the grate, Jillian eyed the cars and checked the parking space Mason always used, the one MacGregor had indicated. A new white Mercedes was parked in it. "That's his space but I don't know what he drives. I would assume it's his."

"Then let's pay him a visit."

"You have to have a key. It's electronic—"

"I know. We just have to wait a few minutes, I'm guessing."

And he was right. They bought coffee from a nearby shop and waited. Within minutes the gate opened to allow a long Cadillac to exit. Mason helped her into the garage before the iron bars clanged shut. The door to the elevator was never locked, and once inside Jillian pressed the button for the fourth level, just as she had years ago when she'd been with Mason.

The elevator car climbed slowly, without any stops, its doors parting on the fourth floor, where couches, lamps and potted plants were arranged in alcoves around the windows. Using MacGregor as her crutch, she walked unevenly down the carpeted hallway to the tiny indentation that served as the entry to the private unit.

Jillian felt strange and out of place, as if she were trespassing, though for a few years she'd walked into this very unit laden with groceries or dry cleaning or a bottle of wine.

How odd it all was now.

"So it's now or never."

"Let's go with now," she said, and rang the bell.

For a second she heard nothing. No sounds stirring within. She almost thought no one was home. But she

gave it another try, pushing on the button and hearing
the familiar dulcet tones of the electronic chimes.

"Coming!" Mason's voice preceded him.

Jillian braced herself as the door opened and she
found herself standing face-to-face with her ex.

"Jillian!" he said, surprised. "Oh my God, what're
you doing here? I wondered how you were. I was going
to call, but I thought you might need time to heal."
Then he stopped gushing as his eyes landed on MacGregor. "What's . . . what's this all about?" In a heartbeat
he'd changed from the overly and sickeningly concerned ex-husband to the quiet, suspicious attorney.

"Mason? Who's here?" a female voice asked, and
Sherice appeared, wearing a red bikini and flimsy, see-
through cover-up. A few days before Christmas, when
the temperature was somewhere around minus-four.
"Oh." Sherice's avid, pretty face clouded for a second as
she recognized Jillian, then was masked with a perfectly
set smile, the kind you see on kids in beauty pageants as
they parade in all those sequined costumes.

"Hi, Sherice," Jillian said, then, stepping closer to
MacGregor, she said to Mason, "this is Zane MacGregor.
He's the man who saved my life when some psycho tried
to kill me."

"But you're okay?" Mason asked.

"Kind of." She stared hard at the man to whom she
was once married. "We think the guy who did it might
be from Spokane, and so, since you're here, I'd like to
talk to you about it."

"Because?" he asked, and Sherice, standing next to
him, visibly paled.

"Because you're here a lot."

"And you think—what? That I . . . ? That I had something to do with it?" He held up both hands. "That's
crazy, Jillian. I have no reason to harm you. I mean, you
couldn't possibly think that I . . . Oh, for the love of God."

"Not you, Mason, but maybe someone you know."

He shook his head. "I don't know what you thought you'd accomplish by coming here, but this is nuts."

"Bear with us," MacGregor said as his cell phone rang and he saw the number. "Just a sec." He answered. "Yeah?"

"Jillian," Mason said, his voice lower. "What is this?"

"I just need your help," she admitted, letting down her guard.

Behind Mason, Sherice rolled her eyes. "Isn't that crazy wacko after you?" she asked, then turned to her husband. "We don't want any of that kind of trouble. That guy, that Star-Crossed Killer, I've been reading about him, and he's really a nutcase. Look, I'm sorry you were left in the woods and all, but we . . . Mason, he can't help you."

"What is it you want?" Mason asked, not happily, but at least not stiffly either.

MacGregor said, "Yeah, great . . . I got it. I'll call you back." He hung up and Jillian knew he'd been talking to Chilcoate. No one else had the number of MacGregor's cell. She glanced up at him and he nodded. "We're certain the information that was sent to Jillian, photos that lured her here, were from Spokane, so what I want to do, Rivers, is hire you for my lawyer, mine and Jillian's, for the next hour or so. That way everything we say will be kept under client-lawyer privilege."

"Wait a minute," Sherice interrupted. "You can't."

But Mason nodded. "All right. Sherice, why don't you go down to the hot tub and wait for me . . . or put some clothes on and go shopping downstairs at that shoe store you like so much."

"Are you kidding? Are you trying to get rid of me?"

"It's business," he said, meeting Jillian's eyes.

"No way. I'm not putting up with your ex-wife pulling your strings and—"

"Sherice!" he shouted. "Don't make a scene. I need some time with my clients."

She recoiled as if he'd hit her, and her jaw slid to the side as she sized up her alternatives. "Fine," she finally said, "I'll change and get my purse." *This is gonna cost you big-time* was never spoken but certainly implied. Mason invited them in and offered them wine as they sat at a large, round table with a gleaming lacquer finish and a huge centerpiece of pine, white hydrangea, red candles and sprigs of holly.

A few minutes later Sherice reappeared in jeans, heels and a short, faux-rabbit white jacket. "I'll be downstairs at the shoe shop. Call me when you're finished."

"I will," Mason promised, and bristling, she stormed out of the apartment.

"Now," Mason said as the door slammed shut, "why don't you tell me what you want and make it short. My hourly fee can't begin to touch the damage she can do to my credit card in fifteen minutes."

So predictable.

Regan Pescoli, tough-as-nails detective for the Pinewood County Sheriff's Department, had a very visible Achilles heel: her kids.

How lucky am I to learn about their abduction or . . . would it be abdication?

She, of course, won't take it lying down.

And the closest route to her ex's house is through the mountains . . . how perfect.

As if God is making up for all the trouble with that Jillian Rivers woman. So I wait. Dressed warmly, my shot clear despite the snow, I know exactly at what point the Jeep will be most vulnerable. She'll drive up the hill and try to make the corner that she's driven a hundred times or more. But she'll be distracted, not really expecting any ice. Maybe listening to the police band. More likely fuming, seeing red.

I've done my homework.

The road is slick.

I'm positioned on the ridge.

My shot is clear.

And I hear the rumble of a deep engine.

Not that of a small car, no, but of a truck or an SUV.

I feel a little heady.

This one . . . this one is important.

Not that they all aren't, but Regan Pescoli, oh, excuse me, Detective Pescoli—her participation is key, and there's an irony to her being part of the plan, a sweet, sweet satisfaction. Maybe she'll be the one. Maybe I'll allow myself the pleasure of her. Once she's in my control, of course. Only after she's mentally broken down to the point that she sees me as her savior. Then, perhaps, when she's lying naked on the mattress, her wounds healing, when she begs me . . .

But I'm getting ahead of myself.

The beams of headlights appear, though it's not yet quite dark, and the Jeep growls as it claws its way up the hill.

A finger of anticipation slides down my spine, and I lick my lips, feeling the frigid air upon them. I'm warm enough in my white down outerwear, but I love the feel of the winter against the few parts of my skin that are exposed.

It adds a little zing to the moment . . . oh the moment.

It's so near I can almost taste it.

Come on, come on.

My hand is steady, my gloved finger upon the trigger, my eye pressed to the sight of the rifle, the crosshairs in perfect position.

Come to Daddy.

Chapter Twenty-Nine

What was the line from one of the old *Airplane* movies? This wasn't the week to give up smoking? Or drinking? Or sniffing glue, or whatever? Well, in Pescoli's mind, this was not the week to give up smoking. She felt for her "last resort" pack and found it empty. Crumpling it in her fist, she threw it on the floor of her Jeep.

She was mad. And yeah, a little hurt. She felt like after all that she'd done for her kids, her wonderful children, after all of her sacrifices to give them what they wanted, to keep them safe, to make a home for them when one father died and the other took off, that they, those precious little people she'd adored with all of her heart, had turned out to be traitors.

She even understood it, kind of, as the Jeep climbed the ridge of hills separating her place from Lucky's. How many times had she thought to herself, if only the hills would grow and become a real barrier, insurmountable spires that would lock him away from the kids forever? She'd had that dream several times in the past, when he'd forgotten Bianca's birthday and left her waiting for a shopping trip that had never happened, or when he'd promised Jeremy tickets to a ball game or a trip to Denver that, of course, never came to pass, or when he gave Bianca earrings that he'd "picked out special for my little girl," only to have Bianca find out, with a slip of the tongue, that he'd bought them for Michelle and she hadn't liked them.

Yeah, a real prince among men, our Lucky, she thought, setting her jaw as the Jeep bucked and lurched a little, sliding more than she expected. The snow was coming down and piling up on this unused stretch of road, but the vehicle was in four-wheel-drive and this had never been a problem before.

She held tight to the wheel, and each time the wheels didn't grab, she didn't panic, just eased her way through. She'd been driving in this stuff for years. When the tires found traction again, and the road had straightened a bit, she made a quick call to Alvarez, who didn't pick up.

"It's me. Hey, I've got a personal issue to deal with. Lucky and the kids. It might take a while, so cover for me, will ya?" She clicked the phone off, confident Selena Alvarez, rock steady, without all the pitfalls of ex-husbands and rebellious children, would pick up the slack. Besides, Pescoli would do the same for her. It was understood.

Rather than turn on the radio, as the reception was crappy in these hills and canyons, and she was sick to the back teeth of schmaltzy or cheery Christmas carols, she slid in the first CD she came to and, as the first notes of a Tim McGraw song played through the speakers, felt betrayed all over again. This was one of Lucky's damned CDs, one he'd forgotten to take with him when he left. She ejected it and tossed it onto the floor in front of the passenger seat to join the discarded, wadded cigarette pack.

Wasn't there anything else?

Oh damn, the wheels were sliding again. What the hell was this? Ice? She was near the crest of the hill, only a few more feet to climb, then around the corner and she'd start down, except the rig insisted on slipping every so often.

"Losin' your touch," she chided herself.

Crack!

Pescoli automatically ducked at the sound of the rifle blast and reached for her sidearm. She felt the bullet hit her tire, even heard something ping against metal. She straightened behind the wheel as she registered what was happening. *The killer? Hit . . . me?*

The car spun, turning wildly, rotating around and around. The edge rushed up. *Oh no!* Faster and faster, the Jeep spun out of control. The canyon rim came nearer. She scrabbled for the cell phone, grabbed it just as one wheel slid over the edge and then the second followed.

A second later, her world spun dizzily as the entire Jeep slid and then tumbled, over and over, rolling down the hill. Pescoli dropped the phone but her fingers were tight on the grip of her gun.

Terrified, knowing that she was probably going to die, that she'd never see her kids again, she held fast to the pistol. If, somehow, she survived this, she thought, panicking, her heart beating so fast she thought it might explode, she was going to shoot the son of a bitch.

Straight through his sick heart.

"I can only tell you what I know and it's nothing," Mason Rivers said, and MacGregor believed him. He didn't doubt for a minute that the slick attorney could lie easily, that he was as slippery as an eel through rocks, but right now, staring at Jillian, Mason Rivers was telling the truth.

And the damned thing was, Jillian's ex-husband was still in love with her. He tried to mask it, of course, but it was there, plain as the nose on his face, the interested way he looked at her, the slight cock of his head, the manner in which he seemed about to touch her hand, seated as she was next to him, but restraining himself. And when he thought Jillian wasn't looking, he stared at her and sighed.

Whatever problems he and Jillian had endured during their brief marriage, MacGregor suspected it was nothing compared with what he dealt with on a daily basis with the churlish, young and jealous Sherice. The too-often quoted "be careful what you wish for" warning ran through MacGregor's head.

He had nothing against younger women. Hell, he'd had two friends who had married women who were over fifteen years younger than they were, but in each case, the woman had been equal to her partner in intellect and personality. Their marriages had worked and were working. But never had he seen it work when the young woman had never quite matured from the "it's all about me" phase, a place Sherice Rivers not only had found but intended never to leave.

"I'll check around," Mason promised Jillian, barely making eye contact with MacGregor. But he loaded up his computer, jumped onto the Internet and searched out everything he could about Aaron Caruso, googling him with Spokane, Missoula and then Washington, Idaho and Montana. Of course, MacGregor and Chilcoate had run these searches themselves, but MacGregor had wanted to see all Mason Rivers's cards. He hadn't completely written him off the suspect list, and the gun in his jacket pocket was proof enough of how little he trusted anyone who could be involved in this deception and near-homicide.

But in meeting with Rivers, and seeing that wistful spark in the attorney's eye, MacGregor had decided Mason Rivers wasn't their man.

And Chilcoate had called with interesting information.

A few minutes later MacGregor and Jillian took their leave. Jillian's ex walked them outside, leaving them on the snowy sidewalk as he turned into a trendy store showcasing purses and shoes with a sign promising "Fine Italian Leather." The windows were decorated in gold and silver balls, tinsel strung between the purses sitting on beds of white, glittery fake snow.

"Christmas, ya gotta love it," Jillian said, and seemed relieved that the conversation with her ex-husband was behind them. "Now what?"

"How about a hotel?"

"A hotel?"

"Uh-huh, with hot water for a decent shower, room service for an overpriced meal and Wi-Fi."

"Wi-Fi? Why do we need an Internet connection?"

"To find out about your first husband."

"Just like that?" she asked, snapping her fingers and arching an eyebrow.

"Well . . . maybe not that quick." But the truth of the matter was that he wanted a little anonymity. If Jillian's attacker had anticipated they might hunt him to Spokane, then it was logical to think that Mason's condo and work might be watched. And he wanted to share with her what he'd learned in his phone call with Chilcoate.

Here in Spokane, things were definitely not what they seemed.

Zane turned the collar of his jacket up and helped Jillian back to the truck. She was walking better, her ankle able to bear a little weight, but he still felt protective of her, maybe even a little responsible for her. And though he hated to admit it, his thoughts had gone down the fantasy road with her more than once. He'd considered kissing her, really kissing her, and seeing where it would lead. He'd imagined feeling her fingers on his bare skin, her breath against the crook of his neck, the way her nipples would tighten if he touched them. He'd even gone so far as to think about sliding into her warmth, but he trained himself to come up with other thoughts, darker ones that reminded him they weren't safe. And it would be smarter, a whole lot smarter, if he let his fantasies stay where they belonged, locked away and never acted upon.

Yeah, sure, like you haven't already figured out that tonight might be the night. Why the hell do you try to kid yourself, MacGregor? You want to jump her bones and do it with her all night long. You've wanted to from the moment she opened her eyes in your cabin and you caught her checking you out.

You know she might go for it.

But then again, you know that once you cross that icy bridge, there just might not be any coming back.

"Come on," he said, looking over his shoulder, making certain they weren't being watched. Twilight was casting long shadows over the city and the street lamps were glowing as snow swirled around them. It worried him that here, in the city, he felt more vulnerable than he did in his cabin in the wilderness.

And how safe was that? Wasn't Jillian attacked outside the cabin? Wasn't Harley shot less than a hundred feet from the back door?

Still, he was a loner by nature, and he had only to remember what had happened in Denver to distrust this city, even one that seemed calm, almost serene with the nightfall. Colored lights drew his eye to a park, and if he let himself, he might just feel a little Christmas cheer.

But that would be foolish.

The twinkling bright beads of illumination could easily be a false front. He felt the pistol, heavy in his pocket, and was glad for the bit of peace of mind it offered.

Who knew what lurked in the gathering dusk of this unfamiliar city?

"Pescoli never showed up again?" Sheriff Grayson was walking toward the exit, with Sturgis only a step behind. The black Lab looked up at Alvarez, and she petted his head, all the while thinking again that she should get a pet of some kind. A cat or a dog or even a bird. Something, a living, breathing thing that she could care for.

"No," Alvarez said. "She called and left me a message. Something came up. Family."

Grayson looked tired. Worn down. He nodded. "Well, I guess she put in enough overtime," he said, squaring his hat on his head. "We all need a break on this one."

"I'm afraid we'll have to make one," she said.

"Bad news about the Estes woman," he said, and he rubbed his jaw, the sound of his five o'clock shadow scratching under his fingers. "The only person we know of who could ID this son of a bitch."

"I know."

"Heard from the Feds?"

Alvarez nodded. "Chandler called in. I took the call. She'll be back in the morning."

"We all will," Grayson said, and touched her lightly on the shoulder. "Go home, Selena." He showed the hint of a weary smile. "We'll catch this guy tomorrow."

She smiled. "In a bit."

"I mean it."

"Gotcha."

He looked as if he didn't believe her, but whistled to the dog and headed toward the exit. She wondered about him, the recently divorced and elected sheriff. At times she thought him an odd choice of the people. Affable and smart enough, he was a bit of a loner, not one to glad hand or attend any event the least bit political; he left that to the higher-ups and to his undersheriff. Cort Brewster loved the limelight that seemed more of an unwanted duty to Grayson, an obligation rather than a privilege.

The press was still camped out around the building, looking for new angles, hoping for something they could print or air. They were smoking, drinking coffee, being coddled by Joelle whenever she showed up. It was all a freak show in Alvarez's estimation, and if the damned goody-two-shoes receptionist didn't stop feeding the entire press corps, they'd never leave. Not that they were all bad. The news helicopter had helped locate one of the victims, and the sheriff had used the press in order to seek the public's help in identifying the killer. But so far, they were striking out.

Grayson would have to pass by a straggling reporter or two on his way to his rig. But he could handle it, Alvarez believed, glancing toward the doorway as he left with the dog on his heels.

Yes, he was an interesting man, she thought, and even smiled at herself. *Off limits, off limits, off limits.*

But then, weren't they all?

Leaning back in her chair, she rubbed the kinks from her neck. The department needed a break in this case in a big way. If they didn't nail this guy's ass and soon, there would be more victims. She knew it. The knot in her stomach was her constant reminder.

Ignoring the headache that pounded behind her eyes and the fact that she couldn't stop her nose from running, she went over the notes one last time and all the things that should make sense: Orion's belt, "BEWARE THE SCORPION," the hunter. They were all jumbled in her mind as she looked at the pictures of the victims for the umpteenth time. Beautiful women who had been terrorized in near-fatal car accidents, then kidnapped and kept alive. For what? Not sexual pleasure. It must be just so the monster could exert his power over them, bend their will to his and then, eventually, when the time was right, usually around the twentieth of the month, leave them in a frozen forest to die.

Her throat was really hurting now. No amount of lemon water or throat lozenges eased the pain, not really, despite all the claims she'd heard on television. It was time to call it a night; all too soon, she'd be calling it a morning.

Her muscles ached but not from working out, and she felt a little bad that she couldn't spend an hour on the elliptical machine or treadmill, then go into the gym's sauna and sweat out this crud that seemed lodged in her lungs.

Tonight she would have to settle for a bitingly hot shower in her own apartment, more tea and hot lemon water and some send-you-into-a-near-coma cold-symptom medicine for the night. Just to knock her out until the morning.

The room was quiet, only a few people left, including Zoller, dutifully manning the task force phones until her relief showed up in a few hours. God, they needed to get this guy, before he killed again.

She picked up her purse, wrapped a scarf around her neck and slipped into her jacket. She was a little worried about Pescoli and had expected her to call in. But then, she was having trouble with that loser Lucky Pescoli, as well as her kids.

Who could blame her?

Alvarez thought about leaving a message but decided not to bother. It wasn't as if she had any news anyway. They'd connect in the morning.

Throat aching, Alvarez walked out of the sheriff's department and saw the shiny letters that Joelle had strung near the door: Merry Christmas and Happy New Year.

Well, maybe for someone, she thought, coughing, as she crossed the parking lot, her lungs thick, her breath fogging in the night. Snow fell lightly all around her as she made her way across the parking lot. She saw large footprints and pawprints in the fresh snow and thought of Grayson and Sturgis, cutting through the lot after dealing with the press, the only set of fresh prints disturbing the snow.

She couldn't help wondering if Grayson was going home to the house he'd once shared with a wife. Or was he stopping off for a meal at one of the local places? Nah. He wouldn't leave the dog in his rig, not in this cold weather. He was on his way to his rustic cabin in the foothills.

As she unlocked her rig's door, she thought about her bare apartment; she hadn't even bothered with a small tree this year. It would be empty and cold.

Sliding behind the wheel she decided, yeah, she really should get a pet.

"A four-star hotel," Jillian commented, taking in the grand façade. "Trying to impress me?"

"You only live once," MacGregor told her as he handed the keys of their beater of a truck to a valet.

In the reception area, the marble inlaid floors and crystal chandeliers looked to be over a hundred years old. MacGregor had no change of clothes, just the laptop he'd procured from this friend, Chilcoate, who seemed to be some kind of local techno geek to the nth.

Though MacGregor was traveling lightly, Jillian did have a small suitcase filled with her things, and then there was, deep in each of their pockets, their guns. It was odd to be carrying a weapon—make that an illegally concealed weapon—through this stately old hotel. But no one had seemed to notice the bulge in her jacket pocket or the few bruises that remained on her face.

Their room was on the fifth floor and elegant, with its matching four-poster beds, gas fireplace, high ceilings and view of the Spokane River as it rolled by, dark and swollen.

Thick carpeting stretched past an alcove by the fireplace where a desk, small table and two side chairs were arranged in a cozy living area. The beds were positioned in front of an armoire that looked as if it had been carved in the nineteenth century, though it housed a televison and complete game system. Through French doors she found the bath, complete with shining marble, Jacuzzi tub and a tile shower with a clear-glass door.

"I thought we needed a break," he said as she checked out the room's appointments. "Besides, it's safe here. Security guard and cameras."

"You think someone is following us?" she asked nervously.

"I think we need to keep you safe. Chilcoate agrees. Looks like Spokane is a dangerous place for you." He walked to her, draped an arm over her shoulders and pressed his forehead to hers, their noses nearly touching.

So close.

So familiar.

So male.

"Should I be frightened?" she asked.

"I'm just being careful."

"And spending a fortune."

His lips, close enough to kiss her, stretched into a wide smile. "I couldn't let you stay in a fleabag, now could I?"

"No, sir, not after that high-end bar you took me to this afternoon. What was it called?"

"The Elbow Room, and it just so happens to be one of my favorite places to get a beer." His eyes held hers for a heartbeat and she thought that he might just kiss her, that his lips, for just a second, might brush over hers. He hesitated, then drew back and crossed the room to lock the door. "Order room service. I'll take the biggest steak they have and a loaded baked potato."

"I'm willing to bet they have something fancier, like pheasant or veal or—"

"A steak, medium rare." He was on his way to the bathroom. "I'll be in the shower." One eyebrow cocked in invitation. "You could join me. . . ."

In her mind's eye she saw them together, wet, naked bodies, slick from the soap that lathered between them as hot water washed over their bare flesh.

"I, uh, think I'll order dinner."

"Your loss."

Her stomach did a slow little flip when she thought what might have been.

"Oh," he called through the open doorway, "and would you mind having these sent down to be cleaned?" He tossed out his sweater, jeans and boxers. So she knew that, on the other side of the door, through the clear panes, if she looked, she could probably see him naked.

She cleared her throat. Licked her suddenly dry lips. "So I take it that money is no object."

"Not tonight, darlin'," he yelled through the open doorway, his voice beckoning. "Tonight I figure we owe it to ourselves to let loose."

"Owe it to ourselves?"

"Something my dad used to say. Will ya call for the maid to pick up?"

"Your wish is my command," she mocked.

He laughed then, and she smiled as she turned to the phone on the desk. She didn't so much as peek through the door he'd left open, not even when he started singing slightly off-key in a deep baritone voice.

You're falling in love with him, her mind warned, not for the first time. Tonight, she didn't care. She eyed the two beds, a nod to the fact that they weren't lovers.

Yet.

"Oh Lord," she whispered, picking up the phone with trembling hands.

The night was still young.

Snow fell all around.

Great, white lacy flakes swirled, danced and twirled in the blue light cast by the street lamps. In the distance carolers sang "God Rest Ye Merry Gentlemen" as traffic moved through the city streets.

The hotel, six stories of nineteenth-century grandeur, a landmark in Spokane, rose high into the dark heavens. Snow was piled upon the gables and dormers, covering the gutters. Lights washed the stone walls with a warm glow and millions of tiny, jewel-like bulbs glittered in the bare limbs of the trees and the arched entrance to the grand old building.

The Spokane River, swollen and dark, rushed by, wind blowing across the swift water, icy and cold. No

stars could be seen in the opaque sky; no moon cast its
silver glow.

She was inside the hotel.

Jillian Rivers . . . no, Jillian Colleen White Caruso
Rivers.

How long has that name been an anathema, a poi-
son filling the air, suffocating all it touches, forever
haunting and teasing and laughing?

Oh, Jillian, you should have died long ago . . . so
long ago.

And now you will.

I stared at the historic building. Though the hotel is
a stone fortress, there were ways inside, keys to all the
locked doors. Keys I have used many times in the past,
keys that I had the foresight to copy, keys that jangle in
my pocket like the cold, crisp bells of Christmas.

Thank God this hotel retained all of its "Old West
Charm," which included metal keys and locks and skele-
ton keys used by the staff. No fancy electronic cards.
Not here.

So Jillian was not safe.

Her face came to me and, once again, I spoke to her.

"Yours will be a quiet death, Jillian.

"An intimate death.

"Not by a loud gunshot. No, that would attract attention.

"Ruin everything.

"A knife. Yes, a knife!

"With a razor-sharp and perfectly wicked curved
blade.

"Drawn quickly across your neck, a knife will do the
trick, exposing a thin seam of blood, which will run hot
and red as you gasp."

I felt a little thrill at the thought of this. I've waited so
long for this moment, planned so many times to rid the

world of her, to take away the threat of her and finally, with the Star-Crossed Killer, I got my chance.

But now my mind would not let me forget that she had escaped me once before.

You should have killed her in the woods. Made certain she would die. You were foolish then, weren't you? Do not make the same mistake. This time she must be dead and then, finally, you will be free.

"I will not fail," I vowed, and I couldn't help but tremble with anticipation.

Feel the snowflakes kiss my cheeks.

Soon, my torment would be over.

Biting my lip, I fingered my weapon and smiled in the darkness as I spoke to Jillian, my enemy, in a whispered promise. "The slash will be deep. Your blood will pulse out in thick, dark spurts.

"Your lifeblood will stain the crisp sheets, spattering against the century-old walls, pooling beneath your head upon the soft, freshly vacuumed carpet.

"You'll be silent then. And finally, you will haunt me no more."

Chapter Thirty

Jillian had forgotten how heavenly civilization could be.

For the first time since leaving Seattle, she dined on a meal that wasn't cooked over an open fire in a cabin, tasteless from a hospital kitchen or grabbed on the run at a tavern. They ate steak, picked at salads and potatoes, even drank wine, despite the warnings on her pain-medication bottle.

And she noticed Zane MacGregor.

Oh, how she noticed him with his dark hair, wet and curling over the back of the plush white hotel robe that was his only article of clothing. It gapped a little over his chest, black chest hairs visible over olive-toned skin.

And he smelled so good.

Of soap and some cologne and that crisp, clean male scent she'd forgotten about.

They ate and drank from a bottle of smoky Cabernet Sauvignon. She took her wineglass into the bathroom, drew a bath with thick, foaming bubbles and relaxed. She removed the tape from her ankle, which seemed far less swollen than a day ago, and eased into the fragrant warm water.

Sinking under the surface, she wet her hair and shampooed it, rinsing it under the faucet as best she could and thinking, for a second, that out of the corner of her eye, she caught a glimpse of Zane, his pale reflection in the glass panes as he sat at the desk. Could he see her as well, a ghostly image caught in the elegant old doors?

If so, who cared?

It wasn't as if she didn't let her eyes wander to his muscular legs and bare feet.

Afterwards, wrapped in her own robe, her hair drying in untamed curls, she shared the last drops of the bottle with MacGregor, who gestured for her to sit down at the desk.

"Take a look," he said, all business while the smell of him enveloped her. On the laptop screen blow-ups of the photos she'd received, enlarged by Chilcoate, who had e-mailed them to MacGregor.

"I photo-shopped these myself," Jillian said, "but I couldn't find anything."

"You're not Chilcoate," he said, adding, "thank God. I won't bore you with the details. Bottom line is, he managed to enlarge this parking meter, which seems to read 'Spokane Municipal Meters' underneath. That puts the photo in Spokane. Besides that, he got this from the reflection in this store window. The letters SEAU."

She nodded. "The rest is cut off, but it seems to be a shop sign."

"Exactly. Which means this man is in Spokane, at least he was for the photo."

Jillian felt a thread of hope. Was it possible? Were they really going to ID this monster who had drugged her and dragged her into those frozen woods to die?

She stared at the photo, at the image of the man in the cap. Aaron? Or someone else entirely? Was she closing in on the man who had stolen investors' funds, then faked his own death and left her not knowing for years? Or was she just being pulled deeper into an incredible hoax used for the purpose of killing her?

She felt an anger, deep and hot and dark, surge through her soul. Not only at the man who had abandoned her, but at the person who was trying to ruin her, kill her, and blame her death on another sick monster.

MacGregor, as if he understood what she was feeling, placed a big hand over her shoulder, the warmth of his fingers permeating the thick terry cloth, seeping into her skin. She tried not to think too much about his touch, not when they were so close.

"Don't tell me," she said, surprised at the emotion she heard in her voice. "Chilcoate's already found the shop, located the street corner here in Spokane."

"Even *he* has his limits."

"You're kidding."

"He promised that by tomorrow morning. When he gives us the location, we'll get to this street."

"And then we'll be at the spot where Aaron, or someone who looked like him, stepped across the street. We won't necessarily find him."

"It's not the answer, Jillian, I know, but it's a start." He rotated her chair so that she could see his face, and for a second she lost herself in his gaze, imagining that he was talking about more than locating her supposedly dead husband. "That's something, right?"

"Right."

"And we're closer now?" he asked.

"To the truth?" she repeated, her voice a little rough because she guessed he was, in fact, not discussing the case any longer. "Yes," she nodded, meeting the unvoiced questions in his eyes.

One of his brows quirked. A silent invitation.

She smiled faintly.

"Ya think?" he asked, as if to make certain.

"No thinking about it, MacGregor. I know."

"That's what I like, a humble woman."

"Just as I like a weak man." Her smile widened as she goaded him, and she saw a flicker of desire in his eyes. She was treading into dangerous territory, but then, didn't she always?

She felt safe with him, trusted him, and a very vital and feminine part of her wanted him. She'd been attracted to him from the first time she'd watched him stoking the fire, when his shirt had lifted to expose a slice of bare skin. But she'd been careful. Cautious. Rightly so.

But not now.

Not when she was certain he was on her side, probably more a partner to her than either of the men she'd so foolishly married.

"I asked for two beds," he reminded her.

"I was wondering about that."

His eyes slid her a sideways look in sexy invitation. "I didn't want you thinking I intended to take advantage of you." The room seemed to shrink around them, becoming more intimate.

"Do you think you could? I know tai kwon do and all kinds of martial arts," she warned.

"And you've got bruised ribs and a sprained ankle. And I outweigh you by nearly a hundred pounds." His gaze skated down her body. "Maybe more."

"You're saying you could take me?" she challenged.

He let out a low chuckle, barely heard over the hiss of the fire. "Careful, woman."

"Why?"

"Because it might be the smarter thing to do."

She stood then, wobbling just a bit, but facing him,

toe to toe. She tilted her chin up a fraction to keep his gaze. "Let's review, shall we? Not that long ago, I thought I was going to die," she said, more serious. "And then you came and saved me and I've been trying to sort out feelings about that ever since. But the real thing is this: life is short."

His smile faded a bit and she noticed the streaks of color in his eyes, the peppery flecks of his beard shadow. "You're making it damned hard for me to be . . ."

"Oh, please!" She laughed, tossing back her head, her wet hair brushing down her shoulders. "For the love of God, MacGregor, I guess I just have to throw myself at you."

And she did.

She wrapped her arms around his neck and kissed him with all the pent-up emotion that had been plaguing her for days. The room tilted a bit and he caught her, his arms steel around her waist as the robe slipped off her shoulders.

She wanted him. Body and soul. And she didn't give a damn about tomorrow or the consequences.

Maybe it was the wine.

The pain pills.

But she wasn't about to let this moment, this one special minute, slip from her. She heard him groan as his arms tightened about her, his big hands splayed across her back.

"Do you always get your way?" he asked into her open mouth.

"I sure hope so."

He laughed, then carried her to one of the beds and lowered her onto the mattress. Stretching out beside her, he kissed her again and this time his tongue pressed against her lips until she opened her mouth eagerly. Hungrily.

The back of her neck heated instantly, desire spreading through her, rushing through her blood, pounding in her ears. It had been so long since she'd been touched and never had she felt so impatient, her body rousing with each sensation.

"Take it slow," he growled when she started tugging at the belt cinching his robe. "We've got all night." And then he showed her exactly what he meant, skimming his hands along her body, slowly loosening her belt, so gently around her sore ribs, peeling off her robe while kissing her. His lips moved downward as the fabric parted and suddenly she was naked beside him. He touched her breasts, holding them, sliding down to take one in his open mouth and causing her blood to swirl and heat deep within. He suckled freely, his hands rubbing her back and slipping along her spine, finding her buttocks and pulling her tight.

Once he stopped to gaze down at her sprained ankle, but she pulled his gaze back to her, assuring him that there was no pain, only pleasure. Then his calloused hands slid lower, over the crest of her rump, fingers exploring and paving a trail for his mouth, oh God, his hot, wonderful mouth.

Jillian moaned as her eyes closed and she felt as if she were losing touch with reality. She touched him as well, biting his shoulder, caressing the wall of his chest, playing with his nipples until he sucked in his breath.

His erection, thick and hard, pressed intimately against her. She started to pull him to her when he stopped his ministrations to stare at her. One hand covered hers, the other pushed her hair away from her face. "You think this is a good idea?"

"No."

"Me, neither."

A second passed and he whispered, "Oh hell." Then he drew her to him and kissed her with an urgency she'd never felt before. His mouth ground against hers and his body lengthened, fitting perfectly, long legs, hard, strident muscles, firm skin rubbing against her.

She couldn't think, could barely breathe. Her thoughts were centered on him, on joining with him. He rolled onto his back and pulled her atop him, careful of her ribs. Staring up into her eyes, he rocked his hips, rubbing her so that she felt nothing but want.

"MacGregor," she whispered, opening her legs to take him.

He drew her body to his and thrust inside, pushing upward, parting her.

She gasped.

Then groaned as he withdrew, using his hands to manipulate her hips, starting the rhythm of movement that drove her insane. Heat flowed through her bloodstream. Desire curled deep inside as Zane MacGregor, lying beneath her, holding her gaze with his own, made love to her as if he never wanted to stop.

Her breath was lost somewhere in her throat and she began to perspire, to gasp, moving, faster and faster, nearly panting. He, too, was breathing quickly, his skin moist, his eyes glazed, his mouth parted slightly.

"Jillian," he whispered hoarsely. "Jillian . . ."

He bucked upward and gave out a hoarse, wild cry.

A shudder ripped through her, as if from the inside out.

The room seemed to disappear, splintering into a million pieces. He released her and she fell down against him, her ribs aching a bit, her lungs desperate for air.

Her world, she was certain, would never be the same.

She wanted to tell him she loved him, but that seemed rash. It was too soon, though it felt as if she'd known him, been waiting for him, all her life.

Neither of them spoke. MacGregor just held her tight against him for the rest of the night, the second bed unused, as he sighed into her hair and she clung to him, certain she'd never been so safe in all her life.

Jillian blinked open a blurry eye and saw that she was alone in the rumpled bed. *Where the hell was MacGregor?* Images of making love to him flashed through her mind and she stretched lazily, blushing a bit, as she glanced at the clock. Eight in the morning and he was gone, no sound of him in the adjoining bath.

Rap! Rap! Rap!

A female voice called, "Room service." This time she sounded a little impatient.

"We didn't order any . . ." Oh. Of course! Grinning to herself, Jillian rolled over and her bruised ribs, tender ankle and a new soreness between her legs reminded her all over again why she was so tired. MacGregor had probably gone downstairs for a second, maybe to ask about his clothes, she decided, before seeing his robe discarded over the back of the desk chair near the fireplace where flames were still burning softly.

How odd.

"Hello? Are you in there? Room service."

"Yes, yes. Coming," she called. "Just give me a second." She found her robe and flung it over her bare body. Her stomach rumbled at the thought of juice and coffee and French toast, or pancakes or bacon and eggs. It didn't matter. Whatever MacGregor had ordered would be great. Suddenly starved, she cinched the belt of her robe and made her way to the door with only a little difficulty. She nearly unlocked the door before thinking twice.

Someone had tried to kill her recently.

Peering through the peephole, she spied a tall woman, arms crossed over her chest, looking pissed as hell. She was dressed in a black skirt, black vest and white blouse, and yes, the waitress was pushing a cart, a corner of it was visible through the fish-eye. Also a name tag was pinned to her vest, and it appeared to be one of the tags that she'd seen on the staff. As she watched her, the woman checked her watch and looked about to knock again.

Jillian thought about the gun in her jacket, but decided she was being paranoid as she cracked the door open. "Who ordered this?"

"You did."

"No, not me." Jillian leaned against the threshold, peering out the sliver of open door.

"No?" Frowning, the waitress said, "Well, let's see." She appeared perplexed as she opened a long leather receipt holder monogrammed with the hotel's logo. "Well, no, not you. You're not Zane, are you?"

"No, but . . ." The waitress reached for a cell phone tucked into her pocket. "I'll straighten this out." She glanced at the number mounted on the door. "Sometimes the kitchen messes up. But this does say Zane MacGregor and this is the right room . . . " She flashed a smile. She was a tall, athletic woman with curly brown hair, a few freckles and the etching of worry lines across her forehead and around her eyes.

The cart beside her, covered with a linen cloth, held two place settings, silver-covered plates, a large pot of coffee and a small vase with a red rose inside. Though the waitress's perfume was a little on the sweet and noxious side, the scent of the coffee and what smelled like bacon did Jillian in.

"Come on in," she said, opening the door wider, allowing the woman, Falda, her name tag read, to push the cart inside. "I'm sorry about the mix-up," Jillian went on, as the door clicked shut behind the woman. "MacGregor didn't tell me he ordered breakfast—"

The minute the words crossed her lips and she'd

mentioned MacGregor's name, she knew she'd made a mistake. MacGregor would never have ordered anything using his first name.

She spun. "Wait a minute," she said, but was too late.

As Falda reached for something on the tray, a scar on her inner arm caught Jillian's eye. A small, reddish crescent on the inside of her wrist. "Oh, Jesus."

Fear sliced through her heart.

This was the woman who had left her in the forest to die!

She snatched up a table knife and started to yell for help.

But Falda snagged the rag and lunged, cutting off Jillian's scream before it began. Jillian gagged at the odor, twisting her head away.

The cart toppled. Hot, black coffee sprayed over the floor, scalding Jillian's arms. She tried to back away but her ankle twisted under her. Pain shot up her calf and she cried out.

Falda was quick. She pressed the soaked rag to Jillian's face, then straddled her quarry. Her skirt ripped, threads popping to expose her strong, muscular legs.

No! No! No!

Jillian gripped the table knife and swung wildly. She sliced at Falda's arm, while writhing and trying to break free of the madwoman's grasp. All the while the sweet, sickening scent of ether was forced into her lungs and esophagus, choking her. She coughed. Her eyes burned. The hotel seemed to sway.

Oh, God, please don't let this happen!

Red-faced, nearly maniacal, Falda pressed harder. "You miserable bitch. Why couldn't he forget you? Why the hell did you have to haunt him? Haunt me?"

What was this deranged lunatic talking about?

Jillian tried to scream, but the sound was muffled. She swung at her attacker, wielding the knife in one hand, striking out with her useless fist. Though she struck at Falda again and again, her blows were weak and glancing. Bruising, not cutting.

Oh, God, please, please, please give me strength!

But the room was spinning. Growing fuzzy. Everything surreal.

The Amazon used her weight to hold Jillian fast against the floor.

"He'll never be able to think of you again, never want you," she hissed, her eyes burning with a hot, seething rage Jillian didn't understand.

What the hell was she talking about? The bed seemed to wobble in her vision, her crutch dimly in view. She thought of MacGregor and wondered if she'd ever see him again. *I love you*, she thought, nearly giving in to the overpowering urge to close her eyes, to let go.

Still she flailed, sensing the tiniest ounce of satisfaction each time Falda winced or squealed.

"He never stopped loving you, never stopped wanting to call you to explain," she hissed, and Jillian was only half following. What was this maniac raving about?

"Well, it's over now. Carl will never have another fantasy about you."

Carl? Who the hell was Carl?

As if reading her mind, Falda hissed, "Carl's my husband. Do you hear me? *Mine!* And he's never going to go back to you. You get that? Never!"

Carl? Sweet Jesus, this woman was nuts! Totally insane. The only Carl Jillian had ever known delivered her newspaper back in Seattle . . . a fortyish man in an aging Toyota pickup that scared her cat. Oh, Lord, she wanted to sleep . . .

"Oh, that's right. You don't know him as Carl, do you?" This horrible woman sounded smug. Pleased with herself. "You'd still call him Aaron, if you had the chance."

Aaron?

In that moment of clarity Jillian's heart nosedived. A thousand sharp images of her first husband darted through her mind, cutting painfully into her brain. Aaron standing at the front of the small chapel in a rented tux, swearing he'd love her forever. Aaron at the helm of a small raft shooting down the rapids of the Colorado River. Aaron smiling and sweating as he reached the summit of Mt. Hood. Aaron making love to her so hard and lost in himself, she'd thought she could be any woman. Aaron leaving on that last fateful hike in South America.

She glared up at her assailant. "Aaron is alive."

Falda's smile was pure, dark evil. "So now you get it, right?"

And she did. As she struggled and flailed, her strength zapped from the ether, her mind slow and dim, she did realize that she was being weighted down by the psycho who had lured her to Montana, this woman who was in love with Aaron and that the bastard who had disappeared years ago was, indeed, very much alive.

"I'm his wife," Falda said victoriously, as if she'd won a great prize.

So Aaron, the bastard, not only was alive, but had remarried.

"And that's never going to change," Falda was saying. "He's not going back to you, not begging your forgiveness."

As if Jillian would ever want the lying, cheating, son of a bitch she'd once claimed to love. Oh, God . . .

Fight, Jillian, fight!

She swung her arm upward, but Falda deflected the blow and the table knife fell with a dull thud onto the thick carpet.

Falda clamped the rag firmly over Jillian's mouth as she positioned one knee over Jillian's throat, choking her, nearly crushing her voice box, denying her the very air that was thick with the ether meant to subdue her.

Though Jillian bucked and writhed, the larger woman held her fast, pinning her down as she gasped for breath.

Jillian became weaker, her blows hitting off the mark, her struggles pathetic as the biting ether slid through her nostrils and into her lungs.

The world swam as she stared upward, looking deep into the eyes of a woman she hadn't known existed.

"It's over, Jillian," Falda assured her, straddling her weakened body. "This time, trust me. You *are* going to die."

Chapter Thirty-One

MacGregor knew it was him.

The man who showed up at the sporting goods shop at five minutes before eight had to be Carl Rousseau. Chilcoate had given him a description and, besides, the man wore a baseball cap and the very jacket he'd worn the day the fateful picture had been snapped, the photograph someone had sent to Jillian from Missoula. Idiot.

It was light now, snowing lightly in tiny, hard flakes as Rousseau walked down the street carrying a paper cup of coffee. As he made his way to his shop, he dodged a woman walking a Greyhound and kept his gaze trained on the sidewalk in front of him, trying to avoid icy spots.

From the cab of the truck where he'd been waiting for Rousseau's store to open, MacGregor watched in silence, the visor tilted down to darken the pickup's interior. Just in case the son of a bitch caught sight of him.

Rousseau was reaching into his pocket with his free hand, probably searching for his keys. MacGregor felt the urge to strangle the life out of the bastard who had let Jillian think him dead. The guy had bilked investors out of their life savings, faked his own death, left Jillian to deal with the fallout. Then, somehow he had the gall to be living what seemed a normal life here in Spokane.

A prick of the lowest order.

MacGregor's back teeth gnashed. He'd love to tear the guy limb from limb.

The bastard deserved it.

But there were still too many questions. Who sent the photographs to Jillian? This man? A guy who seemed to be going about his work day as if he didn't have a care in the world? If so, why? And who was the photographer? A tripod on a timer?

No friggin' way.

Something wasn't right, and MacGregor felt a niggle of apprehension deep in his gut.

He waited for a sports car to roar past, heavy music throbbing, then opened the door of his truck and stepped into the street where snow, and slush, and gravel crunched under his boots and the cold winter air held the city in its grip.

Caruso/Rousseau didn't appear the least bit concerned as MacGregor jogged toward him, one hand firmly in his pocket, the fingers of his gloved hand wrapped around the handle of his pistol.

"Carl?" MacGregor called, forcing a smile that felt so fake he thought it might crack.

Rousseau looked up, his expression blank, snow on the shoulders of his jacket. "Yes?"

"Carl Rousseau?"

"Yes." He was a little irritated now, but not aggressive as he juggled his steaming cup of coffee and tried to insert a key into the lock. "Is there something I can do for you?"

A delivery truck rumbled past, belching blue smoke as it turned the corner too tightly, one big tire rolling over the sidewalk, a huge fender narrowly missing the street sign.

"Yeah," MacGregor said. "There is." He was nodding. "There's someone I want you to meet."

"Who? No, wait a minute." The key slid into the lock and as he pressed a shoulder to the glass door, it swung open. "Do I know you?"

"Not yet."

Caruso visibly tensed. "Who are you?"

MacGregor felt a cynical smile twist his lips. "Trust me, Caruso, you don't really want to know."

"Caruso?" Some coffee slopped over the lip of Rousseau's cup and onto the wet sidewalk, an area protected by the awning of the shop. Stunned, he said in a low whisper, "What are you talking about?"

"Your real name. The one your parents gave you. Aaron Caruso. Remember?"

"What? No. I'm Carl Rousseau—" he began, but he blanched and his eyes moved quickly from side to side, as if he were a trapped rat searching for a quick escape.

"Your name is Rousseau *now*," MacGregor corrected, his blood beginning to boil. "But that's not real and we both know it, so don't bother trying to argue. The truth is, I don't know how you wrangled that, but your real name is Aaron Caruso. You're forty years old. You were married to Jillian White, then you took a hike in Suriname and didn't come back. Faked your own damned death and took off with other people's money. Left Jillian holding the bag. The empty bag." His hand curled over the butt of his gun. "What kind of a coward are you?"

"I'm not—"

"Like hell." MacGregor snapped. He shoved Caruso into his shop, forcing him out of the street and into the dark interior that smelled of dry goods and oiled wood.

A bell over the transom jingled and the surprised storekeeper stumbled over a male mannequin dressed head to toe in the latest fishing gear in a display made to look like a camp site. The mannequin's tackle box clattered against the hardwood floors, brightly colored fishing flies and lures spraying at MacGregor's feet, a jar of salmon eggs rolling toward the counter. For a second Caruso flexed, rounding on MacGregor, his eyes glittering with fear and hatred. His hands were curled into tight fists.

Good!

MacGregor would like nothing better than to punch the guy out. One fist clenched and his other tightened over the gun in his pocket. In a sizzling second, his brain flashed back to the fight in Denver, to Ned Tomkins' bloodied face and his own arrest. He still wanted to knock this bastard over the goddamned moon. To hell with the consequences!

"This is about Jillian," Caruso whispered, the truth finally dawning on him as he stood, a little dazed.

"No shit, this is about Jillian!"

All the starch left Caruso's body as he stood in his shop, surrounded by displays for tents and backpacks and boots. Canoes hung from the high, exposed ceiling while fishing rods and hunting rifles were displayed high on the walls, illuminated dimly by soft fluorescent security lights still glowing and humming.

Just when MacGregor was about to get into it with him, to knock the bastard to hell and back, Caruso, the coward, crumpled, his two clenched fists relaxing. "Oh Jesus." He lifted a hand to his face. "I don't know what to say."

"Say you've been stalking her."

"What? Stalking Jillian?" Caruso shook his head as if confused. He swiped at his brow, his fingers trembling. "No, why would I—?"

"You deny it?"

"I haven't seen Jillian in . . . Oh dear God." In a second he aged fifteen years. Instead of trying to argue or fight, he just nodded his head, his shoulders slumping

as if he bore the weight of the world—an Atlas, over-
taxed and overburdened. He fell onto a stool in the display near the fake campfire. "I would never."

"Yeah, right." MacGregor didn't believe him, but something was wrong here. Caruso's reaction wasn't what he
expected. This was a man who had tried to kill Jillian,
and MacGregor had expected a fight. He'd looked forward to it. So what was with the whipped-dog act? At
least now, he was in charge. Just to make certain that
Caruso didn't pull a fast one, that he realized MacGregor meant business, he hauled the pathetic lump of
misery to his feet and pulled out his pistol, shoving the
barrel into Caruso's jacket, just under his ribs. "I thought
maybe you'd like to see your wife again. Let's go." He
nudged Caruso toward the door with the gun. "And
maybe before we get there, you should figure out just
who the hell you are."

Jillian kicked. Hard. Her thoughts were a dizzy tangle and the world was going black, but she drove her leg
upward in a fury. At the same time she threw one hand
at Falda's face, scratching her cheek before her fingers
twined in Falda's thick hair. She yanked with all her
might and the woman pinning her down bit back a scream.
Momentarily distracted by pain, her hand slipped a little
and the rag over Jillian's nose and mouth slid, enough
that Jillian could suck in some fresh air.

Yanking hard on Falda's hair, Jillian bucked upward,
trying to get into a position she could use, one she'd
learned in martial arts.

Falda was caught off guard.

Jillian rolled to one side, her movements still clumsy.
If she could just get into position and her head would
clear, if she could gain more control, she was certain
she could take this sick woman down.

"You sick bitch," Falda hissed, one hand trying to loosen Jillian's hold on her hair. "I knew you'd be trouble."

Jillian flung her head and the rag soaked in ether slipped off her face. She tried to scream for help but her words were only pained whispers from an injured throat. No one would be able to hear her, but surely someone would hear the struggle or Falda's scream if Jillian could wound her.

She had to free her legs!

Ankle throbbing, pain burning through her body, she struggled in an attempt to make as much noise as possible, so that someone, please, anyone would hear them. For a second she thought of MacGregor. Where was he?

In a horrifying instant she imagined that Falda, whoever she was, had found MacGregor first and killed him. Her heart went stone cold. No! No! No! She couldn't believe it. *Wouldn't!* He had to be safe. Oh God, please.

Twisting violently, one hand still tangled in the woman's coarse hair, her other arm free, she beat at her heavy assailant. Adrenaline sizzled through her blood as she slammed her fist into the woman's nose.

Falda shrieked in pain.

Blood spurted and rained down on Jillian's face.

She squirmed away, trying to get some leverage by dragging Falda's head backward, exposing her throat. One blow to that soft spot and—

Falda wrenched her head away and squealed in rage as a handful of her hair tore from its roots.

It was Jillian's chance.

She kicked upward, ignoring the pain, forcing Falda forward. Then she grabbed at her arms so that she could initiate an upa mount escape she'd learned in jiujitsu.

She flipped Falda over and Jillian was on top. Now if she could just—

Falda moved suddenly, and Jillian couldn't react fast enough, the effects of the ether still causing her to be sluggish and uncontrolled.

Quickly Falda rolled away and onto her feet. "You miserable bitch. Why the hell won't you just die?" she demanded as she withdrew a knife from a pocket of her torn skirt. Her hair was wild and standing on end. Blood was smeared over the lower half of her face and it stained her blouse and vest.

With her intent, ruthless gaze and bared teeth, Falda paced between Jillian and the door like a predator stalking maimed prey.

Jillian thought of the gun in her jacket pocket, but it was too far to reach. The phone, too, was on the far side of the room by the bed, and even if she had the time to dial for help, Jillian couldn't speak, couldn't say a word.

And Falda, seething with her twisted fixation on killing Jillian, stood squarely between Jillian and freedom.

Jillian felt cold to her bones.

Every muscle in her body cried out in pain, but she wouldn't give up. She refused to stop fighting.

With a cruel, determined smile, Falda stepped forward. Her eyes burned with her obsession. Her face was taut with anticipation. The hunting knife, with its wickedly curved handle and serrated blade, was clutched tightly in her strong fingers. "It's over, Jillian," she hissed. "And long overdue."

MacGregor tromped on the accelerator. The truck roared through the city as he drove with his left hand, the gun in his right leveled at the man to whom Jillian had once been married.

"You don't need that," Caruso said, staring at the gun. He seemed defeated and tired, his skin pasty and sallow.

MacGregor wasn't buying it. For all he knew this con man could be acting crushed, all the while hoping for an opportunity to grab the weapon and turn the tables on MacGregor. No way. MacGregor kept the muzzle aimed at the man's heart as he sped through the cold streets bustling with people making their way to work. Traffic was heavy, taillights glowing red on wet pavement. Snow fell in bitter tiny flakes, freezing hard on the road where the warmth of engines and exhaust hadn't melted it.

If Caruso made a move, then they might both die, but MacGregor knew he had the advantage. If the guy tried to get out of the truck, MacGregor would be after him in a second. Aaron Caruso wasn't getting away. Not again.

Thankfully the hotel wasn't far.

He'd already called the local police but hadn't waited for them to appear. Instead he told the dispatcher he'd meet the officers at the hotel. It galled him to bring in the authorities, but he had to for Jillian's safety, even if they felt the need to arrest him for all the laws he was currently breaking, speeding being the least.

He just didn't give a damn about anything but ending this.

And ending it now.

The truck wheeled around a corner and MacGregor tromped on the accelerator, speeding through a yellow light. He passed a Volkswagen bug, steering clear of pedestrians, bikers and other vehicles as his wipers slapped the snow from his windshield.

"You're MacGregor, right?" Caruso asked, as if finally putting the pieces together. "I read about you. You saved Jillian from that psychopath they call the Star-Crossed Killer, the guy who leaves his victims to die in the wilderness. What a sick son of a bitch."

So the guy was still trying to wriggle out of it, deny

that he was the one who had lashed Jillian to that tree, intent on letting her freeze. Caruso was trying to deflect his guilt. Which was just plain bullshit.

And yet . . .

"Don't give me that crap about her being abducted by the Star-Crossed Killer. We both know that's just a cover-up. You took Jillian out there to the woods. *You're* the one who lured her there, then used the killer as a smoke screen. *You* tried to make the crimes look like the others, but you failed, Caruso."

"What? No!" He seemed stricken.

"Cut the act. We both know what you did. When we get to the hotel you can explain it all to the cops, try and feed them your line of bull and see if they buy into it. But you'll have some major explaining to do, not only for kidnapping and trying to kill Jillian but for all the havoc you wreaked on the lives of all those people you stole from. You're going to have so many investors and insurance companies crawling up your ass, you'll never be able to sit again!"

From the corner of his eye MacGregor saw Caruso's face drain of all color. He looked as if he might piss himself. "No."

"Yeah, right."

"Seriously. You have to believe me. I was here, at the shop. You can check. I didn't have anything to do with . . ." As if he suddenly understood the magnitude of his crimes, he let out a long breath and stared through the windshield. But he wasn't seeing the taillights of the truck a few feet in front of them. No. Caruso was searching inside his soul and finding something that scared him to death. "Oh, no . . . no, no, no," he said so quietly it was barely audible over the growl of the truck's engine and the noise of traffic rolling through the streets.

"You can't deny any of this, you sick prick."

"No, I . . . Look. Yeah. You're right. I did steal the

money, I did disappear," Caruso said in a rush, as if suddenly confessing his darkest sins to his parish priest. "But I never did anything to Jillian. I would never—"

"Oh hell!" MacGregor wanted to smack the guy. He was driving five miles over the speed limit when the light ahead turned yellow and he was stuck behind the idling furniture delivery truck. "Didn't do anything to her? What about leaving her alone? To think you were dead? To face your investors, the ones you stole from? To try and convince the police that she wasn't in on your scam?"

"But—"

"Then, years later, something must have triggered you into thinking she would find you, so you lured her to Montana so that you could kill her. It's as simple as that." But even as MacGregor spoke the words, he realized the flaw in his logic. His gut went cold.

If Caruso wanted to stay hidden, to remain Carl Rousseau, why send the pictures? Why entice Jillian into leaving Seattle to find him?

MacGregor's hands tightened over the steering wheel.

He saw the horrified, fearful expression on Caruso's face and knew the guy was holding back. "Wait a sec," he said, his heart drumming with a new fear. "I'm wrong about who sent the pictures, aren't I?"

Caruso closed his eyes and bit his lower lip.

MacGregor could almost see the wheels whirling in the man's brain.

"Dear God," Caruso whispered, his head slowly moving from side to side, as if he were denying the turn of his own dark thoughts. "I didn't think she'd go this far."

"What, you sick bastard! Who?" MacGregor demanded as the truck in front of them finally began moving again. "What is it you know?"

"It's Falda," Caruso said, his jaw tight.

"What?"

"Falda. My wife. My *second* wife. She's . . . she's been

gone lately, but she's back in Spokane now." A muscle in the side of his jaw worked. "You'd better step on it, MacGregor," he advised. "When Falda wants something, she doesn't let anything get in her way, and I'm damned sure she wants Jillian dead."

MacGregor gunned it.

Heart-thudding, adrenaline sizzling through his bloodstream, he peeled around the truck, narrowly missing a parked car and eliciting a loud, angry honk from the delivery vehicle as he headed for the hotel. Caruso had a jealous wife, a wife so jealous of his first one that she would try to kill her?

Christ, how sick was that?

"Where's Falda now?"

"I don't know." Caruso shook his head as he chewed on his lip and stared out the window. Suddenly MacGregor didn't doubt Aaron Caruso or Carl Rousseau was telling the truth, and it scared the living tar out of him.

"Does she know her way around a rifle?"

"Oh yeah."

"Can you call her? Does she have a cell?"

"Yes . . . but she won't pick up."

"Try."

Rousseau scrounged in his jacket pocket and pulled out his cell. MacGregor still had his gun aimed at his heart. The hotel was less than a mile away, up a slight hill. With one eye on the road, and the other on his passenger, MacGregor threaded through traffic, the big truck lurching as he braked suddenly to turn. Caruso nearly dropped the phone as he dialed.

"Come on, come on, pick up," he said, but they both knew it was no use.

"Where are you taking me? What hotel?" Rousseau asked.

"The Courtland. Why?"

"Of course," he said, silently indicating that the

Courtland was without question, the best hotel in the city. "She's there."

"What?"

"Falda. She's at the hotel."

"How do you know?"

"I just know. It's just a feeling I have. If Jillian's there, Falda will hunt her down."

Cold fear knotted MacGregor's stomach and he told himself that Caruso could be bluffing, trying to derail him, but there was a severity in the man's face, a horrified conviction that convinced MacGregor that this con man might just be telling the truth.

"It makes sense," Caruso admitted. "I met Falda years ago, while I was married to Jillian. We had an affair and together decided I would just disappear with the money. Well, that's long gone. I spent a lot of it hiding my identity, and investing poorly and Falda . . . oh, hell, she's been jealous of my first wife for a long time. From the beginning. Even though she and I cooked up the disappearing act and pulled it off, even though I left Jillian, Falda never thought I stopped loving Jillian." He hesitated, then added, "Maybe she's right."

MacGregor saw red. His jaw was clenched so hard it ached. He jetted around a slow-moving minivan and, at last, the hotel's massive stone façade loomed two blocks ahead.

"I don't have time for this," MacGregor growled. Jillian's life was in danger.

But Caruso shook his head, now totally convinced. "Just six months ago, Falda was cleaning the shop. She found pictures of Jillian in an envelope in my desk. Photos I couldn't quite give up. I've had them since we were first married."

MacGregor scowled at the man, wishing he could beat the tar out of him right here and now. This was why Jillian's life was threatened. Because of some damned pictures?

"What happened?"

"Falda went ballistic. Out of her mind. Even though I swore that I'd forgotten I'd saved them, she cut them into tiny pieces in front of me, then threw them in my face. She was . . . beside herself."

"You idiot."

"I kept them because I wanted to remember a better time. The truth of the matter is that I'm dying. Cancer. It's terminal. Lately I've been thinking it was time to put things straight."

MacGregor still didn't trust him. This could all be an act. But the guy did appear a bit jaundiced. "Put things straight how? By what? Coming forward? Confessing?"

Caruso didn't answer, but MacGregor guessed the truth. "You were going to contact Jillian, weren't you?"

Again, silence. Just the sound of the truck's engine and slap of wipers against the snow. Caruso's Adam's apple bobbed.

"And do what? Ask her forgiveness, so you could go to your grave with a clear conscience?"

"Something like that."

"Did you tell Falda what you were planning?"

Caruso shrank further into himself, but he gave a short nod. "Yeah."

He may as well have signed Jillian's death warrant and the fucker knew it.

"It was a mistake." Caruso hitched his chin toward the hotel. "Falda used to work here. At the Courtland," he said. "She still has the uniform. The name tag. And a pass key."

MacGregor's heart turned to stone as he sped through the entrance to the hotel, past two tall stone pillars bedecked in colored lights. The back of the truck fishtailed as he took the corner too fast and narrowly missed a taxi lurking at the end of the drive. The driver jumped out, raised a fist and yelled something.

MacGregor barely noticed. His heart was pounding, his mind blind with fear. "She couldn't know the room number, couldn't gain access," he said.

"Don't kid yourself. She has friends who work here. A cousin who runs off at the mouth. You don't know Falda, MacGregor. If she wants inside the room, she'll get in, even if she has to break the door down herself."

"Then it'll be your fault, Caruso." They rocketed toward the portico where valets were standing, staring at the truck careening toward them. MacGregor stood on the brakes. "Whatever happens to Jillian is on your head."

"You'll never get him," Falda swore, inching forward, raising her knife.

"Here's a news flash," Jillian tried to yell, but her voice was still the barest of whispers. If only she could get to her pistol! "I don't want the son of a bitch."

"Yeah, right." Falda wasn't buying it, and she was still blocking the damned door. If Jillian tried to run past her, she'd be caught. If she went for a window, she'd be attacked.

But she had to do something.

"I found pictures," Falda told her. "Of you. Two of them showing you half naked."

What? Don't be distracted, Jillian. Go for the gun. Get the damned gun!

"I don't know what you're talking about." Maybe she could lunge for the desk chair and send it crashing against the wall. Or kick the toppled cart and make someone outside this room come running.

"They were taken when you were married. You know, he might have been taking photographs of you, but he was already cheating on you, with me."

But Jillian didn't remember. Too many years had passed for her to recollect any of the snapshots of her marriage to a man she'd tried hard to forget.

"Even so, he kept those snapshots. Looked at them when I wasn't around. Probably jacked off to them."

Jillian cringed, but Falda wasn't finished with her rambling. "He never got over leaving you, that's the problem. Felt guilty about it. Shit, why? And when the money ran out, his guilt really got to him. Started saying crap like, 'I shouldn't have done this to Jillian, I shouldn't have done that to her. She didn't deserve it.' That's what I had to live with. And then when he got sick, found out he was dying, he thought he had to see you again."

Aaron was dying?

Jillian felt nothing.

He'd been dead to her a long, long time.

"If he did that," Falda said, still advancing, "if he tried to, and I quote, 'make things right,' he might feel better, get some peace before he died. But what about me? The police, they would blame me for all that money Carl took. I'd get thrown in jail. While Carl is sucking up to you. You're the one he wants to confess to, you're the one he wants to forgive him."

"Never," Jillian whispered vehemently, though her mind was still racing, searching for a way to thwart this maniac.

One side of Falda's mouth lifted and her eyes glittered with pure hatred. "You're right about that. If you're not around, he won't feel compelled to see you again, will he? He can die in peace."

"You're sick."

"Yeah? Well, you're dead." Quick as a cat pouncing, Falda lunged.

Jillian feinted, but her ankle buckled and Falda was on her again, the knife raised, the two of them rolling on the floor. She fought, but the stronger woman slammed the knife into her shoulder. Pain ripped through Jillian's arm and she screamed, but the sound was only a garbled, pitiful mewl. Over it all, she thought she heard the wail of a siren.

Don't give up!

Footsteps pounded in the hallway. Shouts. Voices yelling her room number.

She rolled toward the bed, blood flowing, as Falda yanked the knife out and jabbed again. This time Jillian was able to squirm away, wiggle enough that the blade didn't pierce her skin, just caught on the sleeve of her robe. She grabbed Falda's wrist with her hand, but she was weak, agony ripping down her forearm.

"It's over," Falda hissed, her bloodied face twisted in triumph. She raised the knife once more. Jillian noticed the rubber tip of her crutch, lying where she'd left it near the bed. She didn't think twice but grabbed it with her good hand, fingers wrapping around the metal. Falda raised her arm to strike again, the blade glinting gold from the light of the fire.

Jillian didn't hesitate.

She swung the crutch upward with all her strength.

Craaack!

The shaft struck hard against the side of Falda's head. Still clutching the knife Falda fell forward, staggering, then crumpled atop Jillian.

Jillian shuddered in revulsion as she wriggled out from beneath the woman's body, barely aware of the sounds in the hallway growing louder, sirens outside screaming closer.

Hugging herself, she glanced down at her attacker. From the glassy stare of Falda's eyes, she knew it was over. She then saw the knife sticking from Falda's chest.

She scrambled to her feet and limped toward the door just as a key rattled in the lock and the door burst open.

MacGregor, ashen faced, gun drawn, flew into the room. "Jillian!" His voice cracked as he wrapped his arms around her.

She fell against him, collapsing against the warm wall of his chest. She was bleeding, her body battered, her mind threatening to lose consciousness, but here in MacGregor's arms, she was safe.

Oh God, she was finally safe.

It was all she could do not to break down. Relief flooded through her body as she clung to him. "Mac-Gregor."

"You're bleeding. Let me see."

"Falda!" A male voice called weakly, brokenly.

Jillian stiffened in MacGregor's arms. She looked over MacGregor's shoulder to spy Aaron Caruso fall to his knees. This broken man was the one she'd pledged her love to, the jerk who had abandoned her and faked his own death. He looked sick and pale as he cradled his second wife's bloodied head.

"Oh God, Falda," he whispered. "What have you done?" He held her body next to his, smearing her blood upon his jacket. "Oh Falda, why? Why, why?" He rocked with the corpse in his arms as a siren screamed in the distance.

People gathered in the hallway. A few hotel guests and staff spilled in through the doorway. An armed security guard cut through the crowd, stepped into the room and turned to hold the onlookers at bay.

"Back! Everyone, please step back!" He assessed the situation and told MacGregor, "The police are on their way up."

"Good."

From the floor, where he sat cradling his dead wife, Aaron looked up.

For the first time in years, Jillian's eyes connected with him—the first man she'd ever loved. "I'm sorry," he said, as if he meant it. Tears welled in his eyes and he blinked to stem them. "Oh, Jilly, I am so, so sorry."

She didn't answer. Couldn't lie. She wasn't sorry for what they'd shared so long ago . . . or for the fact that Falda was dead.

She felt MacGregor's arms tighten around her.

"I never meant for this to happen," Aaron said.

Her jaw tightened.

"I'm dying. Falda's gone. She won't hurt you ever again." He appeared so frail that her heart did ache a little for him, just as it would for anyone facing his own death. He'd be arrested, tried for any crimes where the statute of limitations hadn't been exceeded, but, she suspected, he would die first. He was pathetic, and she wouldn't wish what he was facing on her worst enemy. "I feel so bad," Aaron said contritely. "Can you ever forgive me?"

"Forgive you?" She thought of all the pain he'd caused, of how he'd left her to fight his battles, to face the press, the bilked investors. All while he went off and married the woman with whom he'd cheated. He'd been a parasite, living off other people's money, mindless of the pain he'd inflicted. And even as she'd stood by, mourning his disappearance, he'd taken a second wife, if Falda could be called that since technically Aaron was a bigamist. He'd attached himself to a psycho who had drugged Jillian and left her in a frozen forest to die. When that hadn't worked, she'd tried like hell to kill her and had damned near succeeded.

"Forgive you?" she repeated, shaking her head. "Not today," she said, "but that might change. Maybe someday. Right before hell freezes over."

Epilogue

So they found the pretender.

Good.

Outside, the wind picks up, blowing hard through the trees. Inside the cabin, I sit naked, sweat glistening on my skin from my recent workout. I stare at the television screen and sip from my drink, the ice cubes clinking softly in my glass as I watch the police haul a handcuffed man named Carl Rousseau from a grand hotel—the Courtland in Spokane, Washington. They stuff him into the back of a cruiser, careful not to bump his head.

The police are proud of themselves.

They've caught one of the bad guys.

The camera pans wider to show a van from the medical examiner's office at the scene. A half dozen police cars fan over the street, their lights flashing, strobing the snowy lawn of the grand hotel. A woman is dead, and it's presumed that this woman is the moron who tried to copy my work.

A woman!

She had the cops fooled.

Well, that's not so hard, is it? They are, after all, imbeciles.

My stomach roils that anyone would try to take credit for my work.

That the police would consider for a second that an imposter could copy what I've spent years creating. My fingers tighten over my glass and I force myself to calm down. After all, the fraud has been exposed.

Angrily I snap off the television and walk to the table where I have started work on my next notes. Perfectly penned, painstakingly created, ready to be left nailed to a tree for the cops. A way to let them know that I am still hard at work, still eluding them, still their nemesis.

Near the neatly stacked letters are photographs of the women I've blessed by choosing them, pictures taken when they realized their fate. Their images stare up at me and I remember them all, how they thought I would protect them, save them . . . how they offered themselves and begged like the whores they are.

They are just the beginning.

There are so many more to be sacrificed, and the sheriff's department will need to be reminded that it's not over.

The police will discover that I am still at work, and I know how to get their attention, even their respect.

The copy-cat will strike no more.

I hear a noise from the room down the hall.

She's stirring . . . maybe even crying.

I finish the drink and know it's time to play my part, to put on my clothes and my sympathetic smile, to assure her that everything will be all right once the storm passes.

That I am her savior.

Little does she know that already she's been chosen to die.

Dear Reader,

Okay, so now that you've finished LEFT TO DIE, you realize that although Jillian Rivers's and Zane MacGregor's story is finished, there are still a few loose ends to wrap up.

CHOSEN TO DIE, my next original paperback, coming out in August 2009, takes up where LEFT TO DIE left off. All the same characters will show up, of course, even crazy Ivor Hicks and ethereal Grace Perchant and we'll be back at the Pinewood County Sheriff's Department in Montana.

CHOSEN TO DIE is Regan Pescoli's story. I love this woman! The minute I started writing about Pescoli, she jumped right off the page to shout into my ear while trying to steal every scene in the book. With all the problems with her kids, job and ex-husbands, she is screaming for her own story.

She's got it in CHOSEN TO DIE, where she is face-to-face with a sick killer. All the usual crazies and suspects from LEFT TO DIE will appear again, including Nate Santana, the man Regan hates to love, as well as the deputies and detectives of the Pinewood County Sheriff's Department and all the eccentric locals in the area that give them fits. I hope you'll have as much fun reading Regan's story as I had writing it. Look for it next summer.

And, in the meantime, I've got other exciting projects. First, let me tell you about WICKED GAME, the story I co-wrote with my sister, Nancy Bush. It's set in the Pacific Northwest, back at St. Elizabeth's parochial school, which was first introduced in MOST LIKELY TO DIE, a book I wrote with my friends Beverly Barton and Wendy Corsi Staub. There's more trouble at the site of Saint Lizzy's where a body is recently discovered, presumably the skeleton of a girl who disappeared years before. The case has gone stone cold, but now is the focus of a new investigation that includes a group of friends who seem to have a murderer in their midst. WICKED GAME will be available in February 2009, so give it a look.

In March the mass market paperback edition of my *New York Times* bestseller LOST SOULS will be on the stands. This is Kristi Bentz's story, a thriller set at All Saints College in Baton Rouge, Louisiana. All Saints is Kristi's alma mater, where she's attending grad school while writing her first true crime book centering on the disappearance of coeds at the school. As she investigates the missing girls' lives, she becomes embroiled in a secret vampire cult and catches the attention of a twisted psychopath. Soon, the hunter becomes the prey and Kristi's running for her life! LOST SOULS leads into my new hardcover, MALICE, available in April 2009.

MALICE is Rick Bentz's story. Detective Bentz, a man thoroughly based in reality, thinks he's being haunted by the ghost of his first wife, Jennifer, who died years before. Or at least he thinks she died. But his visions of Jennifer are so real, so vivid, he can't help but feel that Kristi's mother is very much alive and teasing him. He becomes obsessed with finding out the truth, even going so far as to reopen the investigation into her supposed suicide. Did she take her own life? Was she murdered? Or did she somehow survive the automobile crash and if so, who is the woman interred in her grave and why is she choosing now to haunt him? MALICE is a roller-coaster ride of insinuation and innuendo, where the lines of truth and lies blur and Bentz's life is suddenly not what it seems.

I loved writing this book. It was one that literally haunted me for years. I hope you enjoy it as well.

Keep Reading,
Lisa Jackson

Please turn the page for an exciting sneak peek of
Lisa Jackson's
CHOSEN TO DIE,
coming in August 2009!

"Oh God, save me," a frightened female voice whispers through the darkened hallways as I finish my exercise routine.

Ninety-three. Ninety-four. Ninety-five.

I count off each of the push-ups as sweat runs into my eyes and my arms start to shake, my hands flat against the cold stone floor, the fire hissing and casting the room in shifting golden shadows. Outside the night is raw, a storm howling through this solitary canyon, hard beads of snow adding to the feet that have already accumulated.

"Please, help me . . ."

I hear the desperation in her cries and it's soothing to me even as it breaks my concentration.

Ninety-six. Ninety-seven.

My form is military perfect, my back level, my muscles gleaming with sweat, my shoulders and arms screaming, but the pain feels good, the sweet torment of my muscles straining, of mind over matter.

Ninety-eight. Ninety-nine.

She's crying now. Mewling and whimpering in the

small bedroom. Like a lost kitten whose eyes have not yet open, searching in the darkness, calling out to the mother cat.

How perfect.

I pause, but only for a second as I savor the last push-up, slowly, painstakingly lowering my body until my chest nearly brushes the floor, then just as determinedly, shoving my weight upward. I hold my body in the final, perfect, suspended position and study my reflection for a minute. Flawless, strident muscles, thick hair, a handsome face staring back at me, veins bulging with the effort.

One fucking hundred.

"Someone, oh please . . . can anyone hear me?" she moans.

It's time.

I release the pressure on my muscles and silently roll to my feet. From the back of a chair I retrieve my towel and dab away at the sweat as I listen to her cry. The longer she waits and worries, the more quickly she'll learn to trust me.

I'm coming, I think, knowing I must respond, play my part, act as if I truly care. I'll give her comfort and pain killers, offer her hot tea and a kind embrace, so that she will want more, will turn to me for comfort, to save her. She will be difficult, I know, a stubborn, intelligent woman not easily turned, but I'll find a way to break her, to make her trust me, to give herself body and soul to me.

Not that I'll accept it.

Still, she will beg for me to take her, to hold her, to whisper that I love her, when, of course, I will not. I imagine the hope in her eyes, the quiver of her full lips, the touch of her hand as it slides slowly down my body in seductive invitation.

But I'll resist.

As I always do.

I add another log to the fire, sparks spraying, hungry flames licking the dry wood, coals glowing blood red and giving this primitive cabin a warmth, a coziness. I head to the small bathroom, walk quickly through the shower, soaping off evidence of my workout, then slip into jeans and a sweater.

She's sobbing quietly in the other room as I walk barefoot to the tiny kitchen where hot water is already steaming on the woodstove.

Perfect.

I pour a cup, add a tea bag and watch as the water turns the color of tobacco. A faint memory flits through my mind. It's a picture of a woman long ago as she dunked a tea bag into a chipped cup. She'd been a pretty woman with pillowy breasts and lips always colored a shimmering peach and forever turned down at the corners. She'd smelled of cigarettes and perfume and had pretended to be my mother.

But she, like so many others, had been a fraud.

Quickly dispensing the ugly memory, I carry the cup through the living area where I've just finished my routine and down the hallway to my captive's door. She's quieter now, as if trying to disguise the fact that she's been crying. As if she's trying to pull herself together.

Which she never will.

I tap lightly on the panels and open the old door slowly, a crack of light cutting into the dark interior.

She's lying on the bed. Frightened. Her eyes wide. Tears visible, tracking down her cheeks.

Am I her sinner or saint?

Her savior?

Or the embodiment of evil?

Soon, she'll know.